7X 9/15 LT 1/14
7X 8/17 LT 1/14

6 X 4/ 12 LT 10/10

BORROW
TROUBLE

BORROW
TROUBLE

MARY MONROE

VICTOR McGLOTHIN

KENSINGTON PUBLISHING CORP.
http://www.kensingtonbooks.com

DAFINA BOOKS are published by

Kensington Publishing Corp.
850 Third Avenue
New York, NY 10022

All Kensington titles, imprints, and distributed lines are available at special quantity discounts for bulk purchases for sales promotion, premiums, fund-raising, educational or institutional use.

Special book excerpts or customized printings can also be created to fit specific needs. For details, write or phone the office of the Kensington Special Sales Manager: Kensington Publishing Corp., 850 Third Avenue, New York, NY, 10022. Attn. Special Sales Department. Phone: 1-800-221-2647.

Dafina and the Dafina logo Reg. U.S. Pat. & TM Off.

Library of Congress Card Catalogue Number: 2006929171
ISBN 0-7582-1223-2

First Printing: December 2006
10 9 8 7 6 5 4 3 2 1

Printed in the United States of America

CONTENTS

NIGHTMARE IN PARADISE

MARY MONROE

CHAPTER 1

I had been on hold for five minutes when the jailhouse operator came back on and thanked me for my patience. She turned me over to the international operator, who put me back on hold for another five minutes before she connected me to my home telephone number in the States.

I was afraid that I was going to faint again and end up back in the same roach-infested detention infirmary where I'd spent last night. I had fainted during my arrest. I'd never been in jail before in my life until now. And it was all because my "innocent" one-night stand with a local man constituted prostitution by the island's standards. I was surprised that I hadn't suffered a nervous breakdown last night, too.

"Leon, please answer the phone," I begged, whispering to myself in a voice that was getting weaker by the second. My wrists were still throbbing from the handcuffs I'd had on earlier.

The officer who had removed the cuffs stood next to me. He flicked a crude lighter and lit a long cigar that was dangling from his thick lips and started blowing smoke in my face. Despite the fact that he was doing it on purpose, I managed to smile at the officer, anyway. He just glared at me, the same way they had all been glaring at me since my arrest.

My head was spinning, pounding, aching, and ringing. I was silently praying that if I did faint again, it would be after I'd communicated with my husband in Ohio. Ohio was my home, but I'd always complained about its dullness. All of my life I had cursed the severely cold winters and fantasized about jaunts to tropical locations. Well, I had finally made it to a sun-kissed, palm tree–lined beach paradise. But never in my wildest imagination did I think that my fantasy would turn into the vacation from hell. And I was not in one of the many crime-ridden foreign hot spots where careless Americans were always getting into one mess or another. Like the war-torn Middle East or one of the Asian countries where some Americans had paid for their illegal indiscretions with their lives. I was in a little, Mickey Mouse country that I had never even heard of until a few weeks ago!

It was an island in the Caribbean called Paraíso, which was Spanish for paradise. Up until last night, it had been the vacation paradise that I'd been dreaming about all my life. It had beautiful weather, beautiful people, fantastic drinks, all-night parties, and beaches lined with palm trees that went on for miles. I couldn't believe that I was still on the same island. It was now the last place on the planet that I wanted to be. I was going to kiss the ground as soon as I made it back to Ohio.

"Hello," my husband Leon's eager voice on the other end of the line finally greeted.

"Baby, it's me," I started. I was sniffing, itching, and trembling all at the same time.

"Renee? Hey, girl! I am so glad to hear from you, honey. Forget all of that shit I said before you left. I really do want you to have a good time."

Leon paused, and I jumped in before he could continue.

"Baby, I need to tell you something," I began, struggling to keep my voice level.

The three officers in the room with me were getting impatient. I could tell by the way each one kept glancing at the large clock on the wall and his watch, clearing his throat, and giving me more dirty looks. I ignored them all. There was nothing more that they could do to me to make me feel any worse.

The international telephone connection was bad. There were spurts of static and a faint whistling sound coming through the line. "Leon, can you hear me?"

"Uh-huh, but hold on, honey. Let me get my coffee." Leon was back on the phone in less than a minute. "How's the weather down there, honey?" he asked, making a slurping noise.

"Leon, let me talk. Please don't say anything else until I finish." I took a breath so deep, my chest ached. "Honey, I am in trouble. I am in real trouble."

"What? Are you sick?" my husband asked in a worried voice.

"Uh . . . well, kind of. I spent last night in an infirmary," I stammered.

"Shit, baby! Was it something you ate? Are you all right now? I want you to come on home now. I don't trust those third-world doctors." Leon grunted, and then he let out a sharp laugh. "I hope you didn't drink too much of that exotic island joy juice." It was good to hear him laugh. Especially since it would probably be a while before I heard him laugh again after he heard everything that I had to tell him.

"Leon, it wasn't something I ate, and it wasn't too many margaritas. I fainted last night because of something that happened. Something stupid," I moaned and rubbed my stomach.

I didn't know how to interpret the brief silence on Leon's end. "Renee, will you get to the point?"

"I'm . . . I'm calling you from j-j-jail," I stuttered, speaking so low, I could barely hear myself.

"Baby, you need to speak up. This is an overseas call, and I can hardly hear you as it is. It sounded like you said you were in jail." Leon laughed again.

"Buhhh . . . buhhh . . . ummmm . . . I . . . I," I mumbled. Gibberish was all that I could manage.

"Shit! Renee, take a deep breath!" There was a lot of concern in Leon's voice now. "Take your time, honey, and tell me what's going on."

I held my breath and looked up at the ceiling. "Leon, I've been arrested."

CHAPTER 2

"Renee, I don't have time for games. If this is your idea of a joke, you need to do better than this. This is not funny," Leon said in a steely voice.

"Baby, this is no joke. I got arrested last night," I whimpered.

"Wait a minute, wait a minute. What do you mean, you got arrested?"

"I'm at the police headquarters now. They brought me out of my . . . cell so I could call you." The words felt like bullets shooting out of my mouth.

"What in the hell have you gotten yourself into, woman? I told you that women shouldn't be running around loose on a vacation without a man along to keep an eye on them! I told you not to go off down there with that wild-ass Inez. Now, what kind of a mess did she drag you into?"

"This has nothing to do with Inez. Well, in a way it does—"

"Stop beating around the fucking bush, and tell me what the hell happened down there! What in the hell did *you* do that got you arrested? I've never even known you to jaywalk, or break any other law!"

I took another very deep breath and then forced the words out of my mouth like vomit. "Leon, they've arrested me for . . . prostitution." The silence that followed for the next ten seconds was excruciating. I could not imagine what was going through my husband's mind. He was an auditor for the IRS, and he often shared some lovely job-related stories with me. Some involved a group of sophisticated call girls who serviced some of Cleveland's most powerful officials. When they did their taxes each year, each woman listed her job as self-employed "public relations coordinator." Leon had audited some of these women and was appalled at how they always managed to slink out of identifying mysterious "business-related" expenses with the help of their powerful friends. I knew that prostitutes were a patch of major thorns in my husband's side. Now here I was confessing to him that I was one.

"*What . . . did . . . you . . . say?*" Leon drawled in a slow, tentative tone of voice. Five more seconds of silence followed. "What the hell is going on down there? Where's Inez?"

"I don't know where Inez is. We had a fight the day before yesterday. She got mad and moved to another hotel. I was so pissed off and confused, I needed to do something to get my mind off what had happened with Inez." I sniffed so hard that the inside of my nose burned. I had to rub and hold it for a few moments. "So I went to this club by myself last night. This guy, one of the locals, was there. I'd seen him around the beach and at a few other places. He seemed real friendly and safe. He joined me, and I told him why I was so upset. Well, one thing led to another. I went to his room with him to, uh, calm down. Next thing I know, uh, I am in bed with him." I paused because I was losing my breath. I thought I was having a panic attack. I couldn't even hear Leon breathing. "Honey, are you still there?" I asked in a meek voice.

"I'm listening!" he roared.

"This man, he was setting me up. He works for the police."

"This man you fucked?"

"Uh-huh."

"This friendly and safe man you hopped into bed with willingly?"

"Uh-huh."

"How was he setting you up if you went to bed with him without being forced?"

"After we finished . . . after I got back into my clothes." I had to pause again. This was the part that was the hardest for me to deal with. "He offered me some money. I only took it because . . . because he was so bad in bed. That's the *only* reason I took the money. Well, I did ask him for cab fare, but that was all I asked for. Anyway, he handed me two hundred dollars . . . and . . . and I took it. I didn't even realize what I was doing until it was too late."

"But you did it, anyway?" Leon's voice was so detached and cold, it made me shiver in the hundred-degree heat. The bad connection made it seem even worse. In addition to the static and whistling noises, now there was an echo each time one of us spoke.

"Well, yeah. This is a crazy place, baby. Down here, my taking that money made it prostitution by the laws on this island."

"Renee, I am sitting here listening to you, but I don't believe my ears! Are you telling me that you—a married woman with a child and a job teaching little kids—didn't know any better? What in the world were you thinking? Is this the way you women behave when you go on vacation?" Leon sounded ominously calm, and that frightened me even more.

My body was so tense and rigid, I didn't think that I could even bend myself enough to sit down, even if I had wanted to. "Leon, this is the only vacation I've been on without you since we got married. This is not what you think."

"Then what is it? You go halfway around the world to sell your pussy, and you end up in jail. What am I missing here?"

"Leon, I can't talk too much longer. You can say and do whatever you want to me when I get home. But we can't go into all this over the phone. You need to get down here as soon as you can and pay my fine. They said that if I pay a ten-thousand-dollar fine, they will release me. I will get deported immediately, and I can never visit this island again, but I don't want to come back down here again, anyway. If I don't pay the fine, I could go to jail for three months," I sobbed.

"Is there anything else about you that I don't know?" Leon sneered.

"What? Like what?" I sniffed, holding back more tears.

"You tell me. I've known you all these years, and I'm just now finding out that you're a prostitute. I'd like to know what else you are keeping from me."

"Leon, we are wasting valuable time. I have never done anything like this before in my life. There is nothing else that I am keeping from you. You need to get off the telephone, get the money, and then get on a plane to come down here. But I think you can wire the money if you can't get a flight right away," I said hopefully.

"You no-good bitch, you! You goddamned, black-ass, slutty-ass, cocksucking heifer! Why should I come get your whoring ass?" Leon's words stung like a whip.

My eyes were burning; I felt like I was going to collapse. I had never been called such vile names before in my life. I wasted ten more precious seconds composing myself.

"Leon, you have to come get me out of this mess because I am your wife. Look, school starts next month. I can't stay down here for another three months!" I wailed. My heart was about to thump right through my chest. At least, that was the way it felt to me.

"You knew all of that before you made a fool of yourself! It didn't stop you. So why should I bail you out?"

"I just told you! Because I'm your wife! You are supposed to take care of me!"

"Sister, you better come up with a better reason than that!"

"What do you mean by that, Leon?"

"What the fuck do you think I mean? Goddammit!"

The officer standing closest to me tapped the desk where the telephone was located with a baton. I glanced up at him, and he pointed to his watch. I ignored him. My legs were so wobbly, I had to hold on to the top of the desk to keep from falling.

"Leon," I whimpered, sweat pouring down my face and back. "If you don't come get me, who will? You know Mama is as broke as a haint, and nobody else in my family has any money. If you don't, I will be down here *in jail* for three . . . three months. I don't know how to deal with that."

"Well, you'd better figure out a way to deal with it!"

"What are you saying, baby?" My mouth dropped open; I gripped the edge of the desk, still ignoring the impatient officer.

"Don't you baby me, you heifer! You got yourself into this mess. You get yourself out! A few months in an island jail might do you some good!"

I gasped so hard, my eyes crossed.

"Leon, are you telling me that you are not coming down here to bail me out and take me home?" I hollered so loud, I almost lost my voice.

"You got that right! Three months is enough time for you to think about what you did and why."

"If it wasn't for you, I wouldn't be in this mess!"

"What? What the hell? How the hell can you blame this shit on me, woman?"

"Because the fight that I had with Inez was about you. Hello?" All I could hear now was a loud and hollow dial tone. Without thinking, or asking permission from the officers, I dialed the operator again. Miraculously, she was able to get a connection immediately. Leon answered on the second ring. "Baby, we got . . . cut off," I started, the words tiptoeing across my trembling lips.

"We didn't get cut off! I hung up!" Leon screeched. His voice was so loud and angry, it sounded like he was in the same room with me.

"Leon, please don't do this to me. You have to help me," I said desperately.

"I don't *have* to do anything except pay taxes and die. Being my wife didn't mean that much to you when you jumped into a strange man's bed!"

"You are not going to help me?" I wailed. Leon didn't bother answering my question. He hung up on me again.

I blinked at the telephone in my hand for a few moments before I placed it back in its cradle. I was in a scary place. A hot, musty, dimly lit room with no windows and with metal furniture. There was a huge, noisy fan hanging from the low ceiling, but it didn't seem to be doing much good. It was hotter in the room than it was outside, where the deadly sun was toasting the rest of the island.

The two male officers stood by the door, with their arms folded, like they were daring me to give them a reason to brutalize me. And the same hostile, hairy-chinned, husky female officer who'd been breathing down my neck like a rapist from the minute I'd been brought to the police headquarters was standing a few feet away from me now.

"My husband is not coming to get me," I announced, directing my attention toward the female. I don't know how I managed to form a smile on my face. I had nothing to be smiling about. But I thought that if I tried to be nice and friendly to these people, they would be nice and friendly with me. I was wrong.

"Brrrrr! I don't blame him much, m'dear. Muck should be left among the muckers," the grim-looking female officer said, folding her thick arms across her lumpy bosom. Like a lot of the women on the island, she was a combination of Spanish and African. She had jet-black hair that was bone straight, and her skin was almost as black as the telephone that I'd just held in my hands. She looked like so many of the sisters I knew back home in Ohio.

"Sister, you don't have to talk to me like that. You don't know me," I wailed.

"Ow!" she yelled, screwing up her face and rubbing her arm like I'd pinched her. "And I don't want to know you," she continued, wagging a thick, gnarled finger in my face.

I couldn't remember the last time somebody had looked at me with such contempt. In addition to everything else that I had to worry about, now I was concerned about this woman, or one of the other guards, getting violent with me. I promptly removed the smile from my face and replaced it with a look of fear.

The big woman cleared her throat, reared back on her ashy legs, and then slapped her hands on her hips. She moved closer to me, her nose almost touching mine. Her sour breath almost made me choke on my own breath. I flinched as the words spewed out of her mouth like bile. "You American women think too highly of yourselves, anyway! Always did and always will. *Sister?* How dare you call me sister! You are no sister of mine. I wouldn't claim you if you came gift wrapped," she yelled, waving her arms. With a grunt that sounded like it came from her bowels, the woman snatched a pair of handcuffs from a wide leather belt hanging from her massive waistline. "Hands back behind your back. Now!"

After she'd cuffed me and spun me around by my shoulders to face her, she smiled for the first time.

CHAPTER 3

I was back in the same cell where I'd spent part of the night before, and most of this morning, staring at the concrete floor. Suspended from one wall by a chain at each end was a narrow cot with a mattress that felt like a slab of cement. A stiff gray blanket was on the cot, but there was no pillow. A large iron pot to piss in sat in a corner, on the floor. There was no lid for the pot and no toilet paper. But there was a roll of brown paper next to the pot, like the kind that butchers used to wrap raw meat. The paper was stiff enough for me to make a lid to cover the pot. There was no window, no sink, and no fan.

I was in the third of four side-by-side cells. In one was a woman who had been moaning and groaning in Spanish the night before. She was silent now. In the other cell next to me was another woman, another foreigner, who was just as dazed as I was. From what I'd picked up from the guards, she was British and had been caught trying to smuggle drugs out of the country. I didn't know what kinds of drugs or how she had tried to get them out of the country. But I felt sorry for her. One thing I did know was that getting caught with drugs could get you executed in some countries.

I didn't know how harsh the foreign laws were when it came to prostitution. I could barely bring myself to think the word, let alone say it. Saying it to my husband had been the most difficult thing I'd ever said to him.

The only reason I was not climbing the walls in my cell was because I truly believed that when Leon cooled off, he'd get one of his lawyer friends, do whatever he had to do, and bring me home.

I was so deep in thought that I didn't hear the door to my dreary cell open. I looked up into the last face I wanted to see: another scowling, husky female officer, jiggling like a float made of jelly. Her humongous breasts looked like torpedoes.

"Come with me!" she barked, snapping her fingers.

I didn't have time to say or do anything. She clamped my shoulder with one of her massive hands and marched me from the musty corridor that contained the four cells into another musty corridor.

We went through several doors and down a darkened hallway before we entered a room that contained a bamboo desk and two metal folding chairs.

"Sit! Sit down now!" the guard ordered nastily, helping me into one of the seats, with a shove so strong, the chair almost rocked over.

"What happens now?" I asked in the same meek voice that I'd been using since my arrest.

"You wait here!" was all the surly woman said before she left the room, locking it from the outside.

Before I could have myself a good cry, another big, husky woman joined me in the depressing little room. She was a hard-looking woman in her forties, but she didn't look like a local. Her skin was a chalky white, and her thick blond hair, twisted into a loosely braided knot on top of her head, was streaked with gray. She had a briefcase in her hand, and she wore a drab gray dress, similar to the uniforms that the officers wore. I was pleased to see that this woman did not have a weapon or a pair of handcuffs hanging off her hip, too.

"Renee Webb?" she asked, with a smile. I was able to relax when she extended her hand to shake mine. "I'm Debra Retner." I let out a sigh of relief when I realized she had an American accent.

"Yes, ma'am," I mumbled, my limp hand still in hers. "Are you from the American Embassy, or something like that?"

"Something like that," the Debra woman drawled, plopping down in the other chair so hard that the tail of her voluminous dress fluttered like a flag on a pole. She let out a loud breath as she flipped open the briefcase, pulling out a few sheets of paper. "Let's see . . . hmmm. . . ." She paused, a disturbing frown on her face. Debra pursed her thin lips and looked at me with pity. Then she fished a pair of glasses from her breast pocket and held them up to her eyes. She looked at the papers again, shaking her head. She let out an ominous groan, blinking rapidly and hard.

"Hmmm," Debra started, scratching her horseshoe-shaped chin. "Looks like you've gotten yourself into a fine mess, huh?" she said, with a chuckle. She parted her thin lips with a grin so wide, it almost divided her face in two. The fact that this woman was able to make light of my situation gave me hope.

"Uh, so they tell me. It's all a big misunderstanding, though. *I am not a prostitute,*" I insisted, holding up my hand. "I have a husband and a child. I'm a schoolteacher. I've never been arrested before in my life, Mrs. Retner."

"Please call me Debra. And is it all right with you if I call you Renee? There is no need for us to be so formal here," the woman said gently, offering me a sympathetic nod.

I nodded back.

"So, Renee, you had a sexual encounter with a man, and then you accepted money for it?" Debra asked, with one eyebrow raised. She tilted her head to the side so that she was looking at me out of the corner of her eye. This gesture of suspicion was universal. My mother, my husband, and even some of the second graders who'd passed through my classroom had given me this look before. "Is that not the case?"

"Well, yes, that is the case. But I—"

"That's prostitution, ma'am. And in this country, it is a very serious charge." Debra removed her glasses and rubbed her eyes. When she put her glasses back on, she gave me a look that made the hairs on the back of my neck stand up.

"Why are you looking at me like that?" I asked.

"Renee, I've heard your account of what happened from the officers. And, for the record, I believe you. However, the man involved tells a decidedly different story."

"What did he say?" All of the trembling that I was doing was probably making mincemeat out of my insides.

"He insists that you propositioned him in the bar, quoted a price, and wouldn't take no for an answer even after he had rejected you more than once. You accompanied him to a rented room, where you demanded two hundred dollars to perform various sex acts."

"That's a goddamned lie! I went up to him in the club, but I didn't say anything to him about having sex with him for money! I just wanted to dance . . . and . . . have a few drinks." I didn't dare tell Debra that I had gone to the club looking for more than a dance and a few drinks.

"He has three witnesses from the club who will back up his story," Debra said, her own anger rising.

"They are all bare-assed liars, too!" I hollered, almost stripping the gears in my throat.

"I know that this man is lying, but I can't prove it. Can you?"

"How would I prove he's lying?"

"Then you can't?"

I shook my head. I gave Debra a hopeless look, and then I started talking out of the side of my mouth. "What happens if my husband refuses to come down here and pay my fine?" I asked, with my teeth clicking together, my lips quivering.

"Excuse me?" Debra said, looking at me with her eyes narrowed into such an extreme squint that for a split second it looked like she'd gone to sleep.

"My husband was really mad when I called my house and told him what had happened. Uh, what I'd done," I said, my face burning with shame.

"I would imagine so," Debra remarked, with a weak sigh.

"Well"—I shifted in my seat and looked Debra straight in the eyes—he was so mad that he said he wasn't going to pay my fine. But, I am sure that he will give in . . . and do it. He'll probably divorce me later on, though," I decided. My voice was fading in and out.

There was a worried look on Debra's face.

"If my husband meant what he said, and I can't pay my fine, what will I do?" I whispered, leaning toward Debra. She looked even more worried. Her shoulders were so wide that when she shrugged, it looked like she had on shoulder pads.

"You will appear in court tomorrow morning to enter your plea, guilty or not guilty," Debra explained.

"But I am not guilty!" I said quickly, almost coming out of my seat. Debra motioned for me to sit back down. "I know I had sex with a man, and he gave me money, but it wasn't . . . it wasn't." I couldn't even finish my sentence.

"No matter what you say, it won't change anything." Debra tapped my hand, then squeezed it. Every little gesture that this woman made seemed sincere. It made me feel hopeful.

"Well, can I plead not guilty and fight this charge? I can explain everything. I was drunk and upset with the woman I came down here with. I thought this man was nice. I'd seen him around, and he seemed like such a nice man. He even paid for my dinner and drinks one evening, before I even knew who he was. Isn't that something like entrapment? He was setting me up from the get-go!" I hollered, groping for words. I couldn't tell what Debra was thinking. "In the club that night, he bought me more drinks, and he listened to me bitch and moan about the fight that I'd had with my friend. I was not in that place looking to sell my body. You have got to believe that. It just . . . it just happened."

"You can plead not guilty and take this to trial. But please be aware of the fact that you can still be held in jail until your trial date, for . . . *up to a year.*"

CHAPTER 4

"**A** year? What the hell do you mean?" I asked, my lips twisted like a stroke victim's. "You can't be serious! Are you telling me that these people can keep me in jail, awaiting trial, for a year? *A whole fucking year?*" I looked in Debra's eyes again, blinking so hard, I could barely see her. But I could still see the hopeless look on her face, and that didn't go over too well with me. Debra gave me a hesitant nod.

"Well, if they keep me in jail for a year, that would be punishment enough, wouldn't it? Why would I even need a trial if they keep me in jail for a year? I was told that if I didn't pay the fine and got convicted, the most time I'd have to spend in jail is *three months.* I know enough about the law to know that locking me up for a year, until they can sentence me to three months afterwards, makes no sense at all."

I looked at the floor. Debra and I remained silent for a full minute before I looked up again, saying the first thing that came to my mind. "The woman that I came down here with, she can be a character witness for me." Now I was really talking crazy. As big a whore as Inez was, even a weak prosecutor could shoot so many holes in her credibility that she'd probably get thrown in jail, too!

"Is this the same woman that you had the argument with?" Debra wanted to know.

I nodded.

"And if it's not too personal, may I ask what you fought with her about?"

My throat was lined with bile, and the rumbling pain in my stomach was almost as bad as labor. "She told me that she'd slept with my husband," I mumbled.

"I see. And where is this woman now?"

"I don't even know," I muttered, with a heavy shrug, a scared look on my face. "After I slapped her, she checked into a different hotel. I can't believe what is happening to me. This was supposed to be the vacation of a lifetime," I said, with a profound shudder. "Women have vacation flings all the time, and they don't get arrested for it!" I yelled. "What is wrong with these people down here? Don't they have enough drug dealers, murderers, and thieves to keep them busy? Why are they making such a big deal out of what I did?" I sobbed.

Debra squeezed my hand again. "Mrs. Webb, let me remind you, you are not in the United States. These little islands are not as idyllic as the travel ads make them seem. If you stay out of trouble, you can really have a wonderful time down here, and in other locations outside of the States. But down here, the laws vary from one island to another. Now if you'd been arrested in Jamaica or Martinique, you'd probably be back home by now." Debra shook her head so hard, a lock of hair fell across her eye. "You picked the wrong island. It's as simple as that," she told me, pushing her hair back off of her face.

"Are you here to help me?" The meek tone had returned to my voice.

"I'm going to try."

"Can I borrow the ten thousand dollars from you? I swear to God, I'll pay you back as soon as I get back to Ohio," I said, so excited I squeezed Debra's hand so hard, she pulled it away.

"I wish things were that simple. I barely make enough to live on as it is," Debra said, with an embarrassed look on her face.

"Can you get me out of this mess, anyway? A woman in your position must have a lot of friends. Can you borrow from them? I have a five-year-old daughter that I need to get home to. School starts in a couple of weeks." I stopped when I realized it was doing me no good to ramble. Despite his flaws, Leon was a good father to our daughter, Cheryl. And both our mothers doted on that child. My daughter was the last thing I needed to be worrying about.

"I am afraid I can't get you out of this," Debra reluctantly admitted, her eyes unable to meet mine.

"Then what the hell are you here for?" I asked, rising again.

Debra motioned for me to sit back down. "I can't get you out of this, but I can make things a little easier for you. You're not the first American I've come to assist, and I doubt you'll be the last. Here is what I can do for you." She paused and sucked in a long, loud breath. Her gray eyes were flat and beady. Like the eyes on a dead fish. "I can speak to the court on your behalf."

"Like a lawyer?"

"If you can afford a lawyer, I can help you find one."

"If I had money, I could pay my fine. I wouldn't need a lawyer. They told me that if I paid ten thousand dollars, they would release me."

"True. But you don't have ten thousand dollars. And that's why I am here."

"What happens if I plead guilty?"

"As grim as it sounds, that would be my recommendation. In your case, as you've already been advised, the penalty would be three-months confinement."

"I see," I muttered, looking at the floor. I started talking out of the side of my mouth again. "Why did this have to happen to me?"

"Don't beat yourself up, Renee. It won't help you at all. You just happened to be in the wrong place at the wrong time. Twelve other women were arrested for the same crime within hours of you; most had been tailed from that same bar. And, by the way, that nice local man who'd been so interested in your tale of woe, he works for the police. Several local women are now serving time because of Jose Garcia, and other men like him."

Jose. The very name sounded obscene to me now. I saw red in more ways than one: his red hair, his red shirt, my red-hot anger. One of the more sympathetic officers had already told me Jose's story. Jose, and other men like him, made money by helping the cops identify prostitutes and get them off the streets. It showed the world that this tiny island was doing its part to fight crime. After the disappearance in nearby Aruba of that pretty White schoolgirl from Alabama, and the shabby investigation, all eyes around the world were on the Caribbean. Some island officials had decided to flex what little muscle they had by making as many arrests for as many different crimes as possible. And I was part of the crime wave.

"That motherfucker. Jose's the one who should be in jail. *He had sex with me.* I thought that all undercover vice cops were supposed to do was get you to quote a price. They are not supposed to actually fuck you!" I shouted.

"Let me remind you again, Mrs. Webb, you are not in the United States. You are on foreign soil, and I am sorry, but you just might be here longer than you want to be."

CHAPTER 5

Before they returned me to my cell, I was ushered down yet another dim hallway into a communal shower, along with two other women. By now my legs felt like rubber. It had been a while since I'd felt my butt. I was surprised that under these extreme circumstances, I was still able to walk and function.

I had seen a lot of large female guards in the compound, but the one who escorted me to the showers, then accosted me with a rubber hose, was the most strapping one I'd seen so far. She was not that much taller than me, but she weighed at least three hundred pounds. A short, severe Afro covered her moon-shaped head like a stocking cap.

Without saying a word, the hefty woman strapped on some kind of a surgical gauze mask and then proceeded to hose me and the other two women down with icy cold water, like cattle. The other two women squealed like injured mice and cursed in Spanish.

"Shaddup! Shaddup you mouths right now! *Rápido!*" the woman with the hose shrieked, her words slightly muffled by the thin mask covering her mouth and nose.

The cold water caused goose bumps to immediately pop up on my flesh. I felt as if I no longer had a voice, so I couldn't scream like the other women. Even if I had wanted to.

All of my jewelry and every other thing that belonged to me had been confiscated. They'd even taken my luggage and passport, and the souvenirs I'd bought, from the luxurious hotel room that I had checked into a week ago. One of the first things that they had snatched was the two hundred-dollar bills that Jose had paid me for my "services." Lord knows, I had earned it. But it was the one thing that I would not retrieve upon my release, even if they offered it back to me on a silver platter.

I had never liked getting my hair permed, so I had always made regular trips to the beauty shop to get my hair pressed. But I owned several hairpieces and wigs, which I wore for convenience. With the weather being as humid as it was in the islands, I knew that a press and curl would not have done much good for my hair. That's why I had brought a few wigs with me. They had taken all of the wigs that I'd left in the hotel room and then snatched the last one right off my head.

The cold hard water and the harsh soap from the hosing down had reduced my hair to its worst state. I couldn't stand to look at myself in the dull mirror outside of the shower. My head looked like a cockle-bur.

One other indignity that I had expected and feared was a strip search. I was surprised that that had not happened yet. When it did happen, shortly after the brutal shower, in another dismal room with no windows, next door to the shower room, I was not surprised. The rubber-gloved fingers that roughly explored the most intimate parts of my body made my flesh crawl. The grimace on the examiner's face made me feel like I was contaminated.

After the humiliating strip search, a pair of thick brown hands tossed a drab pea-soup green smock and a pair of woolen footsies on top of my naked body when I was still stretched out on my back on a slab of a cot. The smock had enough room in it for two women my size. The footsies were long and wide enough to fit the huge, flat feet of any one of the enormous female security guards.

"Can't you at least give me a dress and shoes that fit?" I asked the matronly woman standing over me, removing her rubber gloves. "None of this stuff fits," I complained.

The matron clucked her thick tongue before she spoke. "This ain't a catwalk in Paris, Miss Naomi Campbell. You either wear what we give you, or you wear the suit that Mother Nature gave you," she told me, with a smirk.

On the way back to my cell, I saw the other two women who had been in the shower with me. They were being marched back to their cells, buck naked.

I sat down hard on the side of the lumpy uneven cot and tried to organize my thoughts. That was not so easy to do with all the moans and groans coming from my neighbors in the other cells.

As sorry as I felt for myself, I still managed to have some sympathy and concern for the other women in the cells on my block. I didn't know their backgrounds, but based upon the harsh way they were being treated—marched around naked—I thought that I was the lucky one. I was not like them. And, in my confused state of mind, I thought that being an American was in my favor, and that that set me apart from the others. The fact that they'd segregated us, lodging me in a cell alone, made me think that I wasn't the only one who felt I deserved special treatment.

Dinner was a stale cheese sandwich, some flat black beans, and a ball of overcooked rice, which my body refused to digest. I made trips to that portable toilet on the floor, in the corner facing my cot, every ten to fifteen minutes. About two hours after the gruesome meal, a trustee of some sort, pushing a metal cart with squeaky wheels, came by. With a long-handled pole, she removed the scary pots from the cells and replaced them with empty ones. The stench from the body waste throughout the area was so profound, it made my eyes water and my nostrils burn.

The stiff blanket on my cot felt like it was moving across my body. I couldn't have slept even if I had wanted to that night. I still couldn't believe what was happening to me. What was even harder to believe was the fact that Leon had turned his back on me. But in all fairness to him, I had to ask myself how I would have reacted if he had been the one who'd been arrested for prostitution. I didn't have to think about it too long or too hard. Leon was my husband, and despite his flaws, I loved him. If he had been arrested in any city in the world and called me for help, I would have done everything in my power to help him. Whether I'd have stayed with him after the fact was another story. But the bottom line was, I would never have done to Leon what he did to me. I was still sitting on the side of the cot when morning arrived, still wondering how Leon could have turned his back on me.

With the exception of the guards, I wasn't too clear on who did what. I still didn't know exactly what Debra Retner's job was. I had not seen her since she had met with me the morning before. About an hour later, when she did return, escorted by two armed guards, I was glad to see her.

"What happens now?" I asked, stumbling out of my cell. I didn't realize how exhausted I was until I bumped into her, almost causing us both to fall to the hard floor. Both of the guards drew their weapons and gave me their most threatening looks. My immediate response was to raise my hands high above my head. Debra held up her hand and spoke to the guards in Spanish. I was too muddled to try and interpret, but the guards put their weapons away and fell in behind Debra and me as we made our way down the grim hall.

"I've got to get out of this place," I whimpered, clutching Debra's arm. "You've got to get me out of here. If I have to go to jail, can't they deport me and send me to a jail in America? Don't foreign countries do that anymore?"

"Some do," Debra said in a hopeful whisper.

"I'm going crazy. You've got to help me get out of here," I insisted, wringing my limp hands. Not only had the harsh shower reduced my hair to a frazzle, it had also made my skin so dry and ashy that rashes had already formed on various parts of my body.

"I can't promise you that, but I can promise that I will do everything in my power to make your experience as painless as possible," Debra said, giving me an affectionate pat on the back.

CHAPTER 6

The two guards stayed right on our heels all the way into what I assumed was a courtroom, where Debra led me to a table with two chairs. There were a few other people in the courtroom, including the man from the bar who had wooed me into bed then set me up. Jose. That son of a bitch! He occupied a front-row seat in the spectators' area.

Jose glanced at me, his evil eyes rolling up to my matted, nappy hair. Without my make-up and my wig, I looked nothing like the woman he'd first met. Had I looked like the frump that I looked like now when Jose first saw me, he probably wouldn't have even noticed me. His lips curled up at the ends in what looked like a weak smile. Or a triumphant smile, I should say. I recalled how one of the officers had told me that the men who worked with the authorities to help identify prostitutes got paid for their roles. I felt really let down and unattractive thinking that I'd been approached because of a possible price tag on my head, not because of my beauty.

A scowling bull of a man in a black robe, his face and hands almost as black as his robe, sat down hard on a bench facing us. Sweat was already sliding down his face, and his jaw was twitching. He looked like he wanted to put the whole world behind bars. And this was the man who was going to decide my fate.

A prim-looking stenographer slid into a seat near the judge. Without a word, Debra approached the bench. The judge gave her an impatient look before he leaned forward. He casually rolled up his sleeves and folded his arms as Debra spoke to him in a voice too low for me to hear. Whatever she was saying only seemed to irritate the judge. He shook his head, unfolded his arms, and started waving both, also speaking in a voice too low for me to hear. When his lips stopped flapping, he jerked his head up and looked at me like I'd just organized a coup against his country. With a grunt, he dismissed Debra with a sharp wave of his hand, as if she had turned into a bothersome fly. With her head bowed submissively, Debra returned to my side.

"What were you saying to that judge?" I asked, concerned because the judge was still giving me dirty looks.

"It doesn't matter," Debra told me, both of her cheeks and brows twitching. "It did no good, anyway," she added, her voice cracking.

"And why is Jose here?" I wanted to know.

"Oh. Well, if you plead not guilty, he will be asked to make a statement, refute your version of the events."

I glared at Jose so hard, hoping to see some remorse or compassion. All he gave me was a look that was so smug, it looked like it had been painted on his face.

About a minute later, two men in dark suits approached the bench and spoke to the judge in Spanish.

"What are they saying?" I asked Debra in a whisper. Not only were they speaking too fast for me to understand, too many other things were crowding my mind. "Who are they?"

"The one on the left is trying to talk the judge into simply deporting you. He's trying to talk His Honor into letting you off with just a warning, no fine, no more jail time," Debra told me, talking with her hand half covering her mouth. "Like I just tried to do."

"Is he like a public defender?" I asked.

"He works for the court. His position here is to try and alleviate a situation such as yours, make a recommendation in your favor. Ironically, he gets paid the same whether he wins or loses. This is just a job to him, so don't think that he really cares about what happens to people like you."

People like you? Debra's words almost seared a huge spot in my brain. This is what I had been reduced to. "What about you?" I asked in a steely voice. "Do you care about what happens to . . . people like me?"

Debra smiled. "I do." A painful expression eased onto her face, and she spoke in a soft but hollow voice. "My daughter, Justine, is serving a life sentence in Malaysia. She and her boyfriend tried to smuggle heroin out of the country. She's nineteen. She has been in jail for only a year. She's my only child. . . ." Debra's voice trailed off, and she just stared at me for a few seconds, with eyes that refused to blink. Then she nodded. "Yes, I do care about you."

I bowed my head. "I am sorry about your daughter." I decided to shift the direction of our conversation. The two suits were still talking to the judge, and I still couldn't interpret the conversation. The way the man speaking on my behalf was waving his arms and raising his voice, it didn't sound too good for me.

"Debra, a ten-thousand-dollar fine or three months in jail for . . . uh . . . what I did sounds pretty severe for somebody who's never been arrested," I said hopefully. "I'm a tourist, ignorant of the laws here. Doesn't that mean something to these people?"

"You will find little or no mercy here. These people are not known for their compassion," Debra informed me.

"I didn't hurt anybody. I didn't steal anything. My punishment does not fit my crime," I said, talking in a slow, mechanical way.

Debra slowly shook her head and dabbed at her eyes and nose before she spoke. There was an extremely sad look on her face, and I was sure that it was because she was still thinking about what had happened to her daughter in Malaysia.

"Last year the fine was only five thousand or one month in jail. Two years before that, there was no fine or jail time for first-time offenders. Just probation. That kind of leniency only made the situation worse." Debra let out a loud sigh. "I can't imagine what it's going to be like a few years from now."

I looked back to the two men talking to the judge. "Who is that other man?"

There was a frightened look on Debra's face, which she tried to hide, but as soon as I saw it, I became even more concerned about my fate. "The other man is a prosecutor. He feels that since all of the other women who were arrested the same day as you pleaded guilty, you should be encouraged to do so as well."

"But those other women are real prostitutes," I reminded.

Debra gave me an exasperated look, but then, a split second later, she looked at me with pity. "Do you remember what we talked about yesterday?"

I nodded.

"Let me tell you something about those other women. Jail is a blessing to most of them." Debra sniffed. "So many of them are homeless or involved with men who mistreat them. They have no families to turn to. It is very dangerous on the streets doing what they do. In jail, they have food and shelter, and medical attention if they need it. They look forward to spending a few months, or years, in jail. It's a bleak life to those like you and me, but so many people are not as fortunate as you and me."

Shaking my head, I said, "How should I plead?"

"Like I've already told you, you can plead not guilty and spend up to a year in jail, anyway, while awaiting trial. Or you can plead no contest, or guilty, and accept your sentence."

"They told me that I'd have to do three months if I plead guilty. There is no way I can survive three months in jail down here." At this point, it didn't make much difference to me if I had to face three months or a year in jail. I couldn't imagine doing either one.

"Shhhh. The judge is about to speak." Debra smiled, then gripped my hand. "Let's hope for the best."

As soon as the judge opened his mouth, I sucked in my breath and held it.

"Renee Denise Webb, you have been charged with the crime of prostitution. How do you plead?" the judge asked. His deep, gravelly voice was like the boom of a cannon and seemed to bounce off of the walls. There was not one thing that I liked about this man. He had that smug look I'd seen on the faces of foreigners on the six o'clock news. The angry ones in a position where they could get back at the American government by taking out their wrath on any American.

I opened my mouth, but I couldn't get any words out until Debra jabbed me in my side with her elbow. "Uh . . . guilty, Your Honor," I said, almost choking on my words. That's the last thing I remember, because I fainted. When I came to, in the same infirmary, in the same detention center that they'd taken me to the first time I'd fainted, Debra Retner and two guards were standing by the side of the cot. My forehead was throbbing. I reached up and felt a knot the size of a jaw-breaker, which had formed a few inches above my right eye.

"What happened?" I asked, looking at Debra.

Before she responded, she waved the two guards out of the room. Then she sat on the side of the cot, blinking hard.

"As soon as the judge announced your sentence, you fainted and fell face first against the edge of the table. That's how you injured yourself. You'll have to return to the courtroom tomorrow to face the judge again. Hopefully, you will remain lucid until he passes sentence again and invites you to comment."

"If he's already sentenced me, I don't need to go back to that court-room," I protested, still rubbing the knot on my forehead. It didn't take long for it to become as numb as the rest of my body.

"The court has to be thorough. You fainted before the judge had finished making his comments. I guess this is not your day," Debra said in a weary voice. "I guess the judge is having a bad day, too. He wants to make an example of you. . . ."

"I have to spend three months down here in prison?" I asked, strug-gling to sit up.

Debra dropped her head and nodded.

"I did all I could do for you. I am so very sorry, Mrs. Webb." Debra's eyes were red and swollen. It was obvious that she'd had a bad night herself. She had lost her daughter to a system that few people could understand. Now she was losing me, too. To another system that few people could understand.

CHAPTER 7

U nlike a lot of the Black girls that I knew growing up in Ohio, near Cleveland, I had a pretty good life. Even after my daddy died from stomach cancer when I was thirteen. Mama was eight months pregnant with my baby sister, Frankie, at the time. I missed my daddy, but I was thankful that I still had Mama and a lot of other relatives in the area.

Mama always made sure I had everything I needed. She collected Social Security for Frankie and me, but she also worked part time. Frankie and I never had to wear secondhand clothes or eat meals purchased with food stamps.

I put myself through college by working three part-time jobs and falling back on a couple of student loans. That was enough, but Mama still insisted on doing all she could for me. "I don't want nobody running around here feeling sorry for us," Mama told me more times than I could count.

There were times when all Mama could spare was some loose change. She wouldn't take no for an answer when I tried to refuse to take it from her, telling me, "These few pennies ain't much, but it's a few pennies more than you got." I was lucky that I'd been raised by a generous and caring woman like Mama. It made me have a lot of hope in mankind.

My love life was average, but by the time I'd finished college, I was ready to settle down and start a family. Mama had told me that it would be nice to settle down with a man who could take care of me, but she expected me to always be able to support myself, too. I looked forward to my future.

I had just started teaching second grade at Butler Elementary when I met Inez McPherson. The year before, she had opened Soulful Nails, the first Black-owned nail shop in our neighborhood. It was in a strip mall between the office of a gynecologist and a popular beauty shop, so there was a steady stream of women in the area at all times. Business was good for Inez. The shop was always neat and clean. There was a large TV, reading material, and restroom facilities to accommodate her customers. And most of them tipped well.

Other than our nails, Inez and I didn't have much in common. But we hit it off right away. I enjoyed her company a lot more than I enjoyed the company of my other friends and my family. I was twenty-two, and she was the only person in my life who treated me like an adult at the time. Mama had a key to my place, and she'd sneak in during the week to do my laundry and clean the little one-bedroom apartment I rented above a candy store. No matter how much I told her not to, she never left my place without leaving a pot of something that she'd cooked on my stove. "Girl, you ought to be glad I come over here and cook you a mess of greens every week," she'd tell me. "This way, I know you eating at least one decent meal every week." I didn't like to argue with my mother. I rarely won, anyway. No matter what the outcome, it did me more harm than good. She eventually started cooking for me two times a week. I was lucky to have a mother who cared so much about me. And, I was lucky to have Inez. I had most of my fun during that time because of Inez. If she wasn't the one giving a party, she always knew where a good party was being held. It didn't take long for me to regard Inez as the big sister that I'd always wanted.

"Baby girl, I want you and that fine-ass man of yours to come to my engagement party next Saturday night," Inez told me a couple of months after we'd become friends. Inez was twenty-five at the time. Technically speaking, she was not a classic beauty. She had dull brown eyes and a slight overbite. When she turned to the side, her lips protruded like a carp's. But she had beautiful bronze skin and a decent head of black hair, which she'd bleached blond years before blond hair on a Black woman became popular. She'd had matching blond hair weaved into her own.

Inez was tall and nicely built. I was almost as tall as Inez, but not as shapely. With my big brown eyes and round face, a lot of people described me as cute, or even pretty. But I'd never been called beautiful.

I dropped into Inez's nail shop after work and on weekends on a regular basis, whether I needed my nails done or not. One thing that had attracted me to Inez was the fact that she lived such a fascinating life compared to mine. The first time I saw her, she had on a T-shirt that said: WHEN GOD CREATED ME, HE WAS SHOWING OFF.

"*Engagement* party? Engagement for what? You're already married," I said, amused. One thing I could say was that with Inez, there was never a dull moment.

"It's over with Paul," she announced, with a casual wave. "He's lost three jobs because of his drinking. God made only one man that I'd be willing to support, but they nailed him to a cross."

"Don't most women usually get a divorce before they get engaged again?" I chided.

"I'm not like most women," Inez reminded me, with a wink. "As you know, I don't have many shemale friends. You are the only one who understands me. I need you there at my party, Renee."

I didn't have the nerve to tell my girl that I did *not* understand her, but I told her that I wouldn't miss her party for the world. I was hoping that some of Inez's confidence would rub off on me.

I had never been married. It seemed like I'd kissed nothing but frogs since I was thirteen. So far, Robbie Dunbar was as close as I could get to a prince. We had attended Butler High at the same time, and we had started dating in the ninth grade. He was reasonably attractive, despite the fact that he was bowlegged and had a receding hairline, which had started its premature decline before he even finished middle school. Poor Robbie. I probably could have done better at the time, but the boy was so devoted to me, I got spoiled and comfortable.

I was disappointed when Robbie dropped out of school in the middle of our sophomore year. Even though it was so he could work at a gas station that his uncle owned, so that he could help support his mother and three younger siblings. I admired the fact that Robbie cared so much about his family that he would sacrifice his education, but I thought that he could have come up with a better solution.

Robbie and I didn't communicate much while I was away at Ohio State, but as soon as I finished my education and moved back home, Robbie was waiting for me with a marriage proposal, knowing that I'd had other relationships throughout my college years.

However, as much as I hated to admit it even to myself, men were not lining up to be with me, so I didn't hesitate to accept Robbie's proposal. But right after he'd slipped a cheap engagement ring on my finger during a two-for-the-price-of-one dinner at a Ponderosa Steakhouse, I went into the ladies' room and cried. Not tears of joy, but tears of disappointment and sadness. Robbie was as sweet, obedient, dependable, and loyal as a puppy. I believed him when he told me that I was the only woman he'd ever slept with. But all of his good qualities were not enough for me. As a matter of fact, Robbie was too good for his own good. For one thing, he was way too passive. Not just with me, but in everything he did. He didn't argue with people who tried to cheat him at the gas station. He didn't defend himself, or me, when two thugs overpowered us one night outside of a movie theater and ran off with my purse and his wallet. I was the aggressor in my relationship with Robbie, and even though it was not that obvious, I was on the passive side myself.

"Robbie ain't perfect, but he's perfect for you. I know his mama, and I know she raised him right," Mama told me. I knew my mother like I knew the back of my hand. What she really meant was that Robbie was probably the best I could do. My aunts and a lot of other people in my family never let me forget that all of my female cousins and a few nieces, with the exception of my severely retarded cousin, Eileen, had all found husbands by the time they were twenty-one.

Inez had already been married once before. Right after she'd graduated from Butler High, she moved to Europe with Jeremy Knight, a White boy that she'd been in a relationship with for a couple of years. When she returned to Ohio three years later, she had a new husband, a Black soldier named Paul Dunn, whom she'd latched onto in Germany. She also had two beautiful daughters, one by each of the men she'd married. The older girl, Ingrid, resembled her father: platinum blond hair, very light skin, and blue eyes. The younger girl, Malena, had inherited the looks of her darkly handsome father: dark brown hair, eyes, and skin. Both children were extremely exotic.

Despite her loosey-goosey lifestyle, Inez doted on her children, and she always put them first. She didn't even let her boyfriends spend the night when her kids were with her, which was only 50 percent of the time. Inez's divorced mother and her father and his young wife adored the children, too. Several times a week, the girls spent a few days with either their grandmother or their grandfather. I was proud of the way that Inez was raising her kids. I was proud of Inez, period. I loved calling her my best friend. However, she did a lot of shit that was strange, even for her. Like throwing an engagement party to celebrate her upcoming nuptials to one man while she was still married to another!

CHAPTER 8

Inez divorced Paul and married Vincent Tunney. She kept her maiden name each time she got married, claiming that it helped her maintain her independence.

"When are you and Robbie going to tie the knot?" Inez asked me when she and Vince returned from a romp in Vegas, where they'd celebrated their third anniversary.

"Next year, I guess," I said, with a heavy sigh.

"You guess? Well, you don't have to jump up and down about it. Don't you love him?"

"I guess." I shrugged.

Inez's mouth dropped open. "Look, I didn't want to say anything, because it wasn't my business. But I hope you don't do something you'll regret. If you don't want to marry this man, don't do it."

"I can always get a divorce. I'm sure you can walk me through that," I said, with a touch of sarcasm. "I just don't know if I am ready to give up my freedom for Robbie Dunbar. What if I meet somebody I like better after I marry Robbie?"

"Listen, don't you make any plans for this Friday night. I'm taking you to this club off of Superior in Cleveland. It only takes about fifteen minutes to get there from here. It's where I met Vince. If there is somebody else out there for you, he'll be at the Victory Club."

Inez had her new husband baby-sit her two daughters that Friday night when she took me to the Victory Club. There was nothing out of the ordinary about this club. The décor was typical: dark carpets and furniture, obligatory plants, and murals of handsome men and beautiful women on the walls. The band was a little better than the bands at some of the other clubs I went to, and most of the men had on suits and ties.

For the first hour, nobody asked me to dance. Inez didn't wait for men to ask her to dance, she asked them. And not a single one turned her down. I was on my way back from the ladies' room when I met Leon. I don't know where he came from. There was no man near me, and then, all of a sudden, he was there. It seemed like he had just jumped off of one of the murals on the walls. Luther was crooning in the background, making things even more conducive to a possible romantic interlude with another man. But I decided to be cautious. I told myself that I hadn't come to this club to look for someone to replace Robbie, per se. I *was* on a mission, though, but it was a soul-searching expedition. I needed to be sure that Robbie was the man I wanted to give up my freedom for. I didn't know if my mission could be accomplished in one night, but I had to start somewhere.

"I'll let you play with my toys if you let me play with your toys," Leon said, falling in step beside me. Before I could respond, his arm was around my waist. I was glad that I had on my black dress. Even though it was short and tight, the fact that it was black made me look several pounds slimmer. Not that I had a weight problem, but I was as vain as the next woman. Even at a firm size 8, I was still trying to do home improvements on my body.

"Excuse me?" I said. I had on a pair of panty hose that had a sturdy control top, but I still sucked in my stomach. My admirer had a strong grip on my waist, and it felt good.

"What are you drinking?" he asked, sitting down at my table like I'd come to the club with him.

"White wine," I mumbled. "Do I know you?" I asked dumbly.

"Not yet," he smiled. "I'm Leon Webb." He fished a business card out of the breast pocket of his double-breasted navy blue suit.

I looked at the card, then at him. "You are the first IRS auditor I've ever seen in person, thank God," I said, rolling my eyes.

"Are you surprised to see that I don't have horns and a tail?" He laughed.

"I'm surprised to see that you guys are actually human," I teased.

"No offense, but I've always hoped that I'd never have to face one of you guys."

"Well, as long as you don't try to cheat Uncle Sam, this might be the last time you come face to face with the IRS." Leon paused and smiled. He was already handsome, with his medium shade of brown skin, closely cropped black hair, shiny black eyes, and movie star Blair Underwood–type features, but his smile and expensive suit made him look even better. "In more ways than one," he added, with a wink that made my toes tingle.

"Do a lot of people really lie on their taxes?" I asked, trying to keep the conversation neutral. This man was breathtaking, and I didn't know how long I could keep my hands off of him.

"Sister, if I had a dollar for every lie I've been told by taxpayers, I could retire, move to Italy, and live like a king." He even sounded like Blair Underwood. Compared to Leon, Robbie looked like one of the Muppets.

I sniffed and tried to appear not too interested. "I wouldn't lie to you," I said.

"So if I ask if you're married, you'll tell me the truth? And please tell me that you came here alone tonight," Leon said, with a pleading look on his face. His neatly manicured hand covered mine and squeezed.

"I'm not married," I replied, with a shy smile. "But I am . . . uh . . . there is someone here with me." I didn't see any reason to tell him that I was out with another woman.

Leon released my hand and gave me a disappointed look. "Is it somebody I need to be worried about?" he asked, looking behind him, and then over my shoulder.

I shook my head and grinned. "I don't think so. There is nobody in my life that you need to be worried about." I didn't feel good about what I'd just said. The truth of the matter was, Robbie was no threat to Leon. He was not even a challenge. A feather could have knocked Robbie out of first place in my heart. I felt somewhat better when I told myself that Robbie was too good for me.

Leon took both of my hands in his and led me to the dance floor. And that's where I stayed for the rest of the night in that club, wrapped in his arms.

CHAPTER 9

"**W**oman, have you lost your mind? You don't know a damn thing about this Leon Webb," Inez said two days after the night she'd taken me to the Victory Club. She and I were the only ones in her nail shop. She had closed for the day but had agreed to give me a manicure after hours. "Now here you are planning to spend the weekend with him! What about poor Robbie?" Inez asked, filing my nails so hard, it hurt. I didn't complain or even flinch, because she never charged me to do my nails.

"Forget about poor Robbie. What about *poor* me! Look, you are the one who made me go out to meet other men so that I could be sure I wanted to marry Robbie. And that's what I did. If I don't like Leon and decide I still want to marry Robbie, that's my business."

"I don't like this Leon. If I were you, I'd stay as far away from him as I could get. He's not what you think. Trust me."

"Do you know something that I don't know?" I asked, puzzled. Inez had been acting like a fool ever since I'd told her about Leon. She had been making off-the-wall comments about him and trying to divert my attention.

"I know a lot of things that you don't know," Inez said in a mysterious tone of voice. She blew on my nails for a few seconds. Then she started filing them again, twice as rough as before. This time I did flinch and yell out in pain, but she ignored me and started buffing my nails like she was shining the shoes on the feet of a man she didn't like.

"Do you know Leon Webb?" I wanted to know.

"Um . . . yeah. As a matter of fact, I do know him, and he's not your type. He's a friend of my cousin Earl, the one who has been in and out of jail half his life. You remember Earl, the pimp and drug dealer." Inez kept buffing my nails, glancing at my face every other second.

"But Leon went to Morehouse," I said thoughtfully, defending a man I knew very little about.

"So? There are a lot of educated thugs out there," Inez insisted.

"Well, is Leon a pimp and a drug dealer, too? Like your cousin Earl?"

"Not that I know of," Inez admitted. "But he's not for you. Trust me," she added, as she narrowed her eyes and gave me a quick nod.

"Do me a favor, and let me worry about Leon. I am still a single woman. And I am a grown woman. I can make my own decisions," I said firmly.

"But, Renee—"

"But nothing," I snapped, cutting Inez off. I snatched my hand out of hers. As far as I was concerned, the manicure and the conversation were over.

Leon wore suits and ties most of the time, and I liked that. And, he was very family oriented, one of the most important qualities that I looked for in a man. His wallet contained pictures of everybody, from his daughter to his elderly parents. He loved his family so much that tears formed in his eyes when he talked about them. His only brother, Stanley, had been killed in action during the Desert Storm War. His older sister, Carrie, a bitter divorcée who had packed up her three kids and left them on her ex-husband's doorstep, now lived with his elderly parents in West Cleveland. There was a look of sadness on Leon's face when he talked about how he was ready to settle down. And how he hoped that that would happen, before he turned thirty. He was currently twenty-nine. I didn't tell him, but I was hoping to do the same thing.

Leon didn't take me to the fancy restaurant like he had promised when I agreed to spend the weekend with him at his house. But that didn't bother me at all. His house was the kind that I had been dreaming about living in all of my life: a cozy four-bedroom brick sanctuary on a quiet, tree-lined street occupied by professional people. He took me on a tour of his house, leading me by the hand. Every room in his house had the same thick beige carpeting. Each piece of furniture looked new and expensive. I was glad to see that Leon was also a neat housekeeper. Robbie's shabby apartment, situated on a dead-end street between a greasy rib joint and a place that sold fishing worms, always looked like a train wreck.

As soon as I stumbled back into Leon's spacious living room, he was all over me. He wrestled me down onto a plush brocade sofa, knocking a large potted plant off the end table to the floor, where the beige carpet was so thick, it felt like I had stepped onto a cloud.

"Oh, baby, I've been thinking about doing this all day," he managed, rubbing my breasts. The only time that Robbie ever touched my breasts was when I climbed on top of him. Even after I'd done that, I still had to guide his hands.

I felt like I was made out of rubber in Leon's arms. I was so limp, he could have tied me in a knot. I swooned when he lifted me off the floor and carried me upstairs to his bedroom. He slowly undressed me, kissing me all over. When he ripped off my panties, I knew there was no turning back.

Robbie was an easy man to lie to. I didn't even have to put forth that much effort when I lied to him about why I had suddenly become so unavailable each time he wanted to take me to the Ponderosa Steakhouse or fishing. "I've been tutoring one of my students. The boy has potential, and I want to make sure he takes advantage of it."

"That's nice, baby. I am so proud of you. I hope this boy and his folks appreciate the sacrifices you make. I sure do," Robbie told me.

An hour after I got off the telephone with Robbie, I was back in Leon's bed, wallowing on his satin sheets, and squealing like a stuck pig.

The more I saw of Leon, the more Inez protested. "I don't want you to get hurt, Renee," she said the next time I stepped into her shop.

"What is your problem?" I yelled, grabbing an opened can of Diet Pepsi out of her hand and taking a sip.

"I have a lot more experience with men than you," she reminded.

"Tell me about it," I hissed, finishing her soda with a loud burp.

"I've made a lot of mistakes, and I've learned from my mistakes. I just don't want to see you get hurt." Inez started dragging a broom across the floor, her eyes still on me.

"Then stay out of my business," I said casually, tossing the empty soda can into a trash can by the door.

Inez stopped sweeping and placed one hand on her hip, shaking a finger in my direction. "You make it my business when you ask me to lie for you when Robbie or your mama calls looking for you, girl. You make it my business when you have Leon pick you up from my house so your nosy neighbors won't see you crawling in and out of another man's car so they can run and tell Robbie."

"Let me make one thing clear. When I want your advice, I will ask for it. In the meantime, stop wasting your breath. Leon wants to be with me, and I want to be with him," I said, holding up my hand. I guess my girl didn't want to talk to my hand, because she dropped the subject.

Inez was the only one who knew about my relationship with Leon so far. But it wasn't long before the neighborhood busybodies saw me and him out together and started blabbing.

The following Saturday morning, my telephone rang at six a.m. "You just like your Aunt Denise!" To my everlasting horror, it was Mama. I'd grabbed the phone on the first ring, hoping that it would not disturb Leon. He looked like a man who didn't want his sleep interrupted. I had never seen a person sleep the way he did. His face was frozen in a frown so extreme that his lips looked like a horseshoe. He was curled up in my bed, with his arm around my waist. I preferred to be with Leon at his house. There was no comparison between his nice place and my tiny apartment, which I'd furnished with odds and ends from thrift stores, yard sales, and dollar stores.

"Mama, is that you?" I asked, whispering. I was so groggy, I could barely see.

"What's wrong with you, girl?" Mama asked, her voice full of her usual impatience and nerve. She stopped talking long enough to suck on her teeth. "You know doggone well who this is, gal!" Mama hollered loud and clear. My mother hollered a lot, but I overlooked it because I knew that all the hollering she did was out of love and concern. She had made it clear that no matter how old I got to be, to her, I'd always be one of her babies.

"Good morning, Mama," I muttered, rising. I was not comfortable talking to my mother while I was naked and lying next to a naked man. I pulled the sheet up to my chin.

"You are going to end up just like your aunt Denise: old and as lonesome as a micky ficky. You can't clown men like you doing, girl! Robbie ain't no fool. He ain't going to settle for whatever nasty hind parts you got left when that IRS scalawag takes off."

"I know, Mama," I said, trying to keep my voice low enough for Leon not to hear.

"It's just a matter of time before Mr. IRS realizes all he's got by having you is a woman who cheats on her man. And poor Robbie! He's going to ball up and die when he finds out he's being played."

"Mama, may I call you back later? I can't talk right now," I said, sitting up on the side of the bed, my feet dangling. I could hear Mama and my twelve-year-old sister, Frankie, mumbling in the background.

"You better get yourself sorted out girl. I am telling you that that Dunbar boy ain't no fool. Poor Robbie! It would serve you right if he came up to you and snatched that nice engagement ring off your finger. And you setting a bad example for your baby sister."

"You're right, Mama. Like you always are." There was nothing like agreeing with Mama to calm her down. "Mama, I will call you later, and we can talk more about this," I insisted. "I love you, Mama."

"I love you, too, baby," Mama said, her voice much softer. She sounded like a totally different woman now. "Do you want me to come over there and cook up a mess of greens? I ain't got nothing to do today."

"That's all right, Mama. I'll call you back later," I replied, hanging up.

"What's up, baby?" Leon asked, sitting up. His arm was still around my waist. He placed his long, muscular legs on top of mine. "Who was that on the telephone?"

"My mama. You know how old people are," I replied, with a heavy sigh, waving my hand.

"Unfortunately, I do," Leon said, rolling his eyes. "I hide when I see my mama and daddy coming up on my front porch." He laughed. "I hope we don't end up like them with our kids," he added, giving me a playful tap on my chin.

His last comment opened the right door for me to reveal what was on my mind. "Uh, Leon, I don't know where this relationship is going, but I think it's something we need to talk about," I said in a tentative voice. I held my breath and stared straight ahead. He was taking too long to respond, so I looked at him.

"Where do you want it to go?" he asked. Leon didn't look half as good when he was just waking up as he usually did. Without his neatly combed hair and suit, he was a fright. His hair was matted and full of lint that had rubbed off of my cheap bedspread, and his breath stank like horse shit. I didn't even want to think about how I looked, or smelled, after the long night we'd just spent drinking and fucking.

I shrugged. "I *am* engaged to marry another man. I've told you about Robbie Dunbar. If he doesn't know about you and me already, he will soon enough. If I lose him, and I wouldn't blame him for calling off the engagement, I'll be alone again. That is, if you decide to move on, too. And that's not where I want to be." I paused and turned my head slightly to the side so that I didn't have to see Leon's face. But I couldn't keep my eyes off of him. I looked at him again and blinked.

"Why don't you tell me where you want to be?" Leon held up his hand. "Do you want to be with me?" His eyes were looking directly into mine.

"Of course. But are we going to take this to the next level, or is this it?"

"Girl, if you want me to marry you, just come out and say it." He laughed.

"Is this a marriage proposal? You didn't say anything about love." I looked away again, talking now like I was talking to myself. "I love you, and I've told you so, repeatedly. But you've never said it to me."

At this point, Leon placed his hands on my shoulders and gently spun me around. "I love you, Renee. I would marry you in a minute if I thought that was what you wanted—"

"It is what I want!" I boomed.

"Well, before we do it, maybe I should at least meet your mama," Leon decided. I had already met most of his family. I liked all of them, and as far as I could tell, they liked me, too. I knew that once Mama met Leon, she would come around. He was the most charismatic man I'd ever met.

Inez had made it clear that she would probably never accept Leon. That bothered me, but I ignored it as much as I could. Other than the fact that Leon had once been best friends with one of her thuggish relatives, I couldn't figure out why she didn't like him. But it was just as well, because Leon hated Inez just as much as she hated him.

And that was one thing that didn't seem like it was ever going to change.

CHAPTER 10

As hard as it was to believe, I still had feelings for Robbie. But I knew in my heart that I could not spend the rest of my life with him. It wouldn't have been fair to him, and it wouldn't have been fair to me. He did next to nothing to excite me, and if that was already bothering me, I couldn't imagine how high I'd be climbing up a wall ten or fifteen years down the road. Compared to Leon, Robbie was from another planet.

There was never a dull moment with Leon. In addition to a regular weekly night out at the movies, Leon took me to dinner at least twice a week. Not to any of the greasy rib joints and cheap Ponderosa Steakhouses that Robbie used to take me to with coupons, but to five-star restaurants where the menus didn't show any prices. Then, to show off, I started cooking Leon's favorite foods for him. We both had ties to the Deep South, so we both loved greens, beans, corn bread, neck bones, ham hocks, and candied yams. Robbie was so indifferent, he didn't care if I fed him cold hot dogs or mud pies. And getting honest compliments from Robbie was as difficult as pulling a hen's teeth. The few times that I had tried to pry comments out of him about a new outfit or a new hairdo, he'd always said the same thing, "Baby, you look great!" Even when I knew I didn't.

I had never felt like I had a whole man with Robbie. He seemed more like a half. Because of that, I felt like I had to be a woman and a half just so we'd make a complete couple! I didn't have that problem with Leon.

I didn't have the heart to break off my relationship with Robbie in person. I took the coward's way out and called him up on the telephone. I had played it safe and waited another month, though. I felt badly about it, but I didn't want to let go of one man until I was sure I had the other one securely hooked.

"Robbie, I have something I need to talk to you about," I began, clutching the telephone in the teachers' lounge. I had called him at his job at the gas station. Shirley Blake, a nosy busybody who taught first grade in the room right next to mine, walked in as soon as I got started. "Uh, Robbie, I might have to call you back," I said, both my eyes on Shirley. As soon as she realized I was talking to a man, she came and stood right next to me. Like me, she was well into her twenties and had never been married.

"Ask your friend if he's got a friend," Shirley whispered in my ear, the garlic on her breath almost melting the side of my face. Shirley was one of the most attractive women I knew, and one of the most desperate. She was so anxious to get married that she had already purchased a wedding gown—and didn't even have a steady boyfriend! Her beautiful shoulder-length black hair and soft delicate features had done her little good so far when it came to men. She had not had a date in over a year. Nobody knew what she did that turned men off. Robbie and I had had some interesting conversations, and a lot of laughs, about Shirley. I was going to miss that.

I covered the telephone receiver with my hand and gave Shirley a pleading look. "Do you mind? This is a private conversation," I told her.

"Well, excuse me," Shirley said in a loud, hostile voice, rotating her neck. She waved her hands, shook her head, and muttered under her breath as she rushed from the room.

I watched the entrance for a few seconds before I returned my attention back to Robbie. "Robbie, I need to tell you something," I said, keeping my eye on the doorway.

"Was that Shirley Blake's voice I just heard?" Robbie asked dryly, about as interested in her as I was.

"Uh-huh."

"She still looking for a man?"

"Every day."

"Well, I hope she finds her another one soon." Robbie laughed.

"Um, that's kind of what I wanted to talk to you about," I stammered, turning my back to the door. I no longer cared who heard what I had to say to Robbie. With all of the gossips I knew, everybody would know about the breakup sooner or later, anyway.

"Talk to me," Robbie ordered in a firm voice. He had never sounded this assertive before, so it stunned me for a few seconds. "Well, are you going to talk to me or not?" he said, sounding even more assertive.

I cleared my throat. "Robbie, there is another man in my life. It's pretty serious between us. Uh . . . and I wanted you to hear it from me," I blurted.

"You are too late," Robbie replied, now sounding as weak and passive as ever.

"Who told you?" I gasped.

"Who didn't? Your aunt Vicki that runs the produce stand told me. Your cousin Fred, who buys his gas at my station, he told me. Your mama told my mama, and then my mama told me. Your baby sister even told me."

"Oh. Well, I am really sorry that you didn't hear it from me, Robbie."

"So am I," he said, sounding tired and disappointed.

"Robbie, I wanted to tell you myself way before now, but I didn't know how. I didn't want to hurt you."

"You are a little too late for that, too. And to tell you the truth, I already knew about you and Leon before anybody else told me. I saw you and him coming out of that fancy restaurant on Price Street a couple of weeks ago, hugging, kissing and everything. I got the picture. . . ."

"Oh. Um . . . I know you will find someone else," I said quietly. "And I hope you will be happy with whomever that is. You're a good man, Robbie."

"But not good enough for you." Robbie's voice sounded so hopeless, I almost changed my mind.

"Robbie, don't do this to me, or yourself. I didn't plan to fall in love with another man. It just happened. But . . . I hope that . . . uh . . . you and I can still be friends."

"I still love you, Renee. Whether I marry another woman or not, I will always have a place in my heart for you. You were my first love, and that's something I won't ever forget."

"Robbie, I think we should end this conversation right now. You take care of yourself. Do you hear me?"

"You, too, Renee. And, uh, you tell that IRS henchman that if he don't treat you right, I'm going to whup his black ass." Robbie laughed again. "Bye, Renee."

It would not have done Robbie any good to try and talk me out of breaking up with him. I was a little disappointed that he didn't even try. Now I was glad that I'd severed the relationship. But I had no idea that my decision was going to come back to haunt the hell out of me.

CHAPTER 11

The Sunday following my breakup with Robbie, I brought Leon to meet Mama after she and my sister, Frankie, got home from church. We'd arrived at the little one-story gray shingled house that Mama rented on Maple Street just as she and Frankie were getting out of Mama's old Chevy, still clutching their hymn books. Mama had on a hat that looked like a small umbrella. She snatched it off and started fanning her face as soon as she spotted Leon and me walking toward her.

Frankie, who was as cute and as sly as a fox, stood behind Mama, with an amused look on her face. My sister had already made it her business to meet Leon. She'd come to my apartment several days earlier, interrogating him like he was a suspect. Once she realized how generous Leon was, she didn't waste any time joining his team. She didn't know that I knew she'd called Leon up at work two days ago and asked him for a hundred dollars so she could get her hair braided. I planned to speak to her about that later.

"That's a nice suit you got on, Leon," Frankie chirped, trying hard not to look at me. To a lot of people, a spoiled baby sister was a thorn in the side. Frankie was no different. "Where'd you get it?"

"Don't be nosy and rude!" I snapped, glaring at Frankie, wondering why Mama was taking her time to speak. Especially since she was looking Leon up and down, shading her eyes with her hat.

Mama had told me more than once that she didn't trust men who wore suits outside of a church or an office. "Young man, did you just come from church or work?" she asked, looking at Leon out of the corner of her eye.

"Neither, ma'am," Leon mumbled, giving me a sideways glance. "I wanted to make a good impression on you, ma'am, so I decided to wear my best suit," he added. I had told him how my mother felt about suits.

"Oh," Mama said, obviously pleased to hear this. "Well, I hope you don't spill nothing on it at my dinner table," she told him, with a broad smile on her heavily powdered face.

Getting through dinner was tense. For a while, Frankie was the only one who seemed to be enjoying the turkey wings and greens that Mama had prepared earlier. After a few awkward moments, Leon really dug into the dinner, too.

Even though Mama was polite, she kept rolling her eyes at Leon and giving me suspicious looks. When Leon stopped the leaky faucet in the kitchen sink from dripping, Mama smiled for the rest of the evening.

"I done had two plumbers out here, and three of my nephews. Nary one of them could stop that leak," Mama said, looking at Leon like he had just walked on water. "You, you take a pair of pliers to it, and five minutes later, it don't leak no more. Ooh wee, child!"

"And it won't ever leak again," Leon assured Mama, patting her shoulder. "If it does, I will buy you a whole new set of faucets." He was as slick as a used car salesman.

Mama was beaming. "Renee, run in the pantry and bring out that bottle of wine I been saving," she ordered, with a huge grin. "Leon, I hope you like white wine."

"Yes, ma'am. I sure do," Leon lied. Other than beer and rum, he didn't drink any other alcohol. But it didn't take me long to realize what Leon's strategy was. He was the type of man who was willing to do and say whatever it took to keep people happy.

Everybody except Inez. The first time I saw him angry was when I told him that Inez wanted to be maid of honor in my wedding.

"No way! No way will I let that bitch be involved in my wedding!" he roared.

His words horrified me. "She's my best friend. I know she doesn't like you, and you don't like her. But I love you both, and I don't want to be in the middle of all this animosity. My wedding is a once-in-a-lifetime event, so I want what I want."

"What about what I want? This is a once-in-a-lifetime thing for me, too." Leon had never been married before, but he'd lived with the mother of his daughter for eight years.

"Baby, she wants to be there for me. Until now, she didn't even want to be in the same room with you. If she can get to this point, can't you?"

"Why are we even having a church wedding in the first place? Can't we just go down to the courthouse?"

"We don't have to have a big church wedding. I didn't want that, anyway. That's all Mama's idea. And your mama's, too. If you want us to go to the courthouse, that's fine with me."

"And anyway, every couple I know that had a big church wedding ended up getting a divorce," Leon said.

"Leon, you can stop now. I already told you that getting married in the courthouse is fine with me," I chuckled. "And if you change your mind later on, we can always renew our vows in a church."

I avoided Mama, Inez, and everybody else for the next few days. I didn't have enough nerve to tell them that the big church wedding that they'd been wanting to experience wasn't going to happen. At least not with me.

I got Mama's answering machine when I called from the Hyatt Hotel in nearby Cleveland. That's where Leon and I had checked in right after we'd exchanged vows at the courthouse, six months after our first date.

Leon didn't believe in spending money on frivolous things, like the weeklong honeymoon in Niagara Falls I'd suggested. I didn't argue with him at the time, but I'd pouted behind his back. I decided that it would be to my advantage to keep our disagreements to a minimum until our marriage was more secure.

I didn't leave a message for Mama. But when I called Inez's house and got her answering machine, too, I didn't hesitate to leave a message telling her that Leon and I had "eloped." Before I could hang up, Inez clicked off her answering machine and picked up the telephone.

"I'm here," she said in a low, raspy voice.

"Please be happy for me," I pleaded. "I love Leon, and he loves me. That's all that counts. I never said it, but I didn't want you to marry

Vince. I was happy for you, anyway. Not that I didn't like Vince, but I honestly didn't think that he was the right man for you at the time."

"Well, apparently Vince didn't think he was the right man for me, either," Inez told me.

"Excuse me? Inez, tell me what's going on," I demanded.

"I packed his shit and told him to get the hell out of my house before I threw him out. I filed for divorce yesterday."

"Already? You're practically still a newlywed!"

"Better now than later. He wanted to change me. He started talking about how he wanted me to tone down my wardrobe, stop wearing so much make-up, and get rid of my blond weave. No man is going to change me."

"Are you all right?"

"I am now. Some of my best friends are bartenders."

"I'm sorry I wasn't around to . . . to talk. I swear to God, Inez, if I had known, I would have been there for you."

"You need to be there for your husband now, baby girl. I'll be fine."

"I'll stop by the shop as soon as we get home, day after tomorrow. We can go for drinks," I suggested, feeling guilty because I was so happy about my marriage, and Inez's had just ended—again.

"Where are you?"

"We are at the Hyatt. Uh, Leon didn't want to go to Niagara Falls or on a honeymoon cruise."

"Well if I was him I'd have chosen the Hyatt Hotel in downtown Cleveland over Niagara Falls, too."

"Inez, please don't start that shit," I said, blowing out a plaintive sigh. "You didn't want anybody to make fun of you when you married any of your . . . uh . . . *three* husbands." There was a moment of silence before we both laughed. I didn't know about Inez, but I had to force myself to laugh. "So when and where do you want to hook up for drinks when I get home?"

"I'm getting out of town for a couple of weeks. I'll call you when I get back and we'll decide then. I booked a flight to Barbados this morning. As a matter of fact, the cab's out there now," Inez said, talking fast. Inez had already seen more of the world than any other person I knew. Being her own boss, and having the kind of money she needed to do just about anything she wanted, it was nothing for her to jet off to some exotic location at the spur of the moment.

"Will you call me as soon as you get back home so we can get together?"

"I will. And, Renee, congratulations and good luck. I really mean it."

I was surprised when I turned around and saw Leon standing a few feet behind me.

"That was Inez. She and Vince broke up. He's moved out, and she's already filed for divorce." I shook my head and looked away. But out of the corner of my eye, I saw a cruel smile cross Leon's face.

CHAPTER 12

Leon was the one to break the news to Mama. I didn't even know he had done it until she called the hotel the day before we checked out.

"I don't care what that man do to you, you better stay with him. There ain't never been a divorce in our family," Mama told me. "And your baby sister is mad because she spent her last penny on one of them throwaway cameras, which she bought to take pictures of the wedding with. I hope you know what you doing, gal," Mama said in a gruff voice. I never got mad at my mother when she stuck her nose in my business. I didn't know too many women who didn't go through some of the same things with their mothers that I went through with mine. I usually listened to Mama, with respect and patience. After all, she had made a lot of sacrifices for me. But I was my own woman, so I always did what I wanted to do, anyway.

"I love Leon, Mama," I purred. I had just come out of the shower. One towel covered my body; another one covered my wet hair. Leon was stretched out on the bed, in just the bottom part of the silk pajamas I'd bought him. "I'm never going to let him go," I vowed, giving my new husband a playful kick with my damp foot. "Mama, can I call you when we get home Monday? I am still on my honeymoon."

"And that's another thing. When you was a little girl, all you talked about was going to Niagara Falls for your honeymoon. It's a crying shame you ended up on a honeymoon in Cleveland of all places. Right in your own backyard!" Mama paused and clicked her teeth. "And with all that money Leon makes working for the IRS, the least he could have done was take you off somewhere romantic." After saying such a mouthful, Mama had to stop to catch her breath. And it didn't take her long to do that. She had other things to say that I didn't want to hear, which she whispered. "I heard Leon was stingy. I bet he'll be shoving chicken gizzards down your throat for dinner three times a week. You better hope you don't lose your job at that schoolhouse."

"Mama, I have to go now." I hung up before Mama could get another word in. Mama was the only person I knew who could turn a dream into a nightmare. I tossed a pillow at Leon's head. "You could have waited until I got out of the shower. I wanted to be the one to tell her."

"Well, I didn't. Now get dressed so we can go out and get something to eat," he ordered, rising.

"Baby, wouldn't it be nicer if we stayed in and ordered room service? Don't you just want to lie here and . . . uh . . . you know." I winked.

"Come on. We're going out to get something to eat," Leon replied.

"What if I don't want to go with you?" I said, folding my arms defiantly, my bottom lip poked out like a five-year-old's. I couldn't believe we were already having our first disagreement as a married couple.

"You're going. Now get your lazy butt up and get dressed. Put on that lime green dress I like so much. Sisters with your bronze tone complexion look so damned good in green."

I removed a pair of jeans and a beige silk blouse from the small suitcase that I had packed. Before I could get dressed, Leon snatched the clothes out of my hand and tossed them to the top of the dresser. With a mischievous grin on his face, he flipped open my suitcase and fished out the lime green dress he liked so much and tossed it on top of my head. I slid into the dress without saying a word. I was in too much of a romantic mood to argue any further.

I didn't like the fact that Leon was already making decisions without any input from me. Robbie Dunbar would *never* have done that. As strange as it seemed, I really missed Robbie. I knew that I was going to spend the rest of my days wondering what my life would have been like if I had married him. Poor Robbie. I prayed that he would find a suitable mate.

By the time Leon and I got to the Full Moon restaurant three blocks from the hotel, I had calmed down. Right after our stiff-lipped waiter dropped menus on our table, I excused myself to go to the ladies' room. By the time I got back to the table, Leon had ordered for me.

"I didn't want an omelet," I protested, pinching his arm. "I wanted pancakes."

"Well, the next time we go out to eat, I advise you to order before you run off to the ladies' room to primp," he said, looking at his watch. "And hurry up. There's a game coming on in a couple of hours."

I took a sip of water and forced myself to smile. It dawned on me that Leon was showing me another side of himself, and it was already making me uncomfortable. He liked to be in control, and that was one of the things that had drawn me to him. However, that quality had been a lot more subtle before I'd become his wife.

A cramp shot through my stomach like a comet. All of a sudden, I was concerned about my future with Leon. As much as I had always wanted a man who had more of a backbone than Robbie, I didn't want a man who made all my decisions for me.

Leon had made it clear that he was in no hurry to have another child. He had a nine-year-old daughter by a woman that he had lived with for several years. He loved his child, and he took good care of her, but even though she was only nine, Collette was a mess. Not only was she moody and materialistic, she had a hard time getting along with other kids. She had been kicked out of every elementary school in Butler. Leon had just enrolled her in a swank private school in Cleveland Heights. More than once he had told me that he was glad he had only one child to deal with.

But I wanted a child, and I wanted one soon. That's why I flushed my birth control pills down the toilet as soon as we got back to our hotel room.

CHAPTER 13

Inez stayed in Barbados for ten days. I received a postcard from her, letting me know that after she left that island, she was going to stop off in Jamaica for an additional few days. Unlike Inez, I didn't like to run away from my problems. I liked to sit down with someone who cared about me and talk things over. Inez was the best listener I had ever known. There was not a psychiatrist, or a bartender, in town that I would rather tell my troubles to before Inez.

I was glad that I had made the decision on my own to try and get pregnant, but this was something that I wanted to discuss with my best friend. Not that I wanted her to give me any advice, but it would have been nice just to have her around to listen to me.

I enjoyed being married. I felt like a totally different woman. I looked and acted differently. And other people noticed, even some of my second-grade students. "Miss Beakes, why come you all the time smiling and humming stupid songs now?" asked Walter Marrell, the most obnoxious youngster in my class this year. Walter looked like a gnome, with his lopsided head, long ears, and round, flat nose. But he still liked to draw attention to himself. His small black eyes seemed to look right through me as he anxiously awaited my response.

"Walter, you must remember that I am Mrs. Webb now. No more Miss Beakes. I got married," I said proudly. I stood in front of my class, with the latest Harry Potter book in my hand, preparing to read a few excerpts to them.

"Why did you get married, Miss Beakes?" the same boy asked, with a giggle, his two front teeth missing. "Now you got to sleep in the same bed with a strange man." The whole class snickered.

"Walter, married people sleep together. Now if you don't mind, let's confine our attention to our good friend Harry Potter," I said firmly, holding up the front of the book. I didn't read much for my own pleasure, but when I did, it was usually a novel by a popular African American author, like Carl Weber or Mary B. Morrison. I'd already read most of the classics and more textbooks than I could remember, so Harry Potter was as much a treat for me as it was for my students.

But Walter seemed more interested in my story than Harry's. He occupied a desk at the front of the classroom, right across from my cluttered desk, so he was hard to ignore. "My daddy makes all kinds of strange noises when he's in the bed with my mama," Walter announced, facing his classmates. Then he turned to me. "Miss Beakes, do you and your husband make a lot of strange noises in the bed?" This time the class roared with laughter.

The bell rang before either Walter or I could say another word. And the subject was never brought up again. At least not in my classroom. I wanted to share cute little stories like this one with Leon, but he didn't have a lot of interest in what went on in an elementary school. I didn't bother to tell him about little Walter's comments. However, I told him about the time that Mindy Stargen came to school with a condom she'd found in her father's pants pocket, blowing it up like a balloon during show-and-tell. Leon didn't laugh or even comment about that incident, or any of the others that I shared with him, even though I gave him my undivided attention all the times he held me hostage for hours on end, repeating conversations he'd had with difficult taxpayers. Inez seemed to be the only one who was genuinely interested in my day-to-day life, and that's why I spent so much time hanging around her nail shop.

The two sisters that Inez employed, Pat Jenkins and Shonda Jones, got sick of me coming into Soulful Nails while she was still out of the country, whining about how I needed to talk to Inez. Their impatience and exasperation showed on their faces each time they saw mine. But I didn't let that stop me.

"She didn't tell you what hotel she was going to be staying in?" I asked, looking from Pat to Shonda. Both of them had on more make-up than Ronald McDonald. Like Inez, they thought their shit didn't stink, but in a good way. I was one woman who was not afraid to admit that I admired and envied confident women.

Impatient customers were lined up in chairs along the wall like convicts. Pat and Shonda were both frantically filing and buffing the fingernails and toenails of the two women who occupied the seats in front of them.

"Inez didn't want nobody to know how to find her," Shonda said, tossing her head back so that her blond weave flopped and fluttered like a scarf. She handled the nail drill like it was a Gatling gun, looking up from the customer in front of her just long enough to glance at my shabby nails and give me a disgusted look.

"If Inez calls, tell her to call me," I ordered, curling my fingers into a fist to hide my raggedy nails.

Just when I was about ready to start climbing the walls, Inez came home four days after my last visit to the nail shop. It was Halloween night, so when I went to answer the doorbell, I carried a large bowl that I had filled with suckers and other goodies.

"Trick or treat!" I yelled as I snatched open my door, expecting to see the faces of some of the neighborhood kids grinning up at me. I was shocked to see Inez standing in my doorway, loaded down with gifts and souvenirs.

What was even more shocking was the fact that Leon was with her. "This handsome devil you married was sweet enough to pick me up and drive me home from the airport," Inez squealed. She leaned toward me and air-kissed my cheeks.

"He what?" I mouthed, puzzled. The bowl suddenly felt twice as heavy in my hand.

"I tried to call you, and everybody else I know, to come pick me up. Leon was the only person I was able to reach," Inez explained, with a sheepish look on her face. Over her shoulder, I saw Leon dragging his feet up our walkway. There was an odd expression on his face. He looked like the grinning jack-o'-lantern I had set on our front porch banister a few days ago. "Your honey was sweet enough to bring me by here first." Inez said the word "honey" like it was painful. I looked from her to Leon and back to her, trying to figure them both out. They were not acting like two people who couldn't stand one another.

I didn't know what confused me more: the fact that Inez had suddenly returned and come straight to my house, or the fact that Leon—who had just referred to her as the poor man's Paris Hilton the night before—had picked her up from the airport.

"Girl, I've been dying to talk to you!" I squealed, hugging Inez. I set the bowl of candy on the end table next to my sofa and threw my arms around her. She had lost a few pounds, which made her body look even more luscious. But with her hair hidden under a scarf and no make-up, she looked rather plain from the neck up.

"I want to hear all about Barbados and Jamaica," I told Inez, smiling at Leon as he made his way into the living room.

"I'm going to fix myself a drink. Why don't I fix you sisters something, too?" he suggested, his gaze darting back and forth from Inez to me.

I looked at Leon and blinked. There was a nervous smile on his face.

"I'd like a *large* cosmopolitan," Inez said, flopping down on the sofa, dropping the shopping bags on the floor.

"A cosmo it is," Leon sang. "And I'll fill up the largest glass in the house," he added, with a chuckle. He stepped forward a few feet, with his arms stretched open like he wanted to hug the world. This was one man who was full of surprises.

"And don't be stingy with the vodka," Inez warned Leon.

I was surprised but pleased to see my best friend and my husband speaking in such a friendly manner. It was a reason for me to celebrate.

"I'd like a margarita," I chirped, smiling at Inez as I eased down on the other end of the sofa. As soon as Leon left the room, I turned to her, with both my eyebrows raised. "It takes thirty minutes to get here from the airport."

"True," Inez said, tilting her head to the side, an amused look on her face. She slid the scarf back off her face, revealing mild sunburn on her forehead. "And?"

"And what did you and Leon talk about for thirty minutes?" I wanted to know. I was so pleased to see Inez that I didn't really care what she had discussed with my husband. It was enough for me to see that they had reached such a milestone in their "relationship."

Inez shrugged. "Nothing much. I slept most of the way." She rose, lifting one of the shopping bags. "I got you one of those straw purses you've always wanted."

I sighed, suddenly slipping back into the slight and mysterious depression I'd been experiencing since my marriage. "Let's do lunch tomorrow. I need a sounding board," I told Inez.

She glanced toward the doorway leading to the kitchen, and then she gave me a concerned look. "If you promise not to yell and scream at me about sticking my nose in your business, I can. I'll meet you at the deli across the street from my shop."

"I just want you to listen to me." I leaned toward her and squeezed her hand.

Inez gave me a bleak look, but she nodded. "Fine. We have a date."

She turned all the way around and looked toward the doorway again. I didn't like the look on her face when she returned her attention to me. "Have you seen what's behind his mask yet?" she whispered, grabbing my hand.

I reared back, snatching my hand away from hers like I'd been burned. "What's that supposed to mean? Look, Leon is my husband now. If he is the demon you sometimes make him out to be, you should have told me before I hooked up with him."

"I tried to," Inez wailed, with an exasperated sigh. "He is your husband now, and I do respect that. I can put up with him if he can put up with me, I guess. The fact that he offered to pick me up from the airport says a lot. Don't you think so?"

"I love him and he loves me and that's all that matters," I insisted. A few moments later Leon entered the living room, with our drinks on a tray. He sported a smile that covered almost half of his face. "Baby, Inez was just saying how nice it was of you to pick her up from the airport," I told him, taking a long swallow from my glass.

"It was no trouble at all," Leon said, scratching the side of his head. He plopped down on the sofa, next to Inez, even though there was more than enough room closer to me. It was the first time that I'd ever seen my best friend and my husband within a foot of each other.

I felt better already, and the strong margarita had a lot to do with that. As a matter of fact, I decided that I didn't need to meet Inez for lunch and cry on her shoulder, after all. I needed to be with my husband.

CHAPTER 14

Inez didn't waste any time getting back into the single life. A week after she got back from her latest jaunt to the Caribbean, I heard that she had found herself a new man. An Iranian this time. That didn't surprise me, but the way I found out did. Leon told me!

"Who told *you* that Inez was involved with an Iranian?" I asked him. We were in the new Range Rover he'd just purchased, on our way to Mama's house for dinner that Sunday evening. Mama had called up and invited us, and Leon had accepted without even checking with me. I had planned to spend the day grading papers and doing laundry. It didn't bother Leon when I told him that I didn't like always having to rearrange my schedule at the last minute. All he did was roll his eyes at me and give me a stupid grin.

"Nobody told me anything about that woman and her Iranian. I saw her with him at the Victory Club the other night," he revealed, keeping his eyes on the road.

"I didn't know you still went to that club," I gasped. I removed my arm from around his shoulder and gave him an exasperated look.

"There are a lot of things that you don't know about me, Renee."

"I knew that a long time ago, Leon. The man I met that night in the Victory Club is not the man that I married. I am really getting worried about what other surprises you might have in store for me," I said hotly. My ex, Robbie Dunbar, was meek and docile compared to me.

But I was meek and docile compared to Leon. However, there were times that I was so assertive, I surprised myself as much as I surprised Leon. "I am not your fool, Leon!" I said in a loud voice.

"Don't you start that shit, woman. I am not in the mood for a fight." He gripped the steering wheel, his eyes still on the road. Just from looking at the side of his face, I could see that he was angry. I didn't care, because I was angry, too.

"I'm not in the mood for a fight, either, but you brought it up. First, you tell me something about my best friend that I didn't know. Then, you tell me that you were at the same club where everybody in town goes when they want to meet someone."

Leon turned sharply, giving me a harsh look. "I went there for a drink with some of my boys. You went there to pick up somebody, but I didn't. I just happened to be there that night I met you, doing the same thing I was doing the other night, having a drink with some of my boys."

"Well, maybe I'll go there tomorrow night," I said, with a snort, crossing my arms so that I wouldn't haul off and slap the side of his head.

Leon balled his fist and socked the steering wheel as he glared at me. Saliva was oozing from the corners of his mouth. "Look, woman, that's one place you don't go unless you go with me!"

"You can't tell me where I can go and where I can't go, Mr. Man. I don't tell you where to go," I shouted, giving him the most incredulous look I could manage. "If Inez and other women can go there without their men, so can I. And if you can't give me one good reason why I shouldn't, you can just shut the fuck up."

"I'll give you a damn good reason—I can't trust you!"

My mouth dropped open. "What? What have I done to make you think you can't trust me?" I glared at Leon's head, wanting to slap it on both sides. "I don't cheat!"

"The hell you don't!" he guffawed. "Is that what you told my man Robbie? If I recall, you were still engaged to marry him when I met you. We had quite a few dates before you broke it off with him. Did you forget all of that?"

"That was different," I said slowly, my head spinning. "I . . . I didn't feel the same way about him that I feel about you. I wouldn't cheat on you."

"And I am supposed to believe you?"

"You should believe me. I believe you when you tell me something."

We were silent for the rest of the way to Mama's house.

"Why y'all both looking like undertakers?" Mama asked as soon as we got inside. There was an amused look on her face.

"I don't feel well," I muttered, tossing my jacket onto the plaid sofa, next to my sister Frankie's lap, in Mama's neat little living room.

Leon remained silent and went straight to the liquor cabinet.

Frankie lifted my jacket with a flyswatter and inspected it with a sniff. With a giggle and a slight frown, she tossed it aside. "I don't like most of the mammy-made stuff you wear, but can I have that see-through blouse Inez brought you back from Jamaica?" Frankie asked, her eyes on the television in front of her. My sister was thirteen now and really into BET, MTV, and any other station where she could watch music videos. As much as she got on my nerves, I loved my sister more than words could say. Like Inez, I knew I could count on this nitwit when I needed her.

"No!" I snapped, flopping down hard next to her. I gave my kid sister a playful tap on her head, and then I grabbed a handful of her neatly braided hair.

"Leon must not be giving you any," Frankie teased, saying it low enough so that I was the only one who heard it.

"Girl, you need to slow down," I advised, shaking a finger in her face.

Leon sat down on the wobbly bamboo chair across from us.

"Don't y'all get too comfortable. I got a pot roast in the oven, a pot of pinto beans on the stove, and a gallon of lemonade in the icebox," Mama said, coming into the living room, wiping her hands on her plaid apron. She still had on the white usher's uniform that she'd worn to church. "Leon, I am so glad to have you in the family. I thank the good Lord that I don't have to worry about my baby spending too much of her time with a jezebel like Inez now." Mama let out a disgusted sigh before she started fanning her face with the tail of her apron.

"Inez is not a jezebel, Mama," I said, with conviction, looking at Leon to see his reaction. "Is she, baby?"

"She's all right, I guess," he mumbled, picking up the latest copy of *Ebony* off of the coffee table. "Mama, remind me to take a look at your dishwasher before we leave." I had learned how to tell when Leon was nervous. He would scratch his head a lot and do annoying things, like tap his knuckles on the coffee table. He was doing both now.

"Leon tells me that Inez has got herself a new man," I added, my eyes still on him.

"Already? Didn't she just get a divorce from her *third* husband?"

Frankie laughed. "That sister gets around like a loose wheel! I hope she's using some protection. Me, if I was a man, I wouldn't touch her with a flagpole."

"Frankie, did you finish all your homework?" Mama asked, shaking her head.

"Yes, ma'am," Frankie mumbled, her head bowed submissively. Then she sucked in her breath, sprang from the sofa, and galloped across the floor to the telephone on the stand by the doorway. "Speaking of Inez, she told me to call her up, and she'd make me an appointment to do my nails for free. I'm going to baby-sit for her this weekend," Frankie announced, with a huge smile, as she dialed Inez's number.

"Let me speak to her before you hang up," I said. Leon shot me a hot look, and then he promptly started scratching his head some more. With all of the nervous scratching that he had been doing lately, I was surprised that his head didn't have holes in it by now.

I was glad when Frankie handed the telephone to me.

"Hey, Inez. I'll be by the shop tomorrow after work if you're going to be there," I started.

"Sounds good to me. What's up?" Inez said in a voice that was exceptionally cheerful, even for her.

"You tell me."

"That's what I want you to do," Inez insisted, with a laugh.

"For one thing, I want to hear about your new friend," I said, choosing my words carefully. Even though I was Inez's best friend, she would cuss me out and tell me to mind my own business as quickly as she would anybody else. I softened my voice, making it sound like I was only casually curious, not straight-up nosy. "Uh, Leon told me he saw you with him at the Victory Club the other night."

"He's the one." Inez sighed.

"Ok. He's the one what?"

"He's the man I've been looking for all my life, I think. He's from the Middle East and looks like a young Omar Sharif. His daddy's a sheik—I looked him up on the Internet—and he's worth a couple hundred million dollars," Inez told me. The way she was swooning, you would have thought that she'd reeled in Lawrence of Arabia. "His name is Hassan Hassan. Isn't that an intriguing name?"

"Uh-huh. Like Sirhan Sirhan." I sighed.

"Who?"

"Bobby Kennedy's assassin. He was from the Middle East, too," I chided.

"Don't you start," Inez warned, with a gentle laugh. "And whatever you do, don't make any remarks about him being a terrorist, or any of the rest of that shit that everybody thinks every man from the Middle East is involved in. Mama almost had a cow when she found out that Hassan's from Iran. 'I didn't raise my girl to sleep with the enemy', she told me. And right in front of Reverend Beauchamp. You should have seen the look on his face!" Inez laughed again, so I knew she was not the least bit angry or concerned about what other people thought about her new lover. But she sounded eager to talk about him, so I did.

"Oh. Did you meet Hassan at the Victory Club, too?" I asked.

"Of course, I did. That is the place to go when you want some new meat."

I glanced at Leon. His eyes seemed to be looking straight through me. "That's what I told Leon. He doesn't want me to go there unless I'm with him." I didn't want to say too much in front of Mama and Frankie, so I let Inez do most of the talking.

"Fuck him! He is not your daddy. You can go to that club and any other club you want to go to without him. I tried to tell you that he was going to try and run your life. Tell you what to do. I tried to tell—"

"I'll come by the shop right after work," I said, cutting her off.

I knew that Inez and Leon still couldn't stand each other. Even though they were cordial to each other around me. But I couldn't forget about him being nice enough to bring her home from the airport when she returned from the islands. Despite his macho attitude and his gruff demeanor, he was a good man, and I loved him. I knew in my heart that he was doing his best to tolerate my best friend. And, in her own way, Inez was trying to get along with him, too. She didn't have to accept a ride home from the airport with him. She could have called a cab. But she didn't. And I knew that it must have been difficult for her to sit by herself in the same car with Leon. I was glad that the two of them had made some progress in improving their relationship.

I was also glad that Frankie and Mama dominated the dinner conversation. I didn't have to say too much. Leon hardly spoke at all. But he did a lot more nervous scratching that day.

CHAPTER 15

When I found out I was pregnant, the first person I called up was Inez.

"I am so happy for you!" she squealed. "I can't wait to tell my girls. Those two little monkeys are always asking me how come their auntie Renee doesn't have any kids of her own." Inez paused and then started talking in a low, serious voice. "How is the proud papa taking this blessed news?"

"I don't think he's going to be anybody's proud papa when I tell him," I told her, gripping the telephone in my sweaty hand. "He wanted us to wait." Leon's daughter, Collette, had only been to the house a few times since I'd moved in. I liked the girl. She was no better or worse than any of the other kids her age that I knew. At least, that's the way she was around me. However, Leon had one horror story after another to tell me about how Collette misbehaved when he was alone with her. He'd even told me about an episode at the mall where she had thrown a major hissy fit because he had refused to buy her the new Prince CD. She had stomped out of the music store and run into the mall atrium, screaming, until a burly security guard calmed her down.

"You have to make young kids feel like they are important. Especially girls," I told Leon when he told me about Collette's tantrum at the mall.

"Well, from now on when she comes to visit and wants to go to the mall, you take her," he told me. His voice was cold and steely, and his jaw twitched.

Leon was not a patient man. Even when it came to his daughter. So I knew that I always had to watch my step with him. I eventually reached a point where I could pretty much read him like a book. As long as it wasn't too much of a hardship, I bent over backwards to keep the peace between myself and Leon.

Whenever Collette visited now, I volunteered to take her to the mall before she even asked, and she seemed to enjoy my company. When I refused to buy her something, she didn't even sulk. I had a way with kids, which was why I had chosen a teaching career, and why I was looking forward to having one of my own in a few months.

"Leon is so full of surprises, I never know what to expect from him. But I hope he's happy about the baby. He's been awfully nice lately. And by the way, I am glad to see that the two of you are acting more and more civil to each other these days," I told Inez.

"I'd still keep my guard up if I were you," Inez advised, with a snort. "Leon wears a mask more often than a full-time bandit."

"What's that supposed to mean? Look, I know he is trying his best to tolerate you—"

"Tolerate me? What in the world . . . why . . . That's a strange word," Inez said, cutting me off in mid-sentence. "I have never met a man yet who felt he had to tolerate me. I won't *tolerate* behavior like that from a man!"

"Well, Queen of Sheba, if you feel that way, why should you care if my man only tolerates you? He sleeps with *me*."

I didn't like the silence on the other end of the line.

"Did you hear what I said? Leon sleeps with me," I said in a firm voice.

Inez cleared her throat before speaking again. "Now, yes. But I assure you that Leon wasn't a virgin when you hooked up with him, like Robbie was."

"Where is this conversation going?" I demanded. "How did we get from talking about my pregnancy to talking about Leon and Robbie?"

"I didn't want to go there. You brought up Leon. I didn't."

"No, you brought him up. You started talking all that shit about him wearing masks. What is your problem, girl?"

Inez gritted her teeth and let out a tremendous sigh. "I am sorry,

Renee. I don't like it when people talk trash about my men, so I should know better. It's just that . . . I don't want to see you get hurt."

"Hurt how? Why are you so worried about me getting hurt? What do you think Leon is going to do to me?"

"Renee, let's just drop it. I am happy for you, and I will pray that you have a healthy baby." Inez sniffed. "Where do you want to have drinks tomorrow?"

"That bar on Morrison is nice. Ernie's."

"That's fine with me. But I am telling you right here and now, you will not drink any alcohol! I don't want that baby coming here with two heads and hooves." Inez laughed.

I laughed, too. But a strange feeling came over me. I was not satisfied with her responses as to why she seemed so concerned about Leon hurting me. I knew Inez well enough to know that she was not the type to hold back critical information. Especially when it involved me.

When I arrived at Ernie's Bar on Morrison Street the next evening after work, enduring a bumpy fifteen-minute bus ride because Leon wasn't answering his cell phone and I didn't have money for a taxi, Inez was sitting in a booth in the back. Shonda and Pat from her nail shop were with her.

So was my husband, Leon.

It was too late for me to slink back out of the door without being seen. If Inez had not spotted me and started waving and drawing attention to me, I would have made a U-turn and left that place, running. The way Leon looked at me, wide-eyed and amused, you would have thought that I was naked. I sat down hard next to him, purposely hitting his knee with mine. I pinched his thigh under the table, not surprised that he didn't even react.

"Did I miss anything?" I asked, forcing myself to smile.

"Shonda and Pat insisted on joining us," Inez explained, looking at Leon as she spoke.

He cleared his throat before speaking. "And as I was on my way out, these lovely ladies were on their way in. They invited me to have a drink with them," he volunteered, scratching the back of his head so hard, sparks flew off. Normally, when we ran into each other in public, he greeted me with a kiss. He didn't kiss me this time, and that surprised and disappointed me. If anything, he seemed annoyed by my presence.

"Well, I won't stay long," I said. I was beginning to get used to Leon doing things that surprised me. "Baby, I thought you were going to visit your uncle in the nursing home?"

"I did. But he was so out of touch, he didn't even know me," Leon said sadly. His elderly uncle Martin had been struggling with Alzheimer's for several years now and was in a nursing home in Shaker Heights. I visited the old man more often than Leon.

I patted Leon's hand for the benefit of the others at the table, but as soon as everybody looked away, I pinched his hand and whispered, "You just wait'll I get your black ass home, you nasty buzzard." I planned to read him the riot act. He ignored my threatening words as he delivered a delayed but passionate kiss on my lips, his tongue darting in and out of my mouth like a serpent's. I was glad that I'd eaten a garlic pizza for lunch. My breath was so foul, it made him cough.

As usual, Inez dominated the conversation. She had more adventures than a pirate, and she loved to talk about them all. She and her rich Iranian were still going strong, but she had gone behind his back and spent a night with her second ex-husband, on a mercy fuck mission for his benefit. Everybody at the table, except Leon, laughed as Inez regaled us with one blue story after another.

I didn't know what that woman did to her men to make them so devoted to her, even after she dumped them. I had asked her several times what it was that she did to them that was so potent. Each time she'd just winked at me and told me that whatever it was she did in bed, it was her "fucking" business.

I finally stopped asking her when she told me one day that smart women didn't share their bedroom secrets. I considered myself to be a smart woman. But I knew that I would never have that kind of control over men, even if I brought a gun to bed with me. One of the many things that I was thankful for was the fact that Inez and I had never competed for the same man. And there was no reason for me to believe that we ever would. As far as I was concerned, I was married to Leon for life. And Inez could hop into as many beds with as many men as she wanted to. I just hoped that my girl would settle down and be with one man on a permanent basis before it was too late. I knew of a few elderly sisters in the neighborhood, some in my own family, who had spent the best years of their lives playing musical beds. But now their most frequent companion was loneliness. I looked at Inez and blinked back a tear, hoping that she would not end up in that club. She caught my gaze and gave me a puzzled look. I grabbed a napkin and pretended that I had something in my eye.

I didn't order anything when the waitress came to the table. Instead, I looked at my watch and rose, pulling Leon up by his hand.

"Baby, we need to get going. I need to stop off at the grocery store and pick up a few things for dinner," I said.

Leon was hesitant, but with an annoyed groan, he rose, dropping a wad of bills onto the table.

"You sisters have a nice evening," he said, following me out of the door. As soon as we got outside, he got loose. "Woman, I don't appreciate you clowning me in public like you just did," Leon barked, shaking a finger in my face the same way I often did with my unruly students.

"I don't know what you are talking about. I didn't expect to see you in that bar with all those women," I snapped, hands on my hips. We had reached his Range Rover, parked at the curb. I stood by the passenger's side, with my mouth hanging open. He snatched open the door on his side and jumped in and started up the motor.

"I need to talk to you," I said, opening my door and easing into my seat. I kept my eyes on his face the whole time.

He stepped on the gas, and the vehicle shot off like a bullet. "I'm listening," he said, grunting and glaring at me. He frowned when he noticed that I didn't have my seat belt on. "Don't you need to buckle up?"

"Uh . . . I think I can make it home all right without it."

"Baby, I know you don't like the way the seat belt wrinkles your skirt, but I think your safety is more important. Now buckle up that seat belt before I buckle it for you."

"My stomach is feeling kind of weird, so I don't want that belt strapped against it."

"What's wrong with your stomach? And how come you didn't order a drink? Oh, I know. All of that crap coming out of Inez's mouth made me queasy, too."

"Inez didn't say anything worse this evening than she's said before. I don't think that there is anything she can say that would make me sick," I said, speaking like I was reading a cue card.

"So, what is wrong with you then? Why are you looking and acting like a zombie?"

"Leon, I was hoping to tell you in a more romantic setting, but I guess this will have to do." I stopped and looked at Leon. "I . . . We are going to have a baby."

He shook his head and cussed under his breath. Then he started laughing.

"I know you don't want any more kids right now, but I'm pregnant, and we have to deal with it," I said, crossing my legs. I was losing steam. I was no longer interested in telling him off when we got home.

He laughed again. Then he did something that surprised me more than finding him in the bar with three women. He pulled to the side of the road and stopped. Then he leaned over and kissed me long and hard.

"I hope that means we are not going to fight about what I just told you," I said meekly. I licked my lips, savoring his kiss. "We'll have a beautiful baby. . . ."

He let out a hearty sigh before he replied. "And it better be a boy," he said, with a smug sniff.

"Does that mean you're happy about this?" I asked. I was apprehensive, to say the least. This man was full of too many surprises for me not to be.

He pulled another surprise out of his bag of tricks. He pulled into the parking lot of a motel at the corner, even though we were only a few minutes away from our house.

"What are we stopping here for?" I wanted to know, looking around the deserted parking lot. This was the kind of place that rented rooms by the hour, with nervous couples coming and going at all times.

"Bring your fine ass on," Leon ordered, pulling me by the hand out of the Range Rover. We checked into a room, where he made love to me like it was the first time.

In a way it was. Things would never be the same between us after that day.

CHAPTER 16

My pregnancy was very difficult. My morning sickness got so severe and went on for so long that I had to take my leave of absence from work three months earlier than I had originally planned. I had backaches that would wake the dead. No matter what I ate or drank, it gave me indigestion.

Mama and Inez took turns coming to the house to sit with me while Leon was at work. I was so clumsy and bloated, making love was so awkward that Leon stopped sleeping with me. Even though Dr. Lukas had said that it was all right for us to continue making love up until my eighth month as long as it was not painful or uncomfortable for me. I was just seven and a half months along, but Leon still wouldn't make love to me. Every time I tried to seduce him, he ran. Some nights he even took a blanket and slept downstairs on the living-room sofa.

"I offered to do other things for him," I confessed to Inez during one of her goodwill stops. "He doesn't even want me to touch him," I moaned.

"Well, if that's the case, there is nothing you can do about that," she told me, leaning over my bed to fluff the three pillows under my head. Inez was dressed like she was on her way to participate in a fashion show. Her head was wrapped in a red turban, and the black leather jumpsuit that she had on showed off every curve she had. And, like always, her make-up was flawless. I looked like hell. My hair was all over my head, and my face was puffy, and as dry and rough as sandpaper. My belly looked like I had swallowed a large watermelon whole.

"But I don't want him to get impatient and horny enough to get his lovemaking somewhere else," I said, with a groan.

Inez spoke without looking at me. "Do you think he would?"

"Well, the man is a man. I know you know a lot more about men than I do, but even I know that when a man's in heat, he'll stick his dick in a hole in a wall. If Leon won't let me touch him, I don't know what else to do to keep him out of another woman's bed."

"I can get you some saltpeter," Inez said, looking over her shoulder toward the door. Mama and Frankie were downstairs.

"What's that?"

"It's this shit that they used to sprinkle on convicts' food in some prisons to help suppress their sex drive," Inez explained. "I like to think of it as Viagra in reverse."

"Where do you get it from? Have you used it before?"

"Don't worry about where I get it from. I've told you before that smart women don't reveal all their bedroom secrets. But, yes, I have used it. I used it on my second husband. I had some problems with bleeding when I was pregnant with Malena, so I couldn't get too cozy with Paul in the bedroom. I had to do something to calm him down, keep him from fucking other women."

"Did it work?"

Inez chuckled and nodded her head, standing over me with her hands on her hips. "Oh, it worked all right. And it kept on working, long after I'd stopped stirring it in his food." There was a distant look on Inez's face. "I loved that man. But the last six months of our marriage, he couldn't "cum" if I called him. It would take me an hour just to get him aroused. Then, before he could do anything, his peter would peter out and go as limp as a wet dishrag." Inez threw her hands up in disgust.

"I sure don't want to take any chances with that shit. Especially after it backfired on you and Paul," I said, shaking my head. "All I can do is pray that Leon honors his vows."

"Can I ask you something personal? You don't have to answer me if you don't want to. But if you do, I want an honest answer," Inez said, a serious look on her face. She sat down gently on the edge of my bed, looking at me in such a strange way that I got nervous and scared.

"What?"

"Would you cheat on Leon if the right man approached you? And use your imagination. I'm talking about somebody truly hard to resist. A hot piece of property, like a Denzel or a Will Smith."

I shrugged. "I don't care that much for Denzel or Will," I lied.

Inez held up her hand. "Be serious. And I only want an honest answer."

I shook my head. "I would never cheat on my husband, period. I'm not that kind of woman," I said, meaning every word.

"What if he gave you a reason to cheat?"

"What reason would justify cheating?" I gasped. There were times when I said things that I immediately wished I could suck back into my mouth. The words that I'd just spoken had an ominous feel to them. And not just that. What I'd just said sounded downright naïve. Nothing justified cheating. People either did it, or they didn't. They didn't need a reason.

"Renee, you've got so much to learn." Inez laughed.

"Would you cheat on your man?"

Inez covered her mouth with her hand and laughed so hard, she shook.

"Oh, I forgot," I said, with a sigh, bowing my head. I was embarrassed. Everybody in town knew what a free spirit Inez was. She was still involved with the Iranian, but she was also seeing a man from Jamaica who had followed her home after her last trip. He had sold his business in the islands and was living in a flophouse near downtown Cleveland, just so he could be near Inez. It frightened and intrigued me to know that there were women with that much sexual power. In a way, I was glad I was the way I was. Having that kind of power could be a very dangerous weapon for a confused woman like me to keep under control. It would probably end up controlling me.

"Let me give you some advice, sister. Never say never," Inez quipped, leaning over my bed.

"I don't want to cheat on my husband," I said. "I hope I never find myself in a position where I'd want to," I added hopefully. "My own mama told me that as long as I made my husband happy, he would not have any reason to even look at another woman."

"Little Mama, you are twenty-six years old now, not sixteen," Inez said, her mouth hanging open after she'd stopped speaking.

"So? What's that got to do with anything?"

"You've been to college. You are not some naïve country girl just off a bus from Hicktown, Mississippi."

"I don't need you to tell me about myself. My mama does enough of that. But my mama is a smart woman, and she usually knows what she's talking about."

"Your mama told you that as long as you keep your man happy, he wouldn't go with other women? Well, I know your mama, and I am sure she *thought* she knew what she was talking about," Inez said, with a thoughtful look.

"Uh-huh," I muttered. I didn't have the nerve to tell Inez that when I was around nine, my mother had thrown my daddy out of the house because she'd caught him with another woman. All I could think of was that my mother had not kept my daddy happy. Mama did everything she could to get Daddy back. Until the day he died, she treated him like a king. I loved Leon, but I did have some limitations, some things I would not tolerate. I just didn't know how far I could be pushed before I pushed back.

"Sister, your mama lied to you. You could be the sexiest, best-looking woman on the planet, and your man would still fuck another one!"

"Why would he?"

"Why wouldn't he? Because he's a man, dammit!"

I wanted to slap that damned turban right off of Inez's know-it-all head. This conversation was getting on my nerves, but I wasn't going to change the subject until I'd said everything I had to say. "Well," I started, rolling my eyes up at the ceiling before continuing. "*If* Leon wants to cheat on me, he will. I can't stop him."

"You sure can't," Inez agreed, with a vigorous nod. This was one of the few times that I couldn't wait for her to leave the premises.

CHAPTER 17

Iwas due to deliver my baby any day now, and I was anxious to get it over with. In the meantime, I needed emotional support now more than ever. When Inez's shoulder was not available for me to cry on, I held other people hostage at my pity parties. I lured a couple of the other teachers to my house, who didn't mind listening to me bitch and moan as long as I listened to them. My mother was always interested in hearing my complaints. It gave her another opportunity to dole out more of her motherly advice. The only people I didn't confide in that much were Leon's family. His mother was a nice woman, but she was distant and conservative. Leon's daddy, well, that man didn't even want to listen to his own wife's complaints, let alone his son's wife's. I enjoyed sharing my thoughts with Leon's uncle in the nursing home, but sometimes that poor old brother didn't even know where he was. I kept my thoughts pretty much to myself around the rest of Leon's family. Despite all of the options I had, they were poor substitutes for Inez. This woman was *my* girl.

But my girl was having her problems, too.

"Renee, you think you've got problems. I dare you to walk in my shoes for a week," she challenged me one day.

"No, thanks. Your shoes are way too big for my feet," I teased.

"Maybe I need to get out of town again for a few days," she continued, with a groan.

Inez and I had just come out of Jeannie Frock's dress store at the mall one Saturday afternoon and found one of those damned police boots on the front wheel of her BMW. We had been in such a rush to get into the mall that Inez had parked in a spot that was reserved for police cars only. But because a huge bush obscured the NO PARKING sign, Inez got out of that mess without having to pay a big fine. That little incident was minor compared to some of the others that she had to deal with. A lot of people depended on Inez. She tried to be there for everybody, and she never complained about it.

No matter how much people demonized Inez with their thick, evil tongues, one thing that the gossipmongers couldn't ignore was the fact that this sister gave back to her community by giving free manicures to bedridden women and donating money to various local charities. And she had a long reach. She even helped support a disabled teenager in Somalia. Inez was the one who got me involved in donating money and old clothes to some local charities. A lot of people could learn about compassion from Inez, but few chose to.

Being self-employed was not as idyllic as I had always thought it was. However, it was a position that Inez had dreamed of all of her life, she insisted. She had used her divorce settlement from her first husband to attend a cosmetology school and to start her own business. But owning the only Black nail shop in our neighborhood was a double-edged sword. Not only did the wives of businessmen and other upscale women patronize Soulful Nails, but customers from hell dropped in, too. And those undesirable individuals were not always from the low-income, high-crime areas. As a matter of fact, the poor, uneducated women who came into Inez's shop, clutching the last few dollars from their welfare checks, were usually her most pleasant clients. One Hispanic sister from the Willow Street Projects provided free janitorial service for Inez three times a week in exchange for free manicures a couple of times a month.

To a lot of her customers, Inez was just another nigger, and they made sure she knew what they thought of her. She had a few serious problems with some of these women. Some even considered themselves middle class because they lived in nice homes and had decent jobs. However, they behaved like savages.

Most of the time those loud-mouthed, gum-chewing hussies behaved themselves. But at least two or three times a week, a few crude women came in and got their raggedy nails and ashy feet done, and then refused to pay. They would usually complain about the quality of the work and then start an argument. Other times they would wait until after they'd gotten all of the services they needed done, then claim they left their money at home.

Last month the daughter of one of the most prominent Black lawyers in Cleveland stormed the shop, with a major chip on her shoulder. She got the most elaborate nail job Inez had to offer: miniature pictures of her five kids and the five different daddies painted on each nail. When it came time to pay, she tried to write a check. There was a huge sign on the wall that said: WE DO NOT ACCEPT CHECKS, and it was in English and Spanish. When Inez pointed out the sign to the woman, the woman tried to leave. Inez had had enough, so she attempted to restrain the woman as she hollered for Shonda to call the police. Well, by the time the cops arrived, Inez and that grifting heifer were rolling all over the floor in that nail shop. The cops were going to take only the customer to jail until Inez started mouthing off at them for taking so long to get to the shop. She ended up going to jail, too.

Inez had dumped her Iranian a few days before, claiming that their cultural clashes had become too extreme. But that didn't stop him from running from behind the counter of the convenience store he owned to bail her out of jail. Less than a week later, Inez had another run-in with the law. While she was having dinner with her current boyfriend in a restaurant in the same block as her nail shop, the man's disgruntled ex-girlfriend stormed in and slapped Inez.

Well, everybody who knew Inez knew that she was not the kind of woman you got violent with, unless it was self-defense. Inez dragged her attacker by her hair out of the restaurant to the sidewalk, in front of several stunned witnesses. By the time the police arrived, each witness told a different version of what had happened. Unfortunately, the cops believed the witnesses who claimed that Inez had thrown the first punch. The boyfriend had disappeared as soon as the ex-girlfriend had entered the restaurant. A sharp lawyer got the charges against Inez dropped.

"You need to talk to your girl about taking some anger management classes," Leon commented over dinner the next day. He folded his newspaper and dropped it on the table in front of me. There was a brief account on page three about Inez's performance in the restaurant and her arrest.

I slid the paper back across the table.

"Inez McPherson does not have an anger problem. Just a lot of bad luck," I defended. "She is still better off than a lot of women I know. She looks great, and she has money to burn." As much as I didn't want to admit it, I envied Inez in an "I wish I could be more like her" kind of way.

"That high-maintenance hoochie ought to look good with all the money she spends on herself. And the reason she's got that kind of money to throw away with both hands is because she is a straight-up mercenary when it comes to her relationships. I bet that White boy she married curses the day she was born. She took him to the cleaners and then some." Leon laughed.

"Leon, are you ever going to accept Inez?"

"Accept her for what?"

"Accept her for who she is. And you might as well. She is my best friend, and she's not going anywhere," I insisted, clenching my teeth.

"What if I don't accept her?" Leon asked, giving me a threatening look.

"Then that's your problem," I hissed.

"Renee, what do you want me to do? Move her in here with us? Would that make you happy? You want to bring her to bed with us? Tell me what you want me to do, and then we'll go from there. I am getting sick and tired of your attitude when it comes to that woman."

"That woman is the only person I can count on!" I covered my mouth as soon as I spat out the words. The hurt look on Leon's face made my stomach burn. "I didn't mean that the way it sounded."

"Sure, you didn't," he muttered. "Look, Inez is welcome in this house. And I will always try, uh . . . I *will* treat her with nothing but respect as long as she treats me with respect."

About two hours later, around one that same Sunday afternoon, Inez called me up. She was so upset, she could barely talk.

"I've been waiting for over an hour on my mechanic," she complained. "And I need to get the kids over to Cleveland Heights so they can see their grandmother before she leaves for her cruise this afternoon."

"What is wrong with that pricey set of wheels you just got two years ago?" I smirked. "I didn't think BMWs ever broke down."

"I don't know what's wrong with it. Last night, on the way home from the shop, I heard this knocking noise coming from the back.

The faster I drove, the louder it got. I am afraid to drive it until I find out what's making that noise. You know how long it takes to get a cab to come out here," Inez whined. "I've called everybody else that I know with a car." Inez paused and let out a loud moan before she continued. "I need a ride," she said in a whiny voice that I rarely heard.

I had sold my shabby Ford Escort to one of my cousins right after Leon and I got married. I only drove Leon's Range Rover when I had to because my pregnancy generated too many surprises for me to get behind a wheel.

"Well, I don't think I can help you, girlfriend," I said, truly sorry. One thing I could say about Inez was that she was almost always available for me when I needed her. It saddened me to admit that I was not always in a position to come to her aid. And she rarely asked me for help of any kind.

"Is . . . is Leon there? I'll fill up his gas tank and give him a few extra dollars if he'll give us a ride," Inez said, her words bouncing off of my ears because they were words I never expected to hear from her.

I laid the telephone on the kitchen counter and went into the living room, where Leon was sprawled across the sofa, watching some sports program. He looked up and smiled, which was a good sign.

"Baby, I need your help," I began, my hand rubbing my stomach.

"What's wrong, sugar?" he asked, leaping up. He shot across the floor and wrapped his arms around me.

"I'm fine," I said, holding up my hand.

"What kind of help do you need? What are you craving? You want some ice cream? Some pickles?"

"I don't need any of that. I haven't had many cravings lately," I said dryly. "Uh, I'm not the one who needs help."

"Renee, get to the point," Leon ordered, the look of patience and concern gone from his face. He gave me a puzzled look and lifted both of his eyebrows, dipping his head as he waited for me to speak again.

"Leon, something is wrong with Inez's car, and she's afraid to drive it. She needs a ride to Cleveland Heights."

"Oh," he said, hands on his hips. Then he started scratching the side and back of his head. "You want *me* to give *her* a ride?"

"*She* wants *you* to give her a ride, too. She's the one who asked. If you don't want to do it for her and her kids, do it for me," I said.

"No problem," he replied, with a hearty shrug, his eyes shifting from side to side.

I couldn't understand why just talking about Inez made Leon nervous. I couldn't recall a time when he didn't damn near scratch the skin off his head when she was the subject.

CHAPTER 18

I was too preoccupied to pay much attention to how long Leon was
gone. I had the granddaddy of backaches, and all I could think
about was lying down somewhere. It was a struggle, but I managed to
make it back upstairs on my own, where I literally fell into bed and
slipped into a deep sleep.

I didn't realize I'd been asleep for hours until I opened my eyes
and saw that it was dark outside. Something was happening downstairs. I sat up, turning my head to the side so I could hear better. I
heard Leon laugh, and a few seconds later, I heard Inez laugh. There
was music in the background: Anita Baker, Inez's favorite. It sounded
like there was a party going on in my own house, and I hadn't been invited.

With the belt on my terry cloth robe trailing behind me like the
train on a bride's gown, I made it downstairs to the living room in less
than a minute. I was huffing and puffing so hard, I had to lean against
the wall to keep from falling.

"Girl, you'd better take it easy," Inez warned, shaking a finger as
she moved toward me. She wore a tight black leather skirt and a low-
cut white blouse. Her fake blond hair was in a ponytail. She had made
herself so comfortable that she had removed her four-inch heels and
had left them in the middle of my living room floor.

"Honey, are you all right?" Leon asked me. There were two empty shot glasses on the coffee table. One had a ring of Inez's raspberry-colored lipstick on its lip.

"I'm fine," I insisted, waving Inez back to her seat. "What time is it?" I asked, looking around the room.

"Half past eight," Leon told me, glancing at his watch and scratching the side of his head. "We didn't want to wake you," he added. He didn't volunteer any more information. I was dying to hear where he had been all of this time. And whether or not he'd spent all of that time with Inez.

She must have read my mind.

"Mama's plane to Miami got delayed. Leon was nice enough to offer to wait with the kids and me and Mama at the airport until she boarded her flight," Inez said, shaking her head.

"All this time?" I asked in a raspy voice, trying not to show my discomfort.

Leon and Inez glanced at each other, then at me. They were looking at me like I had just asked them to explain the mysteries of the world.

"We had to swing by that traveling carnival on Willis Road," Inez explained, giving me an apologetic look and then shrugging her shoulders. "You know the one over by Lake Erie."

"Going to that carnival was my fault, baby. I took a different route home, thinking it would be quicker. As soon as the girls saw that carnival, well, there was no getting out of that!" Leon laughed.

"Where are the kids now?" I asked, looking from him to Inez.

"With their fathers," she answered, rolling her eyes.

Inez loved her two girls more than she loved life itself. She even arranged her active love life around them. Other than the three men that she had been married to, no other man had ever lived in her house, because of her two young daughters. Inez's mother, a former Playboy Bunny and a very socially active divorcée, enjoyed having her granddaughters with her. She had been asking Inez for as long as I could remember to let the girls move in with her.

"Did you fix the car?" I asked Leon. My voice came out sounding harsh, so I cleaned that up with a grin as I joined him on the sofa. Inez sat down on the love seat facing us. Like the vixen she was, she crossed her legs and hiked up her skirt, which was already too short, briefly showing her shaved pussy. If any other woman had pulled such a brazen stunt in front of my husband, *in my living room,* I probably would have slapped the shit out of her and then kicked her ass all the way from my house to Michigan. But since it was Inez, I didn't. This was just the way she was, and I was used to it by now.

"He sure did," Inez answered, giving me an embarrassed look, smoothing down her skirt too late. She and Leon burst out laughing at the same time. "Girl, I forgot I had left a cantaloupe in my trunk yesterday evening. It got loose from the bag that the guy at the farmer's market had put it in and was rolling around all over the place. That's what was making all that noise!" Inez slapped her knee and laughed some more. "Five minutes later, my cousin Earl showed up, and he needed a ride to go visit his son in Sandusky. Since Leon had already come to my rescue, I let Earl borrow my car."

"Oh," was all I could say, but there was a lot more on my mind. Like, how come they'd left me on my own for so long with all the problems I was having with my pregnancy? Inez still must have been reading my mind.

"I told Leon we should at least check on you! I could have let him take the kids to that carnival, and I could have come and stayed with you. Or we could have come back to get you and taken you with us. I know you don't leave the house much these days, and you shouldn't. But a couple of hours in the fresh air might do you some good."

"Except for a few back pains, I feel fine," I lied. My whole body felt like it was on fire. But there was something bigger and better going on in my life: my best friend and my husband finally seemed to have put their differences behind them. I didn't even bat an eye when Leon insisted on driving Inez to her cousin Earl's house to pick up her car, even though Earl had called offering to bring the car to her.

As if on cue, as soon as Leon drove off with Inez, Mama called me up. She started her verbal assault as soon as I told her that Leon had spent most of the day with Inez and had offered to drive her home.

"Girl, have you lost what's left of your mind? A woman would be a fool to let her man spend so much time alone with a . . . a . . . meat grinder like Inez!" Mama yelled so loud, it sounded like she was coming through the telephone, feet first.

"Mama, if Leon was going to fool around, it wouldn't be with my best friend," I insisted.

"You know, for a woman who has been through college, and for you to be a schoolteacher, you are the stupidest Black woman I ever met! You ought to be ashamed of yourself! Don't you know that a woman's best female friend is more dangerous to turn aloose around her man than a naked prostitute?" Mama paused just long enough to grind her teeth and catch her breath. "Lord, I sure hope your baby sister don't grow up to be such a fool! You take after them women on your daddy's side!"

"Mama, will you calm down? Inez can pick and choose any man she wants in this town. I've seen her do it. If she had wanted Leon, he'd be with her, not me. Besides, if I can trust her with my life, I can certainly trust her with my man." I rubbed my stomach. "It took all of this time for me to get Leon and Inez to be friends, and I want them to stay friends. Now if you don't mind, I'd like to get some rest," I told her.

Mama didn't say anything else, but she let out an exasperated sigh. When I got her off the phone, I let out an even more exasperated sigh.

CHAPTER 19

Inever told Inez or anybody else, but from time to time, I felt extremely guilty about the way I'd cheated on Robbie and then broke off our engagement so that I could marry Leon. It was one of the few things I would admit to myself that I was ashamed of. In the back of my mind, I wondered if fate was going to pay me back some day. It was not easy, but I forced myself to not think about it that much. I had other unpleasant things on my mind that needed my attention more. Like what Mama had said about Leon and Inez.

As hard as I tried, I couldn't get Mama's words out of my mind. Leon was not perfect, and he loved women. It would have been naïve of me to ignore that important fact of life. So I decided that when Leon returned from driving Inez home, I would come out and ask him if he was having an affair with her. It was painful just rolling the words around in my head. I couldn't imagine how much more it was going to hurt to say them. But I had to if I wanted to get this shit out of my system.

"Leon, are you fooling around?"

"What? Hell, no! I have not been with another woman since I married you!" Leon roared, glaring at me. I'd waited for him to come upstairs when he got back home. I was already in bed for the night, feeling stronger than I had in days. He turned his back to me and started undressing. I could tell that he was pissed off by the way he flung his shirt across the room, letting it land on the floor. He struggled to remove his shoes, kicking them off like they suddenly hurt his feet.

"Are you telling me the truth?" I whimpered. "Are you telling me that you and Inez are not fooling around?"

He whirled around so fast to face me that he stumbled. For the first time, to me, he did look like he had on a mask. Just like Inez had told me so many times before. His eyeballs looked like they were about to pop out of the sockets. His nostrils were twitching, and his mouth was hanging open like a dipper. It was not a pretty sight. This was not the man I'd married. I had to ask myself if I really did know *who* I'd married.

"*Inez?* I don't believe my ears!" Leon quickly looked at the important numbers that I had taped to the base of the phone on the nightstand. Then, he let out what sounded like a growl. He glared at me again and then trotted over to the phone. He hit the speed dial and got Inez right away. "Hey, it's Leon. No, nothing's wrong . . . uh-huh . . . She's fine," he said calmly, one hand in the air, motioning for me to be still. "Listen, I know you are not going to believe this, because I don't." I didn't give him the chance to continue. I leaped off of the bed and snatched the phone out of his hand.

"Inez, it's nothing. I will talk to you tomorrow," I said, hoping I'd diffused a potentially messy situation.

"What the hell is going on?" Inez asked. "Why did Leon call me? Are you sure you are all right?"

"I swear it's nothing. Now let me get back to bed. I'll talk to you tomorrow," I promised. I hung up and returned to bed. Leon stood in the middle of the floor, in his underwear. There was a puzzled, slack-jawed look on his face as he stared at me.

"Of all the women on this planet for me to cheat with, what makes you think I'd touch that bitch?" he asked.

I was so confused that I didn't know what I wanted now. I wasn't happy when he was calling my best friend nasty names, and I wasn't happy when he spent hours at a time alone with her.

"Most men would go out of their way not to spend time with some bitch," I snapped. "You didn't hesitate to chauffeur her from the airport or fix her car."

"She's your friend. I'm trying to make you happy by being nice to her. That's the only reason! Do you think I'd even bother with that woman if she wasn't your friend? I thought you wanted me to get along with her."

"There's a big difference between you getting along with her and you fucking her," I snarled.

"I'll be glad when you drop that load. I know pregnant women act like a fool until they deliver, but you take the cake, woman." Leon flopped onto the bed, on his back. He gave me an impatient look before he reached over and turned off the lamp.

The darkened room and the heat from Leon's body did something to me. I reached over and patted his crotch. I was glad that I got an immediate reaction.

"Leon, this is just the beginning of our lives together. We'll be together for another forty or fifty years, I hope. If we can't be honest with each other now, what do we have to look forward to?"

"I am being honest with you," he said.

I couldn't tell if he was still upset or not, but he was getting more and more turned on as I massaged him. When I got up and turned the light back on and got naked, he decided he was too tired to do anything.

As soon as Leon left for work the next morning, I called Inez.

"What's up?" she asked as soon as she answered the phone in her nail shop. "Why did Leon call me last night?"

"Inez, you are the most straight-up person I know. I can ask you anything, right?"

"True. What do you need to ask me?"

"And you won't get mad?"

"I am going to get mad if you don't get to the point. Shit."

"Well, I just need to know if you are fucking my husband," I blurted out, my heart beating a mile a minute.

The long moment of silence that followed made me more nervous than I already was.

"What did Leon tell you?" she asked in a suspiciously distant voice. I ignored the fact that Inez didn't seem surprised by what I'd just asked her. She'd been asked the same question by other women, so it was no wonder it didn't faze her. But I thought that coming from me, it would have made a difference. She was as cool as a block of ice. "Did he tell you I was fucking him?" she asked in a flat tone of voice. This woman had so much control, it was scary.

"He claims he hasn't been with another woman since we got married," I replied, making sure my voice remained firm.

"Then that should answer your question," Inez told me in a voice that I almost didn't recognize.

I let out a sigh of relief. "That's all I wanted to know," I managed.

"Don't you hang up this phone yet, woman. What the hell made you ask me a question like that? I got enough on my plate. I don't need, or want, Leon." Inez laughed.

"Well, he's getting it somewhere."

"He's not getting it from me," she hissed, speaking slowly. Like she wanted to make sure I understood every word she said. "Why do you think he's getting his cookies somewhere else?"

"That man loves to fuck. We haven't done it in months! I can't turn him on with a pair of pliers. If I didn't know any better, I'd swear that somebody had slipped him some of that saltpeter shit you told me about."

I could tell that Inez was getting impatient by the loud breaths she kept letting out. "Are you busy today?"

"No more than usual. I thought I'd take the bus over to the school to say hi to some of my students and have lunch in the school cafeteria with some of the other teachers so I can catch up on my gossip. Why?"

"Cancel that. Let me take you to lunch."

Inez picked me up a few minutes before noon. However, we didn't make it to the deli on Meyer Street like we'd planned. I went into labor right after we'd stopped at a red light at the corner near my house. Inez sped through that red light, and several more, to get me to the hospital.

Giving birth to the first child was a once-in-a-lifetime event for every mother. It was not something that I wanted to go through alone. Mama had told me that as soon as I felt the first contraction, to let her know so that she could be by my side until it was over. Leon had reluctantly promised that he would be in the delivery room with me, too. But bad timing on nature's part had prevented Mama and Leon from being with me on such an important occasion in my life.

My daughter, Cheryl, slid out of me twenty minutes after Inez got me to the hospital. And like in so many of my other dramas, Inez was the only one there for me. Except when she was off on one of her globe-trotting excursions, Inez *always* seemed to be there when I needed her the most.

CHAPTER 20

My life was finally complete. Each week, month, and year was better than the last. During the next five years, Leon and I refurnished the whole house and added a recreation room so that his older daughter, Collette, had a place to entertain her friends when she came to visit.

Leon and Inez got along most of the time. One of the things that did cause friction between them involved my daughter, Cheryl. Inez spoiled her to death. She never came to the house without something for Cheryl. That was enough to set Leon off.

"I don't want my daughter to end up as spoiled as Inez's girls. She'll grow up thinking that the world owes her something just because she's here," he complained, rooting around in the refrigerator we'd just bought for a beer while I prepared dinner. Cheryl, who was the image of her father, stood right next to him, gnawing on a carrot. She was excited because in addition to being in kindergarten, she now spent her afternoons in a child care center with her little friends across the street from our house, instead of with Mama, in Mama's stuffy old house.

"Inez knows when to quit," I told Leon, water up to my wrists as I stood over the sink, washing some green beans. "That sister just likes to spend money," I added, with a chuckle, admiring the diamond studs Inez had just delivered for Cheryl's newly pierced ears.

"The few Black women who are lucky enough to have a lot of money to spend should spend it more wisely. Not on a lot of unnecessary foolishness. And please tell your girl that I said we don't need her charity. I can take care of my family by myself." Leon paused and tickled Cheryl's cheek.

"What's charity, Daddy?" Cheryl asked, still munching on her carrot.

"Something that people with money give to poor people," Leon replied, with a painful look on his face.

"Cool! I like being poor!" Cheryl hollered, with an eager look on her face as she looked from me to her daddy. I let out a gasp that almost strangled me. Leon stood there with his mouth hanging open, looking at Cheryl like she had just recited the Lord's Prayer in rap form.

"See what I mean?" Leon shouted, waving his bottle of beer. "Inez is a bad influence!"

"We are not poor, baby," I assured my daughter, giving her a serious look.

"Then how come Inez gives us so many things?" Cheryl asked, looking confused.

"Because she loves us," I promptly replied.

I didn't even bother to tell Inez what Leon said about us not needing "charity" from her. And it was a good thing that I didn't. Because when she offered to pay my way to go on a Caribbean vacation once school was out, I jumped at the chance. But I waited until July before I mentioned it to Leon. He and I were celebrating the Fourth of July in our backyard. Frankie had taken Cheryl to see a fireworks event in the park across from Mama's house.

"No, I don't want you going off on a trip without me. Especially to a place like the Caribbean. I know too many brothers from Jamaica, Puerto Rico, Trinidad, and everywhere else down there, so I know what those men are like!" Leon snapped, his fork stabbing at the ribs on his plate.

I sucked in my stomach, and shoved another dollop of potato salad into my mouth, promising myself that I would jog around our block before I went to bed that night. "What about Paris?" I asked, talking and chewing at the same time.

"What about Paris?"

"Inez told me that she'll treat me to a trip to Paris if we can't get a good deal on a Caribbean package."

"That's even worse! The whole world knows that even the homeliest Frenchman can talk his way into any woman's panties he gets a hard-on for. And you Black women are too uppity and loose to be traveling without male escorts. Uh-uh! You are not going to any of those places unless I go with you. Case closed."

I wasn't too upset about Leon not wanting me to go away with Inez. I was happy just spending my time at home with my little family. But the more Leon protested, the more my attitude changed. After thinking about it for a few days, I decided that I did want to go on vacation with Inez. I offered Leon a compromise: I wouldn't go to any of the places he didn't approve of.

"How about Paraíso?" Inez suggested over lunch the next day, after my latest argument with Leon.

"Where is that? I've never heard of it," I said, holding my salad fork in the air.

"It's in the Caribbean, not far from Jamaica," Inez told me, sipping from a tall glass of iced tea.

"Have you been there? What's it like?"

She nodded. "Twice. It's a lot like some of the other islands. The Spanish settled there when they were still taking over other parts of the world. The British joined the party and eventually took over. The locals speak Spanish and English. The African slaves gave the island some color."

"Hmmm. Let me think about it," I told Inez, giving her a thoughtful look. I didn't want to seem too anxious, but this sounded like the trip that I'd been dreaming about all my life.

I couldn't wait to approach Leon with my latest vacation proposal. When I did, his reaction did not surprise me.

"Where the hell is Paraíso?" he asked in a gruff voice, not even looking up from *Fear Factor*, a show he hated but watched every week.

"It's a little rock somewhere in the Caribbean," I said, with a shrug, frowning because the contestants on the screen were eating live bugs.

"Never heard of it," Leon quipped, his back still to me.

"Neither had I until Inez told me about it. It's just some lazy little island country where the people do a lot of fishing and lying around on the beach. Inez is going to pay most of my expenses," I said, sitting on the arm of the sofa. "I'll just have to spend a few dollars out of my own pocket for souvenirs and other miscellaneous things, like postcards, stamps, and stuff."

"You'll do no such thing," Leon yelled, turning to face me. "We need every dime we can get our hands on to get the roof fixed." Leon gave me a guarded look. "And in case you forgot, property taxes are due in a few months."

"Then I won't buy anything," I offered, rising. "The bottom line is, I am going to Paraíso whether you want me to go or not. You are not my daddy. And besides, I don't tell you where to go."

An amused expression appeared on Leon's face. Then he gave me a thoughtful look and a shrug.

"Well, excuse me! I am scared of you!" he said, with a grin.

"Don't tease me. I am serious. I am going on that vacation, and you are not going to stop me," I insisted.

"Oh, all right. I guess you can't get into too much trouble in some little poo-butt place that I have never even heard of before. If you want to go, go. All I ask is that you *behave* yourself and bring me back anything but a T-shirt!" With that, Leon turned back to his program.

I had already told Inez that I was going to Paraíso with her, no matter what, so I didn't call her right way. I called Mama up because I would need her to help Leon take care of Cheryl.

"You are going to Para what?" Mama hollered right after I'd told her my plans.

"Paraíso. It's an obscure little island in the Caribbean," I explained.

"Ain't that where that little White girl on a vacation with her school friends disappeared from last year? That Natalee Holloway," Mama said, with a heavy voice. "Pretty little thing. Every time I see that poor little gal's mama on the television, I want to reach in that screen and hug her." Mama sniffed.

"That girl disappeared in Aruba," I told her.

At this point, my sister, Frankie, who was now a sassy eighteen-year-old, picked up the extension. "Wherever you go, I hope you bring me back something nice," she ordered, with excitement in her squeaky voice.

"I seen a movie on the Lifetime channel about folks snatching females off the streets in foreign countries and then selling them to the sex slave people. I would never get over it if somebody grabbed you and Inez and sold y'all," Mama said, her voice even heavier.

"Renee and Inez?" Frankie guffawed. "Women their ages ain't got nothing to worry about, Mama. The folks involved in the sex slave trade wouldn't pay a food stamp for a couple of broke-down crones like Inez and Renee. They only snatch real young girls. And even if Renee and Inez were young, those folks ain't going to waste their time and money on no Black females. It's mostly real young blondes that they want. There ain't nobody in the world that want *us* for any kind of slave now bad enough to pay cash money," Frankie jeered in a know-it-all way that had been annoying me for years. I rarely let Frankie's off-the-wall comments bother me. No matter how obnoxious and insensitive my baby sister was, she did a lot for me. Like babysitting for free and running errands. But I still had to be firm with her when she talked trash.

"Thank you for your input, baby sister," I snarled, forcing myself not to laugh, because I knew that what she was saying was true. I knew that Inez didn't feel the way I felt, but with us being in our thirties now, I thought our "femme fatale" days were over. The competition was too stiff. But I did hope that someone would find us attractive enough to dance with if we visited the clubs when we got to Paraíso.

"Renee, I wish I was you. You're going to have the time of your life," Frankie decided, speaking in a soft voice that I rarely heard. Coming from her, these were some very potent and positive words.

And like my little sister predicted, I was going to have the time of my life.

CHAPTER 21

I was looking forward to a lot of things. The start of school in September was one. I enjoyed my job now more than ever, even though I often got stuck with some of the most difficult kids in town. Last year I'd had several ruffians who had given me a run for my money.

One day last March, I hid in the cloakroom for a whole day while a substitute tried to tame two of my most unruly students. At the end of the day, when I revealed myself, the two boys in question cried like babies when they realized they'd been busted.

My upcoming trip was also at the top of the list of things that I was really looking forward to. I said as little as possible to Leon and Mama about it, pretending like it was no big deal. Had I not, I was pretty sure that with their negative input, they might have talked me out of going.

Leon had asked me several times if I'd rather wait until he got his bonus from work so that he could go with us. Each time I told him no. I didn't tell him that he was one of the things that I needed a vacation from.

Then, he tried to sabotage the whole thing by telling me about one horror story after another that he'd heard. Each one involved some naïve traveler getting caught up in some outrageous criminal act and ending up dead, maimed, or missing. He even showed me magazine articles about drunken people falling off cruise ships and never being seen again. I paid no attention to Leon's croaks of doom.

Mama was even worse. She came by the house a few days before my departure, with Pastor Mason's wife in tow. Each one had on so much black, even black scarves and stockings, that they looked like ninjas. They hemmed me up in my kitchen and laid hands on me. Then, they prayed over me for twenty minutes.

"We got all of them marauding terrorists roaming all over the world, blowing up hotels, planes, and whatnot. I don't know why anybody, except other terrorists, would leave the house to even go to the store, let alone some foreign country halfway around the world," Mama sniffed after she got tired of praying. She hugged me so hard, she almost squeezed the breath out of me. I loved my mother, and I knew that she meant well. I didn't have the nerve to tell her that she was also one of the reasons I needed to get away for a couple of weeks.

I shopped for my vacation wardrobe as discreetly as possible, hiding the things that I didn't want Leon to see. Like the two thong bikinis and the four see-through tops. I figured that I'd donate these provocative items to my sister when I returned from my once-in-a life-time vacation. And once in a lifetime was exactly what I expected it to be. I never wanted to jump through so many hoops again for Mama and Leon just because I wanted to take an innocent little trip.

"You better take hella condoms. At least two dozen. Those guys down there are always in heat."

I whirled around from the half-packed suitcase on my bed to see my baby sister standing in my bedroom doorway. I had packed and repacked my suitcases so many times that I couldn't remember what I'd packed and what I hadn't packed. I was glad that in less than ten hours, Inez and I would be on our way. I glanced at my watch. Leon was out having drinks with his boss. But he had promised to be home in time for us to have a little fun before the night was over.

Since I'd had Cheryl, my sex life had improved tremendously. I couldn't keep Leon off of me. As much as I enjoyed making love with my husband, I knew that I would be able to go without sex for two weeks without climbing the walls. But I wasn't so sure about him, so I wanted to whip it on him real good as much as I could before I left. As long as I handled my business right, I was now convinced that I didn't have to worry about Leon bringing another woman into the picture. Abstinence was not impossible, even for the horniest people.

"Frankie, don't sneak up on me like that," I scolded, giving my sister the annoyed look that she deserved. "And what do you know about condoms?"

"I know everything I need to know about condoms, and then some," Frankie said, with a naughty gleam in her eyes. "And I hope you do, too." She strolled across the floor toward me. I gave her another annoyed look when I saw that she had helped herself to a beer from my refrigerator.

I had no desire to sleep with any strange men on the island of Paraíso, but I knew that Inez did, with her nasty self! Her latest honey was away on a business trip, and she'd been complaining to me all week about her coochie being wet and itchy from lack of use. And I knew that she had already packed at least a dozen condoms in pastel colors and fruit flavors, so I knew that she meant business.

"I'm a married woman," I reminded Frankie.

"Big sister, you ain't fooling nobody but yourself with that Little Miss Innocent act." Frankie made herself comfortable at the foot of my bed, burping like a seal. "A piece of paper never stopped nobody from getting them a *piece*."

"How did you get in this house, girl? And what do you want?" I snapped.

"Duh? You told me to come pick up Cheryl the night before you left." Frankie rolled her eyes and gave me an exasperated look. "And do a sister a favor and remind your girl Inez that she promised me a trip for my high school graduation before the end of this year. A few weeks on a beach in Hawaii during Christmas break would be nice, but I'd settle for Mexico." I wanted to slap Frankie, but before I could, she walked up to me and gave me a big hug. "Have a good time down there, old woman." She paused and gave me a serious look. "And please be careful down there. You are the only sister I got to ... uh ... *pick on*," she told me, with tears in her eyes.

"I'll remind Inez about the trip she promised you," I said, with a sniff, patting my sister on the back. I knew I didn't have to remind Inez to do anything if she'd made a promise. She had never let anybody down.

I hadn't been able to do much for Frankie's graduation, back in June. As a teacher, I did not make a huge salary. But Leon did. However, a lot of our combined income went to his eldest daughter and her mother, Jimmie Lee. We called her Gimme Lee because she was always demanding something from Leon, chanting, "Gimme this, gimme that." That lazy bitch had not worked in four years! In addition to the child support payments that Leon made, he paid Jimmie Lee's rent and other expenses. If Inez had not offered to pay my travel expenses, I knew that I'd never make it to the Caribbean, or anyplace else, other than some relative's house down South. It was so important for me to take this trip while I had the chance.

An hour before Inez came to pick me up so that we could get to the airport that Saturday morning in August, I received a very strange telephone call.

"Hello, Renee. This is Robbie," a deep masculine voice announced when I answered.

"Robbie who?" I asked, with an impatient yawn.

"Your use-to-be," Robbie told me, sounding more patient than any other man would have. "I've . . . I've been missing you, girl," he said in a voice that sounded like it was coming from a lovesick schoolboy.

"Oh. I thought you sounded familiar," I lied, knowing damn well that I had not forgotten what the man I'd dumped to marry Leon sounded like. There were times when I didn't like some of the things I said and did. But life was not a rehearsal. I had just flattered myself by assuming that Robbie was calling me to try and set up a rendezvous with me behind my husband's back. "Robbie, I love my husband. I wouldn't do anything in the world to hurt him," I said proudly. "Now you have got to understand that it is over between us. You really need to find yourself another woman and focus on her, not me," I said, with a sniff.

"Renee, I am glad to hear you say that. All I ever really wanted was for you to be happy. And I tried my best to make you happy, but I guess my best was not good enough for you, huh?"

"Robbie, is that what you called me up for?" I asked, trying to sound sympathetic and understanding at the same time. "Well, this is not the time for this conversation."

"Renee, I got your phone number from your sister, and I hope you don't mind me calling your house," Robbie said, his voice cracking.

"No, it's all right. I'm alone," I said, puzzled as to why Robbie was calling me after all this time. I had not even thought too much about him since our breakup, but I'd seen him from time to time pumping gas as I drove past the gas station where he still worked. And each time, even with his back to me, I'd have recognized his bow legs even with my eyes closed. "Uh, how have you been?" I asked, stumbling over my words. "Are you all right?"

"I'm fine, Renee. As a matter of fact, I just got engaged to one of the Mitchell twins," he announced proudly.

"Oh. That's nice." I was sincerely happy for Robbie, even though I'd hated the two stuck-up Mitchell sisters all of my life. Even though they were as evil as hell, Jennifer and Janet Mitchell were the prettiest two Black women in Butler, and everybody knew it, especially them. Jennifer had even competed in the Miss Ohio beauty pageant a few years ago. It was kind of ironic that Robbie had ended up with such a prize, anyway. Not to say that I was a Miss Anything, but I knew that Robbie had considered me a trophy on some level. I didn't even ask Robbie which one he was going to marry.

"I don't believe much in dreams, but this one woke me up last night. When I went back to sleep, it repeated itself," Robbie said, clearing his throat.

"Well, was I in the dream?" I asked. I hid my impatience. Not because I believed in dreams, but because I was curious. I glanced at my watch. Then I moved closer to the window and parted the red and gold brocade curtains, which I'd just purchased the weekend before. I breathed a sigh of relief when I saw Inez's car stop in front of my house. "Oh! I have to go now!" I said quickly. "Uh, Robbie, I really would like to hear more about your dreams, but can I talk to you when I get back? I'm about to leave right this minute to go away for a couple of weeks." I patted the cute, short, and tapered black wig that I had clamped in place on my head with a dozen bobby pins. I had decided to wear wigs for the next two weeks, so I wouldn't have to deal with a head of frizzy naps and dandruff.

"I have to tell you this now, Renee." Robbie paused, but not long enough for me to shut him up. "In the dream that I had last night, you kept trying to call me for help from some place with a lot of water around it. Are you about to go off to an island?"

I hesitated for several seconds. "I . . . yes, I am. A place called Paraíso. That's Spanish for paradise. Why would I try to call you from my vacation, even in a dream?" My response came out sounding kind of stern, but I didn't realize that until I'd said it.

"I don't know. I'm worried about you, girl. Just be careful. And, I want you to know that if you ever do need my help, all you have to do is call me." Robbie hung up before I could tell him that the woman he needed to be worrying about was that Mitchell woman he was going to marry, not me.

I felt bad about the way I had talked to Robbie, and the way I had felt about him. Despite his shortcomings, he had been one of the best things that had ever happened to me. But that was something that I would not admit to him or anybody else, except Inez. I had a wonderful marriage, and I had every reason in the world to believe that it was only going to get better.

CHAPTER 22

I had to force myself to not think about Robbie's telephone call. Just hearing his voice had made me a little sad, and this was not how I wanted to start my vacation. And I didn't waste any more time thinking about all of that scary shit that Mama and Leon had tried to fill my head with. That's why I quickly slurped up five martinis during the first three hours on the plane, hoping they would help me keep things in perspective.

"You'd better slow down," Inez warned, giving me a dry look. "You don't want to burn out before we even set things afire. We are going to be in this air at least two more hours."

"Slow down my ass," I burped, rolling my eyes at Inez. She shook her head and groaned, but I still leaned across her lap from my window seat and motioned for the flight attendant to bring me another drink. "You do stuff like this all of the time. This is old news to you," I said, letting out a loud hiccup.

This whole scenario was a first for me in more than one way. It was my first real vacation, my first trip to the Caribbean, my first time to really get loose and not worry about who saw me doing what. Other than Inez, there would be no other witnesses to whatever I ended up doing on the island. I could get shit-faced drunk and run up and down the beach naked if I wanted to. I could do all of the things that I would never even think about doing in my hometown. I could even flirt and dance up a storm with other men, and not worry about it getting back to my husband. The thought of all the possibilities at my disposal brought a devilish smile to my face.

I'd been Miss Goody Two-shoes for too long. Well, those shoes were about to come off. I wanted to be assertive. No, that was too tame. I wanted to be *aggressive* for once in my life. So far, Robbie had been the only person that I'd really been even mildly aggressive with.

I giggled and fanned my mouth with my hand, and then I tried to sound as determined as I felt. "Things are going to change for me. I am going to start enjoying life a lot more. I am going to be . . . uh, more like you." I cleared my throat as Inez sat there looking at me like she wanted to hold up a cross and splash me with some holy water like they did Dracula. I ignored her reaction and kept talking. "I didn't even get a real honeymoon, and if I wait for Leon to take me on a real vacation, I'll be waiting from now on." I was slurring my words, but I didn't care.

Leon's idea of a vacation was for us to drive down to rural Alabama and sit on his aunt Betty Lou's back porch and watch his male relatives kill a hog for us. That's what we had done the past three summers in a row. I wanted to see what it really felt like to let my hair down and get truly loose. I intended to party my ass off on this vacation.

The plane was now flying low above our destination, and I felt like I was in a dream. From the window on my side, I could see water so blue that it was sparkling like glitter under the blazing sun.

"Oh, my God! The island is shaped like a heart!" I turned to Inez and gasped.

"What did you expect with a name that means paradise?" Inez grinned in a nonchalant way, like she did this every day. She did do it often enough for it not to excite her as much as it did me. "And just wait until you see the men," Inez panted. A dazed expression covered her face like a veil.

"I don't want you to embarrass me down here on this cute little island, woman," I scolded, waving a drunken finger in front of Inez's face.

"Girl, don't be trying to judge me. I don't apologize for anything I do," she said, with a pensive look on her face now. "And for your information, I don't fuck every man I spend time with. I'm picky." She let out a snort, snatched the drink that I'd ordered off of the flight attendant's tray, and gulped half of it down in one swallow before she handed the glass to me.

"Aaah, a hoochie with some class," I guffawed, jabbing Inez in her side with my elbow. "You know I don't care what you do. I still love you." I finished the drink, and then I got serious. "I just wish that you could tone it down a little. You can be happy with one man. Look at me."

Inez gave me a disgusted look. She looked at me for a long time before she blinked, and then she looked away. But not before I saw the unbearable sadness in her eyes. We remained silent for the rest of the flight.

I was glad to see that I was not the only person staggering off the plane. I think everybody but the crew was drunk by the time we landed.

The local men, some with women already wrapped up in their arms, started winking and blinking at Inez and me before we even made it to the luggage carousel. It was downright comedic to see a bunch of strange men waving and throwing kisses like they'd never seen a woman before in their lives. I was grinning and waving back at them, but Inez just strutted by like she didn't even see all of this activity going on around us. However, she made a date with a baggage handler before we even left the airport.

"A baggage handler? Aren't you aiming kind of low?" I asked as soon as we got into the cab that was taking us to the Princeton Hotel, which was located right on the beach. "Couldn't you have at least held out for a waiter or a street vendor?" I laughed. But behind my laughter were some real concerns. I didn't want my best friend to let some island Romeo make a fool out of her. Like fucking the hell out of her, and then racking up outrageous charges on her credit cards. One of the homely, middle-aged teachers at my school had met some young guy on a beach in Mexico last summer. When she got back to Ohio, she bragged about her handsome new man. She even sent him a ticket to come visit her. A month later, she married her gigolo in a wedding that was almost as lavish as Princess Diana's. As soon as the bridegroom got his green card, he took off with another woman—in his new wife's new car. And he had run up twenty thousand dollars worth of charges on her credit cards. The homely teacher had a complete nervous breakdown.

"I hope you never meet somebody who takes advantage of you," I said, still thinking about the teacher. "Some of these low-income guys are more interested in finance than romance."

"Girl, my mama didn't raise a fool. I know when a man is trying to get more from me than he deserves. Why do you think I divorced Vince? Anyway, I've had some of my best times with men in low income," Inez informed me. There was a faraway look on her face.

The Princeton Hotel stood out among the other hotels on the beach. Like it was in a league of its own. For one thing, it was the tallest building on the block. And the only pink structure that we'd seen on the island so far. Limousines were double-parked in front of the hotel, dropping off and picking up prosperous-looking men and women. The hotel lobby contained a huge man-made waterfall, live trees, and exotic plants and flowers. It was a place fit for royalty, and that was exactly how I felt.

As soon as we checked into our spacious hotel suite, with its pink and white decor, two queen-size beds fit for two queens, and a mini-bar, I ran out to inspect our balcony. The boy who'd brought our luggage to our suite was still present. Judging from the exaggerated grin on his round, sweaty face, he was enjoying a mundane conversation with Inez. I ignored them and the complimentary champagne and chocolate on the dresser and headed for the bathroom, dying to take a shower. But before I could even get undressed, I heard the boy tell Inez, "My shift ends in ten minutes." I didn't hear the whole conversation, but I had to wonder why he was telling her what time he got off work.

By the time I got out of the shower, Inez was gone. I found her on the beach, right below our balcony. She was stretched out on the white sand, under a beach umbrella, like a throw rug, sharing a bottle of rum with the same youngster who had brought our luggage up to our room.

I didn't bother Inez; I just wandered around until I found a cute little beachside restaurant nearby, where I enjoyed a candlelit dinner alone. I ignored all of the men walking by, tipping their white Panama hats, and giving me the eye. But I certainly enjoyed all the attention.

When I motioned for my waitress to bring my check, she practically skipped over to me and announced, "One of your admirers has already settled it." She gave me a wide grin and a mysterious wink. My mouth dropped open, and I looked around the area, jerking my head so hard, my neck ached.

"Whoever he is, he didn't have to do that," I said coyly, still looking around. "Is he still here?" I asked, clutching a narrow glass that had to be at least a foot long. I took another sip of my drink, amazed at how much more potent it was than the drinks I'd consumed on the plane.

"He is indeed. Let me give you some advice." The waitress, a thin, long-faced woman, with a grin like a mule, leaned close enough to whisper in my ear. "You are obviously from another place. Here, when an attractive woman is on her own and accepts a drink or a dinner, it sends the message. The men on this island have senses that are keener than a dog's. They can hear the message loud and clear."

"What message?" I asked dumbly, dabbing rum and coke off of my lip with the tip of my finger.

My waitress gave me a knowing wink. "Every man present wants to mount you."

It took me a few moments to realize what the friendly waitress meant.

"Well, I am a married woman," I said as loud as I could, hoping whoever had paid for my dinner was close enough to hear.

The waitress shrugged and let out a sharp laugh. "Most of the men on this island are married. At least you have one thing in common with them."

I practically ran back to the hotel room, where I wasted fifteen minutes trying to get through to Ohio so that I could tell Leon how much I loved him. My sister, Frankie, answered my telephone.

"What are you doing in my house?" I demanded. "Where is Leon?"

"The cable went out on our whole street. You know I never miss *America's Most Wanted*, girl. Leon took some lady out for a drink," Frankie revealed.

"Some lady?" I asked, swallowing a hard lump in my throat. "What lady?"

"That big-tittied lady from next door. She was upset. Something about her husband leaving her for his secretary."

"Oh?" I didn't even want to know which one of my next-door neighbors Leon had taken out for a drink. It didn't matter, because the women on both sides of our house were attractive.

"Miss Thing had the nerve to have on some shorts and one of them see-through, low-cut blouses, like the ones you bought for your trip," Frankie revealed. "Girl, you better call back and check your man."

"My husband knows how to behave," I said weakly. I was in the worst kind of denial and had been for years. I finally realized that.

"I bet all of them Kennedy wives said the same thing. Big sister, if you want me to whup that cow's ass when Leon brings her home, tell me. Then, when you get back, I'll hold her so you can whup her some more." Frankie laughed.

"Frankie, do me a favor. Don't tell Leon I called," I said, with a heavy sigh.

It seemed like everybody was having fun except me, and I didn't like that at all. After what I'd just heard from my sister, I had to wonder just how much longer I could trust myself.

CHAPTER 23

I was tempted to leave the hotel again, hoping to see the man who had paid for my dinner. The least I could do was to thank him, and maybe even have a few more drinks, on him. There was nothing wrong with that. And I decided that it would be nice to have somebody to talk to.

I called my house again. This time Leon answered. I hung up as soon as I heard his voice.

I didn't see Inez again until the next morning. Around eight, she tiptoed into the room, with her sandals in her hand, looking like she'd been mauled. Her hair was askew, dark circles surrounded her eyes, and she had what looked like a handprint on her neck.

I had ordered room service and was enjoying a continental breakfast in bed. Even though our suite had air-conditioning, I had opened all of the windows. The smell of paradise was intoxicating. The only aroma I recognized was the scent of flowers, but I was sure that the coconut trees also contributed to the intoxicating hodgepodge that had me savoring each breath I took. The sounds outside, below our windows, were just as amazing. Exotic birds flying past the windows were chirping and noisily flapping their wings. Ocean waves were splashing against the rocks on the beach, and people on the beach were laughing like they didn't have a care in the world. And different types of music—reggae, calypso, Spanish, and even hip-hop—seemed to be coming from all different directions.

Our hotel was located on El Capitan, the tiny island's main street. Almost everything else was, too. Like the shopping center, most of the restaurants and bars, and a beach that ran the length of the heart-shaped island. As far as I was concerned, the island lived up to its name. I was in paradise, and I was going to enjoy as much of it as I possibly could. Everything was too beautiful for me to get upset, but I had to say something to Inez about her antics.

"I hope he was worth it," I snapped, giving her a look that I hoped made her feel like the shameless hussy she was acting like. "And I hope this is not the way the rest of the trip is going to go." I took a sip of coffee and fanned away a gnat that had flown in one of the windows. A large bird, with blue, yellow, and green feathers, and a beak that had to be six inches long, perched on our windowsill.

Inez waltzed over and chased the curious bird away, and then she shut all the windows. "What's the point of having air-conditioning if you're going to leave the damned windows open?" she said, with a profound yawn.

"So, how was your date?" I asked, with a sneer.

"I didn't fuck him, if that's what you mean. I let him get a little cozy with me, but mainly, we just talked. He was a really interesting dude to talk to."

"I'll bet. He must have had all kinds of exciting stories to share about what it's like to work in a five-star hotel." I started to take another sip of coffee and stopped. "Or was it the baggage handler from the airport?" I covered my mouth with my hand to keep from laughing. I was angry, but I was also amused.

Inez shook her head and flopped down on the side of her bed.

"Neither one. Dude from the airport never showed up. And the hotel cutie forgot to tell me about his wife until she showed up with their two kids to give him a ride home. I never felt so punk'd in my life!" Inez groaned one second and giggled the next. "Wait until you see the bartender from the restaurant on the second floor. I bumped into him while he was on his break, on my way to the ladies' room. He's the one I sat with on the beach all last night."

I gave Inez a disgusted look as I tried to find the right words to say what was on my mind.

"Inez, am I going to spend these two weeks waiting for you to come back from one date after another, listening to all the fun you had? What will I say to everybody at home when they ask me what we did down here?"

Inez rose from her bed, stretching like a feline. She slapped one hand on her hip and started wagging a finger at me. "Let's get one thing straight right now. What happens in Paraíso stays in Paraíso." Then she removed her bright yellow halter top and dropped it to the floor, cupping a tittie in each hand.

Before Inez had invested in some serious plastic surgery, the same titties that she was so proud of now had looked like baby elephant ears: small, flat, and floppy. She had specifically instructed her surgeon to give her a bosom identical to Pamela Anderson's. And that was exactly what she got.

Rolling her eyes at me, Inez wiggled out of her denim Bermuda shorts, shaking her naked rump. Her butt was so firm, she could balance a cup on it. And she wondered why she had so few female friends.

I shrugged. "I appreciate your paying for me to come down here, but if you came here to do your wild thing, why did you drag me along?" I pouted, feeling like the ugly stepsister that got left behind.

"You're right. I know how you feel," Inez said, offering me one of her best smiles. "Let's get dressed and go shopping and sightseeing. We'll have lunch, come back to the room, and take a siesta, and then we'll go out for dinner and dancing. Just you and me."

I didn't have much credit available on any of my credit cards. Leon had charged up a fortune buying school clothes for Cheryl and Collette, and his ex had badgered him until he'd purchased her a new refrigerator. I had spent most of my last paycheck paying for the clothes my trip and the new wigs that I'd brought with me. In addition to what Inez had already done to make this trip possible for me, she insisted that I take one of her no-limit American Express cards to pay for some of my purchases.

We literally shopped until we dropped. Somehow we had managed to make it to an outside café near the shops, where we fell to the ground in the sand, our shopping bags landing next to our feet. I immediately kicked off my sandals so that I could feel the soft white sand between my toes. This was as close as I'd ever been to heaven, and I didn't want the moment to end.

Inez couldn't wait for a waiter, so she offered to go to the bar to get us some drinks. I was on my back, stretched out on the ground, with my eyes closed, when I felt somebody tickling the bottoms of my bare feet. I looked up into the eyes of one of the most breathtaking men I'd ever seen in my life.

"What the hell?" I managed, sitting bolt upright.

"It was my pleasure to pay for your dinner last night," the man said, squatting next to me. I could see several different ethnicities in his face and coloring. He was a medium shade of brown like me, but he had sharp Latin features and light blue, slanted eyes. He appeared to be a combination of Spanish, African, and Asian. His thick hair was a rusty red, but it was almost as kinky as mine was under the curly wig I had on.

"So you're the one," I said, feeling clumsy.

The handsome man gave me his hand and gently pulled me to my feet. I thought that I was going to go up in flames when he brushed sand off of my legs and butt. I was patting my wig to make sure it was still securely in place when Inez strutted back, holding a tray with our drinks. Before I could open my mouth, my handsome admirer did a double take and looked Inez up and down. He almost knocked me back to the ground, trying to get to her so fast to remove the tray from her hands. I felt clumsy and in the way, so I sat back down on the ground.

"So we meet again," she said to the man. "I see you've met Renee."

"Not exactly," I said, feeling like a balloon that somebody had just let the air out of. "Mr . . . uh," I said, snapping my fingers.

"Jose," Inez gushed, extending her hand for this man to kiss it. "Jose and I had a wonderful time last night." She swooned, but I couldn't tell whose benefit it was for. "Girl, you ought to see this man dance," she squealed. Jose beamed proudly as he promptly wrapped his arm around Inez's shoulder, squeezing her against his broad chest.

"That's nice," I muttered, putting my sandals back on. The drink no longer appealed to me, nor did this man, with his smoldering good looks and rusty red hair. I felt woefully out of place. "Uh, I think I'll drop my things off at the hotel, then take a walk on the beach," I announced. I stumbled like a wounded lamb as I rose, snatching up my shopping bags in one swoop.

CHAPTER 24

Ipractically ran back to the hotel. As soon as I entered our suite, I got naked. I stood in the full-length mirror behind the bathroom door and tried to figure out what it was about me that made most men lose interest in me as soon as they saw Inez. I was attractive, even more so than Inez. And I had not cheated nature by having cosmetic surgery. I had a few lumps, knots, and stretch marks on my body, which I had no trouble hiding, but you would have thought that I looked like Moms Mabley or Big Mama Thornton when I was around Inez. I knew it wasn't just about looks. Inez exuded charisma, confidence, and sex appeal. I was convinced that even if she had looked like Moms Mabley or Big Mama Thornton, most men would still choose her over me.

There was some justice in my world, some consolation: I had a husband and a strong marriage. Inez had struck out with three husbands and was probably going to end up alone in the long run. I had to be doing something right.

I didn't expect to see her any time soon, so I slipped into my long T-shirt of a nightgown and crawled into my bed. Even though the sun was hours away from sinking into the sea, I was in for the night. The large television in our room had cable, so I could enjoy some of the same shows I enjoyed at home. I laughed to myself, thinking how sad it was that I'd come all the way to the Caribbean and was in a luxurious hotel room, watching an *I Love Lucy* rerun.

I decided that I would get used to ordering room service. And just to add some icing to the cake, I'd order steak and lobster for dinner, and the most expensive wine available, every evening that I spent in the room alone. Hell, Inez could afford it! I let out a wicked laugh, wondering how happy the waiter would be when he saw the huge tip I was going to add to the room service bill every single time.

I had the telephone in my hand, about to order my dinner, when Inez stumbled into the room.

"Girl, what the hell are you doing in bed? Don't you want to go dancing?" she asked, slamming the door shut and marching over to the bed. She dropped her wide-brimmed straw hat to the floor, shaking her hair like a wet dog.

"I thought you had other plans," I said in a bitterly cold voice, placing the telephone back in its cradle.

"I do have plans, and that is for you and me to go dancing."

"What about your new friend?" The words flew out of my mouth like spit.

"You mean Jose?" Inez made a face and waved her hand. "He's too old. He's pushing forty."

"Well, we are not exactly spring chickens ourselves. Did you forget about your thirty-fourth birthday coming up next month? And me, I feel every one of my thirty-one years."

Inez dismissed me with another wave of her hand. "Don't laugh. Old woman or not, I plan to enter that wet T-shirt contest at the Giggling Shark nightclub tonight. They started passing out flyers on the street right after you left. Come on. Get out of that bed, and put on your sluttiest dress, baby."

"I don't dress like a slut, and you know it. I didn't bring any slutty clothes," I complained, trying to convince myself that thong bikinis and see-through halter tops didn't count.

"Suit yourself. But you ought to know by now that if you can't beat 'em, you join 'em. If you wear one of your regular outfits tonight, everybody will know you are a schoolteacher."

"What's wrong with that? I *am* a schoolteacher!" I hollered.

"And that's why I'm the one having all the fun. Get up. Put on that short red dress I talked you into buying today," Inez ordered. She snatched the covers off of me and pulled me to the floor by my arm.

We were dressed, out of the door, and walking into the club less than an hour later.

With eleven other females to compete with, three of them blue-eyed blondes in their early twenties, and one young sister who looked more like Beyonce than Beyonce, Inez walked off with the first prize in the wet T-shirt contest that night at the Giggling Shark nightclub. She won three hundred dollars, plus all the tips that the men had tossed at her feet. And her drinks were free for the rest of the night. The club's photographer took her picture as she stood in front of a large mural of a giggling shark on the wall.

We both had fun that night, and the next few nights as well. We tried some other clubs along the beach, turning down drinks and dances left and right. We reluctantly declined the offers from the many men who wanted to join us at our table in each club. For the moment, we wanted to keep our space to ourselves. "This way we can enjoy each other's company more," Inez insisted, and I agreed. Leon had not called me but I was having too much fun to let that bother me.

By the next Friday night, when we had only one more week to enjoy ourselves, we decided to do more dancing and more drinking. And we agreed that it should be at the club that seemed to be the most popular one on the island, the same club where Inez had won the wet T-shirt contest.

Like before, the men at the Giggling Shark were all over the place, literally grabbing our hands each time we walked off the dance floor after dancing with another man. One thing I had to say about this island was that the men seemed to outnumber the women. At least, that was the way it looked in the clubs, the restaurants, and on the beach.

And I loved the beach in Paraíso. I loved being near water, period. A few family outings near Lake Erie and a couple of family reunions on both sides of my family on the banks of some of the lakes in Mississippi and Alabama had been my only "beachlike" experiences. The white sands of the beach near our hotel were mesmerizing.

I had never worn a thong bikini before in my life, so I was not prepared for all of the attention I got at the beach. When we were not shopping, taking siestas in our hotel room, or visiting the clubs, we spent our time stretched out on the beach. Inez was right at home on all that white sand. But I think it bothered her that I got a lot of attention, too. Because she had a lot more stretch marks on her backside than me, she refused to wear a thong bikini. She was self-conscious about the patch of stretch marks, which resembled a cat's paw, right in the middle of her left buttock. Her plastic surgeon had not been able to remove it. But Inez was the kind of woman who always had a backup plan. Since her bosom was as close to perfection as one could be, she removed her bikini top and started prancing back and forth to the beachside bar, with her breasts jiggling like Jell-O. During the last two appearances that we'd made at the beach, I had felt like her understudy. After a while, I didn't want to go back there with her. So we started spending more time in the clubs. But that backfired, too.

I had to address the situation, which I had been trying to ignore. Whenever a man in a club paid more attention to me than Inez, she reacted in a way that made me uncomfortable. That usually meant that she showed a little more skin and shook her butt a little more than usual. But the straw that broke the camel's back was when she strolled over and plopped down into the lap of a real nice man who had been keeping me company at our table while she was entertaining the huge crowd in the Giggling Shark by dancing on top of a table that Friday night.

After just a few minutes, the man slid Inez off of his lap. He then leaped out of his seat like a jackrabbit, darted across the floor, and grabbed a shapely White woman, pulling her out to the dance floor.

"Now that was a tacky thing to do," I complained.

"I agree. Men of color act like dogs in heat when a White woman enters a place. Some of them at least." Inez paused and grinned. "But I showed those White bitches who was in charge when I won that wet T-shirt contest the other night, huh?"

"I was talking about you," I said, glaring at her. "Not that White woman."

"What about me? What did I do?" Inez asked, with both of her eyebrows raised.

"That man was talking to me. He's a schoolteacher, too, and we were having a real nice conversation."

"So? I didn't stop you from having a real nice conversation. I didn't stop him from talking to you."

"Well, after you plopped your bubble butt down in his lap, what else could he do?"

"Girl, we are having too much fun for you to start tripping." Inez grabbed a napkin and used it to wave another man over to our table. "I'm not going to sit here and put up with your jealous attitude."

"I am not jealous of you, woman. I just don't appreciate the way you behave with the men who are clearly interested in talking to me," I said.

Inez gave me an exasperated look and rose from her chair so abruptly, it fell over.

Things would never be the same after that night. Inez and I did not speak again until we returned to our hotel suite. There was so much tension in the air, you needed a machete to cut through it.

"Inez, I have no idea how many men you have fucked, and I don't want to know. I know how important it is for you to have so many men give you so much attention." I was talking with my back to Inez as I removed my clothes. When I turned around, she was standing in the middle of the floor, with her hands on her hips. "You are the most insecure woman I have ever known, and you don't need to be," I told her, with my arms folded.

"I don't know what in the hell makes you think I'm insecure. I can have any man I want. Insecure? Me? I don't think so. That's what you, and the rest of the bitches who hate me, think." Inez stomped over to her bed and sat down hard, struggling with her sandals, trying to remove them so fast.

"You can't stand for me to get more attention than you. Just like that day when we came back from shopping and that Jose came over. I was really the one he had wanted to talk to." I pouted. I crawled into the bed and pulled the sheets up to my neck.

"Then why didn't you fight for him? That is the problem with you weak bitches."

"I am not weak. I am just as strong as you are. And I don't have to suck dicks or fuck every man I come across to show just how strong I am."

I had never seen Inez look so angry before in my life. She jumped up from her bed and stood in the middle of the floor. Her body looked so stiff and still, she could have passed for a statue.

"And that makes you better than me?" she asked, her voice fading in and out like a dying lightbulb.

"I never said I was better than you. I said I was just as strong as you are." I sniffed. "I just don't show it the way you do. No wonder Leon has such a hard time accepting you in our lives. He thinks you're a bad influence on me."

I heard her let out a deep breath. As far as I was concerned, the conversation was over. But she kept it going.

"Do you want to know why your precious husband has such a hard time dealing with me?" There was a harsh look on her face as she yelled at me. And I didn't like that one bit.

"I know why!" I yelled, throwing the covers back. "Because you are a straight-up whore. That's why. I feel sorry for you."

Inez moved closer to me, looking at me with so much contempt, I flinched.

"Do you want to know why Leon came after you in the first place?"

"What's that supposed to mean?" I asked. "Leon approached me that night in the Victory Club because he was attracted to me, not because he knew that I was an easy piece, like you."

"I had him," Inez said in a calm voice. "I had your man." The look on her face was disturbing. I had never seen such a leer on another human being's face before in my life. For a split second, she looked like a gargoyle. Her words rang in my head like tubular bells.

Inez could not have caused me more pain with those words if she had just stabbed me in the heart with an ice pick.

CHAPTER 25

"Excuse me?" I managed, tilting my head. "What the hell are you saying to me, girl?" I asked, rubbing the spot on my chest where my injured heart was located.

"You heard me." Inez didn't bat an eyelash as she glared at me.

"You had him?" I shifted my eyes and shook my head. "Him who?" I demanded.

"I had Leon."

I froze. I froze everywhere on my body. For a few seconds, the only things I could move were my eyes, and my eyes were on her face. I blinked hard as I rolled and shifted my eyes. The look on her face was now indescribable. I couldn't decide if she looked smug or evil.

"What the hell are you talking about?" I finally managed to ask, my eyes still on her face.

Inez sucked in so much air, her cheeks expanded. She looked like a blowfish until she let out all of that air. "I fucked him inside out." Each word that shot out of Inez's mouth, aimed at me, felt like a dagger. Then an odd expression appeared on her face. She looked like she regretted what she'd just confessed. What happened next surprised me. Tears formed in her eyes, and she started sniffling, wiping her nose and tears away with the back of her hand.

I stood there in slack-jawed amazement. I could not believe what I had just heard.

"Say something!" Inez shouted. I couldn't believe she was actually trembling. Tears were streaming down both sides of her face.

"You slept with my husband?" I managed.

"Yes," she muttered, giving me a look of pity.

"How could you?" I croaked. I didn't realize I'd balled my fists until I looked at my hands. Inez looked at them, too, and took a few steps back, holding up her hands. "My *husband?*" I mouthed, my fists still balled.

"It was long before he became your husband. It was during the time that I was separated from Paul." Inez looked away for a moment, talking in a low voice. "Leon wanted to marry me. He knew I was going to divorce Paul, and he thought it was to marry him. But I married Vince instead. Leon had a fit. He promised me that he would always be in my life, one way or the other." Inez looked at me and paused. I didn't like the look of pity on her face. "I didn't have a sister for him to hook up with, just so he could have an excuse to still be in my life." Her voice cracked open like an egg, and she seemed genuinely frightened for a moment. A look came on her face that irritated me to the bone. She lifted her chin and blinked back her tears, and then she *smiled.* A crooked, mocking smile was on her face. "Once he found out about you, he decided that you were as good a substitute as any." And just as fast as that smile appeared, it disappeared. She looked sad, beaten, and confused. The same way I felt. But I was also angry.

"Woman, are you telling me that the only reason Leon married me was so he could still be around you?" I marched up to her, ready to slap that stupid look off of her face. "How can I believe a slut like you?"

"I am not saying that that's why he married you. Don't put words in my mouth. I know he loves you now, but if it hadn't been for me, he probably would not have given you the time of day in the first place."

"You are a goddamned, lying, whoring ass bitch. I never dreamed you'd stoop this low!" I screamed, my whole body trembling.

"Let's call him," she said in a calm voice, nodding toward the telephone. Before I could stop her, she picked it up and started dialing. I sprinted across the floor and snatched it out of her hand, recalling the night that Leon had dialed her number when I'd asked him if he was having an affair with her.

"Why didn't you tell me all of this shit before?" I wailed.

"I tried to tell you as soon as I found out you were interested in him. But you never wanted to hear anything bad about your man. He and I had several heated discussions about how he was using you just to get back at me. Starting that first night he saw you with me at the Victory Club."

"Why didn't you tell me all this before I married this man and had his baby? Why did you let me live a lie for over six years?" I couldn't believe that the shrill voice coming out of my mouth belonged to me. I sounded like a shrew. I was sure that I looked like one, too, because my face was twisted into such an angry grimace, it ached.

"I just told you! And I tried to tell you more than once. But when it seemed like you both were happy together, I stayed out of your business. And since we're bringing everything out in the open, you need to know that he did everything he could to get back in my bed *after* he married you."

"And did you let him?" I whimpered, so weak that I could barely stand.

"No! Hell, no! I would never fuck a married man. Leon started hating me as soon as I told him what a bastard he was for using you as an excuse to remain in my life."

"You can have him. If what you are saying is true, I will divorce his black ass, and you can move him in with you." I was wringing my hands so hard, they got numb. "But let me tell you one thing. I plan to take him for everything he's got, so you'd better prepare yourself to pay his bills, buy gas for his car, help him keep all those goddamned suits of his dry-cleaned, help him support his other child and her mother, and my child, too. The whole nine yards!" I yelled, shaking my finger in Inez's face and rotating my neck. The bile rising in my throat tasted like poison.

"Renee, I don't want to be with Leon. I am your friend, not his. I have always tried my best to be there for you, and whether you believe it or not, I'll still be there for you." Inez smiled, and I think that's what sent me over the edge. I lunged at her. I slapped her face on both sides so hard that she stumbled and fell to the floor, her long legs flailing like a chicken that had just been decapitated. "Fuck you," she said in an even voice, rising. "I hope you will enjoy the rest of your vacation."

That was the last thing she said to me before she stormed out of the room.

CHAPTER 26

Ispent the next two hours with a bottle of wine in one hand and the telephone in the other, trying to get in touch with Leon. I didn't leave him any messages, because I wanted him to hear what I had to say out of my mouth, not from an answering machine. I was getting drunk, and more disgusted, wondering where in the hell he was.

I finally gave up and went to bed, but I didn't sleep at all that night. I could still hear Inez telling me that the only reason Leon approached me was so he could still be in her life. Each time I replayed her words in my head, I sizzled with rage. I didn't know which one disgusted me more: Inez or Leon.

I knew that some men did some stupid shit when it came to women, but I found it hard to believe that one would marry one woman just to spite another. If what Inez said was true, then the last six years of my life had been a farce. It was hard enough to think that Leon didn't really love me, but where did that leave our daughter, Cheryl?

I had to know, and I had to know before I faced him again. When morning arrived, I tried to call him again, but I was not successful. I finally dozed off for a few hours, expecting to wake up and find Inez back in the room. Around noon, when I checked with the front desk, I found out that not only had she not left any messages for me, she had transferred to another hotel! Housekeeping had been instructed to pack her baggage and send it by taxi to the other hotel. The only consolation was that she had paid our hotel bill in full and had preapproved any additional room service I ordered.

I had a massive hangover, and my head felt like it was about to explode. But my head was not the only part of my body that was in pain. My stomach was in so many knots that I could barely walk in an upright position. I had slapped Inez so hard that the palm of my right hand, and my wrist, throbbed like a toothache. My throat was sore from yelling at her so hard.

When the maid came to clean the room, I went out on the balcony, where I finally broke down and cried like a baby. Now I had to deal with burning, itching eyes, too. My mind was in a frenzy. I swayed every time I stood up, and I had to hold on to the wall to keep from falling on the balcony floor. I was glad that the balcony had such a high railing because it would have been so easy for me to accidentally tumble to the ground. There were two lounge chairs on the balcony. I plopped down on one, hugging my heaving chest as I let the tears roll.

I had to think back over the years and wonder what I had done to deserve such unspeakable betrayal. Other than what I'd done to my ex, Robbie, I didn't think that I had done anything bad enough for my life to be in the state it was. Hell, I'd done a lot more good than most of the people I knew! I was a role model for the kids I taught, I contributed to charity, and I'd even sent my last bonus check from work to the Red Cross to help the victims of Hurricane Katrina. The big question in my mind was, what good had it done me to do so much good? If my marriage fell apart, what would become of me? I was thankful that I'd still have a lot of positive things in my life, like my job, my precious daughter, and the rest of my family. And unless I had a nervous breakdown before I got back home, I'd still have my health.

I didn't want to be pitied. I didn't want people writing me off as just another weak woman who went to pieces because she couldn't handle her business. I vowed right then and there that I wasn't going to let Inez and Leon destroy me. I was going to come out of this mess with some dignity and class. I didn't care what it took; I would do whatever I had to do so that I could still hold my head up.

The longer I remained in the room by myself, wondering where Leon was and whom he was with, the worse I felt. I paced the floor like a caged panther. I didn't know what to do to ease the pain, but I had to do something.

Around seven that night, I called room service and ordered a steak sandwich. It was the first thing that I'd put in my stomach since the evening before. Right after I finished gobbling up the steak, I took a quick shower. As soon as I towel-dried myself, I slipped into a pair of white shorts and one of the see-through tops that I'd packed. Then I was out the door. I flagged down the first taxi I saw and jumped into the back seat while it was still moving.

"Take me to a club where I won't run into any tourists," I told the young taxi driver.

"I don't know if such a club is on this island, senorita. This is a small place," the driver told me, giving me an apologetic glance in the rearview mirror.

"Well, there must be at least one club where I won't run into too many tourists," I insisted. The main tourist that I didn't want to run into was Inez McPherson, of course.

"Well, there are a couple of clubs on the south end of the island that most tourists avoid." The driver gave me another apologetic look before he finished. "They cater to a more, uh, uninhibited crowd."

"Sounds good to me," I chirped, my eyes looking out of the window.

A few minutes later, my driver stopped in front of a small brown building with a green door. I could hear reggae music blasting from inside before I even got out of the taxi.

"This is the Cockpit Club. One of the oldest establishments on this island. If you like to dance, this is the place to be," the cab driver told me.

"Do they speak English in this place?"

"We are a bilingual island. You'd be hard pressed to find someone within city limits who does not speak English." The driver turned around to face me, watching me as I watched a fierce-looking man with a bullet-shaped bald head and bare feet snatch open the green door and enter the club. "Just be careful. An American got himself stabbed to death in this club recently."

"Oh?" I said, removing my hand from the door handle.

"But he was asking for trouble. A room full of witnesses swore that it was a case of self-defense. The police didn't even hold the man who did the stabbing."

"Oh." I shrugged with relief, reaching for the door handle.

I paid the driver and gave him a decent tip. Then I hopped out of the taxi in such a hurry that I almost fell to the ground. As soon as I opened the heavy green door and entered the club, I felt refreshed. There were wall-to-wall men in this place, and all eyes were immediately on me. It looked like a scene out of the movie *Scarface.* Men of all different sizes and shades of brown strutted around in light-colored suits, loud-colored shirts and ties, gaudy jewelry. Some had on white Panama hats, and others had slick-backed hairdos and thick, bushy mustaches. There was so much *machismo* in front of me that I had to blink hard to bring everything into focus.

I got asked to dance three times in English and Spanish before I even made it to a table. And this was just what I wanted: attention.

I wasn't myself that night, in more ways than one. Under normal circumstances, I never would have climbed on top of a table and danced a jig like I did. I paid for my own drinks until I got down to my last ten dollars. From this point on, I boldly asked each man that I danced with to buy me another drink.

I had a table near the stage, where a young DJ was playing all the latest tunes from America, but I spent most of my time on the dance floor. I don't know if it was my age that finally caught up with me, or my senses. But all of a sudden, I started feeling tired and bored. There were a few other women in the club, all of them attractive, and that was the fuel that kept me going. I was holding my own, and better than I thought I could. More men were asking me to dance than any other woman in the club, and that gave me even more confidence and courage.

"Would you like some company later tonight?" a man whispered in my ear from behind. When I turned around and saw that it was the bald-headed, barefooted man that I'd seen entering the club when I arrived, I almost screamed. His teeth were almost as brown as his complexion. His breath was as foul as cow dung.

"I'm . . . uh . . . expecting someone," I lied.

"An imbecile, I presume." Baldhead's English was so pronounced, he sounded British. I found his accent intriguing. However, I couldn't get past his bald head, brown teeth, bare feet, and bad breath.

"Excuse me? Why would you say something like that?" I asked. There was something about anger that gave me courage that I didn't know I had. Anger also made me do things that I would never consider, like go to a strange bar in a strange country by myself, looking for somebody who would prove to me that I was still an attractive woman.

"A man would have to be an imbecile to let such a lovely woman be on her own in a place like this. You've been on your own for some time now. I've been watching you. I know that you are here with no one in particular."

"Uh, my boyfriend had to work late. But he'll be here any minute," I said, rising from my seat, my eyes scanning the room. As if it had been planned, I looked into the eyes of the same man who had caused that first bout of friction between Inez and me: Jose. He looked so dapper in his white linen suit and red shirt. A white Panama hat rode his thick red hair.

I didn't wait for Jose to come to me. I rushed over to him. "Jose, I am so happy to see you again!" I had to yell to be heard over the loud music. He seemed pleased, but surprised.

"Have we met?" he asked.

I nodded. "Don't you remember me? Are you with someone?" I asked, looking behind him. "I hope not, because I want to show you a really good time tonight." I nudged him with my bare knee. I didn't know how to interpret the strange look he gave me. But then he smiled and followed me to my table, with me leading him by the hand.

"You are from Ontario, yes?" he said, sitting. I sat down, too, making sure our knees touched.

"Ohio," I said. "I teach second grade," I said proudly, immediately wishing that I could take my last sentence back. One thing I had learned was not to volunteer too much information about myself, unless it was interesting. Most men were not impressed with school-teachers, unless they were one themselves. Like that man Inez had snatched practically out of my arms the night before. "Are you with someone?" I asked again, hoping he would say no. Some of the men had been pretty aggressive, trying to pull me to their tables or off into a darkened corner. One even tried to drag me into the men's room, kissing me up and down my neck all the way. I had to slap his hand for him to release me.

I felt safe with Jose. And comfortable. Comfortable enough to tell him about my fight with Inez. I left no stone unturned, even referring to her as my *ex*–best friend. Jose listened with wide eyes, nodding, shaking his head, totally in my corner.

"And where is that vixen now?" he asked, scanning the club.

"I don't know where that woman is, and I don't care. She checked out of our hotel, and knowing her, she's probably shacked up with some other woman's man right about now." I gave Jose a weary look. "That's the kind of woman she is. She's just that bold and nasty. You saw how she jumped on you, even though you were talking to me!"

Jose gave me a blank look, but he nodded. Then he said just what I wanted to hear. "She was a bit too forward. And, that artificial hair of hers was notorious!"

"It was?" I said, patting my wig. Now I had to worry about him finding out that I had a head full of artificial hair, too.

"Blond hair on a woman of color is not attractive to me."

"Oh," I said, somewhat relieved. The wig that I had on was black, the same color as my real hair. But Jose didn't need to know that the hair on my head had come from another woman. "I came out tonight to"—I paused and giggled—"let my hair down."

"And such beautiful hair to let down," Jose said, his head bobbing like a cork as his eyes rolled up to the top of my head.

"Thank you." I giggled again, glad that I'd tacked the wig to my head with several hairpins so that it wouldn't shift or slide off of my head.

"I don't know what is going to happen when I get back home," I whined. "So I need to enjoy myself now, while I still can," I added, looking around the club to evaluate my competition. Not only were the other women present attractive, most of them had on outfits that made my see-through blouse and Daisy Duke shorts look tame. One woman was totally topless, bouncing from one man's lap to another. "Damn Inez and Leon. I am not going to let them ruin everything for me! I will enjoy myself tonight!" I vowed, glad that I was able to hold my own with so many other women, younger and prettier, prancing around in the club.

I don't even remember moving from my chair to Jose's lap. His hand started caressing my back and my arms, and then quickly moved down to my naked thighs. What had happened to me in this club so far did wonders for my wounded ego. I had been faithful to Leon. Whether he had an intimate relationship with Inez before or after we were married didn't matter. Just the thought of him making love to her was too much for me to stand! I pictured him on top of her, her legs wrapped around his waist. It was the most disgusting scene that had ever crossed my mind. And it wouldn't go away. I closed my eyes, and that's all I could see. My hand found its way to Jose's crotch. I was pleased to feel such a massive lump between his thighs. I smiled as he spread his thick muscular legs and started rocking in his chair. He removed his Panama hat and placed it on his lap, hiding his erection. He winked at me. I winked back. I ignored the little voice speaking to me from the back of my head, asking me, *Woman, what in the world do you think you're doing?*

Inez had told me to never say never. But I'd still told her that I would *never* cheat on my husband. I didn't feel that way anymore. At least not tonight. All I needed was the right man to help me cross that line. Jose seemed to be the most likely candidate.

"Uh . . . do you want to go someplace else?" I purred. I had an itching to go to the beach with Jose, where we could at least roll around in the sand. However, he had something a little more intimate in mind. And that sounded even better.

"Why don't we go to my room down the way a bit and get more comfortable?" he suggested, his hand rubbing and squeezing my behind. That was all he had to say and do.

I was a woman who had been betrayed by the last two people in the world that I'd expected to betray me. Well, I wasn't going to just sit back and do nothing about it. I was about to do the most logical thing a woman in my position could do to alleviate the pain that they'd put me through—and I was going to enjoy every minute of it!

I felt vindicated already. An obscene grin appeared on my face. I looked at Jose and nodded, sliding my tongue suggestively across my lips.

CHAPTER 27

Jose had been very vague and mysterious about his profession so far. He had hinted that he was a bartender, but a few minutes later, he said that he worked as a cook and a driver. We'd spent hours together, and I knew next to nothing about him. He had shown me pictures of his children, but he had not mentioned a wife or a current lover.

I followed Jose down the crowded street, swinging my sandals in one hand, clutching my drink in the other. I turned around and looked over my shoulder back at the club we'd just left. Some of the men that I had danced with had come out to the sidewalk and were still looking at me with lust in their eyes. Every time my mind wandered back to reality, I felt so light-headed that I stumbled every few steps. But Jose made sure I didn't fall or stray away from him and get lost in the crowd along the way. He kept a firm grip on my arm.

It took just a few minutes for us to reach the small dark motel. This was where Jose said he often rented a room when he was away from his house, on the other side of the island. Despite the motel's dull exterior, exotic birds fluttered throughout the courtyard. There were a few ancient jalopies haphazardly parked near the entrance, and a few dazed and disheveled individuals milling about.

"This is where you live?" I asked, rubbing my nose.

"Aha." Jose laughed and nodded. He had a deep, loud laugh, which seemed to come from within his soul. "It's not a palace, but it holds many memories. I've had some of my best moments here," he informed me, unlocking a narrow, mud-colored door, which squeaked like a mouse.

As soon as I stepped into the dimly lit, musty room with a lopsided bed, a scarred dresser, and hardly anything else, I regretted it. Jose closed the door with his foot and locked it. Then he locked all three of the small, dingy windows. There was a shabby Bible in English on the nightstand, splayed open to a page where someone had underlined the passage *Your trusted friends have deceived you.* Reading that made me want to leave even more. But it was too late. Jose had already started undressing me. It seemed like he wanted to fuck me and get it over with as soon as possible. I had expected him to be a little more subtle and romantic. His odd behavior turned me off, so I pushed him away.

"What is it?" he asked, his voice sounding more like a creature's growl.

"Uh, I didn't bring any protection," I said, rearing back and attempting to unhook myself from his viselike embrace. With all the things going through my head, I had overlooked one of the most important things of all: condoms. Even though Inez had packed enough for five women, I had not packed a single one. I had no reason to. As a matter of fact, I had not had any use for condoms since my college days.

"No problem!" he yelled. He screwed up his face in a way that made his eyebrows look like they had grown together. He yanked open the top drawer in the dresser and plucked out a package of condoms, opening it with his teeth. His merging eyebrows now looked like a big, bushy red caterpillar.

In the dim light, I could now see that Jose was not as handsome as I had originally thought. His skin was as armored as the hide of an armadillo. His teeth were crooked and threatening to turn brown. I had every reason to believe that my leaving was no longer an option. Nor was resisting. From the look on his face, there was no turning back. I gritted my teeth, closed my eyes, and hoped for the best, vowing that I would never put myself in a situation such as this again.

"Can I have something to drink?" I asked, my head still reared back, trying to dodge his sloppy kisses. I was already tipsy, but this was a case that required a serious buzz.

Jose let out an impatient sigh and released me. Then he trotted into a bathroom with no door and came back out, clutching a plastic cup full of cloudy, lukewarm water.

As soon as I finished drinking the water, he was on me again. He bent me backwards so far, my face was level with the cracked ceiling.

This man was, without a doubt, the worst lover I'd ever come across before in my life. That big bulge I'd felt when I massaged his crotch in the club was 90 percent balls. What was left over was about the size of my thumb. I closed my eyes, gritted my teeth, and prayed that he would not be on top of me for too long.

"Thank you," he whispered, rolling off less than a minute later. He belched and farted at the same time.

I felt like I'd been betrayed again. But this time there was nothing I could do to make up for it. Finding another man to sleep with didn't appeal to me. The way my luck was going, he would probably be even worse.

And to think that I had held on to my wig with one hand the whole time Jose was in me so it wouldn't slide off. "Can you call me a cab?" I asked in a tired voice, almost gagging on the stench of his gas. I rose, fanning the air with both hands. "And can you give me some cab fare?" I knew that I wasn't too far from my hotel, but I didn't want to walk. And after all I'd just been through, I didn't want to spend the last ten dollars that I had with me on transportation.

Jose didn't look at me as he rose from the bed and lifted his pants from the floor. I couldn't remember the last time I saw a man get completely dressed so fast. He even buttoned his red shirt wrong, leaving the tail hanging over the waist of his pants flapping like a seal when he walked. His red hair stood up on his head like a rooster's comb. With a grunt and another fart, he flipped open his wallet and removed some bills, dropping them onto the bed next to me.

I sat up and was surprised to see two crisp hundred-dollar bills. Ben Franklin never looked better. I looked at Jose with a forced smile. "Is this all for me?" I asked, feeling that I deserved it and even more.

He looked and acted nervous as he raked his fingers through his hair. He glanced at the door; then he looked at me with his hands on his hips. It was the way he looked at me that was so disturbing. It was the most extreme look of disgust that I'd ever seen on another human being's face in my life.

I didn't have time to react to Jose's sudden change. I rushed back into my clothes and sandals. What happened next happened so fast, I don't remember all the details. Two men in uniforms, and with guns drawn, burst into the room, yelling in Spanish. My mind had shut down for a moment, so I could not determine what they were saying. One stopped in front of me and said in plain English, "You are under arrest for the crime of prostitution."

With a sly grin, the other one grabbed my arm and roughly spun me around to face him. He started fondling my breasts and making lewd comments in English and in Spanish. The next thing I knew, he was clamping a pair of handcuffs on me. That's when I fainted.

CHAPTER 28

"Mrs. Webb, did you understand what the judge just said?"
"Huh?" I could barely speak or stand.

"By pleading guilty, your ninety-day sentence begins immediately. You will be credited for the days you've already spent in custody."

For a few seconds, I didn't know where I was. Then it suddenly dawned on me where I was. No, it hit me like a Mack truck: I was back in a courtroom on the island of Paraíso, with a charge of prostitution hanging over my head like a guillotine. I felt like I had already lost my head.

I didn't feel like myself. And without my wig and make-up, I knew that I didn't even look like myself, either. I blinked, shook my head, and looked around. I felt like I had just woken up from a nightmare, but I was wrong. This was real.

I didn't know exactly how long I had been standing before a Paraisan judge, with Debra Retner, my legal representative, by my side. I had tuned them both out as I stood there, thinking back over all the events that had led me to this point.

Debra Retner, the sympathetic woman who acted as a liaison between the island officials and visiting Americans who got themselves in trouble, was the only American I'd seen or spoken to since Inez's departure. All of a sudden, I felt hopelessly alone and homesick. I glanced at a logo representing the American flag on the front of

Debra's briefcase. My first instinct was to touch it, which I did, and then I burst into tears.

"The court will notify your family—" Debra told me, rubbing my back as she handed me a tissue.

"I want my family to hear about this from me," I sobbed. "Just my mother and my sister. Not that punk ass husband of mine!" If my husband, Leon, had walked into the room, I would have ripped him to shreds with my bare hands. I still could not believe that he had refused to fly down to the islands from Ohio to pay my fine and take me home.

First, it was him sleeping with Inez, and now this. He had betrayed me twice. But I made up my mind right then and there that I would not let his actions destroy me completely. Despite my weaknesses, I was still a strong woman, and if this experience didn't kill me, it was going to make me even stronger.

"You can write to your mother and sister as soon as . . . as soon as you get settled in. However, an official from the court will also be contacting your family. It's standard procedure. There is information that your family will need that you don't know yet. Like visiting rules, what they can or cannot send to you. Other important information as well."

"What if my family can raise the ten thousand dollars?" I blurted, blinking hard as I looked into Debra's sad eyes.

Debra Retner shook her head and gave me a hopeless look. "That option is no longer available once you've been sentenced."

"But that's not fair! I was set up, and these people know that!" I hollered, looking at Debra through wild eyes that felt like they were ablaze.

"True. And I couldn't agree with you more." Debra glanced at her watch and looked over my shoulder. A pained look appeared on her face. I followed her gaze to the female guard walking in my direction, dangling a pair of handcuffs. Debra moved a few steps away from me. "I am so sorry, Mrs. Webb. I know you don't deserve this, but my hands are tied," Debra told me, her voice cracking.

The sour-faced judge dismissed everyone. And not more than a few seconds later, the gruff female guard cuffed me and led me away. Debra Retner continued to stand in the same spot, with the most hopelessly sad look on her face. Somehow I managed to smile at her and mouth, "Thank you."

The bus that transported me, and about a dozen other women, to the detention center at the end of the island shook, rattled, and rocked all the way. It was like being on a roller coaster. None of the other women spoke to me. When they spoke among themselves, it was in machine-gun Spanish, so I didn't know what was being said. And I didn't care, because nothing could make me feel any worse or better.

My new temporary home was a small cell with a barred window too high for me to look out of. For reasons that were never explained to me, I had no cell mate. But every other cell that I could see housed at least two women. And in some cases, three. The first cell that I'd been herded into had been hard to take. But the one where I was going to spend the next three months of my life was even more primitive. It had no sink, or anything else, except a sleeping cot against the wall. There were no toilet facilities. I had to do my business in a round hole in the cement floor that was about the shape and size of a large dinner plate. I could see and smell that someone before me had had a bad aim. There was a metal lid to use as a cover, and a lime green substance that smelled like sulfur had been sprinkled around the edges and into the belly of the hole. For toilet paper, there was a short water hose hanging from the wall.

Shortly after I'd been secured, a cross-eyed trustee slid some paper and a nub of a pencil though the bars of my cell. I scribbled a few lines on a sheet of paper to Mama and Frankie, trying to make light of my situation. I told them that I was in "a little trouble," and that I'd be "in custody for ninety days," and not to worry about me.

I was surprised when I received a response from home six days later. Mama wrote:

Dear Renee,

If you had married that Dunbar boy, you wouldn't be in this mess. He would not have let no wife of his go traipsing halfway around the world like Leon done. Leon called me up and told me what a fool you made of yourself down there! Shame, shame, shame! Your grandma Vera must be spinning in her grave! If she was still alive, she would put a whupping on you that a doctor couldn't take off. I told Cheryl her mama's in a hospital down there in them islands because I don't think she needs to know what a fool she got for a mama. Poor Leon. I will send you some money when I can so you can at least buy you some rock

candy or magazines or something to help you get through this mess.
Your sister, Frankie, said to tell you not to forget to bring her some gifts
home when they turn you aloose. If you forget them gifts for Frankie,
we'll never hear the end of it.

Love, Mom

The letter from my mother was hard enough to take, but the newspaper clipping from the *Butler Review* that she had stuffed into the
same envelope was even worse. The headlines screamed: BUTLER
WOMAN ARRESTED FOR PROSTITUTION DURING CARIBBEAN VACATION!

A Butler schoolteacher was among more than a dozen women
arrested for prostitution last weekend on the tiny Caribbean island
of Paraíso. Witnesses claim that Renee Denise Webb, thirty-one,
entered a local bar frequented by prostitutes and immediately
began to aggressively proposition several men. "She was half
naked, drunk as hell, and all over the place, hugging and kissing
every man in sight," a witness, who asked not to be named, reported.

Prostitution has become a major concern for island officials
in recent years. Last year 40 percent of the prostitutes in custody
tested positive for HIV, the virus that causes AIDS. Since January
of this year, twelve prostitutes have been convicted of assaults,
robberies, and murders.

Mrs. Webb's colleagues are stunned. "I thought I knew her.
She fooled a lot of people, and I am embarrassed to admit that I
ever considered her a close friend. She's a tramp! And I hope
that my association with her will not affect my reputation. I can
never trust her again. I will never associate with her again," said
Shirley Blake, who teaches at Butler Elementary School, where
Mrs. Webb has taught second grade for the past nine years.

Mrs. Webb pleaded guilty at her arraignment and was sentenced to ninety days in a Paraíso women's detention center.
Upon the completion of her sentence, Mrs. Webb will be immediately deported. She will also be permanently banned from
reentering the island in the future.

That Shirley Blake. That bitch. I wanted to scratch my colleague's
eyes out. Then she'd really have a reason to trash me and call *me* a

tramp. For years I'd been her only close friend. I'd lent her money and set her up with single men I knew. Now I knew what Mama meant when she told me that your best friend can also be your worst enemy. But I also had to wonder how that applied to Inez. Was it possible that she'd been both my best friend and my worst enemy at the same time? It was too depressing to think about for too long.

I folded the newspaper clipping and Mama's letter and slid both back into the envelope. The next few letters from Mama were just as depressing as the first one. I didn't look forward to hearing from her.

CHAPTER 29

"I have some very good news to report to you." Talking to me through the bars in my cell was one of the trustees. She was one of the few prison workers that I felt comfortable with. This one was not as husky, drab, and gruff as most of the others. She was a petite, brown-skinned woman with a cap of fuzzy black hair and large brown eyes. So far she was the only one I'd seen in the compound who wore make-up. Her lifelong dream was to one day visit the United States, so she had taken a particular interest in me from the moment I'd arrived.

I didn't react fast enough. The trustee, whose name tag identified her as Luz Capistrano, reported the news before I could respond. "You do not have the HIV virus. Your results came back yesterday, but I didn't get the information until this morning," she chirped, with her arms folded across her flat chest.

I nodded and smiled through dry, cracked lips. I was glad to hear that at least I didn't have to worry about having a fatal disease. Even though Jose had used a condom, it wouldn't have surprised me to hear that he'd pricked a hole in it on purpose before sliding it on. But I didn't get too excited about the news that Luz had just delivered. What I did have to worry about was still enough to keep me in the doldrums. I didn't know what was going to happen to me during my incarceration, or what was going to happen to me when I returned to

Ohio. No matter how I looked at my situation, it was about as grim as it could get.

"I will keep you in my prayers," Luz told me, giving me one of her biggest smiles. "You don't belong in this place. I can tell," she added.

I smiled back. "But I'm still here," I said, with a shrug, my voice cracking. My hands gripped the bars as I faced Luz. "Thank you for being so nice to me. I will never forget it."

"Do you have any little ones?"

"I have a little girl named Cheryl. She's five," I sniffed, picturing my baby's little, round face. I couldn't imagine what she'd been told about my situation.

"Well, you will have her in your arms again soon. Praise God for that." Luz's smile faded, and I didn't even have to ask her why. "All three of my little ones died in my arms before they lived to see one day. One thing or another. No money for medicine or good doctors." Luz paused and let out a loud sigh. "Bad doctors live here on this island, and they did things to my body at times when I was not able to stop them. Some of the same things they do to keep the stray dogs on the street from bringing more stray dogs to our streets they done to me. I am like the stray dogs on the street now."

"I'm sorry," I offered, not really wanting to hear any more depressing news. It was hard enough trying to deal with my own.

Luz gave me a pitiful look. "Maybe when I make it to America, I will visit you at your home," she mouthed, looking at me with the kind of desperation in her eyes that was common among ambitious foreigners whose goal in life was to visit or live in the United States.

"I'd like that, Luz," I said, my eyes on the gummy floor. I was willing to say anything to maintain a positive relationship with Luz. In a place with so much despair and uncertainty, I knew I needed at least one friend. My mind flashed on the one friend that I had always been able to count on: Inez. I don't know why, but in the back of my mind, I expected her to help pull me out of the deep hole that I'd dug for myself. I kept telling myself that had it not been for her, I wouldn't be in the hole in the first place.

"You will love America," I told Luz, my mind flashing on things I associated with my homeland: Big Macs, reality TV shows, Oprah, and the lovable, snaggletoothed second graders who filled my classroom every year. The thought of them beginning this school year with a substitute brought tears to my eyes. I had to turn away from Luz.

I wanted to continue the conversation. But under the circumstances, the only subject of interest to me was living through this ordeal. As nice as Luz was to me and as much as I liked her, I returned to the cot and turned my face to the wall. I kept my face in that direction until I heard Luz leave, the ring of keys she carried jingling like bells.

The prison employees were not as brutal as I had expected them to be. If anything, they seemed just plain indifferent. Luz was the most personable one I'd encountered so far.

I had not had any bad experiences with any of the other inmates yet, but I still had more than two and a half months to go. I was determined to not let my guard down. I had learned from Luz that the most dangerous inmates, like the ones who had committed murder or who had sold their own children, were kept in a separate facility. The "good" criminals, like me and the two dozen women that I interacted with, included just prostitutes and petty thieves. Just like Debra Retner had told me, some of these women seemed delighted to be incarcerated, as opposed to living on the streets. They had a place to sleep, food, medical attention, and even recreational activities. There was a small television set in a large room, with a satellite dish. There was a volleyball net in the yard. Women's magazines were routinely passed out, and the inmates clamored for them, even though most were at least six months old.

To me, the menu left a lot to be desired. Every meal included rice, even breakfast. The bread, a flat, square-shaped biscuit, was always cold and stale. No matter what the meat was on a particular day, it always looked the same: gray and stringy. I couldn't tell when it was pork, beef, or chicken. I skipped a lot of meals. When I did eat, I often didn't know what I was putting in my mouth.

The next letter that I received from Mama included forty dollars, which I used to purchase a few personal items and some junk food from the commissary. I didn't bother reading Mama's letter right away. I was certain that it contained more words that would do me more harm than good, so I decided that I would read it at my leisure. I ended up wishing I had read Mama's letter. If I had, I would have known what Inez was up to.

Two days after I'd received Mama's last letter, Luz approached my cell, clapping her hands. "More good news!" she greeted. I jumped up from my cot and ran to the front of the cell, gripping the bars like

I always did when someone came to see me. That Thursday morning was one of the hottest days I'd endured so far. The temperature was already over a hundred degrees, and it wasn't even noon yet. Sweat was sliding down my face like wax.

"What is it?" I asked, coughing. I had contracted a slight cold a few days ago and was still dealing with a cough and a few other aches and pains.

Luz grinned and shook her ring of keys at me before she opened the door to my cell. "Big surprise," she hollered. "The best surprise for you!"

"Am I going home?" I asked, gasping so hard I almost choked on my tongue. My eyes blinked hopefully.

Luz grabbed my hand and pulled me out of my cell and into the corridor. Then she proceeded to lead me down the darkened hallway, beyond the cell block. The large shoes slipping and sliding on my feet made it hard for me to keep up with her. I ignored the catcalls, grunts, and groans coming from the women in the other cells.

"You have a visitor!" Luz exclaimed, squeezing my hand.

Thursday was visiting day. Three Thursdays had already come and gone, and no one had come to visit me except Debra Retner. I had not expected any other visitors, so I assumed that it was Debra who had come to see me this time, too. Mama couldn't afford to make the trip. And from what Mama had revealed in her letters, the rest of my relatives had said that they couldn't visit me, because they were afraid something might happen to them if they entered a foreign country.

At this point, I was so angry with Leon that he was the last person in the world I wanted to see. It was too late for him to pay my fine and take me home, so there was no point in him coming now. The thought of him kicking back and going on about his life, with me sitting in an island jail, just made my blood boil.

Then I recalled Debra telling me on her last visit that she was going to visit her daughter in that hellish prison in Malaysia this week. I stopped in my tracks and pulled my hand away from Luz. "Who is here to see me?" I demanded. "Is it my husband?" Bile rose in my throat as I clenched my fists.

"No. A pretty woman has come to visit with you. Come about!" Luz yelled, grabbing my hand again.

The waiting room was almost as gloomy as my cell. There were a lot of dusty windows on all four walls. The windows were small and round, and looked like sad, hollow eyes. I felt like I'd just stumbled into a cheap cafeteria in a cheap hotel. It smelled like one, too: musty and stale. The glare from the sun coming in through the windows blinded me for a moment. I couldn't see much until I reached one of several long wooden picniclike tables, where prisoners sat across from their visitors on hard wooden benches. I shaded my eyes and sucked in a mouth full of air.

"Hello, Renee." It was Inez, the one woman that I never expected to talk to again.

Luz patted my shoulder and left immediately. I just stood there staring at Inez, with my hand still shading my eyes, which had tears forming in them.

"What the hell are you doing here?" I croaked, wobbling on legs that felt like they were going to collapse at any moment.

"I would have come back down here sooner. But I didn't go straight home when I left here. I made a detour to Aruba. I didn't know you were still down here until last week!" Inez rose and put her hand on my shoulder, guiding me into the seat across from her.

She looked uncomfortable and frightened as she glanced around the room, and I could see why. There were almost as many armed guards in the room as there were prisoners. An escape was not even a remote possibility. And from what I'd heard about the immediate area outside the compound, it was safer to be inside. Other criminals, wild dogs, and snakes patrolled the area. A week ago a woman who had worked in the laundry room wandered too far away from the prison grounds one evening. They found a few bits and pieces of her body on the ground next to a coconut tree two days later. She'd been raped and beaten and left for the wild dogs to finish off.

"I guess you know how I ended up in here," I said, sounding sarcastic when I didn't mean to. I couldn't control much of anything I said or did anymore.

Inez glanced to the side, speaking with her lips barely moving. "I've talked to your mother and your sister. And ten different other people saved that newspaper clipping about you for me." Inez tapped my hand. "I told your mother to tell you in her letter that I was on my way. I booked a flight as soon as I heard, so I didn't have time to write you a letter first. Besides, I didn't know if you'd accept a letter from me, anyway. I figured I had a better chance of communicating with you if I showed up in person." Inez shifted in her seat and gave me a hard look. It was hard for me not to look away. "Renee, I came back to the hotel the next day after that, uh, that little confrontation we had. They told me you'd just left in a cab. I waited in the lobby all night for you to return. When morning came and you hadn't come back, I went back to my hotel. I hadn't slept all night, so I was out like a light for the next eight hours. If I had known anything about what had happened to you, I would have been there to bail you out, no questions asked. Despite our little spat, I would not have let you go to jail," Inez said, with conviction. And I believed every word she said.

I felt disembodied. My head seemed to be floating above my body. I was stronger than I'd given myself credit for, because I was still able to express myself. I tilted my head and gave Inez a wan smile. "They would have let me go if I'd been able to pay the ten-thousand-dollar fine in time. Leon could have brought it, or he could have wired it down here." At this point, I had to stop talking to catch my breath and compose myself. I felt a panic attack coming on, but a few deep breaths held it off. "Leon hung up on me when I called him. And you know how broke everybody else in my family is," I said tiredly. "Did you know that Jose was the one who set me up?"

"Who the fuck is Jose?" Inez asked, with a grimace. "Did I meet him?"

I nodded. "He was the one who was tickling my feet that day we stopped for drinks after shopping," I said, my angry words burning my lips. Just thinking about Jose made me sick. Talking about that beast was almost impossible. But since Inez gave me such a puzzled look, I kept talking about him. "You had already met him earlier. When you came back with our drinks, he forgot about me and was suddenly all over you like a cheap wig."

"Jose? The older dude with the reddish hair?"

I nodded. "He works for the cops. Men like him help the cops trap . . . uh . . . prostitutes." My eyes wandered off to the side for a moment. "Jose didn't pay for my dinner or flirt with me because he liked me. He was only doing his job," I said through clenched teeth.

"Fuck . . . it could have been me."

"If you had fucked him and accepted money from him, yes. But it wasn't you," I said in a firm voice.

Inez sighed and tilted her head. I could see large tears in her eyes, even though she blinked a lot, trying to hold them back.

"Renee, I am sorry about what happened between us. And I don't blame you if you don't want anything else to do with me when you get home. But I want you to know that I didn't sleep with Leon after he got with you. I know people think I'm a whore, and I don't give a shit. And maybe I am, but I am as good a friend to you as a woman like me can be."

"Did Leon try to sleep with you after he married me?"

Inez dropped her head and nodded. "All the time. And the more I rejected him, the more he hated me; at least that's what he tried to make you think. But I do believe that he did develop very strong feelings for you once he realized what a wonderful woman he'd picked. He married you. You had his baby. That's got to mean something to him." Inez sounded sincere, but that didn't make me feel any better.

"Have you seen or talked to him?" I asked.

"As soon as I found out what had happened to you, I went to see him. I told him that I'd told you everything. He was righteously pissed. But I didn't give a flying fuck. Now I *know* he won't be trying to make moves on me anymore."

"Why did you come back down here?" I asked. "There's really nothing you can do for me now."

"Because I knew you needed a friend to help you get through this mess. Who else was going to do it? As far as I am concerned, you are still my best friend. When you get home, I will do everything I can to help you get back into the swing of things. That's the least I can do."

"I don't want you to pity me, Inez. I'll be fine," I said.

Inez shook her head. "I don't pity you. You are the best friend I've ever had, and I want to be there for you again."

I don't know what made me say what I said next. I didn't even believe the words as they rolled out of my mouth. "I wish I was more like you. I would not have been so quick to settle for Leon. I should have dated every man in sight."

Inez gave me a long thoughtful look. "Why would you want to be like me?"

I shrugged. "At least I'd be happy."

"You think I'm happy?" Inez guffawed. "You think fooling around with a lot of men makes me happy? Did you ever think that maybe the reason I do what I do is because I am unhappy, and I'm trying to hide it? You want to know what one of the few things in my life is that makes me happy?"

I blinked and shook my head.

"You," Inez declared. "I never had any close female friends in my life until I met you. That's why I tried so hard to warn you about Leon. I guess I didn't try hard enough."

"Yes, you did," I rasped. "You did all you could do for me."

I lost it first. I started crying, squawking like a crow. Inez was even worse. She burst into tears and cried so hard, I ended up consoling her.

CHAPTER 30

Inez stayed until visiting hours were over. I returned to my cell, feeling like a new woman, and in a way I was. I knew that I could never go back to being the same meek little housewife I'd been. I didn't know yet what I was going to do about my marriage.

Mama included some vague hints in her next two letters that Leon was thinking about getting a divorce, so there was a possibility that the outcome of my marriage was not going to be up to me, anyway. One thing that Mama had revealed in her letters was that Leon had agreed to let Cheryl stay with her until I returned. That didn't surprise me. I did believe that the man loved our daughter as much as he loved his other daughter, but he didn't have the patience to take care of two young girls on his own. He used to get nervous when both of the girls were in his presence. And that was even with me there taking care of most of their needs.

Another month dragged by, bringing me closer to my release date. But I was more depressed than ever. One of the inmates died in her cell while giving birth two and a half months early. When the guards and trustees found her the next morning, she was hanging sideways across her bed, with the dead baby dangling from between her thighs.

They were still cleaning up the mess when Luz strutted down the hall to my cell, with a familiar grin on her face.

"You have a visitor from America! Come about!" she hollered, clapping her hands like a trained seal.

I had received a letter from Inez telling me that she'd had some unexpected expenses, and because of that, she didn't know when she'd be able to visit me again. But I still assumed it was her.

"He's a nice-looking man," Luz continued. "Nice blue suit."

I stopped dead in my tracks. I didn't think that any of my male relatives had scraped up the money for a ticket and a hotel, and gotten over their fear of something happening to them in the islands. There could be only one other man in a nice blue suit sitting in that visitors' room, waiting to see me: Leon. The way I felt about Leon now, I would have preferred a visit from Jose, or even Osama bin Laden.

"I don't know . . . I don't think I can see him," I told Luz, wringing my hands. "He didn't come when I needed him, and it's way too late now," I told her. I was feeling angry and sad at the same time. I was still angry at Leon for turning his back on me. I was sad because he still had an active role in my life, whether I wanted him to or not. I just didn't know how much of a role he was going to have in my future.

Luz gave me a puzzled look. "But he says he didn't see you for a long time before you got married. . . ." Luz stopped when I gasped and stumbled forward. I almost knocked her down, trying to get to the visitors' room so fast.

He stood there in a blue suit, holding a wide-brimmed hat in his hand, grinning. He looked like a young country preacher. There was a part in his hair, on the side of his head, that was so wide, it looked like a divided highway. His receding hairline made it look even more countrified. The glare from the sun was as strong as ever, so I had to shade my eyes. But I would have known that bowlegged body anywhere.

"Robbie?" I choked, stumbling toward him. Luz helped me to a seat at the table before she disappeared. Robbie came around the table and embraced me.

"Renee, I know I am probably not the man you wanted to see, but I couldn't stay away no longer." Robbie's smile was almost as bright as the sun, which had temporarily blinded me.

"Robbie, you didn't have to . . . I am so glad to see you."

"Renee, Inez told me how Leon clowned you. I told her then, and I am telling you now, if you had called me the same day you called Leon to come down here and pay your fine, I would have been down here that night—lickety-split. There ain't no way in the world I would have left you down here in this place. Oh, I probably would have whupped the holy piss out of your little black ass once I got you home. And I probably would have never let you out of my sight again, but we could have worked through it." Robbie smiled. For the first time, I realized how handsome he really was. He looked like an angel in my tortured eyes. Maybe it was because he had come to my aid that made him look so damned good to me now. It didn't matter. Robbie Dunbar never looked better in his life.

"Robbie, I am so sorry that things didn't work out between us. I know now that I made a big mistake breaking up with you for Leon." I dropped my head and spoke, with my eyes on the floor. "You are worth five of him." I looked up at Robbie. I kept a straight face because I didn't have the strength to smile at the moment.

"I feel you, Renee," he said. The feelings that Robbie had for me were sincere. There was no doubt about that. And I felt and appreciated his feelings. I didn't care if I learned anything else from my nightmare, because I had learned how to be humble. This characteristic was going to be very important in my future.

I cleared my throat. "I was too blind to see that before. I don't know what's going to happen when I get home. But, I really don't know about you and me ever having a relationship again. I am going to need some time to sort out my life and my feelings."

Robbie chuckled and waved his hand. "Girl, you ain't got to worry about me. I'm getting married next month."

I managed a weak smile as I rolled my eyes. I was embarrassed.

"Oh, that's right. I forgot about you and that Mitchell woman," I said, hoping I didn't sound too harsh. Despite the fact that I had learned how to be humble, I still didn't like the fact that a nice, sweet man like Robbie was going to end up with one of the biggest bitches in town.

"But me getting married won't stop us from being friends. I already told Janet that. I swear to God, she's such a good woman." So Janet was the one he'd picked, not her identical twin, Jennifer, the bigger bitch in the Mitchell family. I still didn't like the idea of a nice, docile man like Robbie ending up in that family of shrews. They'd have him baby-sitting, washing dishes, baking cookies, and mopping floors every other day. Just like I would have done if I'd married him. The thought made me want to laugh, but I didn't.

"I need all of the friends I can get, Robbie." I used to think that Leon was my best friend. But when the school board sent a registered letter addressed to me to our house, telling me that I'd been fired, Leon didn't even have the decency to send it to me himself. He sent it to Mama and had her send it to me. "I'm going to have to find a new job when I get home, and probably a place to stay."

"Well, I bought out my uncle, and now the gas station is mine. Mine and Janet's. We can always use a good cashier," Robbie said. "I can front you the money to get you a place," Robbie added, pulling out his wallet. He dropped a wad of bills on the table.

"What's that for?" I asked, puzzled.

"Janet wanted to come. But she came down with the flu the other day and is taking antibiotics. She was the one that told me to give you whatever we could afford so you'd have some spending money to get whatever they allow y'all to buy down here." Robbie paused, looked around, and scratched his chin. "See, your mama and your sister have been going all over town, borrowing money to send to you. Your mama even hit me up for thirty dollars last week." Robbie slid the money across the table.

"You have to give it to the trustee when she comes," I explained. "You don't have to do this, but I am grateful for anything you do for me, Robbie."

Robbie looked away, and I had a feeling that it was because he didn't want me to see the pain in his eyes.

"I meant what I said about us staying friends," he said, squeezing my hand. "I know working behind a cash register in a gas station is a big comedown from being a schoolteacher, but it's better than no job at all."

"Thank you, Robbie." I smiled. "Have you had any more dreams about me?" I asked. When I smiled, my face ached like I'd been slapped. My lips were so dry and ashy, I had blisters.

He shook his head. "Just that one I had before you came down here. The one where you kept trying to call me for help." Robbie gave me a serious look. "I don't really believe in dreams or anything else supernatural. But the Monday after I had that dream, I got my passport renewed, and I put aside some traveling money. And even though you didn't call me yourself, I knew you needed my help."

CHAPTER 31

The last two weeks were the hardest. They seemed like the longest two weeks of my life. A lot happened during the last few days. One woman gave birth in the showers. A few prisoners that I had become friendly with were released. One elderly woman who had been serving a life sentence finally died, and they hauled her away in a gray body bag and then dumped her on the back of the same truck that hauled away the garbage.

Ten days before my release, I received two letters from Mama on the same day. One contained some photographs that she had taken of my daughter, Cheryl, weeks ago that she kept forgetting to send.

I received the first and only letter that my sister, Frankie, took the time to write. She didn't have much to say. Just that everybody in town was still talking about me like a dog. And, she advised me not to forget to bring her a few island gifts.

Debra Retner paid me one final visit, glowing like a lighthouse because she was almost as happy as I was that my sentence was almost over.

"I am sure that you will look at yourself and life from a different perspective from now on," Debra said, giving me a hug as soon as she entered the visitors' room.

I nodded and cleared my throat. "I can't thank you enough for what you did and tried to do for me. I know I probably won't ever see you again after I leave this place, but I do want you to know that this was all just a big, stupid mistake that I made. I am not a criminal. Especially not a prostitute." I held up my hand. "I know what you're thinking. Like you told me before, sleeping with a man and accepting money for it is prostitution. I was mad at my husband and my best friend. I had to do something that night to get my mind off of them. I didn't have much money, and that's why I was trying to get men to buy me drinks. I wasn't trying to get them to take me to bed and pay me."

Debra rubbed her nose until it turned red, and then she gave me a dry look.

"I did need cab fare to get back to my hotel, and that's what I'd asked that motherfucker for. But when he offered me a lot more than cab fare, I only took it because he'd been so lousy in bed. And I thought that I'd deserved something extra for my troubles." I rolled my eyes.

Debra had an amused look on her face. She glanced over her shoulder before she began to speak in a low, detached voice. "I lived in France for a few years right after I got out of college. There were times when I had no job, no money, no place to live. Let's just say I asked for a lot of cab fare, too." Debra laughed and gave me another hug. "Some of us get caught. Some of us don't."

That was the last time I saw Debra Retner. I never saw my favorite trustee, Luz, again, either. One of the other trustees told me that Luz had been transferred to another facility the day after Debra's last visit.

It rained off and on for the last three days of my confinement. Hurricanes had already whipped the hell out of some of the other islands earlier in the year, but so far Paraíso had been spared the brunt of Mother Nature's wrath. I prayed that the storm would not interfere with my release. My prayers were answered.

An hour after I was processed for release, Inez arrived, grinning from ear to ear.

"I thought you'd like some company on the flight home," she told me. She had on just as much make-up as usual, but not enough to hide her red, puffy eyes. She had arrived in a rental car, which she had planned to take me to the airport in. But I was still in custody and therefore not allowed to ride to the airport with Inez or anyone else other than a prison official. Inez trailed behind the gray prison van as it transported me to the airport, where I would be officially deported.

We got separated once we got to the airport, and I didn't see Inez again until I arrived at my gate.

"It's all over now," she said, giving me a bear hug.

"Almost," I told her.

I got nervous going through customs at the airport in Paraíso. I was so paranoid and afraid that something else would happen that might cause me to be detained. But as a person being officially deported, I had no problem getting out of the country.

I didn't know what I was going home to. I had not heard a peep out of Leon, so I knew I was not going back to the house that I had shared with him for the past few years.

The most logical place for Inez to drive me to once we made it back to Ohio was my mother's house. I couldn't wait to hug my daughter and hopefully undo the psychological damage that she had probably suffered during, and because of, my absence.

It took all of my strength to hold back my tears when I saw the Cleveland Hopkins International Airport from the air. But I lost it when we approached the international section. Greeting me was a gigantic black and white sign that said: WELCOME TO THE UNITED STATES OF AMERICA. There was a large American flag blowing in the wind next to it. The sight of these two symbols of freedom was too much for me. I couldn't stop shaking and crying. I was so overwhelmed, you would have thought that I had just returned from hell. In a way I had. I now knew how prisoners of war felt when they returned to the States. Inez wrapped her arm around me and led me from the plane. I stopped crying when I noticed security guards and other people staring at us.

"Did I ever say I was sorry for slapping you?" I asked Inez, with a chuckle, sniffing and wiping my nose with the back of my trembling hand.

"I think you did. But if you ever do it again, I am going to slap you back," Inez told me, with a straight face. We laughed at the same time for the first time in over three months.

Right after we retrieved our luggage and headed for the exit, I saw Leon. He stood near the exit, with his arms folded and a scowl on his face that was so extreme, it made him look like a baboon. He had on a black suit, a black hat, and a white shirt. Whereas Robbie had looked like a country preacher in his suit, Leon looked like a gangster straight out of *The Sopranos*. My legs were stiff, but somehow I managed to march over to him just so I could look in his face. As soon as I did, I revised my opinion of him and decided that he looked like the devil, not a gangster. He was the embodiment of evil. He had used me for years and then betrayed me in the worst way. I'd done a stupid thing in the islands, but it didn't come close to what Leon had done to me.

He looked me up and down, shaking his head. Inez chose to stand behind me. I could feel her breath on the back of my neck.

"My wife—arrested for prostitution! *Prostitution!* Woman, what in the hell got into you down there in those islands?" Leon hissed, his eyes looking like they belonged on a snake. "I hope you learned your lesson. Any other man in his right mind would tell you to go to hell. Any other man wouldn't take you back on a platter. I am giving you one more chance to act like a wife and a mother—only on account of Cheryl!" he shouted, shaking a finger in my face.

"Hello, Leon," I said, with a smirk, looking him up and down. "Nice suit."

"Don't you try to change the subject, woman," he ordered. I ducked when he reached for me, causing him to give me a surprised look. "Renee, you don't know what you put me through, going down to that island, fucking up the way you did. What the hell was the matter with you? Your little stunt cost me a major promotion! And half of my coworkers won't even look me in the face these days! My mama told me to tell you to your face that she does not want you around my daddy, or even in her house, anymore!" At this point, Leon looked over my shoulder at Inez, looking at her like he wanted to kill her and drink her blood. "And you . . . you! I knew that sooner or later you were going to drag her to hell with you, Miss Inez McPherson! For being such a whore yourself, at least you were smart enough to stay out of trouble!" Leon turned his attention back to me, snapping his fingers in my face as if I were a dog. "Let's go. I need to get your ass home so I can straighten you out. There are a lot of things we have to sort out. I can tell you now, you won't be going on another out-of-town trip without me anytime soon!" he screeched, grabbing my arm. I snatched my arm out of Leon's grip so fast and hard, he lost his balance and fell against the wall.

"Don't you touch me, you low-down, funky motherfucker," I said in a cool, calm voice. Leon let out a profound gasp and looked at me like I had tossed a bowl of acid in his face. "I'm divorcing you, motherfucker. You can visit your daughter at my mama's house, but if you ever come near me again, I'll kill you."

Leon's mouth dropped open, and he stumbled like a drunken sailor. His face looked like somebody had suddenly let all the air out of his cheeks. He had a slack-jawed look that made him look like a hound dog now.

I released a big breath and then motioned for Inez to follow me to the door. When I looked back, Leon was still standing in the same spot, with that same deflated look on his face.

I recalled how Inez used to warn me that Leon hid who he really was behind a mask. Well, that mask had finally fallen off. Now I knew exactly who he was.

Despite her many flaws, Inez was my friend. And, even though Robbie had no desire for me to be his woman again, and I didn't blame him, he was my friend, too.

If that cashier's position was still open at his gas station, and if it was still all right with his wife, Janet, I was going to accept it.

NIGHTMARE IN PARADISE

MARY MONROE

ABOUT THIS GUIDE

The suggested questions are intended to
enhance your group's reading of
NIGHTMARE IN PARADISE
by Mary Monroe.

DISCUSSION QUESTIONS

1. Renee dumped her plain, bowlegged fiancé, Robbie Dunbar, so that she could marry Leon Webb. Leon was movie-star handsome and he had an intriguing job. It took Renee several years to realize she'd made a mistake. When did you realize her mistake?

2. When Robbie called up Renee and warned her about the ominous dream he'd had about her on an island she didn't take him seriously. Did you expect her dream vacation to turn into such a nightmare?

3. Do you think that Inez should have told Renee about the relationship she'd had with Leon before Renee married him?

4. Even though Leon eventually fell in love with Renee, he had started a relationship with her just to spite Inez. Renee was hurt and angry when Inez told her this. Should Inez have kept that part of her confession to herself?

5. Despite her loose lifestyle, Inez had some good qualities. She was a good mother to her children, and she was generous and dependable when it came to her friends. Do you know a woman like Inez? If so, would you be friends with her?

6. Leon tried to make Renee believe that he hated Inez but he still went out to have drinks with Inez and drove her around when she didn't have transportation. If your man behaved like he hated your best friend but he still did favors for her, would you be suspicious? Would you *still* try to bring them together the way Renee did with Leon and Inez?

7. Do you think that Renee should have been more aggressive and demanded more information from Leon about his relationship with Inez?

8. Sleeping with a stranger and accepting money for it was out of character for Renee. Because of that single act of indiscretion she lost her beloved job as a schoolteacher, her husband, and a lot of other peoples' respect. But did you think that her getting

arrested for prostitution and being sent to prison for three months for one stupid mistake was fair?

9. As soon as Inez heard about what had happened to Renee she returned to Paraíso. Not only did she apologize to Renee, she promised to help her through her nightmare in any way she could. Did this convince you that Inez was a true friend to Renee?

10. Inez's visit to the prison surprised Renee. But Robbie Dunbar's visit surprised her even more. After the way Renee dumped him for Leon, was Robbie a fool for going out of his way to support her anyway?

11. Leon did not write to Renee while she was in prison and he didn't visit. Do you think that after enough time he should have calmed down enough to at least communicate with her on some level?

12. Inez kept her word and stood by Renee throughout her ordeal. When Renee and Inez returned to the States, Leon was waiting at the airport. After he'd verbally assaulted Renee he told her that he was going to take her back. But instead of falling into his arms, Renee had a few choice words for him, too. Then she strutted off with Inez. Was this a good way to end this story?

13. A lot of women have vacation flings with men that they don't know and will never see again. Whether you've had a vacation fling or not, would you think twice about doing it after reading this story?

BAD LUCK SHADOW

VICTOR McGLOTHIN

CHAPTER 1

NIGHT TRAIN

A tortuous evening of bowing and shuffling had gotten the best of Baltimore Floyd, just like a one-armed boxer's desire to climb back into the ring got him knocked out every time. Flashing that cheesy grin he hated had left the smooth tan-colored drifter with a mean streak thicker than train smoke. Smiling back at countless blank faces of discouragement while serving a host of ungrateful, highbrow travelers in the last two dining cars on the Transcontinental Steamer had him wishing for better days and easy money. In the winter of 1946, times were hard. That meant tips didn't come easily, and come to think of it, "please" or "thank you" didn't, either. Hearing the train's whistle blow when it crept slowly across the Missouri state line put an awkward expression on Baltimore's face, one that almost slighted his charmingly handsome good looks. Agreeing to sign on at the railroad company as a waiter for an endless collection of snooty voyagers, with nasty table manners and even worse dispositions toward the Negro help, was simply another in a string of poor decisions plaguing Baltimore, who was a professional baseball player hopeful mostly, and a man with troubles certainly.

He'd seen nothing but rotten luck during the past month. The worst of it had happened when the gambling debt he couldn't pay off came haunting around his rented room to collect at about three o'clock in the morning. Two pistol-toting "go-getters" is what Baltimore called the hired thugs who broke down the door at Madame Ambrose's boardinghouse, aiming to make him pay the devil his due or else send him straight to hell if he couldn't. It was a good thing the lady with the room directly across the hall from his didn't like sleeping alone, or he'd have been faced with meeting the devil firsthand that night. With three dollars in his pocket, every cent of it borrowed from the gracious neighbor lady, Baltimore had lit out of Harlem when the sun came up. He'd hitchhiked south, with a change of luck in mind and a bounty on his head.

Unfortunately, the change he'd hoped for was slow in coming, and his patience was wearing as thin as the sole on his broken-in leather work shoes. That awkward expression that welcomed Baltimore into Missouri melted into a labored grin when his best friend, Henry Taylor, a sturdy, brown-skinned sack of muscle, popped into the flat-ware storage room, balancing two hot plates weighed down with porterhouse steaks, mashed potatoes, and green beans. Henry, just as tall as Baltimore and substantially brawnier, presented the dinner he'd undoubtedly lied to get his hands on or outright stole, while maintaining his professional, "on the time clock" persona. His black slacks held their creases, the starched white serving jacket was still buttoned up to the neck, and his plastic Cheshire cat grin, which the customers always expected, made a dazzling appearance.

"Dinner is served boss and not a moment too soon," Henry announced, once the door was latched behind him.

"You ole rascal, I don't care what you had to do to come up with this meal fit for a king, but I hope your eyes was closed when you did it," Baltimore teased, salivating over a dinner much too expensive for the likes of them. "I can't wait to get my hands on—," he started to say before hearing a light rap against the other side of the storage room door. "Here. Put the plates in the bread box, Henry," whispered Baltimore, fearing another waiter wanted to share in their late-night treasure. Some of them were unscrupulous enough to make waves by reporting thefts to the crew supervisor if they didn't get a cut.

"Shut that cupboard door all the way so's they can't smell the taters," Henry mouthed quietly as the light tapping grew into more insistent knocks.

When Henry opened the storage room door slowly, he was surprised to see a white face staring back at his. The man, who appeared to be nearing fifty, was fair-haired, with pale, blotchy skin. He was thinking something behind those steely blue eyes of his, Baltimore thought as he leaned his head over to see who was disturbing the first decent meal he'd had in a week. "Sorry, mistuh, but the dinner car's been closed for hours now," uttered Henry, guessing that was what the man wanted. "We's just putting the dishes away."

"Either one of you boys interested in making a few dollars, fetching ice and fresh drinking glasses for me and some sporting friends of mine?" the intruder asked, fashioning his remarks more in the manner of a request than a question.

"Naw, suh, I'm . . . I'm really whooped," offered Henry in a pleading tone.

"Hell, naw," was Baltimore's answer. "We's retired for the evening, done been retired, and besides, you don't see no *boys* in here." Venom was dripping from his lips after slaving deep into the evening only to incur some middle-aged white man getting between him and a four-dollar plate of food, with an off-the-cuff insult. "You best get on back to those sporting friends of yours," Baltimore added when the man didn't seem too interested in budging.

Henry swallowed hard, like always, when Baltimore got it in his head to sass a white man to his face. He swallowed hard again when this particular white man brushed back his green gabardine jacket just enough to reveal a forty-four-caliber revolver.

"Yeah. You'll do rather nicely," answered the man in the doorway. He was leering at Baltimore now and threatening to take his bluff a step further if necessary. "Now then, I'd hate for us to have a misunderstanding. The head conductor might not like that, especially if he's awakened to terrible news."

Baltimore squinted at the situation, which was brewing into a hot mess he'd have to clean up later. He was in deep because he'd already decided just that fast to lighten the train's load and teach the passenger a lesson about respect he would take to his grave. Considering that the train wasn't due to arrive at the Kansas City station until eight a.m., only a fool would have put his money on that particular white man's chances of breathing anywhere near 7:59. "Well, suh, if'n you put it that way, I guess I'm your man . . . uh, your boy," Baltimore told him, flashing the manufactured beaming smile he was accustomed to exhibiting when bringing customers their dinner bill. "Just let me grab a bite to eat, and I'll be along directly."

"You'll come now," growled the uninvited guest. "And button your clothes. You look a ruffled sight," he added, gesturing at Baltimore's relaxed uniform. "I'll be right out here waiting."

"And he'll be right out, suh, right out," promised Henry, pulling the door closed. "Baltimo', what's gotten into you? That's a white man, and he's got six friends in that pistol, waiting to do whatever he tells 'em to."

"He ain't gonna shoot nobody," Baltimore reasoned as he fastened his serving jacket, huffing beneath his breath. "A stone killer does the doin' and don't waste time on the showin'. I'll be back tonight. You go on and have at my supper, too. Ain't no use in letting it get cold. Be too tough to chew then, anyway."

Henry put his face very close to Baltimore's in order to get his undivided attention. "Ahh, man, I know that look in your eyes, and I hate it. You got trouble in mind, but you told me you was through with that sort of thing."

Baltimore sighed as he eased a steak knife into the waistband of his black work slacks and pulled the white jacket down over it. "Don't appear that sort of thing is through with me, though, does it? Think of me when you eat my share. It'll make me feel better knowing you did."

Waiting impatiently in the aisle, the insistent passenger raised his eyes from the silver coin he'd been flipping over his knuckles when Baltimore came out of the tiny closet, holding a stack of glasses on a round tray. "Good. I was starting to get concerned about the two of you." The man was fond of the joke he'd told, so he chuckled over it, but neither of the black men found it amusing in the least. Both of them saw a dead man pacing in the other direction, wearing an expensive suit and a brown felt hat, and playing an odd little game where the stakes were dreadfully high. It was a skins game, Baltimore's favorite. Killing the white man on their way to the smoking car crossed his mind, but he suspected there'd be money to be had at the end of the night, maybe a lot of it. Before he chased those demons away, he told them to come back later, when he'd have need for them.

"I'm going to say this only once, so pay attention," the man grumbled. "When we get inside, I don't want you to speak, cough, or break wind. There are some very important people in there, and they won't stand for an uppity nigger interrupting their entertainment," he warned Baltimore. "I'll give you ten bucks for your time, when I'm convinced you've earned it." When Baltimore's gaze drifted toward the floor, the white man viewed it as a sign of weakened consent. He had no idea just how close he came to having his chest carved up like the porterhouse left behind in the flatware cabin. "Good," he continued. "Don't make me sorry for this."

"I'm already sorry," Baltimore wanted to tell him but didn't. Instead, he played along to get along, but soon enough he found himself wishing for a seat at that poker table. As the night drew in, and the smoke from those fancy cigars rose higher, so did the piles of money. Baltimore had learned most of the gamblers were businessmen heading to Kansas City for an annual automobile convention. He'd also discovered that the man who'd coerced him into servitude went by the name of Darby Kent, and for all of his gun-toting rough talk, he was the sorriest poker player this side of the Mississippi and spitting out money like a busted vending machine. Darby often folded when he should have stayed in, and then he often contributed to someone else's wealth when everyone reading his facial expressions knew he had a losing hand. After three hours of fetching and frowning, Baltimore was really disgusted. The way he looked at it, Darby was shoveling over his money, the money Baltimore had planned on relieving him of after the fellows were finished matching wits.

"Darby, looks like a bad run of luck," one of the other men suggested incorrectly. It was a run of overgrown stupidity.

"I'll say," another of them quipped. "Gotta know when to say when." After watching Darby toss back another shot of gin, he shook his head disapprovingly. "On the other hand, if you don't mind fattening my wallet, I won't, either." That comment brought a wealth of laughter from other players sitting around the musty room, smelling of liquor, sweat, and stale tobacco.

"I'll agree that the cards haven't exactly fallen in my favor up 'til now," Darby said as he grimaced. "Perhaps I could use a break." He laid the cards on the table, next to a mountain of money Baltimore guessed had to be close to ten thousand dollars. "Come on, you," Darby ordered his reluctant flunky, while motioning for Baltimore to collect his serving tray and an extra ice bucket.

Leaving all of that loot behind was like pulling teeth, but Baltimore forced himself to walk away. Had he not been confined to a moving train, there would have been a golden chance to stick up the card game and make a fast getaway. Unfortunately, there wasn't a hideout to dash off to afterwards, so the idea passed just as quickly as it had entered Baltimore's head. Baltimore fumed every step of the way he followed behind Darby, staggering and sullen. He was mad at himself for not going with his first mind to end their arrangement before Darby had all but opened his billfold and shook out a big stack of money for the better-suited players to divide amongst themselves.

When they reached a nearly depleted icebox inside the abandoned dinner car, Baltimore began filling one of the wooden buckets. Darby steadied his shoulder against the door frame to light up a cigar. He huffed and cussed that he should have been more conservative with his wagers.

"I'm beginning to think, maybe I've taken those other fellows too lightly," Darby opined openly, as if Baltimore gave a damn what he thought. Tired and angrier now, Baltimore sought to put that silly notion to rest.

"Say, Darby, lemme ask you something," Baltimore said, seemingly out of nowhere. He was facing the man while holding the bucket firmly at his side with his left hand, keeping his right one free. "Do you always lose your ass after showing it? I mean, you have got to be the dumbest mark I've ever seen." Baltimore watched Darby's eyes narrow disbelievingly after hearing a much cleaner diction roll off the black man's tongue. "See, the way I figure it, you resort to pattin' that pistol of yours when men like me don't step lively fast enough. I'll also bet the ten dollars you owe me that you're all bark and no bite. Ain't that right, suh?" Baltimore added, showing him how black men were skilled at adapting their speech to fit the occasion. When Darby stopped puffing on the stinky cigar poking out of his mouth, Baltimore smiled at him. "Ahh-ahh, not yet. I'll also bet you a nickel to a bottle of piss, if you go pulling that heater on me, you'll be dead before your body drops."

Darby spat the cigar onto the floor as he reared back and went for the revolver. Baltimore slammed the heavy ice bucket against his gun, snatched him by the throat, and then punched the steak knife into Darby's gut so hard, the handle broke off. Darby's mouth flew open as he anguished in pain. Baltimore watched intently as the white man gasped for breath like a fish out of water and clutched at the opening in his stomach. When Darby fell onto his knees, pain shooting through his body, he began to whimper softly. Baltimore was quick to stuff a bar towel in his mouth to shut him up. "Uh-huh, I knew you were all bark," Baltimore teased as he removed the pistol from Darby's shoulder holster and began riffling through his pockets. "Let's see how much you still have, you sorry bastard. Seventy-two dollars?" he ranted. "I knew I should have stuck you sooner." Suddenly, Baltimore heard someone coming, but there was nowhere to hide, so he raised the dying man's gun.

"Baltimo', that you?" someone uttered from the shadows. "Baltimo', it's me. Henry."

"Whewww, man, I almost blew a hole in you, thinking it was one of them white boys coming to see about the ice," Baltimore cautioned his closest friend. "Here. Hurrup. Help me get his jacket and pants off him."

Henry's eyes grew as wide as saucers. "Why you want to go and do that?" he asked apprehensively.

"'Cause he's just about my size, this here is a damn nice suit, and I don't want to get no blood on it," Baltimore told him flatly. When Darby's upper body started convulsing, Henry was ordered to stop it. "Come on now. Hold his head still."

Struggling to hold the man down, Henry was forced to snap his neck when the groaning grew too loud to bear. After realizing what he'd done, Henry fell over on his behind like a repentant sinner. "Now you done got me involved," he fussed.

"Being my friend is what got you involved, Henry," Baltimore corrected him. "And you came through for me. I won't forget that. Now, let's get him off this train before somebody comes."

Reluctantly, Henry climbed to his feet and helped wrestle off the dead man's suit. He spied the fancy wing-tipped shoes on Darby's feet, but he could see right away, it wasn't any use to take those. Darby's feet were nearly four inches shorter than his. Then, he caught a glimpse of a shiny gold ring on the man's finger as they opened a dining car window to ease his body out onto the countryside. "Hold up, Balt. I'ma take this here ring for my troubles."

Baltimore pulled Darby's legs up to the sliding window and pushed against the cold January winds. "Naw, don't take the ring. It's the same kind the other fellas had on. That could come back to haunt you. Leave it on him. Hell, let the coyotes get it." Henry considered what his partner in crime had told him, pretended to agree, but then decided to swipe it, anyway. He eased the ring off and slipped it into his pocket behind Baltimore's back. As the train whipped around a bend, the wind howled. Henry closed the window while Baltimore neatly folded Darby's suit under his loose jacket.

"Where're you going now?" Henry asked, as he rolled out a mop bucket to clean up the mess they had made doing away with the corpse.

"To sleep so's I can get to dreaming about that steak that's been calling my name," Baltimore answered, slapping thirty dollars in his accomplice's palm. "Send somebody to wake me when we pull into Kaycee. Boy, I sho' am tired." He patted Henry on the back and started off, with a carefree saunter, as if he hadn't moments before goaded a man into a fight and ended his life as a result. Baltimore's ice-cold veneer aided him in sending Darby to another world altogether, but it didn't do a thing in the way of shaking off that bad luck shadow dogging him from town to town.

CHAPTER 2

KANSAS CITY

Later that same morning, the train rolled into Kansas City's Union Station six minutes ahead of schedule. Henry knew that for certain because he was up and stirring at least an hour before. What he and Baltimore had done to that white man might have been despicable to some, but the kind of men they ran with at times, just to scratch a living, would have all agreed that Darby Kent had it coming. And that's exactly what Henry kept telling his self when his conscience gnawed at him from the pit of his stomach. "It couldn't have turned out no other way, because of how the man kept after Baltimo', trying to pinch at his dignity and mash his spirit," Henry thought aloud. "If that's not worth killing over, nothing is." Just then he smiled, pulled the curtain back on his five-by-seven-foot sleeper compartment, and peeked into the one across from it. All he could see was a mess of coal black, curly hair resting on a pillow case. Baltimore was sleeping like a brand-new baby, one with a newly acquired gabardine suit and his share of the seventy-three dollars found in the pants pockets.

After all of the other food servicemen departed for breakfast duty, Henry got dressed and studied Baltimore some more before calling out to wake him. Despite the fact that they were already late to their workstations, Baltimore groaned defiantly. "Come on now," Henry pleaded, "or else Mistuh Sterling's gonna pitch a fit. You know he don't like you much as it is. He ain't ever given nobody a tough time as he gives you."

"Good, 'cause I wouldn't give a bent nickel for him, neither," Baltimore answered eventually, whipping the curtain aside with his arm, then sticking his head out. When he got a look at Henry, dressed in full working attire, he sighed hard and long. "Henry, you can stick around, huckle-buckin' all you like, but I'm getting off here. I heard those white boys talking last night when they thought I wasn't smart enough to listen at the important parts. Most of 'em belongs to this . . . what they call a Motor Assemblymen's Association." Henry was nodding his head, but he had no idea where Baltimore was going with the discussion. Actually, it didn't matter, anyhow. He'd be right there alongside his friend, for life.

"I'd bet there's probably a couple'a hundred of them arriving over the next week for the automotive convention starting tomorrow," Baltimore continued, casually lying on his side in white cotton boxers and a matching sleeveless undershirt. "Just think about all of that money rolling into town with them. There'll be a million ways to hustle up on some cool scratch. Better than slaving for folks who'd just as soon have you locked up for bumping into 'em if they's on the streets instead of on this train. Naw, man, this is the stop for me. Kansas City is where I ditch that shadow that's been hounding me. And the only way to get it off my back is with a heap of good luck to turn it around," he said. "So, you can tell old man Sterling to kiss my ass."

"You can tell him your damned self 'cause here he comes, breathing smoke and chewing nails," Henry said as he peered down the long aisle. Sure enough, the salty and well-seasoned chief of the service staff was rambling fast toward the men's sleeping quarters.

Mr. Thaddeus Sterling was old enough to be a father to most of the cooks and waitstaff on the train, although he was a white Southerner, whose purpose in life was stocking a full crew that took their posts seriously and didn't cause too much trouble. When he reached the bunks in disarray, he appeared mad enough to spit. "Is this the best I can expect from you, son?" he asked Baltimore. "'Cause if'n it is, that dog won't hunt. Not today, it won't."

"Mistuh Sterling, it's not like that," Baltimore answered, in a semi-respectful tone. "Well, not exactly, anyway. I'm beholden to you for letting me on but—" he tried to explain before the older man cut him off.

"But nothing! I knew you couldn't hack it. I could tell it the minute I laid eyes on you. 'There's too much pride in that fella,' I said. 'He'll buckle as sure as my frumpy aunt Fanny's knees,' I said." The supervisor had saliva collecting at the corners of his mouth, he was so upset. Truth be told, he was very fond of Baltimore, and that's why he rode him so hard.

"Mistuh Sterling, I'm actually sorry to hear about your fat ass aunt Fanny's knees and such, though it appears you've been right about me all the while," Baltimore patronized him and then winked at Henry. "But, you can do us both a favor if you run and go put my exit pay together while you're celebrating just how right you was." Henry took a calculated step back and away from Baltimore then, fearing that Mr. Sterling would fire off and slap the taste out of his friend's mouth on general principle alone. He was almost disappointed when it didn't happen.

"Exit pay!" the supervisor yelled, putting his face in Baltimore's like a veteran drill sergeant breaking in a new recruit. "Now ain't that a kick in the head. You've got some nerve, son, some kind of nerve, I swear. The shoes, you owe me for. Three uniforms, you still owe me for, and you eat like a man twice your size. If anything is left in the balance, *Mr. Floyd*, it's you who owes me!" Mr. Sterling had gone and worked himself up into a thick lather all over again, and it was partly due to his associate's rabble-rousing remarks.

"Tell you what, Mistuh Sterling. I'm willing to let it go and call it even," Baltimore suggested, knowing he'd be dismissed as soon as those words rushed away from his lips.

"Uh-huh, that's just what I thought you'd say. Now, get the hell off my train, and be quick about it, before I have you run in for loitering," he threatened, merely for grins. When Mr. Sterling noticed how hard Henry was trying to avoid eye contact, he barked up another tree. "And what's gotten into you? Ohhh no, don't tell me you want to have a discussion about your exit pay, too?"

Henry threw his gaze at Baltimore and then down toward the ground again. "Naw, suh, I wouldn't think of doing no such thing, and I'm obliged to you for giving me a spot on your crew, but I'ma be getting the hell off your train with Baltimore."

"Dammit, I should've known," replied the supervisor as he looked the guys over suspiciously. "This doesn't have anything to do with one of our dining guests jumping the train last night, does it?"

"No siree, we don't know nothing about that, do we, Henry?" hinted Baltimore.

"Naw, suh. Uh-uh, nothing at all. Nothing," Henry answered emphatically. He was certain then he'd made a mistake by keeping Darby's association ring, but he couldn't see parting with it now. Holding on to it, that was his second mistake.

Mr. Sterling eased the black visor back past the cusp of his head and used his skinny fingers to scratch at his balding scalp. "Damnedest thing about the fellow who jumped, his friends say he left a satchel in his drawing room with over fifty thousand clams packed away in it. Oh well, as long as you boys don't know anything about it, try to stay out of trouble, because you won't be welcomed back this way if'n you can't. Don't take no wooden nickels," he added on his way back down the aisle. "And, don't take anything that don't belong to you when you get off, neither."

Baltimore heard Mr. Sterling refer to him and Henry as boys, but there wasn't an ounce of malice in his manner, so he let it fall by the wayside. They had both been caught off guard regarding the opportunity they'd missed by not searching the dead man's stored belongings. Baltimore tried to hide the fact that he was furious while he pondered what might have been had he simply planned and plotted the robbery, instead of allowing his anger to guide it. The next time such an occasion presented itself, the outcome would be substantially more favorable, he decided, substantially more favorable.

After throwing several slightly used toiletries and just about everything else he owned into a small plyboard suitcase someone had left on the train during a short stopover in Denver, Baltimore stepped down onto the platform and smiled heartily. "Henry, the air is crisp, and the women are hot. Let's enjoy one and do something about the other," he strongly recommended.

"Don't look now, but there's the police talking with some mighty impo'tant-looking white folks," Henry replied while peering up the platform in the direction they were heading.

Baltimore grimaced. He knew what had to be done. "Damned the luck," he cussed quietly. "I just got this suit!" He peered over at Henry and felt like crying on the spot when several of the important-looking white men began pointing toward him. "Henry, hand me your travel bag, put this here suit-box back on the train, and step away real natural-like." Henry didn't fully understand why his friend was willing to leave all of his worldly possessions behind, regardless of how meager they happened to have been. Because Baltimore sounded so determined, Henry didn't hesitate to do as instructed. As Baltimore strolled closer to the police car parked alongside the train stop, he glanced over at Henry and then placed a helping hand on his shoulder. "Now, you act like your gut is ailing you something fierce if they start nosing around about that dead fella, you hear?"

"Yeah, I'll play along," Henry answered, hoping it wouldn't come to that.

"Howdy, Officer," Baltimore hailed vigorously as they approached the collection of white men.

"Yeah, that's him, the thinner one on the right," one of the card-players from the night before announced. He looked at Baltimore's casual navy slacks and dark wool peacoat. "He's a bit more relaxed now, but that's the one who left with Darby."

"You deliver ice and refreshments to these men last night?" asked the burly city cop, dressed in a long-sleeved winter uniform. Looking on curiously, his partner was just as stout and a few inches taller.

"Yeazah," Baltimore said quickly. "And that other man, the bad one at cards, said he'd pay me ten dollars, but then he met up with some woman. Told me to wait at the icebox, so I did."

"This woman, what'd she look like?" asked the officer who seemed to be in charge.

During his dissertation, Baltimore kept looking at Henry, waiting on him to go into his shtick about stomach pains. Unfortunately, all Henry could think about was that fancy ring burning a hole in his pocket. "Oh, she was a looker with long brown hair," said Baltimore, when a woman fitting that description entered his line of vision from the station. "She had a style about her, too. Kinda put you in the mind of that one there." He gestured at the woman, whom he'd never laid eyes on until then, and suggested she be questioned instead of him. "But like I was saying, after that man didn't come back, I went on to sleep, as much as I could with my friend here complaining half the night about the piles." When Henry realized he'd been given a cue to chime in, after Baltimore told the bald-faced lie on him whining throughout the night about chronic diarrhea, he went to holding his stomach with both hands.

"Ooh, he's sho' right," Henry howled. "I think I feel another spell coming on. We's on the way to see the doc now." Without waiting on permission to be dismissed, Henry staggered off, holding the back-side of his worn gray corduroy pants. "If y'all getting back on the 219, don't eat the steak 'n eggs." Each of the men looked uncomfortably at one another because nearly all of them had had steak and eggs with their breakfasts before disembarking.

"We'll be back before she pulls off if you want to ask us some more questions about that man," quipped Baltimore, hoping they would be willing to let it go at that.

Continuing on with their course of action, Henry leaned on Baltimore and groaned louder than before. "Awwwe! You gots to get me to the doctor!" he wailed loudly. "Awwwe, I'm about to bust open!" Instead of offering to lend them a ride to a colored doctor's office, the policemen waved the two black men off, figuring them use-less in the disappearance investigation of Darby Kent, personal assis-tant to Pierre Albert, a famous automobile designer.

"How you feel now?" Henry fussed as soon as he limped around the corner of a brick building and out of sight of the cops. "You don't have the man's suit or his fifty grand, neither? All you got is a head full of ideas that almost sent us to the chain gang."

Baltimore stared at Henry, with a concerned expression, because he'd never doubted him before. Something had transpired, and Baltimore wanted to know what it was. "What chain gang? Well, would you look at this? You let a couple of country-ass cops start poking around, and you fall apart like a wet paper sack. Henry, what's gotten into you?" The expression Henry exhibited was a shameful one. Immediately, he began feeling bad for running afoul where unshake-able friendship was concerned. "Haven't I always looked after you?" asked Baltimore. "And, haven't I always shared every last thing I came by with you? Huh? Didn't I get you outta that scrape when Butcher Davis was looking to cut your head off over his oldest daughter?" Baltimore added, laying it on thick enough to spread. When Henry appeared legitimately remorseful, he went in for the kill and nailed the coffin shut. "Then is it too much to ask that you share in *my* mis-ery from time to time? Or is you gonna be a fair-weather friend after all we've been through together? Tell me, because I need to know." Baltimore pouted sincerely, as if he were really taken aback.

Henry contemplated all the trouble Baltimore had gotten him into as well as out of over the past four years, and it teetered on evening out, so he hunched his shoulders and shook his head apologetically.

"In for a penny, in for a pound," he said eventually. "I'm sorry for getting shook up enough to think of turning on you. You've done right by me when I couldn't make due for myself. I ain't gone ever forget that."

Baltimore fought back a smile, biting his lips. "Don't mention it, Henry. Friends shouldn't have to. Let's get out of this cold and scrounge up some grub. There's a diner up on Twelfth Street. Might even have a pretty waitress or two."

"Now you're talking," Henry chuckled. "This time I get first crack at 'em, so don't go latching on to the prettiest one like you always do."

"I wouldn't think of it," Baltimore told him, with fingers crossed behind his back. "I'm aiming to get bigger things on the menu than way-too-oversized waitresses with nothing better to do than eat up all of their tips." Baltimore struck out walking, with Henry looking at him oddly, not sure whether to believe him or not.

"Say, wait up, Baltimo'!" he yelled ahead. "You think all of 'em might be too oversized? Hey, man, hold up. Too oversized for who? A large woman keeps a warm bed. It's the wrong season to be cattin' around after a skinny woman."

CHAPTER 3

HAM 'N EGGS

Abel's Diner, resting on the corner of Twelfth and Front Street, wasn't all that big a place, but what it lacked in size, it made up for with an abundance of character. There was a late-night crowd posted up in the rear booths. Baltimore smiled when his eyes landed on all them folks because he'd gone searching for nourishment, too, after rabble-rousing the night away. There were three bottom-of-the-barrel working girls sitting at the table near the door, licking their wounds and sulking over low temperatures and low-down clients. It had been a long while since Baltimore felt so at ease and at home. These were his kinds of people, and Abel's was his kind of spot. "Table for two," he said to a dark brown, ample-breasted matron dressed in a yellow waitress uniform, with a white hat and apron to match.

"Right this way," she answered gleefully while eyeing Henry especially. "Y'alls new in town, huh?"

"Uh-huh, just blew in this morning," offered Henry as they took a seat at the small wooden table. "We might need some company getting adjusted . . . being new and all."

"Well, I ain't a part of no welcoming committee, but I have been known to help a man get adjusted, if you know what I mean. The name's Hattie," she added, pointing with her thumb toward the name embroidered on her outfit, above her left breast.

"Nice to meet you, Hattie," said Baltimore in a hurried tone. "I'm sure you're a pip at getting men folk adjusted, but we need to eat. I'm powerful hungry." Henry flashed a panicked expression across the table, as if pleading with Baltimore to lighten up on his sure thing. "I didn't mean no disrespect, Hattie, but my friend Henry had himself a hot meal last night. Me, I had to work through the dinner bell. I know a seasoned woman like yourself can understand how I might be a bit testy this morning," Baltimore explained, noting the streaking stretch marks streaming down her cleavage. He considered apprising his wide-eyed friend of Hattie's potential litter of young children at home, but Henry was smiling so eagerly that Baltimore couldn't see himself being the bearer of bad news.

"No offense taken," Hattie said, blushing. "Of course, I understand, sugar. Mens tend to act just like little ole boys when they ain't had enough to eat. I'm about to shove off, but I'll see to it that somebody takes good care of you and your friend." She scribbled some numbers down on an order slip from a thick booklet, then tore off the top sheet. "Here you go, Henry. Call me direct if you want to be my friend, too."

"Yes, ma'am," Henry said excitedly. "I'll be sure to call this evening, once we get settled."

"See to it that you do," Hattie insisted in parting.

Henry watched her wide hips rock from one side of the room to the other, but Baltimore was busy watching the menu. It had been close to a full day since he'd eaten, and he grew seemingly more agitated by the minute. "I wish Hattie would send somebody over and fast. I'm getting light-headed," Baltimore complained. "They can't all be that slow."

"Some of us are faster than others, I would imagine," debated a waitress of slight build, who seemed to appear out of thin air. Her complexion was a dead-on match for Baltimore's, and the way her green eyes slanted up at the outer corners gave the impression that at least one of her ancestors was of Asian descent. A thick black curl dangled from her temple, down past her ear, purposely covering a fresh mark on the right side of her face. Suddenly, Baltimore wasn't as starved as he had been just moments before. He caught himself wondering if the bruise on the woman's face was caused by a careless mishap with a straightening comb or a cowardly man who'd beat on her while trying to make up for one of his own shortcomings.

"I see," said Baltimore finally. "Please order me up a whole plate of flapjacks, a big slice of ham, and a chicken coop full of eggs. Then come back in ten minutes and see what else I have room for."

The waitress smiled, lingering around to hear what Henry had in mind. "I'll have the same," he told her cordially.

"Now, both of you can save a dollar apiece if you're willing to trade ham for sausage," she suggested, cocking her narrow hip in Baltimore's direction. "That's a good deal any way you cut it."

"I'll bet it is, Macy," Baltimore agreed, as he read the name on her uniform before she dashed away to submit their breakfast requests. "Look at there, Henry. A woman who saves a man's money instead of spending it all. She knows how to make a good impression."

"Yeah, I'll bet that's the same thing her husband thought when he decided on marrying her," Henry argued. "Her shirt said Macy, but her wedding band was screaming *missus.*" Concern colored his face. "Baltimo', we came here to get a line on some real money. Getting involved with another man's wife can't do us nothing but harm. Supposing he catches you with her, and you have to kill him?"

"Relax, Henry. I just met the woman, and you've already put us together against a loaded gun. I'm not gonna get behind no trouble over this woman," Baltimore assured him, not believing a word of it himself. He was certain that Macy's situation stood some investigating, but he couldn't share that with Henry until it was too late for him to do anything about it.

After Baltimore sopped up a puddle of molasses with a hot buttered biscuit, Macy pranced around to see if the fellows had had their fill. Henry surveyed the way she took her time collecting the dishes on Baltimore's side of the table. Baltimore picked up on it as well, but it didn't bother him at all. There was something soft about her, genteel, he noticed while making a play to keep her buzzing near just a little while longer. "So, Macy, seeing as how you're situated with a man and all, tell me where a fella who was down on his luck might get his hands on some nice working clothes?"

The waitress giggled, rubbing her thumb underneath the gold wedding band, as if she was still getting used to the jewelry, as well as the idea altogether. "Working clothes, you say? Day clothes or the other kinds?" she asked in such a manner that left no doubt she wasn't as genteel as Baltimore had previously imagined. That made him smile on the inside, deep down where it really counts.

"The other kind, secondhand if we can get 'em," Henry threw in, trying to break up a collision with destiny sure to leave somebody in a deep dug hole before it was all said and done.

"Uhhh, yeah," Macy stuttered. "There is this place over off Vine where a couple of men looking to put in some late hours could get outfitted on the cheap. Ask for Rascal. He's my second cousin."

Before Baltimore had the chance to thank Macy for the tip, she was off to see about another table. Henry hopped up, tossed some money down, and dragged his amorous companion out of the restaurant before the waitress became overwhelmed with the inclination to come back and linger some more. "Man, you're getting to be a handful, pulling on me like that," Baltimore huffed once they were out onto the sidewalk. "I didn't come between you and your lustful eyes for Hattie's buzzums, now did I? No, I didn't. Know why? Because sometimes you got to let a man make his own mistakes so he can appreciate the wrong he did while making them."

Henry was still trying to comprehend the reasoning in Baltimore's logic by the time they came upon the slightly used clothing store. "Who was that we supposed to ask for?" Baltimore asked as they entered the establishment, overwrought with secondhand men's clothes. Actually, the selection was better than either man had anticipated. Some of the suits were in such perfect condition that Baltimore spent all but six dollars on a new wardrobe and a descent suitcase to carry it in, once Rascal got to flouncing around all in a tizzy. Macy had purposely omitted the fact that her cousin, on her mother's side, had a special flare for fashion and a fondness for helping men to look their best, especially the ones who stood out in a crowd. Baltimore fit the bill perfectly.

"Henry, I feel like a man of means," Baltimore gushed, staring at his pin-striped threads in the store mirror, with Rascal standing not too far off.

"Yeah, but you smell like embalming fluid and mothballs," Henry joked, insinuating that the suit had been lifted from a mortuary.

Baltimore sniffed at the lapels and nearly gagged. "Ohh, man. It smells like they just rolled the body out of it this morning. It's alright, though. For the price, you can't beat it. I'll air it out. Tell Rascal I'm taking this one for a walk, a long walk."

"Hell, naw. You tell him," Henry refused. "Man with ways like that makes me nervous. I'll be waiting outside."

All dressed up and no place to go, Henry agreed to let Baltimore work on securing them a warm place to lay their heads while saving their remaining money to eat on. While they were busy deciding on a quick scam to get the ball rolling, a dark-colored taxicab roared past, then slammed on the brakes. Henry backed up on the curb when the tires screeched toward them in reverse. As if on cue, the cab driver climbed out of the four-door sedan like a paid chauffeur. "Baltimore Floyd, that is you!" the short, stumpy-built dust-colored man hailed.

"Well, I'll be," Baltimore replied happily. "As I live and breathe, Pudge Gillis. Ain't nobody slapped you in the clink yet?" As Henry looked on curiously, Baltimore shook hands with the man half his size, dressed in a suit of clothes two sizes too big, as if he was still expecting to grow into them.

"Naw, but that don't stop 'em from trying, though," Pudge answered, peering up at Henry. "Who's this you got with you?"

"Pudge Gillis is the man who knows everything going on south of Eighteenth Street. Pudge, say hello to my good friend Henry Taylor. He's liable to be the next starting catcher for the Monarchs," Baltimore boasted truthfully. Henry was an accomplished ballplayer with a St. Louis farm team waiting on a Negro League charter.

"Hi ya, Henry. That's some mighty high praise coming from Baltimore," Pudge said, nodding in admiration. "You know he's not too quick to hand it out."

"Boy, do I," answered Henry. "But I'll takes 'em where I can get 'em."

"Fellas, what brings y'all to town so soon after the new year?" Pudge asked as his car idled near the curb.

"Let's get in your Ford and talk about it," suggested Baltimore. Once they were inside the taxi, Pudge began sniffing similar to the way Baltimore had in front of the store mirror.

"Smells like a funeral back there," Pudge cackled. "Let your windows down a notch so's that burial suit Rascal sold you airs out a bit."

"Told you so," grunted Henry, relieved to lower his window.

Baltimore smirked at Henry while doing likewise. "You can tell me all day long if you want. These are some mighty fine rags, and I don't give a damn what . . ." he started out saying before pleading for Pudge to stop the car. "Pull it over! Right there!" he ranted hysterically when his eyes landed on a moneymaking opportunity of the sweetest kind. As soon as the car slowed enough to jump out, Baltimore did just that.

The pointy-toed wing tips he'd just purchased were hardly worn, so the leather soles were as slick as ice when they landed on the hard concrete.

After Henry's eyes discovered what Baltimore was chomping at the bit to involve himself with, he feared the worst. He saw a lady, a very beautiful white lady, being manhandled directly outside of a posh department store, where a neatly stenciled sign hung near the entrance. "No Blacks," Henry read, with labored breath. "Ahh, naw, we's going on the chain gang for sure."

Pudge, sitting behind the wheel, threw the gearshift in park and craned his neck to watch. He didn't know what to expect, but it would be something to talk about, no matter how it ended, he reasoned. "Shush now. Just check it out," he whispered in Henry's direction. "Yep, this ought to be good."

The lady tossed her long honey blond–hued hair and wailed at the cleanly shaven middle-aged man dapped in a light checkered suit, with his mind set on holding on to her. A small crowd gathered when Baltimore flew right into the middle of it. "There you are, madame," he greeted the woman, using his best English. Although shaken, the woman maintained her stunning appearance, draped in a fine dark-colored faux sable coat and a chocolate, crescent-shaped cloth hat to set off the ensemble. "We've been searching for you throughout," Baltimore huffed, merely inches from the woman's face. "Mr. Woolworth will be so glad we've managed to stave off another embarrassing setback." The woman continued wrestling with the white man over her large red handbag with polished wooden handles. "We've hired this taxi and looked for you endlessly," Baltimore threw in to boost the swelling lie he'd spun.

"I don't know who you are or what you're talking about, but I'm the store manager, and this shoplifter is going to jail as soon as the police get here," the man asserted firmly. That's when Baltimore kicked it up another level.

"Sir, I'm Elmer Crenshaw. Perhaps we should discuss this inside before you make a dreadful miscalculation and, most assuredly, cause one of the wealthiest men in this country a grave disservice."

The store manager narrowed his eyes at the brash, well-spoken Negro offering to talk up on a proposition. He figured the least he could do was listen and maybe do a lot better for himself on the back end. "Okay, you have one minute, but she comes with us," he demanded, as if he hadn't just given her up by agreeing to hear the fast-talking con man out.

"Thank you, sir, and believe me you will not regret this," Baltimore affirmed. "Mrs. Woolworth, the mister sent me after you, hoping you haven't gotten yourself into another predicament like you did back in Chicago." When the manager appeared stunned, Baltimore knew he had him. "Yes, sir, she's done this sort of thing before, I'm afraid. She has a condition," he whispered softly, so as not to add insult to injury.

"Did, you say Woolworth?" asked the white man, loosening his grip on the lady's bag.

"None other, sir. I don't have to tell you how word of this getting out would cause quite a stir. Now, the missus has medicine for her illness, but she doesn't like the pills, as you can imagine. Believe me, we'll return the things she took and pay you a small fee for the misunderstanding. Don't think of refusing, because Mr. Woolworth wouldn't like that. He's good to those who look out for him and his, if you get my meaning?" Baltimore turned and stared into the woman's wild expression. He spoke very calmly to maintain eye contact. "Madame Lilly, you pay the nice man a hundred dollars, and we'll be able to straighten out the rest this afternoon. You can send one of the limousines back and have Harold pick up one of everything this store has in your size. Just like the mister arranged it in Chicago."

"Uh-uh, I will not!" the woman spat defiantly.

"*Every* garment in-in her size?" stammered the store manager greedily.

"Yes, sir," Baltimore answered casually as a police squad car parked behind the taxi on the street. "As I said, she has done this sort of thing before. Let her pay you for your troubles, and we'll get her back to the Waldorf Hotel so the doctor can have a look at her. Her husband will be forever in your debt." The woman caught a glimpse of the police car, and as quickly as you please, she whipped out five twenty-dollar bills. She pressed them into the hand of her captor, turned her nose in the air, and then proceeded to strut past the police officers. The store manager slid the money into his pocket and waved off the cops, just like Baltimore knew he would. "I don't know how you put up with rich white people," Baltimore sighed as the squad car drove away. "They gonna be the death of me."

"Tell me about it," the white man replied, with a pained expression, when he realized the well-spoken Negro's diction had taken an immediate dive. By the time the store manager's better judgment caught up to his bad decision, he knew he'd been had.

Baltimore was in the backseat, several blocks away, and frowning disapprovingly, with the pretty lady on his lap, laughing her head off. Henry gawked at the woman's complexion, which was so white, she appeared to be carved from a bar of soap. And if that wasn't bad enough, she threw her arms around Baltimore's neck, kissed him passionately, and then, without notice, reared back and slapped his face so hard, it sounded off. Pudge had been taking it all in from the rearview mirror while keeping one eye on the road.

"Ouch!" shouted Baltimore, massaging his cheek. "What was that for?"

"That's for the hundred you had me pay that man!" she answered him in a common manner befitting a very common girl. "A hundred dollars is a lot of money and hard to come by, too."

"How many times do I have to tell you, Franchetta? Don't go pushing your luck," Baltimore reprimanded her. "There are two kinds of people who get pinched, them's that's greedy and them's that's stupid. Don't be stupid."

"Alright, Daddy," she cooed. "I'll be on my best behavior now that you've come stumbling back around."

"Okay. Let's see what a hundred bought you, other than your freedom papers," Baltimore jested.

Franchetta slid off Baltimore's lap and wedged herself between him and Henry. She unfastened her ritzy three-quarter fur coat and pulled one expensive necklace out of her lacy panties after the next as the men looked on. Henry was speechless, and Pudge nearly wrecked his taxi, twice. "Aren't you forgetting something?" Baltimore said knowingly.

"Shoot. I should have known you saw that, too," the woman pouted. She fished around inside a hidden compartment in the lining of her coat and came out with the store manager's wallet." Baltimore let that woman kiss him again after she handed the wallet over as a gratuitous fee for saving her. While en route to her place, Henry was so confused that he started to mist up around the eyes. Baltimore shook his head as he recited what had gone on inside the department store with the manager and how he'd pitted the man's greed against him. "Any con man worth his salt could have pulled it off if the pigeon was inspired properly," Baltimore said solemnly.

"Gentlemen, I'm proud to introduce you to Miss Franchetta St. Jean, my first love . . . among other things, and as you just seen, a first-rate pickpocket." He'd neglected to include other pertinent vital information, which allowed her to bring the other men up to speed, if and when she saw fit.

"Baltimore, please tell this fool before he floods this cab with those crocodile tears," she sniped, without regard for Henry's feelings.

"Okay, okay," Baltimore agreed. "Henry, Franchetta here ain't what you think. She's as black as you and me, on the inside, where it matters most."

Franchetta went on to tell them how her mother was mulatto, and that although she didn't know her father, it had always been assumed he was a white man, though this had not been confirmed or denied before she ran off from home at age sixteen. Since meeting Baltimore in lower Maryland as a young girl, she'd become quite the chameleon, learning how to wear her hair and pass for white during the day to survive, while kicking up dust and devilment with her own people as soon as the sun set on the city. Another of the things neither of them mentioned straightaway was Franchetta's full-time occupation. They both agreed, with a sly wink, that it was better to save the best for last.

CHAPTER 4

FORGET ABOUT HEAVEN

After the taxi stopped in front of a small, two-story, wood-framed house painted a pale shade of yellow, Henry helped Baltimore with the luggage from the trunk, while Pudge stared at the backside of Franchetta's swanky coat swaying all the way up to the worn screen door.

"Tomorrow morning, Pudge. All I need is 'til then!" Baltimore yelled over the rattling muffler before he slapped the rear fender to send Pudge on down the road. Baltimore figured it would take him that long to get in good with Franchetta all over again while catching up on old times. He had no idea what she'd begun cooking up inside that busy head of hers as soon as she saw him leap out of a moving car onto the pavement to rescue her from an imminent arrest.

As Baltimore headed up the walkway, Henry pulled on his new secondhand wool coat. "That Franchetta, she's sweet on you, but how long do you think she's gonna let me hang around? We done spent up just about the whole knot on these new digs."

Baltimore shrugged off his question before seeing his way to answering it. "You'll be welcome as long as I hang around, I guess. Don't go worrying about a thing, though. Franchetta's as good as gold, only twice the fun getting to hold. She's got friends, you know," he said, leaving a pregnant pause to hold Henry's attention. "Nice ones," he added, with a sly smile, as they marched up three cement steps to reach the elevated porch. Before Henry had time to process the loaded comment, he was faced with meeting Franchetta's friends firsthand as they looked out of that charming pale yellow house.

A slight woman, the shade of hot tea, met Franchetta at the door after undoubtedly watching her climb out of a taxi with two strange men. There were only three rules that governed the house, which was occupied by four young, enterprising women. One of them was picking up after themselves, another was having their share of the utilities on time and without fail, and the third one was simply no men, not ever. That's why the thinly built woman, in khaki slacks, brown loafers, and a blue long-sleeve pullover sweater, shot a questioning glare at Franchetta as she bounded happily through the door. "What's with the strays you brung with you?" the woman asked Franchetta, simultaneously mean mugging her visitors.

"This here is Charlotte Bingham, but the girls call her Chick. Now move over a beat so we can get a good look at what the cat drug in," Franchetta demanded playfully, with a smile parked on her face. She shrugged her coat off and tossed it on the arm of the sofa next to the door. Now, standing shoulder to shoulder with her apprehensive roommate, Franchetta winked at the men, relegated to standing on the dust mat. "Those fellas ain't no strays at-tall, Chick. The big lug is the sensitive type, so go easy on him. Henry Taylor, say 'good day' to the lady," Franchetta instructed him. After he nodded uncomfortably, without too much yakking, Franchetta nudged Chick from the side, as if to say "lighten up" while she had her fun. "Good boy, Henry," Franchetta giggled seductively. Henry smiled awkwardly and then looked over at Baltimore for a clue, but his friend was enjoying this little game as much as he knew Franchetta did. "And that steamy dream standing there in one of Rascal's redos is Baltimore Floyd. He sho' is nice to look at, ain't he?"

"He's a thriller alright, but he kinda smells like this undertaker I used to know," Chick said, rubbing a forefinger beneath her narrow nose. "I guess he'll be alright as long as he don't have cold hands. That always did give me the creeps." Chick sucked her teeth rudely, still unsure if letting the men camp there was a good move. Despite her petite frame, Chick was as tough as nails and handled herself like a much larger woman. She always said, "A colored girl's gotta carry her own weight and a lot more if she wants to make a dent in this world." In Chick's case, her bite was a lot worse than her bark, a lot worse.

"Melvina, Daisy!" Franchetta hollered loudly to summon the others. "Come and see what I went out and got for the house!" A bit aggravated and growing colder on the front porch, Henry sighed when he realized the game wasn't over, not by a long shot. Baltimore understood fully. Franchetta was in control the entire time, but she wanted the other women to feel as though they had some say in the matter, when, in actuality, she was going to do what she always had: whatever she damned well pleased. When the two remaining roommates appeared behind the first two, Henry's mouth watered at the thought of sleeping under the same roof with four beauties.

"What's with them standing there like statues?" Melvina asked as she peeked at the men over Chick's shoulder. This one made Henry nervous in the worst way. Melvina Hicks was a saucy brown thing with a sturdy frame, the kind that made a man change his religion and his name. Her soft brown eyes and generous breasts were hard on a man's constitution, and his bank account, once she got her hooks in him. One look at Henry and no one had to guess what he was thinking. His face resembled one big wagging tongue.

"What you looking at!" Chick scolded him, sensing that Henry's hormones were firing up. "Let's get something straight. Ain't gonna be no fooling around if we do decide to let y'all in."

"Daisy, what you think about my bright idea to let these pals of mine flop here awhile?" Franchetta asked the youngest of the four.

Daisy Wilson, satin brown with an hourglass figure, stuck her neck out and looked the men up one side and down the other. Baltimore and Henry tried to stare straight ahead during her inspection instead of allowing their horns to show. One renegade glance made Baltimore wish he hadn't. Daisy was no more than twenty-one years old, but she'd been hooking for three years, since her mother threw her out into the streets for screwing around with her stepfather. Now, there was no proof of the affair, but everyone in town knew he'd been after Daisy for years, and from the day she celebrated seventeen, he couldn't seem to find his way to his wife's bed. A week later Daisy was out on her own and entertaining in a cathouse, before she met up with Franchetta and the girls. "I ont rightly know," Daisy answered quietly. "Where they's gon' sleep?"

"With me?" Franchetta answered assuredly. "Won't that be cozy."

Melvina smirked her displeasure over Franchetta's blatant disregard of her vote. "Wait a minute, Frannie. Just how is it that you get both of 'em?"

Franchetta cast a glint at Chick from the corner of her eye. "Appears to me, Chick, we just done decided." Before walking away from the interview of sorts, Franchetta made her position plain. "Come on in out of that cold, boys. We've got a lot to talk about."

"You telling me," mumbled Henry as the ladies retreated inside. "Baltimo', would you look at that. This house has more ass than a team of mules."

"Just don't go getting in no hurry trying to ride them all at once," Baltimore suggested. "Wait and see. Take it slow. You have to treat sporting women a certain kinda way when they's off the clock. Trust me. I know what I'm talking about. I ain't wrong about this. You'll see."

Henry's eyes widened when his friend's words hit home. "Baltimo', you can't mean all of 'em are sporting women?" Henry couldn't believe his good luck as Baltimore eagerly entered into the front room. "Hey, Balt, is all of 'em?" Henry queried softly, heavy on Baltimore's heels. "Ahh, man, when I die, forget going to heaven. I'm coming back here."

Once the men were comfortably inside, both of them surveyed the house with a wandering eye. Right away, Henry saw that the fireplace was in desperate need of repair, as were many other amenities. The hardwood floor that covered the first floor needed corking in several places, the curtain rod over the big bay window needed to be rehung, and Henry had never been in a woman's home that didn't have a leaky faucet or two. Baltimore glanced at Henry, pretty near reading his mind, because he was thinking the same thing: how it would be a privilege to help the girls fix up their humble abode while taking advantage of their hospitality.

"Here. Please take care of my hat. It's the only one I got," Henry said, handing it over to Chick.

She took the light-shaded Stetson from him and eyed it like he should have selected another one. "Don't mention it. I'll put it in the safe," she scoffed.

"Franchetta, do you by chance have any carpentry tools or a handyman's box?" Baltimore asked before he set the luggage on the floor.

A thankful smile danced across Franchetta's thin lips when she looked around the living room area to evaluate what the men saw. "I know it could use some work. It's small, but it's ours. Yeah, y'all can find a box of hardware, hammers, and nails out in the car shed. The previous owner didn't have any further use for them. Why on't y'all change in my room and have at whatever you see broke." Henry followed Baltimore into the bedroom at the bottom of the staircase and closed the door.

"Huh? Henry looks to be worth his keep, but your friend Baltimore is too damned pretty to be any good with his hands," Chick cracked at the first opportunity. "Least not around no workman's tools, I'd bet," she added on second thought, still not completely sold on them invading her safe haven.

"Oh, he's full of surprises, ladies," Franchetta answered for the other women who might have been wondering how useful Baltimore could be in the maintenance department. "Chances are, anything you can think of, Baltimore has already come up with three ways to pull it off, work it out, and make it holler."

Daisy peeked over her magazine and giggled, but Melvina was inspired and liked what she heard. "Is that so?" she asked, hoping it was. "We are still talking about tending to things around the house, right? 'Cause I'd hate for a girl to build her hopes up and be all a shamble behind a heap of disappointment."

"There's not an ounce of letdown in him," Franchetta asserted. "Uh-uh, not one little ole pinch of it. Not one."

After the fellows walked over every inch of the four-bedroom house and compiled a list of things to be attended to, they agreed on who would be responsible for each task. They were fast at work in a jiffy and glad to do it. Franchetta changed into comfortable house clothes: a white long-sleeve cotton blouse and a pair of hunter green polyester slacks. She displayed everything she'd copped from the department store by laying it out on her bed while sharing how Baltimore had literally jumped from a moving car and rescued her. "Sure, he did," Franchetta boasted when Melvina and Chick made it obvious they thought she was embellishing the story. "Don't y'all be looking at me cockeyed like that. I'm not putting on. I'm telling you straight. The taxicab was still moving when he leaped out and dashed over like a comic-book hero to come and see about me." When the other women laughed, Franchetta agreed that she'd gone too far with that one. "Anyways, Baltimore saved me from that store manager with some of the slickest talking you ever heard."

"What'd he say, Frannie?" Daisy begged to know.

Franchetta pounced off the bed and began strutting around the room, with her fists anchored on her hips. "This is how he strutted up, all dignified like a college boy," she told them as she pranced. "He said, 'Excuse me, sir, but I do believe you have my white woman, and I want her back.'"

"He did not," Chick argued, wide-eyed but refusing to believe it.

"Of course, he didn't, or I'd be in the clink for sure," Franchetta confessed. "But he may as well have by the way that cracker, who was holding on to me by the wrist, stared at him. Baltimore says right out of the box, 'There you are, madame. We've been searching for you hither and thither, or something just as hoity-toity. Then he busted out about how Mr. Woolworth would be so glad that I didn't get myself into trouble again, on account of my kleptomanium."

"Your which?" asked Melvina.

"You know, that brain glitch some rich white folks get that makes them steal what they could pay for outright," Franchetta answered the best way she knew how.

"Oh yeah, I have heard of that," Melvina remembered. "That was good thinking. What else did Baltimore do?"

"Yeah, what else?" asked Daisy, bright-eyed and all aglow as Chick sat there with her arms folded across her chest.

"Well, Baltimore waved over at the taxi, telling the white fella how my husband, the Mr. Woolworth, would spare no expense getting me to the Waldorf safe and sound. Yeah, he laid it on about how they should get off the sidewalk and step inside the store to discuss how my stunt could cause one of the wealthiest men in America a certain dreadful miscalculation . . . something or another, you know, to really get the man's mind off of me. The way Baltimore was tossing those five-dollar words around, I almost believed I was entitled to a rich white man's money myself. And once the store manager bit down on the hook, it was all over but the crying. That's when I lifted his billfold. I figured that belonged to me for my troubles, but I gave the take to Baltimore for getting me out of the jam."

"Wow, that's something alright," Daisy said in amazement. "So if he didn't happen by when he did, Frannie, you'd be in the pokey right now?"

"No doubt about it," Franchetta answered soberly.

"Okay, so you paid the man his due," Chick said, reasoning that that should have been enough. "So why bring him and his friend all the way out here?"

"I'm glad you asked, Chick. Remember how we ended up sitting on our empty pockets when the pipe fitters' convention came through last year, only because we didn't have anyone to promote us to over three hundred plumbers looking for something *different* to do? A man like Baltimore is a good man to know and a pitch above perfect in the negotiating area."

"Uh-uh, I don't need no pimp," Chick objected adamantly, although Melvina felt the same way.

"And I'm not getting us one, neither," Franchetta informed them. "We could use a promoter for the automobilers coming into town by the train- and busloads. Now, a smart man could keep us busy every day for a week. There will be some big spenders rolling in, a lot of money to be had, and we should be looking to get some of it before it's gone." She peered at Chick, then at Melvina, and lastly, at Daisy. Franchetta could tell they were lamenting over the dry spells they'd had to endure from time to time. Once she'd adequately baited her line, she decided to let it ride the current until the time came to get out the net. "I'm going into the kitchen to put something together for dinner. Y'all think on it a while. You'll come around." Franchetta disappeared, closing the door behind her so the girls could discuss their interest in acquiring a potential promoter. Franchetta's insides fluttered when she heard the comforting clomps of manly footsteps throughout the house. It almost felt like having a man of her own, with four big feet.

●

CHAPTER 5

IN MY RECOLLECTION

Thirty minutes after Franchetta called the corner grocer with her delivery order, a young, pimply-faced teenager arrived on his bicycle with two bags stored inside a wire-framed handlebar basket. Franchetta paid and quickly sent the boy away. She floated around the small kitchen while setting out cutting boards, mixing bowls, and seasonings. It didn't take too long before Melvina and Daisy joined her, with Chick dragging along behind them, like it pained her to do so. Daisy's face brightened when she saw the preparations for a grand dinner spread. "Ooh, Frannie, you must really like having that man around?" she asked knowingly. "He must have been heavy on your heart once upon a time."

"Hmmm," Melvina sighed pleasantly. "Seems to me, he still is."

"The older y'all get, the more you'll realize how some things never change," Franchetta said, then blushed. "Now who's gonna peel those potatoes?" she asked, motioning over to a five-pound sack resting on the oatmeal-colored Formica countertop.

"Uh-uh, not me," squealed Daisy, "I've never been good at peelin', but I wouldn't mind pulling on some snap peas." She plopped down happily onto a metal chair with padded blue vinyl cushions.

"Is that sage I smell?" asked Chick, with a measured amount of reluctance. "What you know about corn-bread stuffing?" she teased Franchetta, assuming that was what the spice had been used for.

"You think you know better?" Franchetta replied, licking a smidge of stuffing from the tip of her finger.

"Ooh!" howled Melvina. "If you can't stand the heat, get the hell out of the kitchen."

"Oh, I can stand it alright, but what if things get too hot for all of us?" Chick offered, speaking of Baltimore handling the promotion end of their business over the next week.

"Let me worry about that," answered Franchetta, with a stern eye.

Melvina nervously rubbed her open palms along the ridges of her curvy hips as she drew in a measured breath and frowned. Daisy stood silently, with her hands buried deep in a plastic bowl of snap peas. "Chick's got a point, Frannie," Melvina said, siding with Chick for the time being. "I mean, Baltimore seems like a real nice man, but all we know about him is what he did to keep you from getting pinched today."

Finally, Daisy looked up from her duties to share in the conversation. "Frannie, how'd you come to know Baltimore in the first place?" That question put a subtle shine on Franchetta's lips as she thought back to the very day she laid eyes on him.

"Well, I'd run off to see the world, since I couldn't decide on what I wanted to do with my life. At sixteen, I came of age and realized I was a woman. I took up with this traveling carnival that pitched a tent in Beaumont, Texas, where I hired on as a popcorn girl. I made a little money and bought me a couple of dresses, you know, to help me appear older than I was."

"Too bad they don't make dresses to help a woman to appear *younger*," Melvina quipped as she chuckled heartily.

"Wouldn't that be something," Franchetta agreed. "Well, we rambled up the eastern seaboard before winter set in and then, one day, pulled into the tiniest little tick on the map, called Whiskey Bottom, Maryland. I was bored and growing eager to sell more than just popcorn, but the headman wouldn't let me outta his sight until I turned seventeen. He said so's I could get those girlish notions out of my head before I found more trouble than I bargained for. My second day in Whiskey Bottom was much like all the others, hawking boxes of corn and keeping clear of the slugs who worked on the machinery, 'cause they had some bad habits and a taste for young girls. It was half past three when the sun shined on a brash eighteen-year-old strutting around like a prized peacock, with three girls on his arms and spending money like he was snatching it down off of trees."

"That was Baltimore?" squealed Daisy as she became noticeably more excited than before.

"And that was ten or so years ago, but, yeah, he was a fine young thing and so sure of himself that lots of grown men at the carnival sneered at him something fierce, but they was just jealous, and he knew it. That didn't stop him from showing those girls of his a grand afternoon and smiling about it while rubbing the other men's noses in it. Before nightfall, I caught his attention and asked if I could speak to him, alone. The next day, he showed up without his arm pieces, but he was just as generous. He won so many Kewpie dolls and stuffed animals that we couldn't carry them all. Hell, I didn't know what was going on until it happened. That boy had me so sweet on him that my teeth hurt every time I said his name. And, that was just for starters." Franchetta went on to explain how she stayed awake at night, thinking about being with the smooth youngster she'd met just south of the Baltimore, Maryland, county line. She wrote down his address and wrote to him for months. He didn't return any of her letters until she sent him a postcard from Santa Fe, New Mexico, informing him that she was now seventeen, legal, and desperately fighting off the carnival headman's advances every night. Within a week, Baltimore caught up to the troupe, setting up camp in El Paso. He'd boarded a train and subsequently stolen a late-model automobile, and there he was, standing right outside the popcorn stand a few minutes before opening time. It appeared that he hadn't slept in days, but his beige cotton blazer and white linen slacks were as crisp as a new dollar bill. "Before I could speak," Franchetta continued, "he held out his hand and told me, 'Come on, baby girl. Let's go home,' like I was supposed to up and fly off to Lawd knows where with him."

Melvina was breathless, while Daisy actually held hers, awaiting the outcome of Franchetta's fascinating tale. "So, after he came all that way, trotting behind you, what did you say?" asked Chick, now drawn in as well.

Franchetta tilted her head back, closed her eyes, and giggled. "I didn't say a damned thing. I up and flew off to Lawd knows where with him, like I was supposed to."

The small room, which smelled of cooking spices and a barely noticeable commingling of reasonably priced department store perfumes, roared with unbridled cackles from the women, including Franchetta, who said, with her head cocked to the side for emphasis sake, "My mama didn't raise no fool." None of the girls knew it, but Baltimore and Henry had been listening to their conversation from a mouse hole they'd begun to cork in Daisy's upstairs bedroom.

"He was into saving women even back then, huh, Frannie," Melvina said, as a fact instead of a question.

"That's not the half of it," Franchetta responded, thinking back, with her face now wearing a saddened expression she couldn't shrug off. "After we ditched the car and caught a rail all the way back East, I learned that Baltimore had a slew of chippies working for him, seven girls in all. I begged him to teach me the business and put me in his stable so's I could earn my keep like the others. He fought me on it and told me it could be a hard life sometimes, but if I was sure, he'd do it. It seems like a million years ago and only yesterday, both at the same time. I kept after Baltimore until he made love to me, taught me how to do it right, and put me on the stroll, like I wanted. It was so much fun, for a while at least, all the shopping and partying we did. Every week was kinda like Christmas."

"Wow, it all sounds swell," Daisy cooed, her eyes cast upward as if she was picturing the best times a young girl could ever have.

"Yeah, he's always been a swell fella, too, as far as swell fellas go," Franchetta added proudly. "Although he's no slouch, loving a man like him is harder than picking up a dime off a marble floor."

"Is that why ya'll parted ways?" Daisy asked innocently. "Loving him was too hard?"

"Nah, he up and left one morning while all of the girls slept. He shelled out three hundred dollars apiece of his own money to send us on our way," Franchetta remembered unpleasantly. "None of us had to ask why," she said. "Baltimore simply quit the business when he got tired of calling on men after they'd beat up on one of his women. That sorta thing riled him up something terrible. He said a man with the taste of a woman's blood in his mouth would keep after it until he'd killed her. Baltimore wasn't about to let that happen, so he'd protect us by leaving a cold body behind each time he had to call on one of those woman beaters." When Henry considered Franchetta's heartfelt words and his friend's troubled past, he climbed to his feet and left Baltimore there to deal with it, alone.

An awkward smile eased at the corners of Melvina's lips as she tried to make sense of Baltimore's plight. "It must be hell, carrying all that around inside him."

"Yeah, I think I fell in love with his misery before I fell head over heels with him," Franchetta thought aloud.

"I'll say," whispered Daisy.

"Tell me about it," Chick said, before turning her head away to hide her sorrow. "Tell me about it."

As Franchetta squirted butter on two whole chickens with a turkey baster, she perked up, as if that time in their lives had come and gone. "Every so often, Baltimore comes back to me, and don't ask me how he does it. In Chicago, he showed up at a stage play I had a small part in. One summer in Springfield, I was managing a cathouse for a sick old lady too mean to die and too ornery to trust anybody else with the money other than me. Low and behold, who strolls in with a baseball team barnstorming up and down the state, playing fairgrounds and city parks to scratch a living? Oomph, that was a nice weekend, but Baltimore never stays for long. One day I figure he might stay for keeps, when he's tired of running maybe." Franchetta peered up from the chickens to see three sets of eyes staring back at hers. She answered those wondering eyes before any of them had to ask. "Sure, I'll take him in after he's seen too many cold days and rainy nights to continue going at it alone. I'd be a fool not to. I just hope he can locate me when that happens." She crammed the corn-bread stuffing inside both birds and slid them into the oven. "Baltimore put his brand on me. Ain't nothing ever gon' change about that. If something could, I wouldn't want it to, nor would I be willing to let it," Franchetta surmised, while summing up her affections for the first man to share her love and break her heart.

Hours later, dinner was served as everyone sat around the table in evening attire: long sleeves, dressy slacks, dresses, and heels. Henry said grace, thanking God for good food, good friends, and the wrongs He promised to forgive in the end, amen. During the meal, Baltimore teased Franchetta about the look on her face when the store manager had his paws dug in. She laughed so hard, she nearly choked on a chicken bone. Henry slapped her on the back and dislodged it, although she was concerned his technique might have left a bruise.

Baltimore helped Franchetta with the dinner plates afterwards, while Melvina served heaping helpings of hot apple pie. Henry took one look at his slice, turned his nose up, and adamantly refused it, making a grand spectacle of himself. "Uh-uh, apple pie is the root of all evil!" he ranted. "And I know what the preacher say, but he's wrong on this account. Some men say money is the root of it all, others charge that it's women who's got money beat by a mile. But think about it. Ever since Eve brought Adam that apple pie from out the bushes, men folk haven't seen nothing but troubles. Go ahead on and think about it."

"Ooh, Henry, you ought to be shamed," hollered Melvina, tickled as she could be.

"Well, I'm not," Henry asserted. "Though I am still itching for something sweet. I know. I'll run down to the corner and fetch some ice cream."

"But it's cold out," Daisy argued as she forked another bite of pie in her mouth.

"Good. Then it won't melt before I get back," said Henry, with his mind set on sitting down to something that had nothing to do with Adam, Eve, apple pie, or the bushes he was sure Eve had baked it in.

As Henry hit the door, Chick opened the cabinet on a slightly used RCA Victrola stand-up record player and stereo. She slowly adjusted the radio tuner until the sounds of a Chicago broadcast came through nice and clear. "Hey! The Johnny Otis Quintet is performing live with Little Esther. I hope they shake up some of those 'Low Down Dirty Blues' like that time they hit Kansas City and almost burned down the Atlantic Club. Remember that, Frannie?" Chick danced to the soulful sounds coming out of the stereo speakers until she realized no one had answered. "Frannie?" she called out before turning to catch a glance of Franchetta ushering Baltimore through her bedroom door and closing it behind him.

"Chick, I've talked to Melvina, and I know how Daisy feels, but I want your say-so before going in there to convince Baltimore to promote and look after us with these out-of-town white men here for the automobilers' convention," said Franchetta. Daisy dried off a dessert saucer with her apron as Melvina looked on from the thick brown corduroy-covered divan.

"Well, we could do worse, I guess. I'd feel good about having him at our back if something came down," Chick submitted. "Think he'll give in and go along with it?"

"We'll know soon enough," Franchetta answered, with good loving on her mind. "I've learned a lot of new tricks since Chicago."

Franchetta had been in the bedroom for an hour, while Daisy and Melvina listened just outside of the door. Chick pretended to be disinterested in whatever had Franchetta moaning passionately and screaming wildly, as if she was being tortured, in a good way, despite having lowered the volume on the stereo several times in the past five minutes. Then, suddenly, it quieted down on the other side of that door. Daisy hunched her shoulders and shook her head at Melvina, her snoopmate. "I on't know Mel. It sounds like she's laughing 'bout something."

"Forget this. I'm tired of being left out," Melvina complained. "I get men to pay me by the minute, and Baltimore's got me standing out here, wishing." She tapped at Franchetta's bedroom door, hoping someone answered. "Hey, is it alright to open up?" she yelled against a wall of oak.

"Yeah, girls," they heard Franchetta reply somberly, as if sedated. "Come on in."

When the door cracked slightly, Daisy pushed Melvina from behind, and the door flew open all the way. It slammed against Franchetta's expensive armoire. The girls had their mouths fixed to apologize for the loud disturbance until their eyes discovered a sight to behold. Franchetta was lying on her heavy iron-framed bed, at the foot of it, with her head facing them. She was totally nude, and so was Baltimore, who was busy spreading peanut butter on Franchetta's behind and licking it off while she caught her breath. Hence, all of the giggling emanating from the love nest. It appeared that Baltimore had picked up a few things since Chicago as well.

"Uh, we was kinda wondering if you had finished convincing him yet," Melvina said slowly, her trepidations fading fast.

Raising her head just enough to view two of her roommates salivating, Franchetta smiled wearily. "Sounds to me like you wanna help some."

When Baltimore sat up to return the peanut butter jar back to the nightstand, Daisy saw his thick penis lying on the bed, between his legs. "Frannie, don't mean to tell me Baltimore's been riding you around the mattress all this time on that big ole red thang?"

"Uh-huh," she answered, falling off to sleep. "You ought to try convincing him some." That was the go-ahead the onlookers needed to join in the business negotiations.

Melvina kicked the door closed with the heel of her shoe when

Chick didn't get up to put in her bid. "Hey, Baltimore, I just got to know. Do you sleep with a sock on it?"

Henry returned home minutes later to soft music playing on the radio and a familiar aroma in the air. He took off his coat, put the carton of ice cream down on the coffee table, and began sniffing the air. "What's going on, Chick? I done gone all over hunting up some ice cream, and now everybody's turned in."

"Nah, they're all in Frannie's room, talking business with Baltimore," she informed him from the other side of a half-empty brandy glass.

"Oh, that don't make no kinda sense," Henry reasoned. "Business, huh?" He marched over to the bedroom and put his ear to it just as the ladies had done. When the laughter started, Henry turned the knob and eased the door open. Through the thin crease, he saw Melvina smearing what appeared to be peanut butter between Baltimore's legs. "Oh, my good-goodness," Henry stuttered softly, trying to get the door closed without being detected. He turned to Chick, licking his lips. "They got a jar of brown spreading butter in there. How's about us getting some strawberry preserves and going upstairs to talk the sorta business they's got going on?"

Chick wrinkled her nose, sipped from her glass, and then went back to the magazine Daisy had left behind. "You're outta luck, Henry," she said coldly. "Let me tip you off to something so we don't have to travel over this road again. I'm off tonight, and if I ain't in the mood to sell it, I'll just keep sitting on it before I'd give it away."

Henry was fuming as he traced his steps back to Franchetta's door. "Aw man, if three's a crowd, there can't be no more room for me," he said to no one in particular. "Hey, Chick," he called out. "Tell Baltimo' I'm going to run downtown and see Hattie. He'll know what I'm talking about."

"You tell him yourself in the morning," she snapped rudely. "He's likely to be in there getting convinced all night long, and I'm going to bed with my forty-four," she added, just in case Henry got the bright idea to come upstairs and try his hand at convincing her.

"'Night, Chick," he said on his way out of the front door, shrugging on the coat he'd only moments before taken off.

"Night, Henry," she said softly after he was out of the door and gone.

CHAPTER 6

A FOOL'S PARADISE

It was just after seven in the morning when Baltimore found himself sitting behind a steaming cup of black coffee at the kitchen table. He'd showered and changed into dark slacks and a dress shirt, and he felt good about shaking off that bad luck shadow that'd been hounding him. Once the jar of peanut butter had been scraped out at about the same time as the girls' will to continue, Baltimore had begun to think out his strategy for making the most of the next five days of his life. He smiled awkwardly, considering something his Bible-preaching father had said before disowning him at the age of eighteen. Following a thunderous argument, the pastor's words had rung out like a loud clamoring against the sky. "Runnin' women, drinking, and gambling all night long ain't nothin' but a fool's paradise!" his father had shouted and then had thrown Baltimore's clothes out onto the lawn. Now, more than ten years later, he was preparing himself to play the fool again, if he took stock in what the old man had to say.

Baltimore chuckled while staring into the cup of murky liquid sitting on the table. He remembered his own response to his father's venomous rants. "Don't think I on't know about the black side of your devilment, too, you hypocrite!" Baltimore had growled back at him. "I'd rather be a fool in paradise than a preacher cabaretin' his way to hell with the flock's money burning a hole in his pocket. You damned right I run women. It's good work if you can get it. You ought to know better than anybody, Brotha Pastor!" In all of the years he'd been away from home, the one thing Baltimore regretted was saying those vile things with his mother looking on from the bay window. Embarrassment had masked her expression, and it had nearly stopped Baltimore cold, but his father's hatred had spurned him on. "See you in hell, old man!" he'd cussed loudly, dodging hard-soled shoes hurled off the front porch. "If I get there first, I'll tell the fellas you'll be down directly and have 'em save a spot for you!" Full of piss and vinegar, Baltimore had been too grown to hold up under another man's roof and rules. He never made the same mistake twice.

Henry stomped through the front door, rusty and reeking of alcohol. Baltimore glanced over at him as he plopped down at the small wooden kitchen table. "Where you been that's got you looking all spit out?" Baltimore inquired suspiciously. "Seeing as how you passed on joining me and the girls last night, I figured you and Chick was upstairs getting acquainted."

"Hell, naw, Chick wouldn't have nothing to do with me, and I don't pretend cottonin' to brown butter spread nor trying to satisfy a crowd, neither." It was obvious that Henry was exasperated over something, but Baltimore didn't have time to concern himself with it.

"Here you go, Henry. Start off by drinking some of this," Baltimore suggested to him. "Then you need to get your head straight, 'cause we've got a mess of business to get on today."

"Done spent most of the night getting my head straightened over at Hattie's, and then I woke up with somebody jiggling on the bedroom doorknob, wanting to get in," Henry explained. "I reached for something to strike back with but came up nellow. I was about to let loose and fly, with my Johnson dangling, when three of the ugliest little children kicked the door in and commenced to hopping up in the bed."

"Three of 'em?" Baltimore asked. "What'd you do then?"

"Who me? I hid in betwixt the covers and kept quiet," Henry answered, glaring at Baltimore, who was trying to hold his laughter down to a mild roar. "Man, it wasn't nothing to laugh about. Hattie could've told me she had three of them monsters all younger than school age; a mama with the gout, living in her basement; and a man who done run off last fall. That ain't the worst of it, though. When Hattie peeled of her clothes, she had more stretch rings than a mighty oak tree."

Laughing again, Baltimore sipped from his cup before asking an obvious question. "When are you going back again?"

"We got another date tomorrow night," Henry replied nonchalantly. "Yep, can't pass up on all that, especially this thing she does where her yams flap together. All night long, it sounded like somebody was in the bed with us, cheering me on."

"Catch a bath, and get on back down, Romeo. I'll put on another pot of coffee and start up breakfast. It won't be long before the girls wake with a powerful want for something to eat."

"I'll bet they're tired as hell of that brown butter spread," sneered Henry.

"Don't matter none. We finished that off around five or so this morning. It took me damned near an hour to get all of it off everything I aimed to keep," joked Baltimore as he opened the round-faced icebox to hunt for ham and eggs.

By nine o'clock everyone had eaten and discussed Baltimore's strategy to best utilize their time throughout the week. Before Pudge arrived, Baltimore explained how he and Henry would set up an office to take the calls and prime the cow from both ends and in the middle; that meant working the men and the money. If he went about his business the right way, he figured to have everyone up to their eyeballs just after dinnertime the same day. Baltimore understood how some white men liked to let their hair down while out of town and sample some of the local delicacies in the process. He also understood how quickly those men would pass the word around, raving about how good the steak would be if he did an adequate job of selling the sizzle. So, that was what he and Henry set out to do when Pudge pulled up to the curb and tooted on the horn.

"Hi ya, fellas," Pudge hailed from the driver's side of the taxi. "Where are we off to first?"

"Hey there, Pudge," Baltimore hollered back as he approached the long blue and beige automobile.

"I'd like to know that myself," Henry said, breaking down the front part of the brim of a light-colored felt hat.

"Run us over to Unca Chunk's," Baltimore decided as he counted his money over again, as if it had multiplied in his front pocket since the last time he counted it. "Me and Chunk's got unfinished business." When Henry heard the cold tenor in Baltimore's voice, he was glad he'd borrowed a hammer from the car shed out back of Franch-

etta's house. He never could tell when he might need to bring something along with him that was harder than Baltimore's head.

Uncle Chunk's was a watering hole and pool hall on the east side of
town, just off of Troost Avenue and Eighteenth Street. The building
sat on the corner like a shady gangster surveying the intersection,
with a broad gray brick face and a high roof that flattened off way up
on the second floor. The establishment was the most popular hang-
out among local and visiting jazz musicians looking for a redhot jam
session after they'd finished playing paying gigs earlier in the night.
Uncle Chunk's offered everyone who walked through the door a no-
holds-barred good time, as the music burned brightly until daybreak,
and frequently deep into the next morning.

Baltimore knocked at the door, with his head down. He was already
working on his next stop after getting what he needed from the bar
and grill's proprietor. "Come on now. Open up!" he shouted. "Pull
your pants up and tend to the door. I know you're in there, you fat
bastard, 'cause I done busted out all the windows on that shiny
Cadillac you so affectionate about parked across the street!" Pudge
watched from the taxi while Baltimore looked at Henry and motioned with his head. "Henry, when he comes rambling out of there,
you get to the right of his shooting hand."

Suddenly, the large oak door flew open. Baltimore leapt to the left
side of the door, reaching in his waistband for the dead man's gun
he'd taken off the train. Henry stood pensively, confused, quaking in
his shoes, with a carpenter's hammer raised above his head as an
older dark-skinned man came waddling out onto the sidewalk. At several inches above six feet, he was just as wide as he was tall. The big
man's pants were zipped but unfastened at the waist, and his shirttail
flapped in the breeze. The long-barreled pistol he stuck in Henry's
face was steady, and his aim locked on. "Who the hell are you to be
busting up my car and . . . ," he said, interrogating Henry before
Baltimore eased the steel revolver he'd brought along against the big
man's right temple.

Baltimore frowned at the man's poor decision to dye his hair coal
black to cover the gray beneath. "How many times I got to tell you to
draw from the right and aim to the left, you old reprobate?" Baltimore warned him as he pulled back the hammer on his gun. The
large man sighed slowly and lowered the pistol to his side. "Look at

there, Henry. Have you ever in your life seen a head that big? It's fatter than a fifty-dollar bag of pennies."

"B-Baltimore Floyd?" the large man stammered, turning cautiously toward the man who'd gotten the drop on him. "If you ever play with me about my Caddy again, I'ma plug you and this handyman you brung with you," he huffed, while tossing a nasty glare at Henry's weapon of choice. "Now quit that acting out, and get on inside before John Law shows up, thinking you mean to do me harm. You know they's on my payroll." He shook his meaty head at Henry and sneered. "What you aiming to do with that hammer? Build a barn?"

As they followed Uncle Chunk into the spacious building, Baltimore rolled his eyes at Henry. "Man, put that thing down. Can't you see we's among friends?" Baffled over Baltimore's idea of a practical joke, Henry was glad not to have ruined his day by peeing his new pants. Although Henry felt foolish, he felt better about breathing. "You look good, Unca Chunk," Baltimore offered sincerely to the mountain of meat walking ahead of him. After he noted that he'd indeed interrupted the man's early morning exercise, more than likely with the newest waitress, Baltimore quickly put his gun away. "I see you haven't changed your ways."

"Don't plan to, neither," Uncle Chunk answered slyly. "That's why they's *my ways*. They suit me just fine, and so did the piece of tail I was riding on my lap before you come breaking it up."

Once they were inside, the smell of rank tobacco and spilt beer filled Baltimore's nostrils. There was a stage to the right, seven or eight tables in the middle of the front room, and several tables along the far wall. Generally speaking, it was a relatively dazzling joint, with a grand jukebox stationed against the wall nearest the stage. As Baltimore surveyed what was referred to as the lounge, he stopped to take a closer gander at the owner, whose tolerance was a bit strained. "Go on back to it then. We'll wait," Baltimore suggested, on his own account. "Where is she at, anyway? In the office? Lemme see her."

"Hell, naw, I don't want her hugging on that snake of yours until I'm good and finished with her," the older man argued. When he saw Henry listening in and smiling, he got his dander up. "What's the matter with you? You see something funny."

"No, suh, Mistuh . . . Unca Chunk," Henry said, cowering. "I'm just trying to keep up with the strangest carrying on I ever did see, is all."

"I know one thing. I'm still waiting on him to tell me why he's beating down my door at this time of the morning," the weary owner said, without actually asking.

"See, me and Unca go back a ways," said Baltimore, looking around to see if anyone was in earshot before he brought up some mighty delicate information. "We've done business in the past, and it always turned out alright, huh, Unca?" The man kept an ear peeled to Baltimore as he leaned against the marble bar top, while tossing generous glances at the closed office door, behind which was where he'd rather be. "Unca, you still got that illegal phone line hooked to the back room?"

"Why you asking?" Uncle Chunk grumbled hastily. "It's not like I'm fixing to let you do some wrong with it."

"Come on, Unca. I need you to loan it out to me. Let's not forget what we've been through." Baltimore squinted and stared at the floor, trying to appear more disappointed than he actually was. "Wasn't I the one to tell you how somebody had wrecked your sedan downtown?"

"Yeah, but you're the one wrecked it!" Uncle Chunk grunted loudly.

"Okay, that was a bad example, but . . . but I was the one who tipped you to another mule kicking in your stall, and I wasn't the one doing the kicking," Baltimore fired back, reminding Chunk that he'd learned of the man's wife's infidelity with the insurance agent. Now, Baltimore watched his annoyed expression grow even dimmer. He could see right off how that might not have been a sterling example, either. "Alright, I got a good one. In case you forgot, I stepped in and played three sets with a damp fever when your piano player up and broke his back from slipping off the stool stone drunk. Seems like you ought to be itching to have me around." Sufficiently secure with his argument, Baltimore let his eyes rest on Chunk's, expecting an amiable response, but it didn't turn out quite like he intended. Instead, the burly man wiped saliva from the corners of his mouth with a folded handkerchief.

"Uh-uh, it seems to me like my troubles only come calling when you do. I don't want nobody getting themselves killed messing around with you in that back room, or else they won't be the last one," Chunk threatened. "Get my meaning, Baltimore?"

"Sure, Unca," Baltimore answered, grinning and nodding his head eagerly. "You won't have no trouble out of me. Uh-uh, not one speck. Besides, what could I do wrong in the few days I'll need it?"

When the gruff old barkeeper stood away from the bar, it indicated that the time had arrived for his visitors to find some other place to be. "I'm trusting you this last time, and the number to the back line ain't changed. But if you knew what was good for you, you'd get the sidekick of yours a rod or something he can really use. Don't nobody scare too easy from no hardware tools."

Although Henry didn't care much for his hammer being slighted in the least, he was smart enough to hit the door before Uncle Chunk changed his mind about letting them use the back room to facilitate their new enterprise. As they hopped back into the car with Pudge, Henry wrinkled his forehead before speaking out. "Hey, Baltimo'?"

"Yeah, what it is?" Baltimore answered, looking at some notebook paper he'd unfolded.

"Was that Unca Chunk really gonna shoot me?"

"Probably not," Baltimore replied honestly, before changing the subject, as if it didn't matter one way or the other since Chunk didn't actually pull the trigger. "Hey, Pudge, is that bellhop Ashy Corvine still at the Marquette Hotel?" he asked, settling into the backseat.

"Yeah, old Ash Can ain't liable to go too far from the 'Quette. He's been there 'round ten years now."

"Good. Then he ought to know a few other hotel hawks who can help our situation," asserted Baltimore, pulling his suit coat closed at the chest. "Let's see what he's up to this morning. The last time I was in Kaycee, I put a lot of money in his pocket but didn't get the chance to benefit from it. There was this girl he hooked me to. She got herself killed dead as Moses when a beer truck ran her down. She was minding her own business, too, just crossing the street to my rooming house. I didn't even have the pleasure to see what all of the fuss was about. I found my way to the funeral, though, looking to get a refund from old Ash Can or at least some of my money back." Baltimore rubbed his chin as he thought back to that very day with regret. "Funny thing, he didn't show up, though."

"Don't figure I would've, either," Henry reasoned. "Seeing as how he was partly the cause of her meeting that truck of suds head-on."

"I never considered that," Baltimore replied sympathetically, his brow furrowed like he was really thinking it over for the first time. "Hmm, I guess I won't hold that against Ashy then."

Henry fiddled with a baseball in his right hand as the taxi idled against the curb outside of the Marquette Hotel. Seeing how he'd spent so much time with one in his palm, he didn't realize it was there until an ashy soot–colored shrimp of a man exited the hotel in a mint green and black bell captain's uniform. The man's eyes widened when he came out to inform them the hotel was "white only" and found Baltimore, with what appeared to be an enforcer accompanying him. "Hey, Baltimore, glad to see you," he said nervously, reluctant to move his gaze from Henry and that baseball he was massaging.

"If you's so happy about it, why are you afraid that my friend here is gonna do something bad to you?" Baltimore asked him, after predicting correctly that was why the little man was so afraid. "Unless you give him a reason to shove that baseball up yo' intestines, you won't have to worry about it." Henry looked at Baltimore and then turned his face away, as if he wasn't willing to ruin his perfectly good baseball. "Now then, Ash, I missed you at that girl's burial, but I know you had bad feelings about what happened to her. I'll let it pass if I can count on you for something very important." Baltimore took out a small notepad and a short pencil chewed on the end. Within ten minutes, he'd squeezed out vital information concerning other hotels' guests, late-night parties, and the going rate for back-door female entertainment. He jotted the names of other black bellmen in the area and then moved on as quickly as he'd appeared, to grease their palms. Getting the word out that he had some clean dark meat for white men interested in jungle love was all he had to do before the money would come rolling in.

After Pudge had chauffeured him and Henry to the ritziest downtown lodging spots, Baltimore had the feeling that most of his business would come from Hotel Phillips, a twenty-floor establishment; the Marquette; and the Hereford House, which wasn't too far from the predominately black entertainment district. Baltimore also mentioned to each of the bellmen, after promising a dollar per referral, that there was a hefty bonus for contacting him about big-stakes, after-hours poker games. He'd say, kind of smooth and sly, "If you was to hear something, we'd be much obliged and willing to pay for the privilege of knowing the time and location." Of course, the baggage carriers understood he wanted a line on the big-money games. They also appreciated the risks and rewards associated with staying in his good graces for a shot at the big payoff. With a lot of planning and a little luck, everyone involved could hit the jackpot.

CHAPTER 7

GOT MY MOJO WORKIN'

Daisy hid her face when she overheard Baltimore explaining to Franchetta why he needed a room closer to the action. She fully understood how emotions sometimes got in the way when sex for profit was up for discussion. It was best for him and Henry to pick up and move south, nearer toward downtown, but that didn't stop Daisy from missing Baltimore before he'd gathered up his things and hit the avenue. Franchetta noticed that she wasn't the only one with a long face. Melvina wore a vacant expression, too, trying to shield the uncomfortable twinge in her stomach over a man she hardly even knew. "Buck up, girls," Franchetta suggested sternly. "Baltimore says it'll be hot and funky in the old town tonight, so get your heads on straight, and I mean that." As Daisy sulked toward the staircase, Franchetta tossed her a bone. "Hey, baby girl, just because he's not here doesn't mean he don't care. He's figured out a way to deal down on this hustle, and it'll all come up aces." When Daisy hit the steps, Franchetta saw the broad smile piercing her lips. "I know how you feel, Daisy. I go through the same thing every time I see him grab his hat and coat."

Back at Uncle Chunk's, Henry dragged a card table into the back room. He took a seat, and then he took his time stacking a sandwich with several leaves of lettuce, cold cuts an inch thick, and half a dozen pickle slices from a gallon-sized jar he'd pilfered from the kitchen pantry. When he heard footsteps heading his way, he cleared his throat loud enough to get Baltimore's attention and then laid his plate aside. "You ready for the introductions?" he asked, with a thorough amount of caution standing behind it.

"Yeah, I'm itching to get acquainted," Baltimore answered softly, as if his mind was on something else. He sank deeper in his folding chair as Pudge entered into the small room ahead of the others.

"I told you I could round them up before dinnertime," Pudge boasted. "These are some good men, every one of them committed," Pudge asserted in a calm, deliberate manner, leaving no doubt that the spare parts he'd brought in were willing to see a real money-making heist to the end, despite potentially unfavorable circumstances. The largest of the usual suspects stepped forward first. Baltimore recognized his chiseled face, with knots and thin scars over both eyes. "This is Dank Battles, y'all," Pudge said proudly, as he presented the man like a prized bull. Henry looked the bull over as if he knew what to look for. Dank's deep-set, piercing eyes and dark leathery skin, black as a Virginia coal mine, caused Henry to nod his head agreeably. He rationalize that Dank was the kind of man he'd want backing his play, considering what might lie ahead.

"Dank here is an ex-boxer," Pudge announced. "Maybe you heard of him. Once killed a man in the ring when he was a top contender."

"Yeah, I seen Dank put that man down for good in Tulsa," Baltimore admitted finally. "If I recall, it was on a Fourth of July. Dank sure did emancipate the hell out of him." Baltimore signaled he was satisfied with this selection by shaking hands with the genuine article, as far as legitimate head thumpers were concerned. Another of the men looked familiar, but Baltimore was certain he didn't know the third one. "Who's this here?" he asked, referring to the obvious stranger.

"I'm Louis Strong, Mistah Floyd," the man answered on his own behalf before Pudge had opened his mouth. Louis was in his early thirties, closer in age to Dank and Pudge, and medium brown with straight, slicked-back hair. His eyes were dark and narrow. The undertone in his skin was a peculiar shade of orange, and he was built like an old man, thin and wiry, but he had a reputation for having fast hands and an even quicker temper. His evil temperament more than accounted for what he lacked in size.

"Ole Louis is a real craftsman, a second-story man," Pudge contended. He had to say something to help sell Louis better when it appeared that Baltimore wasn't all that impressed. "We calls him "Slow Fuse" on account he's so quick with his hands once the fuse burns down. You know, one of them there ironies."

"First off, I go by Baltimore. There won't be no need for titles among us. We's all equal here," said Baltimore. Eventually, he walked over to get a closer look at the other familiar face in the trio, circling the man and carefully apprising what he saw. This fellow was a nut-colored man, shorter than the other two, at about five-ten or so, with arms as thick as oilcans. From the back, he appeared to be cut from a pillar of stone. His broad shoulders and solid legs reminded Balti-more of a wild boar he had to kill many years ago. The scar raked across the back of his neck insinuated that somebody had jumped him from behind, but the mere fact that he was still walking around meant the other fellow got the worst end of the altercation. Baltimore smiled when it came to him that he'd met Rot Mayfield in a Joplin, Missouri, county jail cell. However, he doubted that the man remembered their brief stint sharing a worn-out cot and concrete floor overnight.

When Baltimore came face-to-face with him, Rot grinned as if he had remembered. Despite his foul-smelling breath, which reeked of chewing tobacco and cheap liquor, those were the two things that reminded Baltimore of his old pals from home. "Rot, it's good seeing you again. How long did they keep you?"

"Two months, after you took off with the sheriff's secretary," Rot told him, cackling at the memory, which had returned for the first time since the event occurred long ago. Everyone in the room laughed heartily as the tension finally loosened its hold over the tiny room and everyone in it.

"Sit down, fellas, and take a load off," Baltimore offered once the pleasantries were completed. "We've got a lot of things to talk about." Around the wooden table, rectangular in shape and ragged from years of careless use, they listened attentively as Baltimore recited one honey of a plan, explaining in full detail how they would take down a major high-stakes card game. On the back of a napkin, he diagramed where every man would most likely be stationed and what duties they'd be responsible for. "We'll need one man outside the exit door at street level, one at the base of the stairs, and one inside the room with me and Henry so the folks we're party-crashing won't get any fancy ideas. After we make the getaway, we'll meet up at a safe place I decide on and split the take equally since every one of us is risking the same thing."

Wisely, Baltimore never discussed the most important aspects involving where or when the robbery was to happen until it was time to strike. He didn't want any of his cohorts to go get any fancy idea, either. As long as they were kept in the dark, none of them would be tempted to crawfish on the deal and pull the stickup with another crew, leaving him out in the cold.

After everyone agreed to the arrangement, they scribbled phone numbers down where they could be reached. Before Baltimore sent the men away, he advised them to stay sober and wait for his call. The pieces were in place, and now all that Baltimore needed was the right card game to hit. Waiting and wondering, that was always the hardest part.

Uncle Chunk waddled into the back room as the men passed by his office. The stern leer he saddled on Baltimore conveyed what he didn't have to say with words. The older man was serious about keeping his establishment out of the headlines and off the district attorney's radar. Henry turned his eyes away and pretended to read the newspaper, but Baltimore acknowledged his concerns.

"Ain't none of this gonna come back on you Unca. You have my word on that. Those men are helping me to set up a floating cathouse is all. Just that all them opened legs we're positioning is bound to ruffle some feathers." Baltimore knew right off, the crafty bar owner didn't believe him for a minute, but the scheme had only moments before been hatched. That early in the game, even the thinnest lie was better than the whole truth.

Henry, feeling out of sorts, decided to plug in the black rotary telephone, with hopes of making Baltimore's lie seem more plausible. As soon as he plugged the long cord in the wall jack, the phone started ringing and didn't stop until very close to midnight. Business was booming. Baltimore gave Franchetta the job of recruiting five new girls and managing the back end of the operation because the demand necessitated new stock to keep up with the growing clientele. Pudge's brother hired on as a secondary driver to shuttle the women between the "white only" hotels, while giving them a minute to freshen up at a black boardinghouse nearby.

Money was coming so fast that Baltimore doubled the companionship rate to ten dollars. Oddly enough, the phone calls didn't tail off a single bit. Bellmen made money on both ends, from Baltimore and the customers alike. Some of the working girls cleared one hundred dollars that first night, when, typically, it would have taken a month to knock down that amount. Henry couldn't believe how many white businessmen were practically standing in line to try out what others were talking about over breakfast the following morning. On the other hand, Baltimore knew that the novelty would wear off at about the same time those businessmen's wives expected them to catch the homebound train. The more things changed, he thought, the more they stayed the same.

Around about one in the morning, when Baltimore couldn't see taking any more requests for late-night company, he unplugged the cord to the illegal phone line and stretched his legs. "Franchetta, I'm getting too old for this line of work," he joked, as if he was the one actually putting in the work. He peered over at her when she didn't respond. At first glance, the longing in her eyes was a giveaway. Baltimore suspected what played on her mind. "Alright, alright. I know that look," he said, chuckling warmly. "I need to talk at Henry, and then we can slide by Club De Ville or the Blue Room. Now, I can't close it down tonight. Someone has to see to it that the money makes it all the way home by morning."

Baltimore had his stable of hostesses give their drivers two dollars after being sneaked up the side entrance to deal personally with customers' most intimate needs; then he would collect the money at the end of the night from them and issue kickbacks to the bellhops on the following morning. And, because he and Franchetta set up each appointment and dispatched the talent personally, there was no way for the taxi drivers or the girls to circumvent the process. He'd be the wiser immediately. It was nice and easy, just the way Baltimore thought it up, and Franchetta was glad she'd successfully persuaded him to engineer it, along with the help of friends who didn't mind joining in to make it hop.

Although Baltimore's outsourcing cathouse idea was rolling along without a hitch, stepping away from the grind was a pleasant detour. Club De Ville was a ritzy nightclub, where those who considered themselves hip went to spend the spare change they did have. The doll of a hatcheck girl smiled at Baltimore as he handed her a woman's fur coat and a whole dollar to make sure she'd guard it vigi-

lantly. That didn't slide by Franchetta's eye, but she wasn't at all concerned, because that young lady was simply admiring what she'd
brought to the party.

"Over there, Baltimore," Franchetta cooed in his ear, while pointing toward an open booth near the bandstand. "I'm going to powder
my nose," she told him before sauntering off in the other direction.
Baltimore attempted to hand her a few dollar bills for incidentals, but
she smiled and declined, thinking there was nothing in the restroom
she'd want to blow money on. There was something refreshing about
hitting a nightclub with a date and a sense of normalcy. Franchetta's
smile glimmered as she washed up in the porcelain washbasin. "A girl
could get used to this," she heard herself say aloud. "If only for a little
while."

As soon as she exited the ladies' restroom, a slick-dressed stranger
pulled at her arm. "Hey there, gorgeous," he said, easing up closely
beside her. "I seen you come in. Why on't you take me up on a discussion about me and you getting lost in each other at my place?"

"Huh, since you saw me come in, you had to see me come in with
him," Franchetta said politely as she stared lovingly at Baltimore, who
was watching the band prepare for another set.

The snazzy stranger ogled Baltimore peculiarly, as if he didn't necessarily approve of Franchetta's taste in men. "Can't say I know his
face. What's his name?"

Franchetta batted her eyes and grinned brightly. "Who? That tall,
skinny papa on my hook? I calls him Daddy."

The fellow was persistent. He pulled her even closer so he could
whisper in her ear. "Don't tell me that sly cat is your man?"

"He's my man when I'm wit' him," she answered quickly, wrestling
her arm away from his grasp. "That's more than enough for me."
That'll teach him to rough handle a lady, she thought. *Especially one who's
already nuzzled up on a date for the night.*

Franchetta celebrated an evening on the town until she'd had her
fill of joking around the dance floor, with Baltimore hot on her heels,
as if he'd never had his way with her before. The sensual way he held
her close to him, all the belly rubbing and carnal grinding, drew the
attention of several other couples sharing the same music, time, and
space.

A woman sitting next to the dance floor pouted continuously at her husband. "How come you don't move me like that anymore, Harry!" she spat. "Wait until I get you home. You've got your work cut out, mister. Go get my hat and coat."

Baltimore escorted Franchetta back to the table, and they collapsed, perspiring and pleased to let their hair down. The night went perfectly until another couple, seated a few tables over, began arguing loudly. "I don't give a good goddamn what you think you saw," shouted the tough-looking man with gold caps covering his two front teeth.

"You trying to tell me, I didn't see you slip that bitch three dollars for a pack of fifty-cent cigarettes when you ain't brought groceries home in weeks?" the woman fired back. Most of the onlookers tried to ignore common alcohol-induced lovers' quarrels, but that one caught Baltimore's attention when he recognized the woman's face from Abel's Diner. It was Macy, whose husband had a handful of her skin clinched in his fist, underneath the table.

Without thinking, Baltimore moved to slide out of the booth, but Franchetta had been watching the couple squabble as well. "Uh-uh, Baltimore. Please don't," she begged, stifling his interference. "We're having too good a time for you to get tangled in that man's affairs. Besides, his business don't have nothing to do with you." When Franchetta sensed that Baltimore's indecision teetered, she practically climbed on his lap to discourage him from causing a scene and ruining the first night out she'd had with a noncustomer in over a year. "Don't be a dope behind a girl who won't use the good sense God gave a dog to walk away after somebody's kicked her in the head the first time." Franchetta's summation was correct. Baltimore had seen enough of mean-spirited men who acted out against women. He decided on the spot that Macy's husband needed a rudimentary course in anger management, even if it killed him.

CHAPTER 8

THINGS PEOPLE DO

When three a.m. rolled around, Baltimore had seen enough of the flashy women and loud music for one night, so he made his way out front and hailed a cab. An orange Continental taxi pulled up to the curb. It quickly whisked him and Franchetta off to the north end of town. Franchetta, very intoxicated, snuggled up next to Baltimore in the spacious backseat, like a woman who was utterly in love and couldn't get enough of it. However, the man she couldn't seem to get enough of was seeing red, blood red. He was counting the seconds until he'd render Macy's husband sorry for handling her that way, especially in public. Baltimore would find a way to meet up with him and pull on his coattail for a discussion, man-to-man.

In the meanwhile, he had Franchetta on his arm and a bunch of money that needed to change hands. When they reached the pale yellow–colored house, Baltimore helped his date up the stairs. Franchetta laughed riotously when she came dangerously close to falling off the cement porch.

Daisy opened the door after hearing a commotion out front. "What happened to her?" she asked, wearing a childlike smile across her lips.

"Too much whiskey and beer," Baltimore replied, struggling to hold Franchetta up.

"Looks like she fell in the bottle, but good," Daisy concluded as

Baltimore ushered Franchetta into the bedroom and closed the door behind them.

"Uh-huh, we're out there peeling white boys' peckers, and Frannie's tripping the light fantastic," Melvina snarled, objecting wearily from the divan. "Ain't that a bunch of nothing?" she added, having not too long ago made it in herself.

"What's that?" asked Chick, returning from upstairs in her flannel housecoat and slippers. "Who done peed down your leg now?" she teased, plopping on the divan, next to Melvina. Chick lifted her legs and anchored her tiny feet in Melvina's lap. Instinctively, Melvina began massaging them.

"Nobody, child," Melvina answered. "Frannie done went out and had herself a grand old time with Baltimore, and I would be up bitching about it, but I'm just too tired to care."

"Tired ain't even the name for it," Chick sighed, laying her head back against the divan. "I've had the damndest time trying to figure out what one of those white fellas wanted from the next."

"Isn't that something?" Daisy contended. "Two of the mens tonight just wanted to look at me. Nothing else."

"Look at what?" Melvina hollered in a comical manner.

"I on't rightly know," Daisy said and chuckled. "We started kissing and fooling around. Then I gets naked, and they just stood there looking, like it was their first time doing that sorta thing."

"Ahhh-ha," Melvina laughed, still working the tension out of Chick's barking dogs. "I wish I could get my fee while a man was wasting his time gawking. I had three fellas in a row who all just rather squeeze and suck on my teets. Then, of course, I opened my legs and let 'em touch on it, too, expecting 'em to pull their peckers and go to work. But, they sat there, spilling their sacks while holding the little pink things in their hands. What a mess it was," she said, curling her lips like she could have done without all that. "Although, it made for cleaning myself a jiff." Encountering white customers wasn't such an infrequent occurrence, but those men were in the habit of cruising for dark-skinned entertainment and were a lot more comfortable in their midst. Some of the white men Baltimore had booked were well-to-do executives and captains of industry, as opposed to nine-to-five working stiffs looking for a diversion from their normal deviant trysts. But as far as the girls were concerned, it was all pretty much business as usual. Well, almost.

"What about you, Chick?" Daisy asked, watching Melvina rub away at her heels.

"Huh?" answered Chick, semisedated. "Oh, tonight was different, alright. The men paid up front, and there wasn't no haggling on the price, either. I guess because I'm small, white boys wasn't so flabbergasted after seeing me with my clothes off. Although my last customer, he was an odd one. Offered me an extra twenty if I's to slick my toes down with grease and then ram them up his lily-white behind."

Daisy, who had been drifting off, tried to imagine such a spectacle. "So, what'd he say when you told him to go jump in a lake?"

"Nothing," Chick muttered, half asleep during one heck of a massage. "I took the money, slapped some grease on my ones and twos, and mashed my foot so far up his tail that my ankle damn near got stuck."

When Melvina realized what that meant, she flung Chick's feet from her lap and hollered frantically. "You nasty heffa! Got me rubbing your hooves what's been shoved up in some man's filthy crack. I'm gonna go and soak my hands in a tub of bleach. You'd do the same if you knew what was good for you."

Daisy's eyes flew open wildly. She hoisted her leg up and peered at her size 10 foot, hoping she'd have an occasion to run into a customer with the same fetish. "You gotta admit, that's one for the books!" she wailed. "The white man paid Chick good money to put her foot up his ass. I know plenty of colored men who'd gladly stomp a big hole in it for free."

"Oomph, he might like having it done at that," Chick mused. "Y'all should have seen him, just a squealing like a pig and yanking on his privates, like nothing I ever seen. I took the money from off the dresser, got my clothes, and left him laying there, balled up like a baby, slobbering on his thumb."

Baltimore walked away from Franchetta's room, tired and hungry. "Hi, y'all. What's all the noise about?" he asked, buttoning his dress shirt to cover his bare chest underneath it.

"Nothing you'd want to know about," Melvina jested. "It's just that Chick got her foot stuck in the mud."

"Oh, good," Baltimore answered, scratching the top of his head. "I thought maybe one of your customers asked for something kinky, like a full-foot screw." He didn't see Daisy about to bust a gut holding in her laughter behind him, but he did notice Melvina's face lighting up with surprise. "Well, then, I'll take the cab drivers' and the bellhops' tips now so's I don't have to bother with waking y'all when the sun comes up." After accepting the money and thanking the girls for their business acumen and efforts, Baltimore made himself a turkey sandwich. When he returned from the kitchen, with the sandwich on a saucer, Chick was the only one stirring downstairs.

"So, it looks like you and me tonight," she suggested shamefully, after playing impossible to get the night before.

"I'da thought you'd be all spent after taking in three more pricks than the other girls tonight," Baltimore assumed.

"Nah, I was saving my best for last," Chick replied seductively, without as much as a hint of shame to speak of. She tossed Baltimore a come-hither stare, and then she playfully pushed him down on the divan.

"As I recollect, you passed on the party in Franchetta's room last night."

"Well, I don't share their fondness for peanut butter," Chick informed him, raising her housecoat to straddle him. "Besides, I like to ride alone. That way nobody gets bent out of shape if'n I'm not in the mood to let up off the pedal." She unzipped his pants and manipulated the situation to suit her. "Oh yeah, that's the way I want to go, Daddy," she groaned tenderly. "Now, mash on the gas."

Baltimore continued mashing on the gas until Chick coasted off to sleep on top of him, broken down and bewildered. Henry came in afterwards, angry and out of sorts, as Baltimore eased Chick aside. He laid her down gingerly before pulling up his pants. "What? You want me to wake her and see if she can stand some more attention?"

"Uh-uh, I'll pass," Henry declined. "I followed behind you once before and made a fool of myself. Chick looks plum tuckered out, anyway, and ain't likely to be able to *stand up* until around noon."

"Fine by me," Baltimore said casually. He sunk his teeth into the sandwich he'd made before Chick prolonged the late-night snack. "Where've you been, anyway?"

"Working on a little something I met over at Unca Chunk's when you and Franchetta ditched me," Henry barked halfheartedly. "We shared on everything, from canned meat to big-chested, brown-eyed triplets, but we need to talk about being stacked up in this house. Let's get to town and find a spot to stretch out."

Considering Henry's pleas, Baltimore nodded assuredly and tore the sandwich down the middle. He handed his best friend an equal share to devour. "Okay," he said evenly, "we'll move out in the morning."

Morning came soon enough. The fellows were both packed up and gone when Franchetta awoke to find Chick in dreamland on the divan, bundled up comfortably beneath the thick, multicolored quilt Baltimore had found in the downstairs storage closet. Stumbling into the kitchen, Franchetta stretched and yawned before discovering a note scribbled on a piece of wax paper. *Faye, me and Henry are going to stay in town for the rest of the week*, she read. *Signed, B.* Franchetta stood there, staring at her middle name, written in block lettering. She predicted that Baltimore was up to something he'd be sorry for later and was merely getting at the apologizing part early. Franchetta also suspected that whatever he had on his mind to do wrong, she'd be there to forgive him afterwards. She was convinced he'd do the same for her. He had already proven that too many times before to see it any other way.

After two hours of catching up to bellboys and prostitutes to make the scratch come out right, Henry was tired of watching Baltimore play facilitator for what amounted to fifty dollars worth of compensation to be split between the two of them. "That's enough Baltimo'. Let's knock off and go have something to eat," Henry suggested, while massaging his empty stomach.

"Okay. That wraps up last night's dealing, anyhow," Baltimore replied, sitting next to Henry in the back of yet another cab. "Do I have to guess where it is you wanna have something to eat?"

Henry leaned back against the vinyl seat cushion and smiled. "I have heard of this one place where they serves a mean plate of chicken and grits."

"Well, then, we'd better get over there before Hattie gets off work." Baltimore snickered lightly. "'Sides, I always did like grits." Henry glanced at him from the corner of his eye, wondering who he was trying to fool, knowing full well Baltimore couldn't stand the sight of grits.

Movement inside the diner was sluggish at best, probably because the time of day landed somewhere between breakfast and lunch. The idea of brunch hadn't caught on so well with Negros, so the waitresses sat around clowning about the men in their lives and those they wanted out of them. "Nah, don't put the suitcases down at the door," Baltimore told Henry as he lowered his cheap travel bag to the floor.

"I aim to keep my hands on what's mine." Too bad he didn't hold the same opinion for what belonged to other men.

"Ahhh, there he is!" shouted Hattie, with her hands outstretched, pretending that Henry was too much to touch. "You said you was coming by last night, but you lied. I had put Mama to sleep by nine. The chillums was down and out soon after that."

"Hattie, now don't be that way," Henry pleaded. "I was busy working 'til late. Don't you know if there was any way for me to get loose, I would have?" When she began to wobble her round head from side to side, like she was mulling over his blatant lie, Henry grinned big and wide. "Yeahhh, that's it. Ain't nobody for me but you. Go on back there, and get some fresh coffee for me and my friend."

"Okay, lover man," she sang, before fixing her eyes on Baltimore, as if he'd just appeared out of thin air. "Oh, uh-huh, I remember. You's Ham 'n Eggs from the other day," added Hattie. "Macy say she remember you from last night, though." As soon as she sauntered off to the back of the restaurant, Henry moved his luggage aside with his hard-soled shoe in order to lean in closer to Baltimore.

"I thought you were with Frannie 'n 'em last night," Henry commented, marveling at how proficiently Baltimore seemed to be getting around. "I caught the last act with you and Chick, but when did you have time to work Macy in?"

"I didn't. Macy was having some trouble with the man who took her to Club De Ville," Baltimore answered. "He was more than likely her husband, seeing as how they was out in the open scrapping and such."

"They were fighting at the club?"

"He was doing a large part of the arguing," Baltimore recounted, "snatching on her at the table. If I had the chance, I'd show her something different altogether."

Squinting down the long aisle with square tables on either side, Henry smiled to himself. "What if, just sayin' what if, she was to show up this morning? What would you say to her?"

"Don't matter. Macy was out later than me, so there ain't no way she found her way in here this early," answered Baltimore, unaware that Macy had been at work for hours and was actually heading his way. "But if she had," he continued, "I'd have to make it known that I planned on making her life a little better after awhile, if she'll let me." Baltimore didn't mind playing this what-if game Henry initiated, because it did give him a chance to talk about Macy as if she could become more than a conquest, if she decided to give in. Baltimore couldn't understand why a man who couldn't provide love and affection didn't up and leave the woman alone, instead of making the situation worse by getting violent.

"Oh, I see. You'd take Macy in your arms and then do what wit' her?" Henry prodded while Macy filled a sugar bowl behind Baltimore, at the next table.

"One thing, if I wasn't still bushed from satisfying two women last night, I'd look to giving Macy a run for her money," Baltimore boasted unwittingly. Henry tried to wave him off after hearing the discussion headed in the wrong direction. "Man, what's gotten into you?" Baltimore whooped suspiciously. When Henry placed his head in his hands, Baltimore had a good idea what was askew. "Macy's standing right behind?" Henry nodded assuredly that she was. "And, she just heard me bragging 'bout laying down with more than a fair share of hens?" Again, Henry nodded, glancing up at Macy, who had her hands balled against her hips.

"Ham 'n Eggs," Macy said, stepping into Baltimore's view while trying not to laugh. "I seen you last night at the De Ville, but with only that high-yellow thing hanging from your zipper. I'm surprised she let you tip out later on, unless you had 'em both at the same time."

"Nah, they was . . . separate," Baltimore admitted, slightly nonrepentant. "They live at the same house, though."

Somewhat mystified, Macy shrugged her shoulders and begun fiddling with her apron strings. "Is that where you live at?" she asked. "With the two of them women?" Despite Henry's disbelief, Macy appeared turned on at the thought of Baltimore getting more than his fair share of feminine affection.

"Nah-uh," Baltimore uttered. Slowly, he came to the understanding that Macy was the type of woman who was very interested in a man who could pull off such a feat and didn't think twice about bouncing back for a third. "I don't have a place to lay my head," he informed her honestly. "Got my luggage right here."

"Slow down, Ham 'n Eggs," she teased. "I'll be off work in another hour. We can see what you got to say about it then."

After Macy disappeared to the far end of the diner, Henry stared at Baltimore endlessly, worshiping and despising him simultaneously. "Baltimo', I done seen you pull off a lot of thangs, but for this here occasion, I ain't even got the words for it."

CHAPTER 9

WHAT THEY CALL YOU?

Macy yelled for the taxi driver to pull over when he rounded the turn at Euclid and East Seventh Street. "Stop here. This is it!" she shouted from deep in the backseat, with Baltimore's fingers dancing beneath her waitress uniform. "Go on now, Ham 'n Eggs," she chuckled, stepping out of the long blue Oldsmobile in front of the Euclid Terrace Hotel. "We's just getting around to knowing each other. Don't start to acting like this is gonna be a regular thing."

Baltimore's smile gleamed brightly. He pulled his thin suitcase from the floor of the taxi and then whispered in Macy's ear. "All I need is today." Macy stared at him. A nervous glint flashed in her eyes. She must have believed every word, because she ran flat out of objections. In fact, she didn't have anything else to say until her uniform was thrown across the cloth-covered chair in room number six, at the end of the hall.

Her heart pounded with anticipation as she watched him unlatch the pull–down style Murphy bed from the wall. "I don't know what you think of me, but I ain't in the habit of cattin' off with men to strange hotels," Macy said eventually, in a way that told Baltimore she was being truthful. "I'm a married woman, but things with my husband are not like they need to be, is all." When Macy tried to explain her situation at home and justify stripping down to her slip and brassiere, Baltimore quieted her with a warm embrace and heated kisses.

"See, Macy, I don't have to know why you decided to come here with me," he uttered passionately, running his wet tongue along her neckline. "It just means I get a chance to show you how happy I am that you did." Baltimore wanted to sweat the sheets with Macy for two reasons. He figured she needed a kind hand on her body instead of one bent on bruising it. He also figured she deserved it. Again, Macy thought well enough to keep her mouth closed, as best she could with a chorus of enthusiastic shrieks and screams pouring out of it. Macy's displays of blissful intimacy, resulting in a myriad of high-pitched moans, continued to seep through the walls of room number six during a good part of the afternoon. During a much-needed intermission from the devilment scattered about, Baltimore washed his face in the small sink next to the kitchenette. "Macy, what do you say to me running down to the corner store for a coupla bottles of pop, or something stronger, maybe?"

"Uh-uh," she objected. "I ain't gonna let you outta my sight until I can't stand no more of that good stuff you been pleasuring me with. No, suh, I was sorry in the beginning for messin' around, but you done changed my mind about that but good."

Baltimore looked over his shoulder at Macy, wrapped in moist sheets. For the time being, she didn't have a care in the world. "I'm happy to oblige," he reminded her. "Told you that from the jump."

"Yeah, you did." Macy blushed, lighting up a store-bought cigarette. "You was right, too. I feel like a million. Tell me one thing, though, and I'll shut up again for about another hour. I think I can't stand at least that much more."

Easing back onto the bed, his naked body lying next to hers, Baltimore caressed Macy's shoulders with his strong hands. "Okay, shoot."

She flicked cigarette ashes on the hardwood floor next to the bed. "I've been clowning around and calling you Ham 'n Eggs so's I wouldn't get too personal. I does that with customers down at the diner. It also helps me to recollect what they like to eat, if they come in again, you understand."

"Sure, I do," answered Baltimore. He wondered where she was headed with this discussion, but he didn't want to rush her to the point. Conversely, he decided on meeting her whenever she arrived there on her own. "That sounds like a smart way to go about things."

"I guess so," Macy said plainly, with her mind plainly on something else. "Well," she sighed, with her fingers fondling the back of Baltimore's thigh. "Huh, I stepped in quicksand the moment you showed up this morning, and I've been sinking ever since."

"So?" Baltimore said, waiting on the important part of her comment. "Some would say, 'That's a good way to go'," he joked.

Macy's full breasts shook as her laughter spilled out unbridled. "And, I'd be one of 'em, too, but the problem is, I don't even know your name, and you've spent the better part of the afternoon driving me wild."

Sitting up on his elbow, Baltimore wrinkled his brow as he considered the possible ramifications of Macy's epiphany, until he reasoned there weren't any. "You know they call me Baltimore, or did you forget?"

Macy turned her head toward him and sighed again, although this time hesitation stood behind it. "Naw, I haven't forgotten. I guess I'd feel better knowing *who they* were and *why they* do. I don't mean to pry, but what kinda name is Baltimore for a man like you? I dare say your mama calls you by the same."

"What's all of this talk about what's in a name?" he replied, annoyed with Macy's interest in something that didn't concern her. "Ain't no need for nobody to bother with that, except the undertaker and the woman who's crying over me when they's lowering my bones into the ground."

"I see," answered Macy, with the wind taken out of her sails. Before putting her cigarette out on a flat tin ashtray she'd placed on the floor beside the bedpost, she tried to calm the unexpected burst of emotion causing knots to develop in the pit of her stomach. "I'd better get going, you know. I'd hate to overstay my welcome."

"If you leave right now, you're gonna under stay it," Baltimore submitted, in the best way he knew how to ask a woman who wasn't his to hang around.

"A little while longer," Macy agreed silently seconds before she was back to shouting. This go-around, "Baltimore," was the only thing she wanted to say, in about a hundred different ways at that. From slow and mellow moans to bold and bawdy hoots and hollers, she traded in her marriage vows that day when calling his name like no others. Unfortunately, that would be her undoing.

Not long after Macy woke up from a catnap, collected her clothing, and dashed off for home, Baltimore was in the hotel lobby, on the telephone. He'd made several calls, including the ones to get a line on Henry. Eventually, Baltimore caught up to him at Franchetta's, where she had been steadily grilling him for information purposely being withheld from her. It was a good thing the phone rang when it did because Henry was wearing thin under the intense interrogation tactics Franchetta administered. There were several ways to make a man sing like a sparrow; questioning him while wearing nothing beneath a sheer negligee was a good one. When Baltimore arrived at her front door, he didn't have to wonder why his pal sounded all shook up on the line, stammering timidly.

"Why'd you bring your big, thick head back over here if you didn't want Franchetta attemptin' to waggle some news out of you?" Baltimore fussed, dragging Henry out of the house, with his pants down around his ankles.

"A few more minutes and I'da had him talking, Baltimore," Franchetta yelled from the front porch, her negligee swaying in the winter wind.

"If I wanted you to know what I was up to, I'd have told you myself," Baltimore hollered back in her direction. A colored mail carrier on his route stopped dead in his tracks on the sidewalk when his eyes discovered what he thought to be a practically nude white woman jawing with a smooth-looking black man. "You ought to be shame, Franchetta!" Baltimore scolded her playfully. "I told you Henry's got a weak constitution for pretty girls."

"Yeah, I know!" she screamed, pretending to be stomping mad. "That's what I was counting on."

When it didn't appear the wide-eyed mailman was interested in vacating his spot on the cold concrctc, Baltimorc stared him down. "Something up on that porch belong to you?" he asked harshly.

"Huh, oh naw, suh," said the mailman as he backpedaled, cradling his bag. He didn't know exactly what was going on, but Baltimore's tone suggested he forget about it and get on about his business. Before Pudge's taxi stormed off down the residential street, the postal worker was long gone, and so was any chance of Franchetta learning what she'd almost pulled out of Henry: information about the heist.

After Baltimore retrieved Henry, he had Pudge drive him back over to the Marquette Hotel to meet with Ash Can Corvine, the reluctant bellhop. The taxi rested against the curb on the Holmes Street side of the hotel, where there would be fewer interruptions. The message left at Uncle Chunk's suggested that the big news Baltimore had been waiting for had finally come through. "Ash Can!" Baltimore hailed gleefully as the apprehensive older man stepped out of the side door, with a cigarette trembling from his lips.

"Hey ya, fellows. I sho' wanted to thank you for putting some extra money in my pocket," Ash Can said, as a matter of record. "Been a long time since I had enough money to blow some of it. I'm just saying, much obliged. Those white men are crazy for the girls you been sending over."

"Don't mention it, Ash," Baltimore responded, watching the unlit cigarette bounce up and down as the man rattled on. "What I want to hear about is the word you left at Chunk's concerning a sporting event set to go down."

"Oh yeah, that. Well, you said before there was some pay tied to the privilege of knowing if I happened to hear something." There was a pregnant pause, which annoyed Baltimore. He pursed his lips over the deliberate ploy to stall for a payoff on the front end. Ash Can struck a match, but he was far too nervous to light up what he'd whipped out to smoke. "Okay, I can see you're a man of your word. I'll just come out with it then."

"You'd be wise to do that," Baltimore agreed, growing more impatient by the second.

Leaning in, the bellhop shared what he'd overheard some men discussing about putting the hospitality suite to good use. Ash Can went on to explain that several smaller stakes games had cropped up, but this was by far the most promising, because Mr. Houston Olds, heir to the Oldsmobile fortune, would be one of the participants. Now that the bellhop had Baltimore's full attention, he dropped the bomb. "The onliest thing you might have to worry about is a city cop who likes to pal around with these stuck-up rich boys. He won't be able to sit at the same table with them, but he's liable to come and watch a spell."

"That's good, Ash Can," Baltimore said sincerely, mulling over what he'd been told. "That's real good. Here's a ten spot. If this pans out, I'll lace your palms with more than a year's pay. For that, you've got to forget this conversation ever happened and ever knowing me in particular."

"I done already started working on forgetting about knowing you," Ash Can replied before thinking. "I mean, I-I-I'll do-do that, Mistah Baltimo'," he added, flicking the dampened unlit cigarette into the gutter. "This here be the end betwixt us?"

"Yeah, this is where we part company," answered Baltimore from his seat on the front passenger side wheel fender. "Thanks for calling me, and only me, about this." He threw in that last comment to dissuade the aging bellhop from thinking of selling the same information to anyone else. That kind of mistake was a killing offense, and Baltimore needed to make sure the man understood that. A square deal was a square deal, even in the midst of planning a high-profile robbery. There was such a thing as honor among thieves, after all.

Speaking of thieves, Baltimore called an immediate meeting in Uncle Chunk's back room. Immediate meant some time later that same day because it took Pudge a few hours to round up the boys. Dank Battles, the ex–prize fighter was found at his sister's house, busting up a chord of wood in the backyard. Rot Mayfield had gotten himself thrown in jail overnight on a public disorderly charge, which he swore was an absolute misunderstanding between him and the barmaid who refused his drunken advances. Louis Strong had lit his slow fuse and was perfectly contented to snuggle up next to her until Pudge came banging at his door. Louis had no qualms about tearing himself from a hot woman and the comforts of a warm bed, especially when the rent was due. He'd agreed to go in with the moneymaking scheme, believing that he shouldn't have to work too hard to pull it off. It was easy money as far as he was concerned, although he'd done enough wrong to know that keeping it was often another story entirely.

Honor, a strange bedfellow to most criminals, was one of the things Baltimore cherished whenever going in with other men on a caper. The heat of battle affected people in different ways—some cowered in its wake and others charged right through—but Baltimore could always count on a stack of money bringing out the very worst in men, the very worst. He'd have to choreograph the takedown and consider making preparations for the contingency of someone freezing up or getting it in their minds to freelance. Although there was no surefire way to guarantee everyone coming out alive, Baltimore persuaded the men that he'd come up with the best method to "snatch and grab" more loot than any of them had ever seen. And, if they kept their cool in the process, living long enough to spend it, it would make be worth their trouble. Everyone agreed, but somebody lied.

CHAPTER 10

DOWN AND DIRTY

"She's something to see alright," Baltimore said as he peered through the crowd of customers at Uncle Chunk's bar and billiards. "But I'd watch my step around a woman like that if I was you. She looks to be the kind who might get froggy long before it's time to jump." Baltimore was leery of the medium brown–toned, petite little number, with a high-class attitude, sitting at the end of Chunk's bar. She was turning her nose up at everyone, and at the proprietor in particular. When he saw her scowl at Uncle Chunk as if he were a dirty drinking glass, Baltimore was satisfied that she'd been involved in a slow grind with the older man that ended a lot worse than it began. However close to the truth that was, he didn't see putting that idea in Henry's head when it was obvious that he was falling for her. "If you ask me, she's trouble," said Baltimore, making his way over to the wooden table. He unplugged the illegal phone line in the back room when he needed a certain amount of quiet to collect himself.

Henry eased up to the crack in the door to steal another glimpse at his new acquaintance. "Yeah, well, that might be so, but Estelle's the kind of trouble I've been looking to get into. Oh, here comes Frannie," he informed Baltimore. Strutting through the crowd, Franchetta stared straight at the thin crease in the door as if she could read Henry's mind on the other side of it and didn't approve of his

thoughts. "That woman's got ice water in her veins," Henry said, turning toward the small table.

"Too bad I can't say the same for that chippie of yours," Baltimore
said and sighed casually.

As the door swung open slowly, noise from the dance area spilled
inside. Franchetta's lips were pursed, although she tried to conceal
her salty disposition. "Hey, fellas, what's the skinny on tonight? Rain's
threatening to come down like sifted flour, the radio forecaster predicted."

"I see you made it in alright," Baltimore joked as he stood to greet
her with a cordial embrace and friendly kiss on the cheek.

Franchetta smirked, knowing Baltimore's heart wasn't in it. "Yeah,
I had the driver drop me right by the front door so's my sugar would-
n't melt none." While amusing herself, Franchetta cast a looming
glare at Henry, hiding in plain view. "Henry, is there something between us I need to know about?"

"Nah, I've been trying to shake the last time I saw you from my
mind," Henry answered, avoiding eye contact.

"Ooh, Henry Taylor, I do declare . . . You're blushing," she sang
pleasantly. "You are one of a kind."

"Only thing is, ain't nobody been able to name it yet," Baltimore offered, looking upside Henry's head for chasing behind a woman with
the wrong kind of composition for his liking.

"Go on now with all of that, Baltimo'," Henry growled. "I'ma stroll
out yonder for a quick look-see. Be back in a jiff."

"Franchetta, take a load off," Baltimore said, gesturing with his
hand toward the seat opposite the table from his. She smiled as best
she could but refused his offer, though not entirely.

"Thanks, but I'll sit here." She took the seat closest to him. "I want
to get a clear picture of the lie you're about to tell me."

"I've never kept anything from you unless it was for your own good,
but I won't fix my mouth to hold no lie. You know me better 'n that."
Franchetta lowered her head, feeling a slight bit ashamed of chal-
lenging Baltimore's integrity as a good friend and a man who had
been nothing but honest with her in the past. "Here is it, down and
dirty." He was second-guessing himself on the other side of a stone
poker face. "Me and a few local boys need to handle something
tonight. I want you to work the phone and keep business flowing as

usual. It'll be a might heavier 'cause of the rain, but that's okay. I'll be back 'round about midnight. Then we can all go out and have a ball . . . me, you, Melvina, and Daisy. Hell, Chick can even come along, too, but she's gotta wash her feet. Yeah, I heard about that."

A strained chuckle sputtered from Franchetta's mouth. "We've tried dousing them with everything but turpentine already."

"If it was up to me, I'd have gone for the turpentine straight away. Ain't too much worse than some funky ass feet," he mused. He set a stack of writing paper by the phone for Franchetta to arrange host-esses. No sooner had the plug gone into the wall jack than the black rotary phone rang like it had been waiting every second of the past half hour to do so.

"I guess we're open for business," Franchetta said, leaning forward to pick up the receiver. "Yes, this is the right exchange," she said into it, somewhat puzzled. "Oh yes, Baltimore, he's here." She pressed the receiver against her chest and shrugged. "Somebody named Ash Can says he needs to speak with you personally and right away."

Baltimore's chest tightened when he took the call. "Hi ya, Ash. This is Baltimore. Yep, yep," he answered in a manner that insinuated he was being purposely secretive and running scenarios around in his head. "Now, I'm counting on you. Give it to me neat. Uhhhh-huh. Are you positive that's how it is? Yep, we can make that. Alright then. Alright."

Ash Can gave it to Baltimore straight, with no chaser, just the way he liked it. The big game he'd been asking about had already gotten underway, according to the second-shift men's room attendant work-ing the lobby. He'd overheard some of the hotel guests getting all worked up over a chance to take some of their competitors' money, along with a decent amount of their pride to boot. Chances were, the game would continue on deep into the night, but Baltimore wasn't willing to sit by and wait that long. He couldn't risk the rain letting up when it served as the perfect seventh man on the job, aiding in their setup and getaway. Even though Ash didn't mention anything about police protection, Baltimore accounted for the possibility of their in-terference, nonetheless.

Before Franchetta contemplated how much trouble awaited Baltimore on the other end of that phone conversation, he'd had a short conference with Uncle Chunk and snatched Henry up and away from the woman he didn't trust. In less time than it took Franchetta to remember how much she loved everything about Baltimore, he was out the rear exit and into a mounting storm.

Two blocks away, in the alley behind an abandoned cotton mill, Henry jiggled opened the padlock on the iron back gate with a crooked piece of metal wire.

"Come on, man. We got to move," Baltimore insisted as he ducked inside the large warehouse, constructed of little more than rusted tin and rotting lumber. "Chunk's done put a call in to Pudge by now," he said. "They'll be here before long."

In the meantime, the two men worked diligently, cleaning and inspecting the guns Baltimore had copped from Rascal at the second-hand clothing store. There were two hardly used thirty-eight revolvers, a shotgun, and two stainless-steel forty-five-caliber canons, which Baltimore called *persuaders* because the mere sight of them often caused the hardest men to back down. Henry wiped the sawed-off double-barrel shotgun with a dry rag. He put it aside so he could open the boxes he'd stored in the corner a couple of hours before. Inside them lay bundles of police-issue raincoats, dark-colored vinyl coverall pants, and black rubber boots. When a car horn sounded after they'd been there nearly forty minutes, Henry dashed over to the large iron garage door to open it.

The lights on Pudge's taxi blinked twice before the car pulled in. Henry secured the garage door once the car cleared the entrance. Louis Strong was the first to hop from the car. He tried to appear calm when he rounded the front fender on the passenger side, but his eyes darted left and right continually, not sure what to expect or what was really expected of him at that point. Dank Battles made his way out of the back door on the driver's side at the same instance Pudge decided to get out and join the others. Pudge, a whole foot shorter than Dank, put Henry in mind of somebody's kid brother trying to hang with the big boys. The vast disparity in their sizes almost made Henry laugh, but he didn't. If they were going to execute a successful job, every man had to pull his own weight despite his physical dimensions.

Rot was the last to climb out of the long sedan. He looked pitiful, like death warmed over, tired and sickly around the eyes. Baltimore noticed right off and decided to keep an eye on the man, who'd likely gone off the wagon. He was likely to come down with a bad case of the shakes before the night was through. A sober drunk was better than one with a snoot full, Baltimore reasoned, so he decided to put his concerns on the back burner for the time being.

"Hail, hail, the gang's all here," Baltimore said, with a heaping dose of trepidation when his bunch of scoundrels came across like a ragtag bunch of miscreants. There was no time to go out recruiting a better crew. He had to make his bed with these, although he had a bad feeling about going through with it.

"Yeah, yeah," Louis replied, after taking a long gander at the guns on display. "We's ready, too. Y'all sho' got some fine heaters."

"Where're we going, anyway?" spouted Dank. "I need to get me some money."

After pushing one of the boxes across the cold cement floor, Henry began taking off his damp jacket. "You'll know when we get there," he said, as if Dank had said something out of line.

"He's right, Dank," Baltimore chimed in quickly, so as not to cause dissension from the outset. "It's better that we get down to the nuts and bolts and save the where-ats until we understand how the plans are put together for a reason and don't need to be changed. Now then, Dank, you'll come inside with me and Henry. Rot, I'll need you to keep an eye on the side door to the street. Louis, you'll be posted between the side door and the money room. You don't let nobody get the jump on us from behind. And, Pudge, course you'll be the wheelman. When the money bags reach the car, that means it's time to catch hell outta that place because we'll be coming out hot." Each of the men was nodding agreeably. Louis kept an eye on the shotgun because it was bound to speak the loudest if danger reared its ugly head. "Go on and get it, Lou," said Baltimore, "if you can handle it."

Louis leapt at the chance, grabbing a handful of shells for backup. After all of the other guns were allocated except for one of the heavy forty-fives, Baltimore whipped out the one he'd taken from Darby Kent the night he and Henry killed him on the train. "I'll pack this one with that persuader so's it don't get lonely. Why on't y'all get on some of those rain clothes and take a handkerchief from this pack." He held out a small plastic bag, and each of the men took one as instructed. "Hold on to it until we get around the corner from the spot. Now, let's load up." When the men began digging into the boxes with rain gear inside, Baltimore pulled Rot aside so the others couldn't hear their conversation. "I know this must be hard on you, Rot. Here, take a little nip to settle your nerves." Without hesitation, Rot accepted the fifth of gin bottle from Baltimore and took a nice swig.

"Thank you, Baltimore. It's good to see you haven't changed a bit. You still have a kind heart. I don't know if I could've made it without a li'l taste."

"I need you to be right on this, Rot. Can I count on you?"

"You can put your life on it," Rot answered, with a thin remnant of liquor rimming his upper lip.

"I hope so 'cause that's exactly what I'm doing," replied Baltimore, before patting him on the back. As the men prepared to take off, Henry opened the garage door for the taxi to pull out of the warehouse. When he returned, wet and a bit musty, Baltimore stared at him to see if he was mentally dialed in or simply going along because of his loyalties. There was nothing but resolve masking Henry's face as far as Baltimore could tell. Neither of them knew that resolve would be their trump card when the last chip fell.

CHAPTER 11

'ROUND ABOUT MIDNIGHT

As the taxi idled in the alley a few streets over from the Marquette Hotel, rain began pounding the streets in sheets, like the radio weatherman had forecasted. Baltimore was glad he'd gotten his predictions correct for once. "Now, this is the way it goes," he announced. "There's a heap of money piled up on a table in the hospitality suite over at the 'Quette. I know they don't allow no Negros up in there unless they carrying bags, so we'll abide like they want us to, only we'll be carrying 'em out." Baltimore reached beneath the front seat and pulled out two large canvas mailbags. "C'mon, Pudge, let's get it over and done with."

At 11:15, a taxicab with five gunmen packed inside parked along the curb on Holmes. It was as quiet as a cemetery on the lonely one-way side street, while very few cars passed in front of the hotel on Twelfth. "Good. No innocent bystanders to get in the way on our way out," Baltimore reveled as he peered at the deserted intersection. "Pudge, we'll be back directly, so keep this old clunker fired up. Dank, Henry, I got only two things to say before we go in. Don't hesitate to shoot, but only if we have to, because there will be some men whose families will stop at nothing to catch us if one of them was to get killed."

"That's only one thing, Baltimore," answered Dank, with a perplexed expression. "What's the other one?"

Baltimore held up his handkerchief and then folded it diagonally. "Don't be stupid," he responded casually as he slipped it on to conceal his face. "Tie 'em on now. Let's get this show on the road." Just before the men piled out of the car and stepped into the puddles on the sidewalk, Baltimore checked both of his guns again and flashed a glare at Pudge. "If this car ain't here when I get back, you'd better keep on driving all the way to hell." He didn't wait on a reply after making his point crystal clear.

Dressed in dark, police-issued garb from head to toe, and with handkerchiefs tied just below their eyes, they exited the car one by one. Henry found the side door unlocked, just as Ash Can had promised it would be. He cracked it open, peeked in, and waved for the others to come forth. Dank and Baltimore eased inside. So far the coast was clear. There was no one to be seen. The well-made plans had been discussed in strict detail, and the time had come to follow them to the letter.

Rot, just about evenly tempered after that quick hit of gin, was as steady as he was going to be. Louis climbed the backstairs behind the other three, who were going after the cash. He stopped halfway up the second flight, where he could tiptoe and see if anyone was coming down the long corridor. Baltimore signaled that that was the perfect place to stay put, but close enough to help mow someone down if it came to that.

Moving in formation, as if rehearsed, Henry and Dank followed closely behind their leader, with their guns drawn. Baltimore crept along the wall in the direction of the hospitality suite situated in the middle of the second-floor hallway. His heart raced faster as adrenaline filled his veins.

With each step he took, the uncertainty of what awaited on the other side of that wall intensified, although he couldn't allow that to deter him. If he wanted to shake that bad luck shadow for good, he'd need money to cinch it. With the right amount in his hands, Baltimore figured to change his luck for a long while. He'd climbed off of that train to make it happen. This was his chance to redirect his fate, and there'd be no turning back.

Directly outside of the door leading into the suite, Baltimore motioned for Henry and Dank to stand on either side of it while he rapped on it three times. It wasn't that he knew of any friendly signal; three knocks had always gotten him into any speakeasy he wanted in, so he went with it. The door opened quickly as a thin, neatly dressed white man wearing a gray suit saluted his contemporaries, with a contented grin and a stiff drink in his hand.

"Night, fellas," the white man hailed loudly. "I'm going up to spend some of my winnings with a choice piece of jigaboo tail that bellboy ordered up for me." With the door wide open and cigar smoke clouding the room, he failed to read the eyes of the men inside, who saw reason to be alarmed. "Why the dirty looks?" he asked, totally unaware. "These nigger bitches are supposed to be cleaner than a Safeway chicken." The cocktail he held flew into the air when Baltimore kicked him square in the behind with the sole of his rubber boot.

"What in the hell is this, Horace?" asked one the older men seated at the poker table. "You said this was a safe game." Not one of the other seven men inside the room moved a muscle. They simply gawked, with their mouths hung open, at what appeared to be three renegade colored policemen.

"It's okay, Mr. Greenly. This must be some sort of prank," the one called Horace surmised, standing up from the dip he'd worn into the love seat. "Right, guys? Isn't this a joke?"

"Hell, nah, it ain't!" Baltimore shouted, giving the room a once over to see if there was anyone hiding. What he did discover was a bigger stack of money than he'd witnessed on the train, possibly twice as much. This was the jackpot, and soon he would walk away with it, barring no one tried to stop him. "I want everybody to get up, shake your pockets out on the table, and then step away from it." When no one acted as if they were going to comply, Baltimore cocked the forty-five and shoved the canon in the face of the one they called Horace. "I'm not in the mood to say it again."

On cue, the middle-aged white man, wearing a scowl and a cheap brown suit, raised his hands reluctantly. "He-he's serious!" Horace said, his voice rattling noticeably. "Just do it. Whatever he says, do it!"

"I can't believe this," remarked the other man with enough gall to speak up. With three guns aimed in his direction, he stood up and raised his stubby arms in the air. "Horace, you're fired. We've paid you for three days to protect us, and now that we actually need your sorry ass, you're as useless as tits on a bull."

"Now that's funny," Baltimore said, moving all of the men to the far side of the room by fanning the pistol at them. "Let's get what we come for and leave peaceful, if these gentlemen wanna cooperate."

Baltimore shook his gun in Dank's direction for him to gather up the money covering the circular wooden table decorated in green felt.

"Horace, you a house detective?" Baltimore asked while Henry stood just inside the doorway. "Do me a favor and put your gun on the table with all of those greenbacks."

The chubby man in the roach brown suit pulled a weapon from his side holster in a slow, careful, and deliberate manner. "Uh-uh . . . a Kansas City detective!" he barked angrily. "That's why you'd best forget about busting in here and taking what doesn't belong to you."

"Ain't that just like a cracker?" Louis quipped, entering the room from Henry's flank. "Man's gotta rod pointed at his snoot, and he's still tryin' a call the shots."

"Uh-uh," Baltimore grunted in order to shut Louis up, when he was supposed to be covering their exit from the staircase. "Get back to your post," Baltimore demanded.

"Not before I get even for all the hell ol' Horace Spivey over there put my baby brother through some years ago," Louis debated. "I was standing out there on the stairs, wondering what was taking y'all so long. Then I come up to see for myself. And I'll be damned if you didn't get the drop on the crookedest cop in Kaycee. I always said if I ever got the chance, I would bust all the teeth out of his mouth." When the other white men heard Louis's vicious declaration, they moved decidedly away from Horace. "See, this pecker would come around every time somebody said, 'A nigga did it,' but he couldn't find nobody to answer for the crime. Yeah, he'd blame all kinds of muck on me and my kid brother, until he got a murder rap to stick."

"That may be so, but we didn't come for that," Baltimore argued insistently. Dank raised two mailbags stuffed with bills to signify it was time to depart. "Let it go. We're done here."

"I on't think so," Louis refused. "Teddy was killed in the pen because of that rat bastard getting an eyewitness to lie on him."

"That's it!" Baltimore yelled to everyone involved. "Y'all take the bags and wait outside in the car!" Dank and Henry didn't waste another minute taking the money and exiting the same way they came in, hurriedly. Dank was glad to be out of there, but Henry knew that it wasn't over. If he had to bet on it, Horace wasn't the only one who was going to die that night if Louis kept after it.

"Horace likes to keep a throwaway in his ankle holster so he can plant the spare on a dead body he shoots in self-defense," Louis educated the room. "Ain't that right, *Dee-tective Spivey*?" Suddenly, the detective's eyes grew broad with terror. He was genuinely scared now, and it showed on his face. "Something wrong, you fat, lazy stiff?"

"I thought I recognized your voice," Horace Spivey confessed, to his own detriment. "You're Louis Strong. I put your punk of a little brother, Teddy, away," he spat, trading venom for fear.

Baltimore took a calculated step to the right when he heard the detective's revelation, knowing what the next move would be. "Damn you, Louis!" Baltimore hollered, preparing to do what had to be done.

"What!" Louis fussed, before the hot lead from Baltimore's gun ripped through the detective's skull. Several of the men bolted for cover, hoping they wouldn't be next. "Dammit, man," Louis complained, turning toward the shooter. "You're crazy for croaking a cop. They'll hunt you down like a mad dog."

"Not if my trail ends with you," Baltimore enlightened him, a split second before blowing two giant holes in Louis's chest. Baltimore made sure he took a steady aim so Louis's mother would still have the option of an open-casket funeral for her son. However, he didn't hold the same respect for the detective's family. "Everybody on the floor, and count to a hundred before you move," he ordered to a completely compliant room.

As Baltimore lit out of the hospitality suite, other hotel guests poked their heads out of their rooms after hearing the thunderous blasts. The only thing on Baltimore's mind was getting to Pudge's taxi before something else went awry. He knew the car would be right where it was when he had climbed out of it, unless one of his misfits went left and put a hole in Henry. Baltimore's breathing labored increasingly when he neared the side door leading out into the street. He wasn't into the backseat a full second when he screamed at Pudge. "Move, man! They's coming. Let's get outta here!"

Pudge stared out of the fogged-up window, waiting on Louis to come pouring out of the same door Baltimore had. "Hey, where's Lou?" he shouted, mashing on the gas pedal.

The other men braced themselves for a barrage of gunfire. Baltimore surveyed the car for his two hefty bags of newly acquired currency. It was only after he'd located the mailbags that he thought it necessary to explain about Louis. "That detective he was needling recognized him and called out his name. That old boy had a snub-nose strapped to his leg. I tried to get Lou outta there, but that cop shot him while he was mouthing off. He didn't make it," Baltimore told them, as if he was torn up about it. "But then, neither did that cop."

Henry was correct, after all. Louis was as good as dead the minute he deviated from Baltimore's instructions, allowing personal issues to creep in and corrupt his plot. The mere thought of police catching up with Louis and forcing him to spill the beans on his cronies had compelled Baltimore to ice the trail at the feet of a dead loudmouth, who didn't know when to shut up. Looking back over his shoulder for the next ten years was not a viable option. Unfortunately for Louis "Slow Fuse" Strong, there were no two ways about it, there just weren't.

There wasn't another word uttered between the remaining thieves inside Pudge's taxi as they sloshed through streets of rising water. Just as he'd done previously, Henry hopped from the old Ford in order to open the huge metal garage door at the cottonmill. "Pull it all the way in, Pudge!" he yelled, taking a moment to scan their immediate surroundings. Riddled with mixed emotions, Henry yanked on the looping link chain to lower the garage door afterwards, thinking how close they were to pulling off the perfect crime without a hitch.

Dank rocked back and forth as he stood over the fire he was told to start in the deserted cottonmill's smokestack. "All of a sudden, I caught a chill," he said, to no one in particular.

"Hurrup y'all and get out of those wet clothes before we all catch our death o' cold," Henry ordered harshly.

Baltimore situated himself in front of an elevated concrete slab once used for stacking pallets of cotton headed for northbound freight cars. He nodded his head while dividing the bills into various denominations. "Henry's right. There's nothing like a man getting himself killed and having to deal with a heavy storm to stir your insides. Get off everything tying you to this stickup and toss it into the fire. Oh yeah, and I'ma need those guns back. Henry, Pudge," Baltimore said in a serious manner, "round 'em up so's we can shell out what the fellows are owed." Rot, sunken down to his knees, dry heaved continually after he vomited a second time. Dank, there's a jigger of booze in the glove box. See to it that Rot gets a taste." Dank, assuming Baltimore knew best, trotted to the opposite side of the taxi and retrieved the bottle. Rot stumbled to his feet, used his sleeve to wipe at his mouth, and then bent his elbow until the last drop of hooch was gone.

"That Baltimo' is a good man," Rot swore to everyone as he started to feel better immediately. "Yeah, I'll be right as rain in a tick, right as rain."

With Henry posted behind Dank, Rot, and Pudge, Baltimore felt comfortable about doling out the money as he saw fit. If any of the men objected, there'd soon be one less to figure in and more cash to divvy up among the survivors. "Fellas, Louis didn't come out of this on the right end because he brought it on his self," said Baltimore, as a reminder in case they developed other ideas later on. "The total grab was just about thirty-seven thousand dollars," he said, to a chorus of oohs and ahhs in return.

He took out a small notepad and a pencil chewed down to a nub. "Now, there's four hundred for the use of the uniforms and the guns. The bellman, what clued me in, has three grand coming to him." When Dank opened his mouth to protest, he remembered what happened to Louis for opening his trap at the wrong time. "He deserves it!" Baltimore asserted passionately. "Without him, someone else would have taken down the game. Now that leaves thirty-three grand parted six ways," he said, while computing the long division on the small pad.

"Shouldn't that be parted five ways, considering that 'Slow Fuse' done burn out?" Dank inquired. "On his own behalf, mind you." He threw in that last comment so that he wouldn't come across as heartless.

"Yeah, I'm splitting up his share now," answered Baltimore. "Unless you boys have a problem with me getting half of his take for putting a hole in that fat cop, I'll see to it that y'all share the other half equally." Of course, no one made a sound, despite what they might have been thinking. "Good, then we all agree. Here's $5,590.00 for each of you." None of the men had the slightest problem getting handed enough money to change their lives if they made decent investments. Dank had recently spoken of allocating a portion of his money to open his own barbershop and shoe-shine stand inside of Union Station. The others kept their plans to themselves while marveling at their newly found wealth. Baltimore handed Pudge an additional five hundred for chauffeuring him around town. "Listen up and listen well," said Baltimore, as the dirty deed was officially done, and compensation for it had been paid in full. "The po-lice gon' be on the lookout for

Negros out on a shopping holiday. Lay low for a while, until these automobilers blow town in a few days. If you get snatched, you don't know me or anything about this heist. I'd be willing to give up every thin dime to have you put to sleep before I'd let you turn on me." As the others examined themselves, mentally, Baltimore threw his arm around Rot's shoulder. "Rot, get yourself somewhere and lay down. Have a woman you can trust look after you." The confessed alcoholic promised that he would and then climbed into the taxi along with Dank and Pudge. The longhand watch on Baltimore's wrist read ten minutes until midnight.

Henry was relieved as the meeting came to an end without anyone else doing the sort of thing to bring about their untimely demise. He waved at the taxi as it backed out of the garage for the last time. Afterwards, he took a moment to congratulate his best friend on a job well done, although he held his reservations closely to his vest. "At my best estimation, you came away with over eight grand for yourself. The minute we stepped off that train, you said it would be a lot of money, and you got your share," Henry congratulated, fighting the urge to push Baltimore on discussing what actually went on after he was ordered out of the room. "I guess Louis *had* to die?"

"Had to," was Baltimore's solemn answer. "I'm not the kind to spend my life on the run from the law. That man dug his own grave when alls he had to do was keep quiet." Baltimore let the end of his sentence dangle in the air for Henry to chew on, since he seemed to take issue with doing what had to be done. "Let's get on out of here. It's round about midnight, and we best get back to our alibis at Unca Chunk's."

CHAPTER 12

DON'T EXPLAIN

The deadpan expression Franchetta had worn over the past hour disappeared the moment Baltimore followed Henry into that poorly lit back room at Uncle Chunk's. She leapt into his arms with such fervor that he almost toppled over. "Damn, girl," he said, chuckling heartily. "You act like I've been away to war."

"Ooh, I don't care where you been, Daddy," Franchetta replied. "I'm just glad you made it back to me."

Henry watched the two of them put on quite the spectacle. He suddenly felt out of place. Although he was 100 percent certain that Baltimore hadn't shared where they had been with Franchetta, there was no mistaking it; she knew exactly what he'd been mixed up in. "Don't mind me," Henry joked while they continued carrying on like honeymooners. "My head may be round, but I ain't got to put up with being no third wheel." He opened the door and looked out, expecting to see something that wasn't there. Jazz played loudly from a loaded jukebox, and it was standing room only. Hoards of hipsters drank and danced as if Chunk's hosted the last party on earth. Henry couldn't have imaged the joint any hotter than it was that night, but something was amiss, and that bothered him. "Uh, excuse me, lovebirds," Henry said, clearing his throat as if it was necessary.

Baltimore pulled his lips away from Franchetta's without taking his eyes off hers. "Oh, you still wearing that third wheel around your neck?"

"It appears that way," Henry answered irritably and somewhat out of sorts. "Franchetta, has a fine brown thang come back here asking about me?"

"Uh-uh," she muttered, her mouth pressed against Baltimore's.

"Do you even care that I done misplaced the woman I intend on lying to about settling down?"

"Uhhh-uh," Franchetta moaned sensually.

"Yeah, I figured as much," Henry huffed, setting out with hopes of finding her in the midst of the crowd.

Baltimore held Franchetta tightly around the waist. "Oh, that's one hell of a welcome," he whispered in her ear. "Now that Henry's gone, I want to tell you something. It's about tonight."

"Shhh, hush your mouth, Baltimore. I'm not interested in your dealings that don't factor me in." Franchetta was falling in love all over again, just as she had each time Baltimore fell back into her life. "On the other hand, there's something I should tell you. A man came beating at that door a half hour ago. He was an ugly cuss, clean-headed and mad as hell, too."

Baltimore stood back on his heels, flashing a surprised expression. He didn't want Franchetta to see how concerned he was, but it took some doing to conceal it. "A man, huh? He say who he was?"

"Yeah, and that wasn't all he said, either," she offered, with a long pause, thinking how adorable Baltimore looked stewing in his own juices. "The man left his name and a message. Said to tell that no-account Baltimore Floyd that he was gunning for him, and he'd stop at nothing to defend his wife Macy's honor."

"Macy? Who the hell . . . ?" he started to ask before remembering exactly who that happened to be. "Oh," was the only thing that came out of his mouth before he ended up with egg all over his face. "Franchetta, see now. I could get into that, but I'd have to—"

"Quiet, Daddy. Don't explain," she cut him off, planting another soft peck on his lips. "We been a part of one another since the day I met you. That's all that matters to me, only thing that ever did. Of course, you know what kind of girl I am, 'cause you're the one who helped me to be this way. I have no regrets about that. There's not much could hurt me concerning you and another woman, except if she can get you to say, 'I do'." That must have been what Baltimore wanted to hear, because he couldn't stop grinning. He ushered Franchetta to the doorway, then stopped as a random thought entered his mind. The phone hadn't rung once since he had returned.

"Did the storm knock the line down?"

"Nah, it didn't, but me worrying over you did," she answered him plain and simply as they departed from that funky little room for the very last time.

Throughout the night, Baltimore's gleeful smile was plastered on his handsome face. To cinch his alibi, if he needed one, he made sure that everyone saw him dancing cheek to cheek with the high-yellow woman, who some knew to be a fancy-free working girl, but that didn't make him no never mind, considering he was the one who helped her to be that way.

When the sun came up, Baltimore slipped on the pair of striped boxers lying on the floor next to the bed in Franchetta's room. He stretched and yawned his way into the bathroom. Despite cutting the rug for several hours and having to be escorted out at closing time, he was actually well rested. There appeared to be nothing short of sunshine in his future as he washed up in the sink. He caught himself staring back at a man who seemed to have shaken his bad luck shadow once and for all. His pockets were inflated, and so was his ego. Kansas City had been kind to him over the past four days, and the time had come to say farewell and move on. Baltimore's philosophy had him itching to hit the road again. "Never sit too long in one place," he'd told Henry on more than a few occasions after a pretty girl caught his eye and begged him to stick around. "There's a lot of living to do that won't get done if you're stud'n on planting your feet. Next thing you know, somebody will come along and try to cut you down and use your ass for firewood," he kidded. "Now tell me, is that your idea of living, 'cause it sho' ain't mine."

Speaking of Henry, he hadn't shown up at Franchetta's house, nor had he left word at Baltimore's hotel, where a room key was left in his name. It was assumed that he had tied on a good one, found that fine brown thing he was so in a hurry to locate, and spent the night breaking in the new year on his own schedule.

The thought of sitting down long enough to enjoy their good bit of fortune did have its appeal, so Baltimore's mind started working on sharing some of it. Lena Horne was starring in a double feature with

Harry Belafonte at the Landmark Theater. Since Lena was Henry's idea of the end all, be all in black womanhood, Baltimore would take in a picture show with the girls. Unfortunately for Henry, he'd have to hear about it secondhand later on.

Baltimore climbed out of the taxi, accompanied by four good-looking women. It was an unusual scene, Baltimore and his harem unloading at the box-office window to purchase movie tickets. It felt like old times, when he ran women for a living, having Franchetta on his arm, with Daisy, Chick, and Melvina in tow. Several people, white and black, paused to stare, wondering if that lucky man was a Negro League baseball star or perhaps an entertainer. The snazzy new suit that Franchetta and friends had tailored specially for him earlier that day made Baltimore fit the part exquisitely. After the eight large boxes of popcorn, seven soft drinks, and an armful of candy from the snack stand had been consumed, Franchetta fell asleep, with her head parked on Baltimore's shoulder, during the second feature. The other three women sat up, fully engaged, with their eyes glued to the screen until the final credits rolled. They couldn't say "thank you" enough for the break from their normal routine, nor could they stop yapping about the films they'd seen. It was Lena Horne this and Harry Belafonte that, as if they were children on their first field trip. Baltimore understood how mixing up a normal afternoon every now and then was a treat for ladies, young and otherwise, so he enjoyed it as much as they did. It wasn't so much that he had spent a few dollars to make them happy. They had money of their own. The day was special because a kind man came into their lives and considered them worthy of spending his afternoon with—in public, mind you—while expecting absolutely nothing in return.

Later that same day, Franchetta's jaw dropped when Baltimore sprung the news that he had reserved a table for all of them at the famous hot spot Reno Nights, where musicians traveled from far and wide to knock the walls down with the rhythmic beats and sultry tunes of the era. If there was a place to be when the sun set on Kansas City, it was at the Reno.

"How do you like this mug?" Franchetta said, with a kiss.

"Pinch me. I must be dreaming," Chick teased, smiling from ear to ear. "I have just the thing to step out in. Bought me some glad rags last year, and I've been waiting on something special to show them off."

Melvina slapped her thigh when she got the news. "Baltimore, you're not shining us on, are you?" she gushed and hugged him tightly. When she caught a glimpse of Franchetta clocking that twinkle in her eye, she tried to pass it off as a ruse. "Frannie, I knew you said that first night we shared him was a onetime kinda thing, but I have half a mind to fight you for him."

"Go on and knock each other out!" shouted Chick. "Then I'll take on the winner."

Laughter filled the living room of the pale-colored house until Baltimore noticed how a certain somebody seemed to be toting a sad sack. Daisy hadn't said a word either way regarding a night out on the town. After slipping on his coat, Baltimore winked at Franchetta, then signaled for her to follow his gaze all the way to Daisy's flat expression.

"Daisy Mae, what in the world could be the matter with you?" Franchetta asked her. "Haven't you been listening? We gonna paint this town red tonight. Every one of us deserves to let our hair down, spread our wings, and fly! What could be wrong with that?"

Daisy sat on the divan, leaned back, and began wringing her hands. Sensing that something was plaguing the youngest of the four roommates, her friends gathered around to hear her out. "I didn't want to say nothing about it," she whispered, barely audible and visibly distressed.

"You'd better tell us what's ailing you, chile," Chick demanded, taking the role of protector. Baltimore had learned how the women often counted on one another to get bailed out of jail when busted on prostitution charges. There was even a story circulating about how Chick had taken it upon herself to shoot a man six times for sodomizing Daisy against her will and then sending her to the hospital, all torn up, beaten, and bruised. After the assault, Chick caught wind of a man thumping a young working girl to within an inch of her life and leaving her to rot in a nasty alley. Daisy had a broken jaw, and her mouth was wired shut, but her fingers still worked fine. She scribbled down the man's name and where to find him. Chick located him, delivered him alone to the same alley where he'd accosted Daisy. She enticed him to drop his pants before he knew what she had plotted, and then Chick whipped out a small twenty-five-caliber gun. She blew his crusty, gnarled penis clean off and planned on leaving him like that, but he wouldn't stop screaming and calling her demoralizing names, instead of apologizing for whatever he'd done to bring that kind of karma back to his doorstep. The idiot didn't know when to stop talking his way out of a pine box.

As Baltimore remembered that story, Chick instantly assumed the worst. "If I need to strap on my man upstairs, you know I will," she threatened through clenched teeth.

"No, Chick, it's nothing of the sort," Daisy explained before they all jumped to the wrong conclusion. "It's hard to explain, but I'll try." She sighed hard and stared at her hands, one taking turns comforting the other. "See, it been a long time since I've left home. Rooming with y'all here has been more of a home than I had before Frannie took me in, all broke and worried down to a nub. I won't lessen my joy here by making it seem I could have been welcomed anywhere and fit in just the same," Daisy added, glancing up at Franchetta's caring eyes.

"Chile, if I didn't know better, I'd think you was working your way up to leaving us," Melvina said, hoping she was wrong.

"That's a screwy idea," Chick said in a dismissive tone.

"That's, that's exactly what I was fixing my mind to do," Daisy answered sorrowfully. "I was ready and willing to spend the rest of my life with y'all, but then he came along." She raised her eyes and tossed her gaze on Baltimore.

"Ahh hell," said Franchetta, shaking her head slowly. "I know that look."

"Well, somebody needs to tell me 'cause I don't," Chick panted. She was completely clueless as to what had been building since the very moment they opened the door and saw two strange men standing on the porch with Franchetta.

Melvina cast a roving eye on Franchetta, and toward Baltimore, and then returned it to Daisy. "Ahh hell is right. We done slipped up and let this chile fall in love."

Franchetta reached up on the hat rack behind the door and handed Baltimore the first hat she pulled down. When he tried to complain about it not being his, she shushed him and ushered him out of the door. "This ain't none of your business," she told him. "It might have been your doing, but what Daisy's in there torn up about has to be doctored on by women folk. Believe me, it always ends up this way. We spent centuries picking up the pieces behind men, and it don't appear that's about to change now."

"Well, when can I come back?" Baltimore asked, with both hands tucked in his front trouser pockets.

"Yeah, show up around seven or so. We'll do our best to undo what you did to her, although can't nobody fix what you done to me, so it's likely not gonna work on her, either."

As Baltimore backed off the porch, contemplating women and love, he shrugged his shoulders and frowned. "I'm sorry, Faye," he offered, when nothing better came forth. "I didn't mean to hurt her."

"If that's what you think you did, Baltimore, it's just one more reason for Daisy to want herself a man like you." Franchetta felt the wind kick. She folded both arms and held herself tightly. "You big dope. Get off my lawn before you have my nosy, upstanding, church-going neighbor ladies ready to pack up and move on, too. Don't know what I'ma do with you."

"Hold me tight like your bottom dollar, and cry for me when I'm gone," Baltimore suggested, as if she didn't know that song by heart.

Franchetta went back inside to help deprogram Daisy, but it was no use. Baltimore had reminded Daisy that she was a twenty-one-year-old who had a lot to offer a man, although she wouldn't be able to keep a good one on a leash when it came down to it because of her profession. She knew that whores had everything and nothing a man wanted, both at the same time. And, for the first time in her life, Daisy believed she was good enough to fall in love and have that man love her back. It just so happened that the way Baltimore made Franchetta feel had rubbed off on her somehow, and she liked the way it felt. For Daisy, the world wasn't depriving her any longer. It was she who had neglected to strike out and see what it had to offer, as an adult. In essence, Baltimore's arrival had ripped off the veil she'd used to cover her shame from childhood. Now she felt liberated and couldn't wait to live on the other side of that veil. Daisy couldn't wait to be loved like a woman was supposed to be.

CHAPTER 13

IN THE ROUGH

Baltimore had walked four blocks before an empty taxi rolled by to carry him from place to place. He didn't know where to search for Henry, so he leaned against the backseat and told the man to drive. The first place he checked was Abel's Diner. The cabbie waited outside while he stepped in to investigate. As soon as Baltimore hit the door, there stood Hattie on her meaty legs. She hosted a mean leer to stare him down. He hadn't insulted her, not to her face at least, so the crooked demeanor she put on was lost on him.

"Hey, Hattie, how you been?" Baltimore asked apprehensively, behind his best manufactured grin.

"Oomph, I was a whole lot better before that lech'rous friend of yo'n come creeping up my skirt," she answered, too loud, in fact, to be on the job.

"Is that so?" Baltimore grunted, not caring one way or the nother if it was.

"Hell, yeah, it is," she hissed. "He ain't been around since the day before yesterday, and the no account stood me up last night. Had me wash my hair and set out my new dress, and for what? Ooh, I can't stand that lying scoundrel."

Baltimore nodded his head like an empathetic friend who felt her disappointment down to his toes. "Sorry to hear that, Hattie. If you happen to see him, tell him I'm out and about on his heels."

"You know what you can tell him for me?" she quipped rudely.

"I know," he answered quickly. "I have him to call you."

"Would you please, Baltimo'? Tell him to ring my phone right away," she begged, all pretenses aside. "I think we had a good thing going."

"I know, Hattie," Baltimore replied as he hit the door, "I know." He was embarrassed for her, but it wasn't anything he hadn't seen before. A woman nursing a love jones for a man who was finished with her was as prevalent as the common cold and just as difficult to get over.

At 5:17, Baltimore paid his fare and tipped the man. Uncle Chunk's wasn't due to get busy for another two hours, and that made it a good time to settle up with the owner for his hospitality. The front door was unlocked, so Baltimore didn't bother to knock. In the time it took his eyes to adjust from the sunlight to a darkened den and low florescent bulbs, a chunky mountain of a man appeared out of nowhere, wearing three yards of fabric tailored into a giant pair of dress slacks. Baltimore lurched backward when the big man raised his hand to scratch at his vastly receded hairline.

"Man, look at you all jumpy. Musta got hold to some good reefer," Uncle Chunk teased. He knew that Baltimore never drank or smoked, because he felt the vices he did surrender to kept him busy enough already.

"Unca, how's tricks?" Baltimore offered, rubbing his eyes. "You behind on your light bill?"

"Ha-ha, if I had a dollar for every time I heard that lame ass joke . . . I got a good one for you, though," Chunk said, as if it were a proposal as opposed to a riddle. "What do you call a fool with three hands in his pockets?"

Baltimore's gaze drifted toward the floor, as if the answer might have been written down there. "That's a stopper, alright. Three hands, huh?"

"Yeah, two of his own and one of hers," the older man added, assuming the sad truth would slap Baltimore across the head. When it didn't happen fast enough, the proprietor nudged him over the edge. "I'd call it a sucker named Henry."

Baltimore's eyes met with Chunk's dingy peepers. He reared back, objecting to what he heard. "Don't tell me you mean Henry's gotten himself latched to a barracuda?"

"You ain't no genius, but I will give you credit for your timing.

Daddy Warbucks is still back yonder, with a lady's arm shoved so far down his pants, you'd think it sprouted a root." While Baltimore contemplated the most courteous approach to attack his best friend's desperate situation, Chunk's belly started jiggling up and down.

"This ain't no laughing matter," Baltimore asserted.

"I'm laughing at you 'cause yours ain't no better. A fella who goes by the name of Tipton came flying through here with his face all twisted up. Said how he was gonna get even with you for dipping into his honeypot," Chunk informed him, delighting greatly in doing so. "Oh yeah. He was foaming at the mouth and making a big deal about ripping your head off and pissing down your neck . . . or something like that," the wily old troublemaker added, to fan the flame.

"I ain't had the pleasure of meeting him yet, but I sho' am dog tired of him running my name down in the street," said Baltimore, seething with disgust. He was beginning to foam up as well. "This Tipton, what can you tell me about the man, other than his flavor for slapping his woman around?"

"Not much more than his rep for being a hothead at times, his weakness for gambling, and a burning in his gut to kick yo' ass." Uncle Chunk was laughing and jiggling again, although this time it wasn't any funnier than the last time.

"Here. Take this before I up and change my mind," Baltimore warned. He slapped three hundred dollars smack in the middle of Chunk's grubby palm.

"Whuuut? If I'da known you was willing to pay me for poking fun at you, I would've been insult'n you from scratch." Chuck looked at the money suspiciously and then eased it into his deep front pocket. "I don't wanna know what you had cooking in that back room if this here amounts to some of the crumbs. Henry's been tossing around bread all day long, and now you come in with your own bakery, too."

"I'm just saying thanks for the use of your phone line. You did right by helping me, and I appreciate that. Now I need to do the same for the three-handed man."

"And, what if he ain't in the mood for accepting your idea of help?" the wise sage countered, with a raised brow.

"He don't have a choice," was Baltimore's answer, set in stone.

Near the rear exit, Henry lay across a pool table, with his pants unfastened at the waist. Baltimore heard him giggling up a storm, but he wasn't in the least bit amused. The suit Henry sported was a shiny

green, satin three piece, with matching spats over his newly acquired
dark-colored alligator shoes. Baltimore watched a woman's behind
wiggle back and forth, but he couldn't see her face, because it was
pressed against Henry's bare chest. And though Baltimore couldn't
say for sure, the vast assortment of department store boxes piled on
the nearby table affirmed his concerns.

"Henry Taylor, get your thick head off of that billiard table so I can
talk to you!" Baltimore shouted like a man who had thrown both
courtesy and caution to the wind. When his voice bounced off the
walls, Henry snapped his head up and guided the woman away from
him.

"Move now!" Henry growled. "Go on. Git! That's the pal I been
telling you about. Hi ya there, Baltimo'. I've been meaning to look
you up. Got busy, though, picking up some extras," he explained further, with a broad wave of his hand to show off his wares.

Apprising the number of boxes heaped on one another, Baltimore
was getting beside himself with anger. "Henry, don't make me ask you
twice. I need to know every place you been and who you been flashing your money to."

"Ain't that a rip," Henry's fine brown frame spoke out on his behalf. "He's a grown man and don't have to answer to you."

Henry staggered off of the table and gathered his long-sleeve shirt
from the lamp shade in an effort to make himself look presentable.
"Shuddup, Estelle!" he barked loudly. "Can't you see my friend is calling hisself, seeing after me?"

"You can't tell me to shuuudup!" she spat back. "Just 'cause you
bought me a fur coat don't mean you can lead me around by the
nose."

"Not a fur coat, too?" Baltimore thought aloud. "Henry, are you trying to get us pinched? I told everybody, including you, to lay low and
go easy on wide-open spending." After his speech about drawing
undue attention, Baltimore had expected to be on a northbound
train before one of the boys made such a potentially grave mistake.
"Do you still have my gun?" he asked impatiently. "I'm thinking of
shooting myself right here on the spot."

"Uh-huh, I still got it," Henry confirmed, staring blankly at
Baltimore. "You want it now?"

"Hell, yeah, I want it now, before you do something really dumb
and have me coming after you. Henry, what were you thinking? Okay,

you couldn't have been thinking, or you wouldn't have done what I said not to do." Suddenly, a crisp chill brushed against the nape of Baltimore's neck.

"Which one of you is Baltimore Floyd?" a gruff voice fired from Baltimore's left side.

"That depends on who's asking," Henry said rather soberly.

"So you're the low-down snake who's been sneaking around with my wife," Tipton griped in Henry's direction, assuming he was the culprit, after speaking up.

Uncle Chunk pulled up a chair, with a tall can of beer and a bowl of popcorn. Baltimore had watched the previews from the sidelines long enough. "Nah, that ain't the man you're looking for," he corrected Tipton, guessing the visitor had a weapon with him. "I'm Baltimore, but me and Macy, see, we didn't do no sneakin'. We did our business out in the open." He purposely goaded her husband, noting his immediate reaction.

Tipton reached under his jacket and came out with a long saw-toothed knife with a bone handle. He held it up and assumed a fighting posture. "Let's see how you feel with this blade stuck down that big mouth of yours," he threatened.

"Probably about the same as Macy did when I had my peter stuffed down hers," Baltimore growled to hurry the party along. "She couldn't say nothing, you know, but I could tell she liked it 'cause I had to make her climb off so's I could get a nap."

Henry motioned for Estelle to head over to the other side out of danger, with Uncle Chunk. She complied but kept a close eye, without even blinking once. "Baltimo', remember I still got that rod you lent me," Henry said calmly as Tipton began moving in on his prey.

Baltimore backed closer to the pool table. "No, I'll handle this like a gentleman," he objected. "Hey, Tipton, I've done some asking around about you. People say you're quite the duke with a pool cue." When the knife-toting menace hesitated over being complimented, Baltimore knew how to get what he wanted without shooting him. "Say you're a bad loser, too."

Step for step, Tipton circled the pool table, behind Baltimore. They were two men involved in a life-sized chess game. "I don't know of any man who cottons to losing, but what's that got to do with me slicing off both of yo' ears?"

Tension mounted as Baltimore allowed Tipton to draw nearer.

"Nothing really. It's just that I've got five thousand dollars, and I'm willing to play you a game of eight ball for Macy, but no bitchin' when you lose your woman to me." Baltimore had previously baited another man into a game he couldn't win and ridiculed him afterwards, when his initial goal was killing him in self-defense.

Henry knew about it and didn't want to see this one played out the same way. "Why on't you go on ahead and kill him now, Baltimo'!" he urged riotously. "Ain't no sense in fleecing this fella out of his wife beforehand. Plus, I need to get me something to eat, and I can't do that while you's in here fooling around with him."

Tipton took his eyes off Baltimore to glare at the drunk making outrageous comments. "Fleece who? I'll take this chump's money, then carve my name in that pretty face of his."

A scream rang out when Baltimore came crashing down on Tipton's arm with the heavy end of a pool stick. Estelle covered her eyes and hid her face when a bone popped out of Tipton's wrist. "Told you she was skittish, Henry," Baltimore grumbled as he kicked Tipton's knife to the far side of the room. "Get me that claw hammer you took from over at Franchetta's," he demanded. "I've been waiting on you to find me Tipton so's I can teach you what oughta happen to men who likes to hurt women."

Henry returned quickly and waved the business end of the hammer to Baltimore. Tipton groveled on his knees, groaning and trying to push the fractured bone back into place as blood poured from the open wound. Uncle Chunk looked on attentively, chugging on his cold beer.

"Help me. I need a doctor!" Tipton bawled hysterically.

"Nah, you're gonna need more than that," Baltimore replied sullenly. "You need a lesson in keeping your paws off of women, and I'ma help you with that." He cocked his leg and rammed his shoe into Tipton's stomach. When the man rolled over, clutching at his belly, Baltimore held his good hand against the cement floor with his knee. Tipton wet his pants after the hammer smashed his outstretched fingers. A long stream of saliva poured from his lips while he hollered frantically.

"Shuddup!" shouted Henry. "Shuddup. It hurts my empty stomach to hear a man scream like that. Hit him again, Baltimo'. Maybe that'll quiet 'im some." The hammer found its mark a second time amid bloodcurdling shrieks.

"Make him stop!" Estelle panted, as if she was about to vomit.

"Why on't you waltz over there with your new fur coat and make him stop yourself?" Chunk answered, belching crassly after making his declaration.

Baltimore was face-to-face with Tipton. "You get outta here, and if I ever hear of you running my name down in the streets or learn that you've gone back to taking up slapping on Macy, I won't be so nice the next time."

Tipton stumbled mightily to his feet just as a loud shotgun blast exploded. He grimaced, bugged his eyes, and fell on the floor. Baltimore wore the same expression on his face when he looked at the smoking barrel in Uncle Chunk's hand.

"What'd you go and do that for, Chunk?" Baltimore asked, still somewhat shocked.

"I couldn't let him get out and tell people what happened to him here," the owner replied rather casually. "I run a respectable joint. Besides, you give me three hundred dollars. He didn't. Now I've got to call my nephew to run by and pick him up. Lock the front door, Henry, so we can clean up this mess. Estelle, you and me need to talk." The room was spinning as Chunk laid out how important it was that she forget what she'd seen, or the same just might happen to her. She cried until her eyes darn near puffed shut, but she came to make peace with it all eventually. A second fur coat helped out tremendously.

Within the hour, all signs of a struggle and the subsequent murder had vanished. Uncle Chunk's was open for business, Henry was off to dinner with Estelle, and Baltimore headed on about his way, thinking about Franchetta's and hoping that she'd had better luck with Daisy than he'd had with Tipton.

CHAPTER 14

THE DEVIL HIS DUE

Baltimore had already made up his mind to leave town first thing in the morning when he returned to the hotel room he shared with Macy. Tipton's mistake of showing up to Uncle Chunk's, barking like he was going to take on the world, had Baltimore sitting on the edge of that pull-down bed, wondering how the idiot could have been so dumb in the way he went about it. Tipton should have realized that a man with friends had the decided edge before he set foot inside the dimly lit barroom. Unfortunately, he only got the one chance to be so stupid.

It wasn't long before the hot water in the shower ran out, so Baltimore shut it off and snatched a clean towel from the metal rack in the bathroom. While shaving, he stared at his reflection in the dirty mirror and smiled. It was hard not to with nearly eighty-one hundred dollars safely hidden in a coffee can, placed inside the hole he'd cut into the floor of his closet. If he took his time spending it, there just might be a dollar or two left when the spring baseball season started three months later, Baltimore thought to himself. Then he began to chuckle because he knew better than that. He stood more of a chance becoming the governor than holding on to that kinda of money. "Yeah, I'ma get me a brand new coupe, wide whitewall tires, and a stereo to beat the band," he said aloud. "Hell, maybe I'll buy me two," he snickered, "one to drive slow and the other for going real fast."

His spirits couldn't have been riding any higher. As far as he could recollect, there were no other jealous husbands after him, and the colored policemen's association was in an uproar behind some rogue white cop getting killed while trying to stop a robbery. That's how the established newspapers spun the story, anyway, and the whole community was talking about. The papers were investigating Negro officers because of the outfits the bandits wore. It was sheer genius to have everyone looking for dirty colored cops who didn't exist. There had been an article written that identified the slain gunman as a career criminal by the name of Louis Strong, originally from Springfield, Missouri, but the other details were sketchy. Sketchy was just fine with Baltimore. He couldn't have been luckier, although he was prepared to take all of the credit for the way it turned out. As far as he was concerned, the only thing standing between him and Henry getting on down the road was the night of fun and frolicking he'd planned to reward himself with.

Once he'd gotten dressed in that dark pin-striped suit and shiny gold-toned shirt, with a matching necktie and pocket kerchief, that Rascal had made him a great deal on, Baltimore hailed a cab and set out to pick up all four of his dates.

Franchetta was patting on a smidge of light-colored foundation in front of her vanity mirror when someone rapped on the front door. "Melvina, Chick!" she yelled. "Somebody's knocking!"

Chick sipped brandy from a cocktail glass as she made her way out of the kitchen, wearing an enchanting off-the-shoulder number, powder blue down past her knees. "I'm seeing to it now!" she replied at full volume. "You could've gotten it yourself, you know. Other folks got things they want to take their time doing, too," Chick muttered under her breath as she moved the window curtain aside with the back of her hand. "Like this here, for instance," she cooed quietly after discovering it was Baltimore at the door.

Melvina came down the stairs in a red sleeveless dress, formfitting but tastefully designed. "Is that him?" she asked while clipping on a set of dazzling fake ruby earrings to complete her ensemble.

Shortly after opening the door, Chick blushed at the way Baltimore leered at her approvingly. "Uhhh-huh, it's him alright," she answered seductively. "It's him, straight up and down."

"Wow, Chick, get a load of you," Baltimore complimented.

Melvina stepped beside her roomie to see what had softened her around the edges. When her eyes locked on his, her jaw dropped, too. "Yeah, it's him," she mumbled, as if he hadn't been consistently handsome the other times she'd seen him.

Baltimore winked, reading her mind. "Hot damn, Melvina. You look good enough to dream about, but I can't take you glowing at me that way. It might give me the wrong idea."

"That'll do Melvina fine because she ain't got nothing but wrong on her mind," Franchetta presumed correctly as she zipped Melvina's dress up in the back. "Somebody needs to go on and invite the man inside so we can flirt with him some more."

Chick grinned and took Baltimore by the hand. "By all means then, do come in."

"If I didn't know better, I'd think you girls were up to something," he said, making an assessment of the unusual attention being heaped on him.

"You'd better watch yourself, slick. They went out and bought up damn near all the peanut butter in town," Franchetta teased. "Now I see why. You do clean up nicely."

"I can't say enough about you ladies. And, Franchetta, I swear 'fore God that Lena Horne can't hold a candle to you in that gown," Baltimore added, praising Franchetta's movie-star appearance in the black embroidered dress, with spaghetti straps and beaded detail, designed in an attractive beige pattern.

Narrowing his eyes, Baltimore glanced up at the ceiling. "Hold up. Somebody's missing. Where's Li'l Miss Daisy Mae?"

Chick went back to sipping from her glass when she decided to let Franchetta tackle that one. Melvina sat on the divan, adjusting the small rectangular buckles on her sling-back pumps. A hush fell over the living room until Franchetta picked up on the others' reluctance to speak on the subject. "Well, Baltimore, a young girl like Daisy is still impressionable at times. She was a tinge mixed up about matters of the heart, so we, I convinced her that she needed some time to herself, you know, to clear her head," she asserted, with an evil eye, daring the other ladies to utter a single word. "These two chickadees, who're wise to dummy up now," Franchetta said flatly, "well, they didn't necessarily agree about me sending Daisy to the hairdresser for some private pampering while the rest of us got all gussied up to step out and howl."

Chick smacked her lips in objection. "I only meant that Daisy could start getting her head right tomorrow morning, is all, after she's had the chance to spin her wheels."

"What do you know from spinning wheels? The last time you had your hair let down, your mama was pressing it over a hot kitchen stove," snapped Franchetta.

"At least I know my mama," Chick fired back.

"Frannie knows her mama, too," Melvina chimed in. "It's her papa, she ain't too clear on."

Seeing where their friendly sniping session was headed, Baltimore played the diplomat, quickly reining it in before it got out of hand. "Whoa, whoa, maybe we ought to get a jump on the chow line. They don't like holding reservations past the sitting time. Anyhow, Roscoe 'Gatemouth' McSwain is in town from Texas with his boys. That's guaranteed to pack the house." After his cordial effort at maintaining order, a slight calm came over the room. Melvina smiled like she had something else to say but didn't. However, Franchetta did, on the sly.

"Yo' daddy is only the man yo' mama claims to be the papa," she said, sneering behind Chick's back. "I heard tell, you favor the milk-man."

"Heffa!" Chick yelled, pointing her finger so there'd be no misunderstanding who she was insulting.

"Nag!" Franchetta spat back.

"Heyyy-hey!" Baltimore intervened. "I'm not putting up with this all night. Either y'all can stay here and act a trifling mess or come on out with me to the jazziest spot in all of Kaycee. Me for one, I'm hungry, and I got the car waiting outside for anybody else who wants to ball on champagne and chitlins."

"Let me get my bag then," Melvina squealed with delight. "I ain't had no Southern cooking in a good while."

"You can have all the slave food you want. I'll dine on some of them steaks I've been hearing about," Chick said, wrestling on her overcoat. Prepared to hit the door, she found Franchetta hovering over the perfume collection in her bedroom. "Well, you heard 'em. We's going out to feast on slave vittles, so is you coming or is you ain't?" she queried playfully.

"Since you put it like that, I is," Franchetta cackled. "Let me get my coat."

Long after Franchetta had gotten her coat and joined the party inside of a warm taxi, she enjoyed the way people at the extravagant

Reno Nights club fussed over them while escorting the entourage past the long line waiting to be let in and all the way up to a ringside table next to the bandstand. Franchetta couldn't help but feel a little distracted about dissuading Daisy from joining them, although it had seemed like the right thing to do at the time. The girls were right about working on Daisy's bright ideas concerning love at a later date. The empty seat, between Chick's and Melvina's, should have been filled with their youngest protégé. By morning Baltimore would be glad it wasn't.

The evening was electric. Dinner was served as the house band played soft and sultry tunes to serenade the jam-packed dinner club. Couples mingled at tables built for two, and larger parties, like Baltimore's, passed stories among themselves as candlelit centerpieces overheard each one of them. It was a night of wine, women, and song. Baltimore glanced at the doorway every so often, expecting Henry to shake that new chippie of his and hang out with people who really gave two cents about his well-being. By the time the real entertainment was introduced to the audience, all hopes of Henry's late arrival seemed wasteful, so Baltimore sat back, watched the girls enjoying themselves, and tried to talk himself into doing likewise.

A slick-dressed announcer grabbed the spotlight and the microphone. He straightened his black tuxedo jacket and belted out his welcome. "Good evening, ladies and gents. We always like to start the festivities out by thanking you for dining with us and sharing in a good time here at Reno Nights, the jewel of Kansas City, Missurah. Now put your hands together for a true country boy making out nice in the big cities of our great land. All the way from Dallas to jurn us, please welcome Mistah Roscoe 'Gatemouth' McSwain." To thunderous applause, a middle-aged man attired in a purple crushed-velvet dinner jacket and black slacks, with a strip of purple running down the side of each pant leg, stood up from the piano without interrupting the arrangement going on between his fingers and the piano keys.

When the light brown musician smiled, his teeth seemed to be spread out an inch apart. Chick grinned brightly, thinking how his nickname served him right. Baltimore wondered if the famous entertainer remembered meeting him one blistering summer in Texas.

"I used to know that cool cat," he told Franchetta. She didn't dare doubt his words, but Chick was the wiser.

"Go on, Baltimore," Chick said, with a hint of uncertainty in her voice. "You've been around, I'll grant you that, but I think you're shining us." Before Baltimore could plead his case, the piano player that people stood out in the cold to see fell into a slow, rhythmic tune that hushed the crowd.

"Looks like there'll be a hot time in the old town tonight," said Gatemouth, with his patented buttery-smooth pitch. "I just got here on the five o'clock train, but I'm feeling mighty at home. I've been told there's some of Kaycee's very own Negro League champi'ns done made it in to join us. Let's give a hand for Satchel Paige and Ernie Banks, my homeboy from the Lone Star State. Congratulations, Monarchs." Applause rang out as two of the men from the table next to Baltimore's stood and waved. "Now, before I go any further, Im'a do something I haven't been blessed to do in a very long time, and that's saying hello to the youngest old soul I ever met. He probably don't recall the day he saved my life when a snaggletoothed rattlesnake jumped up and bit me while I was helping myself in another man's watermelon patch. I'm forever beholding to him . . . 'cause he sucked the poison out when he could have left me for dead. Now I won't tell you where that old snake nipped me, though. It might embarrass the fella I'm about to introduce. Oh yeah, there's one other thing that bonds us together. Listen up 'cause it's a testimony. Now, I haven't shared what I know about *him* and my brother's wife, and that makes him lucky."

That loaded statement caused laughter to fill the air as he continued. "But, he does know about *me* and my brother's wife, kept it quiet, too, and that makes him my friend." Franchetta looked at her man, fidgeting uncomfortably with his hands. She shook her head at the improvability of it all as the music played on. "He's a man up to his old tricks and, by the looks of it, some new ones, too," Gatemouth said compassionately. "Please show your love for Mistah Baltimore Floyd, ladies and gentlemen."

Melvina's eyes widened as she turned toward Baltimore to express her surprise. Chick puckered her lips, wishing she could have taken back what she'd said earlier about not believing him. "Well, you gonna stand up and let these people get a look at you or not?" Chick prodded gleefully. Baltimore didn't mind being acknowledged among great Negro ballplayers, but that was as far as he wanted it to go. Gatemouth, he had other ideas altogether.

"Baltimore, come on up and help me out with this. I need me a cigarette. You know I don't like to stop once I get started."

"Go 'head on, Daddy," Franchetta insisted when it appeared Baltimore wouldn't budge. "You can't let that man down. He's famous."

The audience cheered as Baltimore approached the stage. He took a subtle bow, and then he took a seat at the piano, next to Gatemouth, who quickly stood up and pointed to his behind, signaling exactly where the snake had dug in. "Sorry, Baltimore, but they wanted to know," he apologized halfheartedly. In turn, Baltimore played along, wiping both lips on the sleeve of his suit coat, as if he were still trying to get the taste out of his mouth. "'Guess I should've washed it first," Gatemouth jested before hugging Baltimore with his free hand. "Now he's goin' to play for you nice people while I have myself a drag." The older man slid off the piano stool before his accompaniment was ready. Baltimore's first note fell flat, so he grimaced while Gatemouth poked fun at him. After he'd found his key, Baltimore sat in on two duets at the entertainer's behest. By the end of the night, Baltimore had considerably more admirers than the three he'd brought with him.

Chick must have told him how foolish she felt a half-dozen times during the cab ride home. Franchetta marveled at how a man who never believed in practicing the piano could've hopped up there at a moment's notice and ripped off one musical number after another without missing a beat, not counting that first one he stumbled over miserably. Baltimore tried to shrug off all of the attention, but there was no use. He had three very captivated ladies in his company, none of whom was ready to stop talking about it. And, if a strange noise at the front door hadn't broken up their merriment, it would have continued for hours.

"You should have seen the look on your face when the man called you up to bang on that piano with him," Melvina recounted joyously. "I thought you was gon' die!"

"What you mean? I was as cool as a cucumber," argued Baltimore, holding out his hands and making them tremble wildly to get a bigger laugh. "Well, I was more settled then."

"Wait. Did y'all hear something?" Chick uttered nervously, staring in the direction where she'd heard the noise. Baltimore reached inside his jacket and pulled out the revolver he'd taken off the man on the train.

"Shhh," he cautioned them, slowly walking over to the door. "I'll check it out." As he lifted his hand to brush back the window curtain, just as Chick had when he'd arrived to fetch them that evening, the door opened. Baltimore cocked the pistol, pointed it, and prepared to fire. Daisy strolled in, sobbing silently. Tears streamed down her cheeks. Baltimore put his gun away and held her around the shoulders. He peeked out into the yard, concerned about what might have happened to her.

"She's ice cold," said Melvina, after ushering Daisy inside like a person who'd lost their grip.

"Ohh, poor thing," Franchetta whined, with a blanket in hand. "Daisy, take your time, but we need to know what's got you quivering like this."

"Did somebody hurt you?" Chick asked hurriedly. That question seemed to bring Daisy out of her catatonic state. She shook her head faintly, then turned her saddened eyes on Baltimore.

"Your friend Henry," she said in a haunting tone. "Your friend, they got him."

CHAPTER 15

IF NEEDS BE

Franchetta's heart began to flip-flop inside her chest. She understood the bond between Baltimore and Henry, his closest friend. Somebody was going to die behind this. Maybe even the wrong somebody. Franchetta got up and retreated to her bedroom and closed the door before Baltimore asked the million-dollar question. Chick and Melvina sought to comfort Daisy, but neither of them had any idea what to say to Baltimore as their eyes darted back and forth to one another.

He cleared his throat to choke back the knot swelling in it. "Hhh-huh, who's got him?" he asked carefully, avoiding eye contact. Daisy's words were running laps in his head. "You said *they* got him. Who?"

"Some fellas over at the Crest Mont Hotel, gangster types with the ones you and him robbed." Daisy was wringing her hands again, although this time she worked at massaging away her sadness for Baltimore instead. "That's not all," she said as a solemn afterthought. "They beat him real bad, too. Say they gonna kill him unless the niggahs who clipped 'em brings all their money back." Daisy went on to tell them how she came about this valuable information. Moments after Franchetta had told her there was more to life than the birds and bees, much more, Daisy had agreed that a hair appointment might serve her well, especially if she was going to catch the morning train to Chicago, like she intended. "See, I was sitting here, on this very spot, trying to decided whether I was gonna grab a hot plate downtown or go straight over to Brenda's for a wash and set," Daisy recalled rather coolly, considering the circumstances. "I wasn't that hungry, so I went directly to the beauty shop. The minute I sat down, two big thugs come in asking Brenda if she'd heard anything about a big poker game getting knocked over. Said they was colored policemen and wanted to turn the whole gang over to these white boys to prove they had nothing to do with it. When they didn't think I was listening, they started popping off about already finding one of 'em with this floozy in a new fur coat and a load of fancy rags. Well, I didn't think much of it until one of the cops mentioned how they haven't made Henry talk yet, but they would break him before long."

Baltimore later learned that Henry had been cocked up in the best suite of a ritzy colored hotel and he had gotten pinched when that new woman of his sent him out for some neck bones and red crème soda. It seems that Henry was showing off an expensive ring that only the white motor assemblymen's members wore, and that was what tipped them off he might have been involved. If Baltimore had known about the dim-witted decision to keep Darby Kent's ring, he would have cut it out of Henry's hand to elude enduring his bad luck shadow's dismal shade.

Baltimore was mad at himself because he didn't see this coming. Conversely, he did recognize the black cop's ploy of sprinkling gossip in the community and hoping to trick Henry's pals into trying to come and break him out. What Daisy thought she overheard was simply bait, but what they hadn't counted on was encountering something too treacherous to pull into their boat.

Eventually, Daisy's tears ceased flowing. Like a small child, she peered up at Baltimore and chose her words before speaking. "Uh . . . you're not stud'n on tangling with them are you? I mean, they could kill you both."

"Yeah," Baltimore agreed. His labored expression was stiff and stern. "But, that don't change a thing, Daisy. Friends is friends. I couldn't roll over on Henry even if I wanted to." He cast a fleeting glance at Franchetta's bedroom door, then grabbed his hat and coat. "Please tell Franchetta Faye good-bye for me. I reckon she can do without hearing that from me. I'm grateful to the three of y'all for taking me in when you didn't know me from Adam. That says a lot." Baltimore didn't stand still long enough to watch them fall apart over how thankful they were for his generosity. He eased on his coat, held the felt hat in his hand, and disappeared into the darkness much like he'd appeared, with a cloud of uncertainty surrounding him.

There were three hours left until the sun came up. Baltimore used all of them to diminish his anxiety. He walked mile after mile until reaching the hotel he'd paid for a week in advance, concerned about being too broke to rent it from day to day when he checked in. Now that the current situation had him firmly by the neck, running short on cash was the least of his worries. The empty room greeted him as the morning sun peeked in through the gap between the curtains. Baltimore drew them closed and peeled off every stitch of clothing he had on. Climbing into bed alone in a strange place always made him yearn for a decent life and family. In a few hours, he'd awaken with a knot in his stomach and a desire to sacrifice ever having either of them.

At nine o'clock, a housekeeper tapped at his door, asking if he needed any new towels. Baltimore stirred, rolled over, and then mumbled "no thanks" toward the door. The maid must have heard him, because she went away without making a further disturbance. Moments later, he yawned and asked himself if it was a good day to die. With a coffee can full of cash tucked away in the closet, he didn't come up with the answer that lent itself to braving a dangerous trap. Baltimore realized he needed to do something that facilitated him coming up with the right answer as he sat up on the side of the queen-size bed, with his bare feet resting on the unkept hardwood floor. "It just don't seem right to check out with that kind of money on hand," he reasoned with himself aloud. After wiggling his toes against the dusty wood beneath them, he decided on a remedy he could live with, or die with, for that matter. "I need to lighten my load," he said assuredly. "Yeah, I got a way to fix that."

Baltimore washed his face, ran a toothbrush through his mouth, and gargled. He didn't bother shaving, though, deciding that the undertaker should earn his funeral fee, if it came to that. After scribbling notes to remind himself of important things that needed to be done, he folded the small sheet of paper in half. A list of places, people, and things lined the page as he shoved it down the back pocket of his dark brown casual trousers. He exited that tiny rented room pretty much the way he'd found it, except for the hole he'd carved to hide his stash in, of course.

With a bundle containing all of his worldly belongings gathered beneath his arm, Baltimore made his first stop along the route to impending perdition. His smile evened out as he passed through the door at Abel's. Macy had seen him when he entered. She was determined to prevent Baltimore from catching a glimpse of her split lip and blackened eye, so she hightailed it to the rear of the restaurant.

Macy ducked into the kitchen, tapping her shoe pensively and praying he didn't see her attempt at eluding him. When she assumed he had gone on, she jutted her head out slowly, only to find Baltimore waiting on the other side of the wall she'd found herself hiding behind.

"By the looks of it, you're not in too big a hurry to see me," he said, knowing she would rather not answer him. "I figured you and Tipton had another tussle when word got out he'd been pacing the streets to get at me. Well, that's what I wanted to tell you." Baltimore was leaning back against the wall, painted a dingy shade of white by someone who'd obviously gotten paid in advance by the looks of the end result. He felt sorry for Macy, and the way she'd turned out, too, as she kept her bruised face from his.

"Something told me, you'd show up," she said eventually, using slow, deliberate words. "And I can't, for the life of me, understand why you'd want to."

Baltimore chuckled, knowing that her self esteem had been kicked and stomped on for years. He was glad then because her life had already begun a metamorphosis before he'd had the opportunity to explain just how that was supposed to happen. "Funny thing about understanding," he offered, "it all finds a way of clearing itself up sooner or later. I came by to tell you I was moving on, and that Tipton caught up to me yesterday." Macy's eyes bucked as fear brushed over them.

"Humph, he got a powerful temper. Did he hurt you?" she asked, roaming his body with her eyes, checking for signs of trauma.

"Nah, we had a sit-down, a pow wow, like injuns, and talked about things like gentlemens," he told her, although she knew that couldn't possibly have been true.

"Uh-uh, Tipton ain't one for pow wowing. He would just assume die first before wasting words after what he beat out of me about you," Macy said, before rubbing the scab on her lip. "But you don't have not one mark on your face," she marveled.

"Told you, we had a sit-down, a meetin' of the minds. He told me how sorry he was for doing that to your face, and he didn't feel right about showing his around here again because of it." Macy flashed a "who you trying to fool" expression back at him, with her arms folded. "Yeah, that's not all." Baltimore reeled off a number of bills from a thick roll he'd brought out of his pocket. "Here's the five hundred he wanted me to give you. Said to tell you he ain't never coming back, so you don't have to worry about that." Moisture began to gather in the wells of Macy's eyes. "Come on now. Don't tell me you're sad he's gone?"

"Shoot, naw, Baltimore. It's just that I don't know what to do first, now that I'm sure he's dead," Macy confessed. "There ain't no way in hell Tipton ever seen that much money at one time, and he wouldn't part with it if he did." She accepted the money just the same because Baltimore was still holding it out there like a handshake and she'd have to be a fool to refuse it. "Is he, is there gon' be cause for a funeral?" she asked, as if it mattered. Baltimore lowered his eyes and shook his head no. "This is a great day in the morning, alright. I always thought it'd be him putting me in the ground."

Someone began shouting Macy's name in front of the restaurant, but she shrugged it off.

"I don't want to blow back through town and find you done went and got yourself another Tipton," Baltimore threatened, with a raised brow. "The next one just might finish the job this one started."

"Naw, suh, I ain't gonna be the same fool twice," she answered, folding the money in half and putting it inside her bra for safekeeping. "I've gotten used to the idea of being single and free already. If another man tries that with me, I'll see to it he don't get off without making it right with his soul."

Macy watched Baltimore cinch up his bundle and head off without so much as a so long, but it was better that way. However, she did have one regret regarding Tipton. She told Baltimore "how sad it was that he didn't have a gravesite, where she could visit, get drunk, raise her dress, and then squat on it whenever she got good and goddamned ready."

Baltimore was still smiling on the inside about Macy's designs on vandalizing her dead husband's final resting place when he stood at a post office–teller window, paying to have his bundle sent to himself in Harlem, New York. If he didn't show up to claim it within a month, it would be sent to a certain pale yellow house, free of charge. Franchetta would stand to receive a nice chunk of change, if that day did turn out to be the one to cash in, after all. Thinking push might come to shove, Baltimore contemplated seeing everyone he'd sent to hell before arriving there himself. He imagined his welcome might cause quite a ruckus at the gate, and he'd make sure of it.

The next stop Baltimore made had him feeling kind of jumpy. Union Station was bustling with hundreds of passengers coming and going. He studied each of the outbound train schedules and then closed himself up in one of seven phone booths, with glass folding doors, placed along the wall. He plunked in a nickel for a local call. Pudge answered it on the third ring. There was a short discussion between the two men, one listening attentively and the other explaining how Henry got nabbed. A seasoned driver was being sought at a cool grand for his skill and availability. Baltimore also let on that he fully understood if Pudge didn't want to throw in with him this go-around. Henry was stupid enough to get snatched up, and by all accounts, he deserved whatever punishment those men decided on inflicting.

"If needs be, I'll go it alone, Pudge," Baltimore said earnestly. "Don't feel like this has to put you in the middle of it. If needs be, I'll tend to it. Either way, I'll be over to Unca Chunk's. There's a few other things I have to work out."

Baltimore strolled into the same bar and billiards joint where Macy's husband, Tipton, had made a deal with the devil and paid with his life. Now it was Baltimore's turn to ante up, although he was hell-bent on outfoxing the man downstairs, who'd been casting bad luck shadows on him for too long. Behind Uncle Chunk's closed office door, Baltimore mapped out a plan to facilitate Henry's safe return. Since there was little to no chance he'd be able raise thirty-seven thousand dollars in exchange for what was left of his friend, he'd simply have to straddle a few hurdles in order to get in and then bite the bullet while shooting his way out.

Chunk liked what he heard overall, despite being 200 percent dead set against any of it. After keeping the details straight in his head, Baltimore stared across the office desk at the overweight thug, who was munching on his second ham on rye sandwich wrapped in wax paper. Chunk chased a mouthful of lunch with a healthy swig of root beer. "So, you think it's got a chance, the way I'ma set it up, I mean?" Baltimore asked, seeking his approval. Just then, Chunk cocked his meaty head back and let out a thunderously grotesque burp.

"Hell, naw," he answered matter-of-factly. "Double hell, naw."

"Glad I got your support on this one, Unca," Baltimore replied, his remarks heavily laden with sarcasm. "I'm really feeling a connection between us right now."

Chunk rolled his eyes and dropped the sandwich on his desk.

"How you gone come at me like that? I was connected to your ass yesterday, when Tipton busted in, outnumbered and outgunned. Now, you can't wait to get yourself jammed up the same way he did. I won't back that play. That's a sucker's bet, Baltimore. Don't believe me. Ask ole Tipton. Oh, that's right. You can't do that, because he got himself me-mor-i-a-lized about as fast as it's 'bout to happen to you."

There was no use trying to get an eighth of an inch inside of Uncle Chunk's thick skull, so Baltimore quit trying. On the other hand, their discussion brought a key issue to the forefront. If he could find out the number of guards they had posted on the room, it might even things out a tad. The question of how to get that information popped into Baltimore's mind as Pudge stepped into the doorway of Chunk's office, with Dank Battles following directly behind him.

The big man slammed his beefy paw on the desktop. "Don't you tell me, this fool done talked y'all into marching in his parade with him?"

"Hey, Chunk, Baltimore," hailed Pudge. He appeared more serious than before, wearing a satisfied grin, soft suede loafers, an off-white Stetson hat, and a perfectly tailored mustard-colored suit with a French-cut shirt and jazzy cuff links. Baltimore wanted to stand and salute him because it was the first time he'd exhibited an impeccable taste in clothing. "Sorry, I'm late," Pudge apologized needlessly. "I told Dank about the trouble, and he wanted to ride along. Though I'd hate to wrinkle my new vines," Pudge added, admiring his own wardrobe.

"That's right, Mistah Floyd. You reminded me of the man I used to be, and then you put some righteous cabbage in my bank account," said Dank, modestly dressed in dark washable clothing he didn't mind getting dirty. "I'll go in with you again."

As Baltimore reached down inside his pocket, Pudge refused it immediately. "I can't speak for Dank, but don't insult me by making this about money. Henry's the only reason you haven't been walking this earth alone. That's reason enough for me. Just tell me how we're gonna get it done."

There was no other way to say it. Pudge had slipped out of his cocoon and turned into a vibrant, confident social butterfly. And, just when Baltimore thought he'd seen it all, Ash Can Corvine appeared with a skinny younger man inching up beside him, like a timid animal.

"Who's this you got with you, Ash Can?" Baltimore asked, hoping he'd be someone with a few of the answers he needed.

"Okay, Im'a say this up front so it won't be no, uh-uh, second-guessing about it," Ash Can stammered apprehensively. "I know y'all was thinking on coming to my house, but this is better 'cause I'm here now. Uh, this is Peedy. He's the night bellhop over at Crest Mont. He's been up to the room where they's holding your friend. Every time they call for room service, the tray is to be left outside the room, on this cart." Ash Can licked his lips and swallowed hard, turning toward his friend for him to cosign on what he'd reported. "Ain't that so, Peedy?"

"Yeah, suh, that's how it is every time," Peedy confirmed. "They ring a food order down, and we hustle it up and leave the cart outside of the room. Only once, I forgot to bring 'em something to wash it down with. That's when I saw they had this man in there with 'em, tied to a chair. He wasn't dead, though," he hurried to report when Baltimore's chest heaved out. "They's keeping him alive on purpose, appeared to me." Before the younger bellman uttered another word, Ash Can hushed him up.

"Okay, there it is, all laid out," Ash Can huffed, squeezing a worn cotton cap in his hands. "Peedy's going in to work now so's he can't be late. I told him this kind of news would be worth something to you," he added quietly. Dank took one step toward the old hotel employee, but Baltimore waved him off.

"He's right, Dank. It's worth a lot." Baltimore peeled out four fifty-dollar bills and handed them to the frightened young man. "'Understand I need you to be right about every piece of this."

"Yeazah," he answered quickly. "Every bit of it is, I swear 'fore God."

Before they parted, Ash Can lingered, as if he had something else on his chest, so Baltimore gave him a forum to get it off. "Say what you got to, Ash. This ain't no time to be mincing words."

"Okay, okay, I'm not meaning this in a bad way, but I hope I never see your face again, Baltimore. People known to fall dead when you come around. I'm just asking to be left alone." All of the men in Chunk's office sided with Ash on his astute observation. Baltimore considered arguing that each one of the people who happened to die because of him had it coming, but it didn't actually ring true for the girl who'd been smashed by the beer truck, so he kept quiet about the whole thing. Ash deserved to make a living without fearing Baltimore or men like him showing up again, demanding information and putting his life at risk. Ash's request was granted like before, but this time Baltimore gave his word.

CHAPTER 16

THE 2:19 TRAIN

As soon as the sun dipped behind the Kansas City skyline, the telephone call Baltimore had been waiting for came through at the Phillip's service station on East Ninth and Park Avenue. Peedy hadn't been on duty at the Crest Mont but twenty minutes when he received a notice that a dinner tray needed to be hustled up to the private suite on the third floor. He rang Baltimore right away, like instructed, and then stalled until he saw Pudge's Ford sedan roll by the Park Avenue side window. As Peedy made his way up the small elevator, with three dinner plates under tin servers to keep them warm, the taxi parked right in back of the "white only" hotel facing Ninth Street. Two colored men walked away from the taxi, draped in black full-length coats buttoned halfway down to conceal the heat they packed underneath them. Peedy's bony knees trembled as he stopped the food cart at the door of the suite. He exhaled slowly and then knocked three times.

"Room service is here, suh!" he announced, leaning in closely to the door. When he heard footsteps approach, he backed away. "Don't mess up, don't mess up," he whispered to himself before the doorknob twisted.

A brown-haired white man opened the door. Peedy made sure not to look inside right away, which was easy to do because the stout fellow with a tree-trunk build blocked his view. "What you doing there, boy?" the white man asked the black one. "You ain't supposed to be hanging around here."

"Nah, suh," Peedy answered, his head bowed. "I'm itching to make a few extra dollars so's I can take my Marigold out to the dinner t'morrow night." His impromptu excuse must have sounded legit, because the tree trunk grinned at Peedy as if he were a child with a crush on a schoolgirl, as opposed to a grown man with a wife and children.

"Marigold, huh?" the man grunted, surveying the dinner plates underneath the tin covers. "Here, take this," he offered, extending his hand, with three nickels and five pennies in it. "Get her a hot dog or something." When the white man turned to maneuver the cart through the door, Peedy took his shot and raised his eyes without lifting his head, as men in his position were accustomed to doing on a daily basis.

"Yeazah, thank you, suh," said Peedy, pretending to unlock the back wheel of the cart. "Marigold likes hot dogs." He caught a glimpse of a large black man slumped back in a chair, bound at the chest and ankles. Peedy also remembered seeing the bottoms of a man's slacks and shoes poking out as he sat down, out of sight and secretive-like. "That's all I could get a look at before it was time to dash off with the twenty-cent tip," Peedy explained to Baltimore at the end of the hall. "The colored man in that room must be a real big shot," Peedy guessed, with four fifties in his possession to confirm it. He quickly informed Baltimore and Dank where the colored man was tied down, where the cart most likely would be stationed inside the room, and about the second man, whose legs he saw from the knee on down. "One other thing, Mistah Floyd," Peedy recalled. "The fellas in that suite forgot to order sodas."

Three meals seemed odd to Baltimore, but he didn't question what Peedy had seen. Perhaps they were feeding Henry to keep his health up until he became expendable or named his coconspirators. There was no time to waste, considering that other hired gunmen could be en route to fortify their position or to move Henry to a more secluded spot. "Thanks, Peedy. You go on and make yourself scarce now," Baltimore warned. "It's about to get real busy in a minute. Come on, Dank. I believe these fellas need something to go with dinner."

There would be no reason to cover their faces on this snatch and grab, because they didn't intend on leaving any witnesses behind.

Dank unfastened his coat and wielded the sawed-off shotgun with his muscular arms, as if it were a child's toy. Baltimore gripped fully loaded forty-fives as he tapped lightly on the door of the private suite. He nodded at Dank, giving him a way out had he changed his mind, but someone approached the door from the other side, and the opportunity to back out vanished. The tree trunk opened the door, but he was talking over his shoulder to one of his partners inside the room. "Yeah, the jig's probably expecting another tip for the sodas," he joked, turning to discover his life was milliseconds from ending. He stood there, with both hands outstretched, expecting to be given a small serving tray of soda pop bottles, and then his eyes widened. "Waaait!" he begged, covering his face in a defensive manner.

The man's voice was gobbled up by the sound of Dank's shotgun cutting him in half. Baltimore tore a huge gash in the man's head as he stumbled backwards into the heart of the room. The food tray was exactly where Peedy said it would be, although most of the food had been splattered on the wall, commingled with blood and brain matter. A second man, whose pants and shoes he saw, was frozen stiff by the surprise of gunfire. He merely sat there in that chair, shaking and hyperventilating, with his mouth hung open and gasping for air. "No, don't get up," Baltimore said coldly. He fired twice, blowing holes in the man's kneecaps before putting him out of his misery. The sound of a lone scream bounced off the walls as a third man poured in from the adjoining bedroom, and then a fourth. Instinctively, Baltimore kicked Henry's chair over to avoid getting him killed in the cross fire. Baltimore leapt behind the overturned sofa, losing sight of Dank momentarily. Bullets whizzed by his head, goose feathers fluttered in the air. Baltimore inched his head up to get a bead on the two men shooting back at him. He saw one of them kneeling against the wall, and the other near the window. "Dank, the moonlight!" he yelled, praying that Dank comprehended what he was getting at. "The moonlight!" he yelled again.

Suddenly, Dank cocked his shotgun and blasted it at the window. The man who'd taken cover there was pelted with chards of broken glass. He stood up, clawing at his eyes and throat. A long, slender piece of glass had arrowed through the back of his neck. Blood squirted out like water spouting from a geyser as he fell to the floor.

"Tucker, they get you?" someone yelled from the opposite side of the sofa that Baltimore was using for a barrier.

"No, I got both of 'em," Baltimore said in a hushed tone that distorted his voice.

"Good. Let's get outta here then," the white man answered back unwittingly. He huffed and climbed to his feet; three gunshots blasted him until he didn't move another muscle.

Dank hopped up and darted over to see about Henry. Baltimore didn't dally. He figured after all he'd been up against, the least Henry could do was live through it. Henry pushed his dry, crusty lips out to speak. "Baltimo', I'm sorry," he gurgled, saliva caked up in the corner of his mouth.

"Nah, you're *stupid*," Baltimore corrected him. "And you'd better not get the notion to die on me, either. Let's beat it outta here before you make a bigger fool out of me." He and Dank cut the ropes around Henry's torso and ankles. The ropes were so tight, they had cut off Henry's circulation. His feet were numb, so they dragged him down the hallway with a bedsheet tied to his waist. When nosey hotel guests stuck their noses out, Baltimore took potshots, sending them reeling back into their rooms. The service elevator stopped on the first floor. Dank headed for the side door, like they had in the initial heist, but Pudge had the car out back, running and ready. "Uh-uh, Dank!" Baltimore prodded. "This way!" Dank sprinted for the back door and kicked it open. He hadn't ever been so happy to see that old, ugly taxi as he was then. With Dank safely outside, Baltimore went back to see what was holding Henry. He raced frantically in the direction of the elevator landing. Two black men were wrestling Henry back onto the service car when they saw help coming to his aid.

"Let loose of him!" Baltimore demanded, his lips dripping with venomous agitation. "I said, let him be," he said, taking aim.

"It's not going down like that," one of the clean-cut colored men replied. "We off duty, but we keeping him. Taking him to turn him over right now."

"Henry, I'm guessing those be colored po-lice what got you," Baltimore hissed. "Yeah, one step above slave catchers." He steadied his aim, with both guns pointed firmly at their heads. "Let loose of him, slave catchers," he warned again, as they used Henry for a shield. Inching forward slowly, the off-duty cops cowered. They were obviously unarmed and praying he wouldn't shoot while they had his friend. When they made a dumb move to drag Henry inside the elevator, Baltimore pumped several slugs at the pulley cables until they popped free from the elevator harness.

Realizing their getaway route had just been shot to hell, they released Henry and commenced pleading for their lives. Baltimore told his friend to get out back, but Henry hesitated. "Fool, these house niggahs was gonna give you over to be hung. Now I've got something to do. If you stick around pining for 'em, that might put you with them," said Baltimore. Henry looked at the men, who'd simply made a terrible decision. They crossed Baltimore. Moments later, the back door slammed shut as Dank helped Henry out to the car. Before reaching Pudge's taxi, they heard four shots sound loudly from the inside.

"Buck up, Henry," Dank told him. "No witnesses. No how."

Henry jerked his arm away from Dank's helpful grasp. "I know. You ain't got to tell me how it be."

Out of nowhere, Baltimore bolted through the door, shouting. "Go Pudge! Go!" he hollered loudly. Dank watched as Baltimore sprinted alongside the taxi and climbed onto the running board as if he'd done it a million times. "We've got to move before every cop in town is after us. Pudge, you might have to put this Ford away for a while, in case somebody got the plate number."

The driver carried on without a care in the world. "Don't pay that no never mind. I change the plates every other week as it is," he chuckled gleefully. "Everything is alright now. We have about twenty minutes if y'all are still gonna make that 2:19 train heading north."

"I know, Pudge," Baltimore said sorrowfully. "And not a moment too soon, either. It won't be long before the station is flooded with policemen searching for two or more colored men who don't belong. We'll be on our way to Saint Louie by then. Don't that sound just jake, Henry?"

Not much on words after causing two black men's deaths, Henry nodded his head, affirming that it was alright with him, as if he had a choice. He'd been pulled from the fire by Baltimore too many times to trick himself into thinking otherwise. *Sometimes a man has to strike out alone*, Henry thought to himself when they neared the Union Station train yard. Oddly enough, Baltimore was thinking the very same thing, but only for another reason. That made the third time he'd almost lost his life trying to save Henry's, and although he loved the man like a brother, that act was getting old. Perhaps the time had come to get some new friends. Either way, their destiny lay together for the next six hours, until the train stopped in Henry's hometown. Come hell or high water; they had to get on it.

Blaring police sirens filled the cool night air as the taxi rambled into the train station. Pudge slammed on the brakes when he became overwhelmed by a stream of police cars pouring in from every entrance. "This is as far as I go, Baltimore," Pudge sighed. "They'll be all over the place in a few minutes. If you were smart, you'd get out now while the getting's good. Come on. Turn around and head back with me and Dank.

Henry moaned, holding his side with both hands. Baltimore craned his neck to look out of the steamed windows. "Dammit, I didn't know this town had so many cops. Pudge, you wouldn't happen to have a bottle on you?"

"Sure, I do," Pudge answered. "You know I keeps a little something on hand for cold nights." Pudge opened his glove box and reached inside it. "Here take it, Kentucky bourbon." Baltimore shook his hand, did the same to Dank, and then accepted the bottle of booze from the driver.

"Come on, Henry. We're leaving tonight," Baltimore grunted when his pal wouldn't move. "Tomorrow ain't promised!"

With that admonition, Henry rolled his body toward the back passenger side door. He looked up at Pudge and Dank, nodded his thanks, and threw himself out of the car. The taxi made a broad U-turn and then sped off in the other direction as winds howled through the train yard. "It's cold out here, Baltimo', real cold," Henry said, his teeth chattering.

"I know. That's what this liquor's for."

"But you don't drink."

"I've got my friends to keep me warm. The lightning is for what ails you," Baltimore answered. "Now let's head on over to the freight-car platform. They'll never look for us among the mongrels."

Despite hundreds of Kansas City police officers searching through the train station, diligently checking each passenger car, not one of them thought to look inside the cattle freighters, where Henry and Baltimore shared the long ride to St. Louis with seventy-three of the foulest-smelling dairy cows from Texas. Funny thing, the cows didn't seem to mind their company at all.

When the train reached the next destination, Baltimore helped

Henry off and bid him farewell for the time being. Tears gathered in Henry's eyes, but he fought the salty sentiment, sensing it was the end of an era with Baltimore, although that wouldn't stop him from doing what he had to. "I ain't gone ever forget what you done for me," Henry said, his voice raspy and low. "Nor what kinds of things we've been through side by side."

"Me, neither, Henry," Baltimore replied, climbing back inside with the cattle. "Me, neither." He was resigned to taking the train due north until someone decided to unload that freighter full of beef. It would give him a chance to think about Macy, Uncle Chunk, Pudge and Dank, Rot, Ash Can Corvine, and even Hattie. All the wrong he'd done in the past week worked on him, like Chick predicted it would, but the good times he'd had in Kaycee blotted those others out like they never even happened.

Reminiscing about Franchetta and the girls made Baltimore feel a little homesick. Maybe he'd slide by Whiskey Bottom and look in on his mother and baby sister, if the old man wasn't around to stop him. But first, he'd have to pay a special trip to Harlem and make good on the debt that had started all of this nonsense in the first place. That ought to stop that old bad luck shadow from easing up behind him for a good long while, Baltimore figured. He was willing to bet on it.

BAD LUCK SHADOW

VICTOR McGLOTHIN

ABOUT THIS GUIDE

The suggested questions are intended to
enhance your group's reading of
BAD LUCK SHADOW
by Victor McGlothin.

DISCUSSION QUESTIONS

1. Do you think that Baltimore Floyd was inherently a bad man or a good one who did bad things?

2. How do you feel about Henry getting involved in the murder of the businessman on the train when he walked into a bad situation growing more intense?

3. Baltimore told Henry that being his best friend involved him automatically? Do you agree or disagree?

4. Soon after Baltimore and Henry reach Kansas City, they encountered a woman being detained from shoplifting. Do you think it was a wise thing for them to do, considering Baltimore's bad luck shadow?

5. Speaking of Baltimore's rotten luck, how much of it was his own doing, from beginning of the story to the end?

6. How does Franchetta's description of her first run in with Baltimore years before help explain his personality, his ruthlessness at times, and his overwhelming generosity and unflappable loyalty at others?

7. Although it appeared that Franchetta loved Baltimore, discuss why she allowed her roommates to share him in bed, among other things?

8. Baltimore shot one of the men in his own crew during the robbery. Do you feel he was justified? Why or why not?

9. Henry was a lot like Baltimore when it came to women. Do you think thy story would have turned out differently if he'd stayed with Hattie instead of taking up with Estelle and then going on the subsequent shopping spree to impress her?

10. Macy, wife of the abusive man whom Baltimore goaded into a fatal battle, didn't quite know what make of the money that she was awarded supposedly by her missing and repentant husband. Why do you think Baltimore lied about where the money

really came from? Do you think Macy ultimately knew the truth?

11. Tough men like Unca Chunk, Rot, Dank, and others from the story offer a rich, dangerous slice of life many of us would steer clear of. Is it possible to understand their plight in life and why they lived on the edge?

Turn the page for an excerpt from GOD DON'T PLAY,
by Mary Monroe,
on sale now from Dafina!

CHAPTER 1

My worst nightmare began with a black snake and a cute envelope. I had no way of knowing that my life was about to fall apart on the most beautiful day that we'd had all year.

The bold morning sun was shining down on my freshly painted house like a lighthouse. I had just had some of the best sex that I had had in years, and there had been no one else in the same room with me.

"You give good phone sex. You should call me up more often," I teased my husband, Pee Wee, as I'd struggled to catch my breath before hanging up the telephone on the wall next to the refrigerator in the kitchen. I couldn't remember the last time I'd enjoyed sex standing up, and nibbling on a Pop-Tart at the same time.

"Well, it is the next best thing to me bein' there," Pee Wee told me, whispering so that his cousins in the next room at his cousin's house couldn't hear him. "Did you get naked like I told you?"

"Uh-huh. Naked as a jaybird," I lied, smoothing down the sides of my muumuu. There was no way I was going to shed my clothes in the middle of my kitchen floor. It was hard enough for me to get naked in my own bedroom. But I did remove my shoes.

"Did you stick your fingers where I told you to stick 'em?" Pee Wee asked with a moan.

"Uh-huh," I mumbled, lying again. The only thing that I'd stuck my fingers in was in that Pop-Tarts box. However, I had massaged a few other spots on my body like Pee Wee had instructed, and that had been enough for me.

I had enjoyed my passionate telephone tryst with my husband, but I was glad when it was over. Not only did I feel downright ridiculous doing some of the things to myself that he'd ordered me to do, but I had started getting cramps in my legs. And I wanted to clean myself up and put on some fresh underwear.

With a satisfied smile on my face, I stepped out on my front porch to retrieve the mail. A large butterfly that had wings every color in the rainbow landed on my hand.

The sun felt good on my face as I clutched my mail and shook the butterfly off my hand. I waved to the friendly, good-looking White couple from down the street as they walked by, pushing their homely toddler in a creaky stroller. Everybody on our block, except for the husband, knew that the homely toddler's daddy was the homely insurance man who made house calls.

A large, light-skinned man that I didn't recognize, with his black hair in large pink foam rollers, waved to me from a shiny black Lincoln that was cruising down the street. I yelled at a stray dog who had decided to lift his crooked leg and water the prizewinning rosebush in my front yard.

My biggest concern that day was trying to decide what to do first: get my nails done, go shopping, do the laundry, or treat myself to lunch at one of my favorite restaurants. I was in a frivolous mood so I didn't want to do anything that was too serious, like go pay bills or visit my fussy parents. But the bizarre uproar that I was about to face would cancel everything else that I had planned to do on that beautiful Saturday. From that point on, my life would never be the same again. What happened to me on this day would haunt me for the rest of my life, because it was the beginning of the end for me in some ways. And it all had to do with a black snake and a cute envelope.

There was nothing that unusual about the cute envelope that had arrived in the mail that morning in late August. I had almost missed it among the usual stack of bills and other unwanted junk—like the Frederick's of Hollywood catalogue with the picture of a beautiful young blonde woman in a white negligee on the cover.

I laughed when I saw the catalogue, wondering what the world was coming to for *my* name to end up on the Frederick's of Hollywood mailing list. I had to give them credit for advertising muumuus, waist clinchers, capes, bras with cups large enough to hold forty ounces of beer, long flowing nightgowns that looked more like parachutes, and other inducements every now and then to appease us full-figured gals. But almost everything else that the mysterious Mr. Frederick— who probably looked like Buddha or worse himself—sold was for women half my size and even smaller. On the first page inside the catalogue were some "one size fits all" panty hose. Yeah, right. The see-through gowns and low-cut blouses were outrageous enough, and I had absolutely no use for crotchless panties. I'd probably be wearing diapers again before I broke down and put on a pair of crotchless panties.

I was not surprised when I flipped the catalogue over and saw that it was addressed to Jade O'Toole, my best friend's sneaky teenage daughter. Some of the clothes that the girl wore every day showed just as much skin as the frocks she ordered from Frederick's that she hid from her parents, so I didn't know what the big deal was. But I didn't have a teenager yet, so I couldn't really judge the behavior of the "in your face" music-video generation. They had their own culture and Jade kept it in my face. I had allowed her to take too many liberties with me so it was too late for me to revise my position in her life. I was no more of an authority figure to her than a cat was. She had started using my address without my knowledge or permission. I shuddered when I thought about what that girl might do next.

Here's a preview of
Victor McGlothin's novel,
Ms. Etta's Fast House.
Coming soon from Dafina!

CHAPTER 1

PENNY WORTH
O' BLUES

Three months into 1947, a disturbing calm rolled over St. Louis, Missouri. It was unimaginable to foresee the hope and heartache that one enigmatic season saw fit to unleash, mere inches from winter's edge. One unforgettable story changed the city forever. This is that story.

Watkins Emporium was the only black-owned dry goods store for seven square blocks and the pride of "The Ville" the city's famous black neighborhood. Talbot Watkins had opened it when the local Woolworth's fired him five years earlier when he allowed black customers to try on hats before purchasing them. The department store manager had warned him several times that clothing apparel wasn't fit for sale after having been worn by Negroes. Subsequently, Mr. Watkins used his life savings to start a successful business of his own with his daughter, Chozelle, a hot-tempered twenty-year-old who had a preference for older, fast-talking men with even faster hands. She often toyed around with fellows her own age when the opportunity to lead one of them around by the nose presented itself. Chozelle's scandalous ways became undeniably apparent to her father the third time he'd caught a man running from the back door of his storeroom, half-dressed and hell-bent on eluding his wrath. Mr. Watkins clapped an iron padlock on the back door after realizing he'd have to protect his daughter's virtue, whether she liked it or not. It was a hard pill to swallow, admitting to himself that canned meat wasn't the only thing getting dusted and polished in that back room. However, his relationship with Chozelle was just about perfect, compared to that of his meanest customer.

"Penny! Git your boney tail away from that there dress!" Halstead King grunted from the checkout counter. "I done told you once, you too damned simple for something that fine." When Halstead's lanky daughter snatched her hand away from the red satin cocktail gown displayed in the front window, as if a rabid dog had snapped at it, he went right on back to running his mouth and running his eyes up and down Chozelle's full hips and ample everything else. Halstead stuffed the hem of his shirttail into his tattered work pants and then shoved his stubby thumbs beneath the tight suspenders holding them up. After licking his lips and twisting the ends of his thick gray handlebar mustache, he slid a five dollar bill across the wooden countertop, eyeing Chozelle suggestively. "Now, like I was saying. How 'bout I come by later on when your daddy's away and help you arrange thangs in the storeroom?" His plump belly spread between the worn leather suspender straps like one of the heavy grain sacks he'd loaded on to the back of his pickup truck just minutes before.

Chozelle had a live one on the hook, but old man Halstead didn't stand a chance of getting at what had his zipper about to burst. Although his appearance reminded her of a rusty old walrus, she strung him along. Chozelle was certain that five dollars was all she'd get from the tight-fisted mister, unless, of course, she agreed to give him something worth a lot more on the back end. After deciding to leave the lustful old man's offer on the counter top, she turned her back on him and then pretended to adjust a line of canned peaches behind the counter. "Like what you see, Mr. Halstead?" Chozelle flirted. She didn't have to guess whether his mouth watered, because it always did when he imagined pressing his body against hers. "It'll cost you a heap more than five dollars to catch a peek at the rest of it."

"A peek at what, Chozelle?" hissed Mr. Watkins suspiciously, as he stepped out of the side office.

Chozelle stammered while Halstead choked down a pound of culpability. "Oh, nothing Papa. Mr. Halstead's just thinking on buying something nice for Penny over yonder." Her father tossed a quick glance at the nervous seventeen-year-old obediently standing an arm's length away from the dress she'd been dreaming about for weeks. "I was telling him how we'd be getting in another shipment of lady's garments next Thursday," Chozelle added, hoping that lie sounded more plausible. When Halstead's eyes fell to the floor, there was no doubting what he'd had in mind. It was common knowledge that Halstead King, the local moonshiner, treated his only daughter like an unwanted pet and that he never shelled out one thin dime toward her happiness.

"All right then," said Mr. Watkins, in a cool, calculated manner. "We'll put that there five on a new dress for Penny. Next weekend, she can come back and get that red one in the window she's been fancying." Halstead started to argue as the store owner lifted the money from the counter and folded it into his shirt pocket, but it was gone for good, just like Penny's hopes of getting anything close to that red dress if her father had anything to say about it. "She's getting to be a grown woman and it'd make a right nice coming-out gift. Good day, Halstead," Mr. Watkins offered, scaling the agreement and extending his cheapest customer the opportunity to slink his conniving behind out of the same doorway he'd tramped in.

"Papa, you know I've had my heart set on that satin number since it came in," Chozelle whined, as if the whole world revolved around her. Directly outside of the store, Halstead slapped Penny down onto the dirty sidewalk in front of the display window.

"You done cost me more money than you're worth," he spat viciously. "I have half a mind to take it out of your hide."

"Not unless you want worse coming to you," a velvety smooth voice threatened from the driver's seat of a new Ford convertible with Maryland plates.

Halstead glared at the stranger, then at the man's shiny beige roadster. Penny was staring up at her handsome hero with buttery complexion for another reason altogether. She turned her head briefly, holding her sore eye, then glanced back at the dress in the window. She managed a smile when the man in the convertible was the only thing she'd ever seen prettier than that red dress. Suddenly, her swollen face didn't sting nearly so much.

"You ain't got no business here, mistah!" Halstead exclaimed harshly. "People known to get hurt messin' where they don't belong."

"Uh-uh. See, you went and made it my business by putting your hands on that girl. If she was half the man you pretend to be, she'd put a hole in your head as sure as you're standing here." The handsome stranger unfastened the buttons on his expensive tweed sports coat to reveal a long black revolver cradled in a shoulder holster. When Halstead took that as a premonition of things to come, he backed down like most bullies when confronted by someone who didn't bluff so easily. "Uh-huh, that's what I thought," he said, stepping out of his automobile idled at the curb. "Miss, you all right?" he asked Penny, helping her off the hard cement. He noticed that one of the buckles was broken on her run-over shoes. "If not, I could fix that for you. Then, we can go get your shoe looked after." Penny swooned, as if she'd seen her first sunrise. Her eyes were opened almost as wide as Chozelle's, gawking from the other side of the large framed window. "They call me Baltimore, Baltimore Floyd. It's nice to make your acquaintance, Miss. Sorry it had to be under such unfavorable circumstances." Penny thought she was going to faint right there on the very sidewalk she'd climbed up from. No man had taken the time to notice her, much less talk to her in such a flattering manner. If it were up to Penny, she was willing to get knocked down all over again for the sake of reliving that moment in time.

"Naw suh, Halstead's right," Penny sighed after giving it some thought. "This here be family business." She dusted herself off, primped her dry twigged pigtails, a hairstyle more appropriate for much younger girls, then she batted her eyes like she'd done it all of her life. "Thank you kindly, though," Penny mumbled, noting the contempt mounting in her father's pensive expression. Halstead wished he'd brought along his gun, and his daughter was wishing the same thing, so that Baltimore could make him eat it. She understood all too well that as soon as they returned to their shanty farmhouse on the outskirts of town, there would be hell to pay. Although whatever Halstead saw fit to beat Penny with, it wasn't no never mind to her. At age seventeen, with scuffed knees and ashy elbows, Penny became a woman that day in front of Watkins Emporium. There was no turning back now.

"Come on Penny," she heard Halstead, gargle softer than she'd imagined he could. "We ought to be getting on," he added as if asking permission to leave.

"I'll be seeing you again Penny," Baltimore offered. "And next time, there bet' not be one scratch on your face." Those words were meant for Halstead. "It's hard enough on women folk as it is. They shouldn't have to go about wearing reminders of a man's short-comings."

Halstead hurried to the other side of the secondhand pickup truck and cranked it. "Penny," he summoned, when her feet hadn't moved an inch. Perhaps she was waiting for permission to leave, too. Baltimore tossed Penny a cordial wink as he helped her up onto the tattered bench seat.

"Go on now. It'll be alright or else I'll fix it," he assured her, nodding his head in a kind fashion and smiling brightly.

As the old pickup truck jerked forward, Penny stole a glance at the tall, silky stranger, then held the hand Baltimore had clasped inside his up to her nose. The fragrance of his store-bought cologne resonated through her thin nostrils for miles until the smell of farm animals whipped her back into a stale reality—her own. It wasn't long before Halstead mustered up enough courage to revert back to the mean tyrant he'd always been. He'd have taken a steaming dump on Penny's head if he thought she'd sit long enough to let him. His unforgiving black heart and vivid memories of the woman who ran off with a traveling salesman fueled Halstead's hatred for the girl his wife left behind. Until his dying day, Penny would be subjected to his angry fits and violent episodes, which always pitted her on the wrong end of a backhanded or a book heel. She'd decided that's what God had planned for her or else things would have been different, because Halstead had sufficiently drilled it in her head how ugly, skinny, and worthless she was.

"Ain't no sane man gon' have nothing to do with you, so's you can git that out your mind," he'd berate her. "You best be glad you're my own or I'd throw you out into the streets myself." Penny didn't want to believe his insults, but there's something to be said for repetition even when its misused for the sole purpose of breaking a child's spirit, and Halstead was determined to destroy Penny's since he couldn't do the same to her mother. He treated his daughter worse than a mangy dog. Penny surmised through the years that a woman and a dog weren't much different if a man beat them both with the same blatant disregard. She'd heard Halstead brag while in a drunken stupor, "You call a dog by the wrong name enough times, he'll come 'round to answering to it soon enough." He called Penny some of the vilest names while beating her, so she figured what he said was true.

"Git those mason jar crates off'n the truck while I fire up the still!" he hollered. "And you might as well forgit that man in town and ever meeting him again. His meddling can't help you way out here. He's probably on his way back east already." When Penny moved too casually for Halstead's taste, he jumped up and popped her across the mouth. Blood squirted from her bottom lip. "Don't make me tell you again," he cursed. "Ms. Etta's havin' her spring jig this weekend, and I promised two more cases before sundown. Now git!"

Penny's injured lip quivered. "Yeah Suh," she whispered, her head bowed.

As Halstead waddled to the rear of their weather-beaten house of orange brick and oak, cussing and complaining about wayward women, traveling salesmen, and slick strangers, he shouted additional chores. "Stack them crates up straight this time so's they don't tip over. Fetch a heap of water in that barrel, brang it around yonder and put my store receipts on top of the bureau in my room. Don't touch nothin' while you in there neither, useless heffa," he grumbled.

"Yeah Suh, I will. I mean, I won't," she whimpered. Penny allowed a long strand of blood to dangle from her angular chin before she took the hem of her faded dress and wiped it away. Feeling about as inadequate as the names Halstead saddled her with, Penny became confused as to which order her chores were to have been performed. She reached inside the cab of the truck, collected the store receipts and crossed the pebble-covered yard. She sighed deeply over how unfair it felt, having to endure such a beautiful spring day in hell, and then she pushed open the front door and wandered into Halstead's room. She overlooked the assortment of loose coins scattered on the night stand next to the disheveled queen-sized bed with filthy sheets she'd be expected to scrub clean before the day was through.

On the corner of the bed frame hung a silver-plated colt revolver. Sunlight poured through the half-drawn window shade, glinting off the pistol. While mesmerized by the opportunity to take matters into her own hands, Penny palmed the forty-five carefully. She contemplated how easily she could have ended it all with one bullet to the head—hers. Something deep inside wouldn't allow Penny to hurt another human, something good and decent, something she didn't inherit from Halstead.

"Penny!" he yelled, from outside. "You got three seconds to git outta that house and back to work!" Startled, Penny dropped the gun onto the uneven floor and froze, praying it wouldn't go off. Halstead pressed his round face against the dusty window to look inside. "Goddammit! Gal, you've got to be the slowest somebody. Git back to work before I have to beat some speed into you."

The puddle of warm urine Penny stood in confirmed that she was still alive. It could have just as easily been a pool of warm blood instead. Thoughts of ending her misery after her life had been spared flew quickly. She unbuttoned her thin cotton dress, used it to mop the floor, then tossed it on the dirty clothes heap in her bedroom. Within minutes, she'd changed into an undershirt and denim overalls. Her pace was noticeably revitalized as she wrestled the crates off the truck as instructed. "Stack them crates," Penny mumbled to herself. "Stack 'em straight so's they don't tip over. Then fetch the water." The week before, she'd stacked the crates too high and a strong gust of wind toppled them over. Halstead was furious. He'd dragged Penny into the barn, tied her to a tractor wheel, and left her there for three days without food or water. She was determined not to spend another three days warding of field mice and garden snakes.

Once the shipment had been situated on the front porch, Penny rolled the ten-gallon water barrel over to the well pump beside the cobblestone walkway. Halstead was busy behind the house, boiling sour mash and corn syrup in a lead pot with measures of grain. He'd made a small fortune distilling alcohol and peddling it to bars, juke joints, and roadhouses. "Hurr'up, with that water!" he shouted. "This still's plenty hot. 'Coils tryna bunch." Penny clutched the well handle with both hands and went to work. She had seen an illegal still explode when it reached the boiling point too quickly, causing the copper coils to clog when they didn't hold up to the rapidly increasing temperatures. Ironically, when it came to Penny that someone had tampered with the neighbor's still on the morning it blew up, a thunderous blast shocked her where she stood. Penny cringed. Her eyes grew wide when Halstead staggered from the backyard screaming and cussing. Now, that wasn't unusual because he was always ranting about this, that, and the other. But this time every inch of his body was covered in vibrant yellow flames. Falling to his knees, he cried out for Penny to help him. "Water! Throw the damned . . . water!" he demanded. She watched in amazement as Halstead writhed on the ground in unbridled torment, his skin melting, separating from bone and cartilage. In a desperate attempt, Halstead reached out to her, expecting to be doused with water just beyond his reach, as it gushed from the well spout like blood had poured from Penny's busted lip.

In the most peculiar act of indifference, Penny raced past a water pail on her way toward the front porch. When she couldn't reach the top crate fast enough, she shoved the entire stack of them onto the ground. After getting what she went there for, she covered her nose with a rag as she inched closer to Halstead's charred body. While life evaporated from his smoldering remains, Penny held a mason jar beneath the spout until water spilled over onto her hand. She kicked the ten-gallon barrel on its side, then sat down on it. She was surprised how fast all the hate she'd known in the world was suddenly gone and how nice it was to finally enjoy a cool, uninterrupted glass of water.

At her leisure, Penny sipped until she'd had her fill. "Ain't no man supposed to treat his own blood like you treated me," she heckled, rocking back and forth slowly on the rise of that barrel. "Maybe that's cause you wasn't no man at all. You just mean old Halstead. Mean old Halstead." Penny looked up the road, when something in the wind called out to her. A car was headed her way. By the looks of it, she had less than two minutes to map out her future, so she dashed into the house, collected what she could, and threw it all into a croaker sack. Somehow, it didn't seem fitting to keep the back door to her shameful past opened, so she snatched the full pail off the ground and filled it with the last batch of moonshine Halstead had brewed. If her mother had ever planned on returning, Penny reasoned that she'd taken too long as she tossed the pail full of white lightening into the house. As she lit a full box of stick matches, her hands shook erratically until the time had come to walk away from her bitter yesterdays and give up on living out the childhood that wasn't intended for her. "No reason to come back here, Momma," she whispered, for the gentle breeze to hear and carry away. "I got to make it on my own now."

Penny stood by the roadside and marveled at the rising inferno, ablaze from pillar to post. Halstead's fried corpse smoldered on the lawn when the approaching vehicle ambled to a stop in the middle of the farm road. A young man, long, lean, and not much older than Penny, the took his sweet time stepping out of the late-model Plymouth sedan. He sauntered over to the hump of roasted flesh and studied it. "Hey Penny," the familiar passerby said routinely.

"Afternoon, Jinxy," she replied, her gaze still locked on the thick black clouds of smoke billowing toward the sky.

Jinx—Sam Dearborn, Jr.—was the youngest son of the neighbor, whose moonshine brewery had gone up in flames two months earlier. After Jinx surveyed the yard, smashed mason jars, and the overturned water barrel, there wasn't anything to do but ask the sixty-four-thousand-dollar question.

"That there Halstead?" he alleged knowingly.

Penny nodded that it was, without a hint of reservation. "What's left of 'im," she answered casually.

"I guess you'll be moving on then," Jinx concluded in a stoic tone.

"Yeah, I reckon I will at that," she concluded as well, using the same even pitch he had. "I haven't seen much of you since yo' daddy passed. How you been?"

Jinx hoisted Penny's large cloth sack into the back seat of his car before responding to her question. "Waitin' mostly," he said, hunching his shoulders, "to get even."

"Yeah, I figured as much when I saw it was you in the road." Penny was one of two people who was all but certain that Halstead had killed Jinx's father by rigging his still to malfunction so he could eliminate the competition. The night before it happened, Halstead had quarreled with him over money. By the next afternoon, Jinx was making burial arrangements for his daddy.

"Halstead got what he had coming to him," the young man reasoned as he walked Penny to the passenger door.

"Now, I'll get what coming to me," Penny declared somberly, with a pocket full of folding money. "I'd be thankful Jinxy if you'd run me into town. I need to see a man about a dress."